BY MICAELA GILCHRIST

The Fiercer Heart
The Good Journey

~ THE ~

FIERCER HEART

Micaela Gilchrist

Simon & Schuster

NEW YORK LONDON TORONTO SYDNEY

SIMON & SCHUSTER

Rockefeller Center

1230 Avenue of the Americas

New York, NY 10020

SIMON & SCHUSTER and colophon are registered trademarks
of Simon & Schuster, Inc.

For information about special discounts for bulk purchases,
please contact Simon & Schuster Special Sales at
1-800-456-6798 or business@simonandschuster.com.

Designed by Paul Dippolito

Manufactured in the United States of America

1   3   5   7   9   10   8   6   4   2

Library of Congress Cataloging-in-Publication Data

Gilchrist, Micaela.
The fiercer heart / Micaela Gilchrist.
p.   cm.
Includes bibliographical references.
1. Kearny, Philip, 1815–1862—Fiction. 2. Kearny, Diana Moore Bullitt,
fl. 1834–1862—Fiction. 3. Generals' spouses—Fiction. 4. Divorced women—Fiction.
5. Generals—Fiction. I. Title.

PS3607.I424F54 2005
813'.6—dc22
2005049794

ISBN-13: 978-0-7432-2282-2
ISBN-10:   0-7432-2282-2

Permission to reproduce illustrations is gratefully acknowledged to:

Frances Loeb Library, Graduate School of Design, Harvard University, Lantern Slide Collection for *St. Louis, View from Lucas Palace* (GSD Lantern Slide, KX1412/b4): 245.
Library of Congress Prints and Photographs Division for *General Scott Entering Mexico City*
(reproduction number LC-USZCU 9950–6173), *The Palace of the Tuileries* (reproduction

THE
FIERCER
HEART

Louisville

One

I T IS A FACT of natural history that a beautiful woman can destroy a man's life with very little effort. I first saw Diana Bullitt in 1838, a year after having been commissioned into the First Dragoons. Shortly thereafter, I reported for duty at Jefferson Barracks, Missouri. Upon arriving, I hunted up the post commander but his aides told me I would find the general and his sister-in-law on the bluffs overlooking the Mississippi River. Riding through the green woods and nearing a clearing surrounded by lilac bushes, I heard the general advising, "Diana, release the bow in between breaths. Now, don't look at me, girl, look at the target."

I dismounted, tied my horse, and walked around the deep shrubbery. There, in the clearing, where the light came pouring through the oak trees, I saw her sitting on a bay horse. She placed the arrow against the bowstring, aimed the bow at the paper target and with vigorous grace, released the shaft. Delighted with her efforts, she turned laughingly to her brother-in-law, the general, as her black hair tumbled out of its pins. She was highly animated, leaning forward on the pommel of her saddle, her dark eyes shining with victory, her face bright and a high color in her cheek. I think she must have caught my movement because she peered in my direction.

But I stepped back into the shadows, felt my chest constrict and a palpitation of the heart that made me double over and gasp for breath. *Goddamn*, I thought, *I am having an apoplectic fit.* I staggered back to my horse, vowing that no woman would ever unhinge me again. I am a soldier first, a man of mark in society and in the cavalry, and could not let myself be distracted by the trifling beauty of a nineteen-year-old girl.

A few days later, the general introduced me to Diana Bullitt. The commander made it excruciatingly clear to me that Diana, being the niece of the famous explorer William Clark, and descended from one of the finest old colonial families, was the sort of girl I might marry but must never lead astray under penalty of losing my testicles and my life, in that order. Autumn dissolved into winter, but still, I did not court her. I visited the commanding general's house on official business every day, and would ride up to see Diana on the balcony, leaning over the railing as she admired me. Yet, through all of those wintry months, I did not touch her. It went no further than talk.

She, being bound by propriety, by her upbringing and her class, would not even take my arm as we walked up the steps together. At regimental cotillions, I did not dance with her as I have utter contempt for dancing fops. Besides, I disliked being lovesick over her, despised my weak feelings of jealousy as I watched her circle the dance floor tormenting the poor set of devils who had fallen in love with her. It was time to be my old self again, moving unfettered and superior to the herd.

In the spring of 1839, President Van Buren ordered me to a cavalry school in France to study mounted warfare. Hoping to be free of her, I left America, and within two weeks of arriving at Saumur in the Loire Valley, I bedded eleven grateful French women. I was certain that Diana would soon fade from memory.

When the Arabs in the military colony around Algiers broke the peace and massacred French troops, I boldly joined my comrades, selflessly dedicated myself to the French cause, and fought the Arab rebels in the Atlas Mountains of French North Africa. For my courage on the battlefield, King Louis Philippe tried to award me a Cross of the Legion of Honor, but being an American army officer I could not accept the medal and the French princes said no dragoon in their army could equal my éclat.

But at night, in camp, when we built fires of mimosa in the blue shadows of the mountains, I could not help but think about Diana Bullitt. I worried that in my absence she had married some dandified millionaire from Ohio who'd made a fresh fortune in quick lime or packthread. Imagining this to be true, I smothered my indignation and with the utmost contempt for her fictional husband, pushed Diana out of my thoughts.

One year later, I returned to New York City and, upon reading the papers, learned that Diana's brother-in-law, the old general, was in town. I called upon him at the Astor House Hotel. With a sly look, the general pulled me aside, swirled the bourbon in his glass, and said, "Why, Lieutenant Kearny, haven't you heard the news? Several prominent men are courting Miss Diana Bullitt. Her mother writes that she would be surprised if Diana is not married by the shut of the year."

Taking two horses and a valise with clean shirts, I bid the general good-bye and sped off immediately for Louisville, Kentucky.

So you see, in my singularly noble way, I was trying to save Diana Bullitt from marrying the wrong fellow, one who was too much her inferior. But my fine intentions nearly destroyed me. Diana pierced my heart like a poison stinger that I spent the rest of my life trying to dislodge.

Two

MY MOTHER SOLD ME into marriage on my birthday, on the thirteenth day of June 1841, for the price of two houses and all of the Chantilly cake I could ever wish to eat. Now, this is the truth. And if you wish to know the truth about any family, you must ask the youngest child—which would be me. I had expected to marry a merchant, a man like my father, and after a long and genteel courtship, go swanning about in yellow lace and orange blossoms. But my new husband told me not to despair. Taking my hand he said, "Come out, Diana Bullitt. Follow me away and you shall stand in bold relief before all the world." Bold relief, indeed! Sixteen years later, I certainly did stand in bold relief before the world and what a disaster *that* turned out to be.

And so it happened that I was married after supper on my birthday without having given the matter any thought upon waking. At Mama's urging, I had been away visiting a friend, and on that day, I came strolling down Jefferson Street in Louisville, Kentucky, with my hat tied by the ribbons about my waist, carrying a basket with a Chantilly cake that my friend's mother had given me.

But as I turned the corner, I saw crowds of strangers milling around on the long stone porch of my house. Large red blankets flagged over the sills of every window fronting the street. I knew what those red rags meant—we had been ruined.

When he died, my father had been the richest man in Kentucky. But now, we Louisville Bullitts were financially deranged. While I was away, our house had been seized by creditors and put up for auction with red banners flying from the windows signaling that everything, including the servants, was for sale. Strangers waltzed through the front door as if they owned the place. Seething with dread, I considered dashing down to the steamer dock, buying a fare to New Orleans, abandoning my home and this humiliating turn of fate.

My panic was whittled to its sharpest point. I could have run away then and my life as I speak of it would have been of a wholly different nature. And I *would have* run away if not for my mother, but I just couldn't leave Mama behind to suffer through this catastrophe by herself. Being the youngest of twelve children, I still lived at home though my brothers and sisters had married and moved on long ago. As the youngest, my first instinct was to run around in circles, throw my hands up in the air, and cry out, "Where is someone who will look after *me*?"

Approaching my house slowly, I hesitated and rested my hand upon the front gate ghosting on its hinges. A group of creditors gathered in the shade of the hawthorn trees and upon seeing me, they lifted their tall silk hats respectfully. But I felt a hot spark of shame and lowered my eyes.

I ran inside and slid over the bare, scuffed floors. Ordinarily, there would have been a middle-aged butler in gloves holding the door open, but I didn't see the servants and didn't recognize any of the people here. Indeed, this didn't look like my house at all. The place smelled of unclean bodies and the halls resounded with the scrape of family heirlooms being dragged away.

From the look of things, the red blankets had been up since the previous day. I pushed through the crowd of strangers and climbed the stairs. Each footfall sounded as though I were dancing on a box. Flies buzzed through the open doors and windows. Upon reaching the first landing, I passed some Lexington farmers conspiring in low tones about buying the Negroes in a lot, preempting the broker before he could assign a price to them. Women knelt before a trunk, removing Papa's shirts and holding them up one by one.

As if walking through a nightmare, I peered into each empty bedroom searching for Mama. In my room, everything had been taken away except the linen blinds, mosquito netting, and the grass mat on the floor. As far as I could tell, my wardrobe was untouched. No one had taken the muslin bug sleeves that the servants had put over the candle sconces to guard against flyspecks. The old walnut floor humped up in the center as if a whale slept under the planking.

I entered the anteroom where a young widow in mourning weeds had thrown wide the doors of the wardrobe as she picked through my gowns.

"Those dresses are mine," I said, closing the wardrobe door.

"You bought all of them?" the widow asked. "Even the corsets? Because they look to fit me real fine."

"I don't think so. I don't think any of my clothes would fit you unless you fell off mightily. All of these are *mine*." I stepped between the widow and my wardrobe and folded my arms across my chest. "I would burn this house down in the dead hour of the night and go running out into the mud in my nightdress before I'd let you have these. Go on, now," I said, and she left without another word. Thus, in my first small victory of the day, I rescued my gowns from the rabble.

But discerning something amiss, I frowned around the room and gasped upon seeing the empty wall above the fireplace mantel. Some stranger had taken our family portrait, *The Bullitt Sisters as the Fates*. In 1834, Mama had commissioned Sully, the famous society portraitist, to paint me and my sisters sitting together in the front garden under an ash tree, wearing summer white dresses and doing needlework.

Sully had depicted us as limpid-eyed temptresses, which said more about him than it did about us. We four sisters had never, a day in our lives looked as wickedly desirable as we did on that canvas, where my eldest sister Mary held the distaff in a shockingly suggestive manner. Beside her sat Eloise, who drew a thread from the distaff as if to measure it, her birdlike head tilted aside and a gleam in her eye. And there, sitting between Mary and Eloise was me, all flushed and agitated as I reached with the scissors to cut the thread in Eloise's hands. Only my sister Anne had not been given a task. Anne Bullitt gazed adoringly at the three of us, her halo of red hair lit all over as if the artist had some premonition of her early leave-taking. Sully had engraved a piece of brass at the base of the frame with the title, *The Bullitt Sisters as the Fates*, thereby celebrating my sisters and me as irresistible sirens luring hapless men into our embraces before mercilessly cutting their lives short.

Well, I felt desperately anxious about that painting. It had given me comfort to know that wherever in the world my sisters might be, we were always together in one place, in spirit, if not in fact. But now some stranger owned my family portrait and she would hang it in her house and make up a story about my sisters and I being her cousins, or something ridiculous like that. Chewing upon my bottom lip in a fit of exasperation, I went to the window and drew deep breaths. My room overlooked the willow thickets, the cottonwoods, and the low swampy part of our land. The green skiff Papa had given me floated on the small pond. Out in the wetlands, I thought I saw Mama leading a calf along a marshy path.

I collected my baskets and then hurried down the backstairs intending to catch up with Mama and ask her how we had come to this ruin. I left through the back door, crossed over the stack yard where the horses stood in the paddock waiting to be turned out into the pasture, and sprinted past them out into the meadow. But Mama was nowhere to be found. Fretting over how I might save the little green skiff, I wandered toward the pond but felt overcome with anxious despair at the sight of it unmoored and adrift. I recalled my fourth birthday, remembered sitting in the boat while Papa held the mooring rope and the sun reflected off the water so that I could not recall his expression, only the glare of light where his eyes should have been.

I sat on the shore, unlaced my boots, and setting them side by side, untied my hat ribbons, and tossed the hat in the grass, then pressed my forearm against my mouth, smelling lily of the valley soap on my skin. Lily of the valley grew wherever Eve's repentant tears had fallen after she was banished from Eden. Mama always said that lily of the valley was the only perfume that was appropriate for an unmarried belle.

Kicking off my petticoats, I left them in a heap beside my hat and waded into the water, talking to the boat as if it were a living thing, "Right there. Don't move now." The rope floated like a bull snake, and I grabbed it and began paddling back to the dock, swimming with my head above the murky surface of the pond. There were flakes of green paint all over my hands, my ivory dress was streaked with algae, and my skirt draggled around my legs.

When I reached the shallows, I walked backward, straining and pulling. The rope scraped against my hands and then, for no reason at all, I felt wafts and flutters in my belly and my heart beating up around my ears. The blood drained from my head and pooled in my feet. Someone was standing behind me.

"Turn around, miss."

I recognized his voice; harsh and Eastern, it came from deep in his cheekbones behind his nose, with sentences like rapid bursts of musket fire. Rat-a-tat-tat.

"Turn around and look at me," he said.

And I did, brushing the hair from my face, staring straight at him, my eyes reflecting the shine off the water. I was thinking, *I gave you up. When you left without saying good-bye, I gave you up for good and have tried to forget you ever lived.*

Lieutenant Philip Kearny folded his coat over his arm. He wore a brown traveling suit, but despite his journey, his clothing was unwrinkled, his cravat crisply knotted, and his shirt, immaculate. He had auburn hair, a high-bridged nose, and under his strongly marked eyebrows, Lieutenant Kearny regarded me in a manner both eager and serious. Possessed of a keen intelligence, he impressed me as a man who reacted to any threat with swift efficiency and yet, something in his expression told me that I had somehow unsettled him. With his hat in hand and his aloof air, the entire effect was of a young man probably no more than twenty-six, but who behaved with the assurance of a man of forty.

We first met nearly three years ago at Jefferson Barracks, Missouri, where I was visiting my sister Mary. One autumn afternoon in 1838, I had been standing on a stepladder in the old orchard by my sister's house, picking apples and tossing them into a basket. And then Philip came striding down the grassy path, proud and swaggering in his dragoon uniform. He bowed, and I nodded. But as he walked by, he kicked the ladder out from under me. I went flying and so did the apples, but Philip Kearny caught me in his arms and declared that he would watch over me and protect me until the end of my days.

Like a fool, I had believed him. Never mind that my footing was secure until he knocked it out from under me. Never mind that I had been reaching up for the fruit I had desired when he came along. He courted me for eight months and everyone predicted that we would marry, but on the day I expected him to propose, he told me he was leaving the country by order of the War Department and hurrying off to a cavalry school in France. Two years had passed without a word from him and now I wanted to ask him . . . Why? *Why did you make me believe you loved me?* But my pride made me stubborn. I would not give Philip the satisfaction of pleading for an explanation.

I broke the silence. "Lieutenant Kearny, how do you do, sir?"

"I am fine, thank you, Miss Bullitt."

"I am in grave suspense," I knotted the rope of the boat to the dock and looked over my shoulder at him. "Did you buy anything at the estate auction?"

"I bought *all* of the paintings, you know, to keep them away from dubious characters. And I have a letter of introduction to your mother. I had no idea you and your mother had . . . I did not know you were in reduced circumstances."

"Mama is nowhere to be found. You may leave your letter of introduction with me, if you like, and I shall see that she gets it."

With a doubtful look, he removed the letter from his coat pocket and handed it to me. I broke the seal and the wax crumbled in my hands. "We can't put you up, nor board your horse. We've had houseguests who've stayed for weeks eating and drinking until they were laid out like dead hogs. It's one of the reasons we are in trouble now. Anyone can see our days of dispensing old-style Southern hospitality are long gone."

"I do not intend to impose."

Unfolding the single sheet of paper with a flick of my thumb and forefinger, I read the letter. In it, my sister Mary wrote that Lieutenant Philip Kearny had recently inherited the largest fortune in the history of the United States from his grandfather. My sister closed with, ". . . and as the boy isn't even passably ugly, Diana really ought to give him due consideration."

"You must have high ranking among God's spies and snoops." He thumped the crown of his hat and studied my reaction.

"I am hardly spying or snooping by reading a letter you put in my hands."

"One intended for your mother."

An anxious stillness fell, as neither of us knew what to say next. I rolled his letter into a tube and rapped it against my leg.

He drew a breath, "May I call upon you, Miss Bullitt?"

"And where will you call upon me, Lieutenant? Here at the pond?"

"You do have a point."

"I guess I do." Misery oppressed me, and consumed by nervous worry over where Mama and I would sleep that night, I nearly forgot all about Lieutenant Kearny. Folding the letter, I tucked it into my wet waistband.

Philip shifted his weight and rested a hand on his hip. "Are you seriously considering anyone . . . anyone in particular?"

Sitting on the dock, and leaning back on my hands, I told a bald-faced lie. "Six local boys have begged me to marry them. Every last one of them *doctors*. Apple-eye boys who can't wait to put a ring on my finger."

"The very air is darkened with doctors."

"What was that you said?"

"Six suitors!" Philip gave me a sly look. "And where will your suitors call upon you in the days to come, may I ask?"

I blew a lock of hair off my forehead and felt perversely unreasonable. "Probably right here by this dock. I shall receive my suitors in my best dock-and-pond-gown." I patted a place beside me. "Now, come sit and tell me what bits of my ancestry you intend to pass off as your own. I am speaking of my family paintings, now."

He carefully arranged his coat and hat upon the dock post and with a neat snapping motion, tugged up his trousers and sat beside me. Philip unlaced his boots and then rolled his black socks into them, giving me a chance to admire his slender ankles and his long white feet with a faint line of auburn hair on the top.

I flirted a look at him because I was good at this sort of thing. But so was he. While in Paris and North Africa, Philip Kearny had probably galvanized French noble tarts every day of the week, drawing them in with his half-sad, half-amused expression and his baffling, elusive abruptness. Suppressing my old feelings of having been wronged and instead, letting nature take its course, I soaked my feet in the water. He kept his feet above the surface.

"What will you do now that you must break up housekeeping, Miss Bullitt?"

"Why, I shall buy the painting of my sisters from you."

"Ah, there is nothing I like better than a little wholesome negotiation. What will you give me for the painting?"

"Ever had Chantilly cake?" I motioned grandly to the cake basket at my side.

He scratched the back of his neck and appeared to think upon it. "No, I can't say as I have."

"The best cake in the world. I shall give you *a cake* for that painting."

Philip lifted the wooden lid and peering inside, sniffed the confection drenched in Lisbon wine. He scooped thick yellow butter icing into his mouth, grinning at me as he swallowed. "I'm afraid it's not enough. How will you earn your keep now?" His eyes twinkled with desire and I knew I had the advantage.

"I do not intend to starve in genteel poverty."

"Starvation ought not to be a problem for a doctor's wife."

I felt my cheeks grow hot; he'd caught me lying about my dismal marriage prospects. "Well now, Lieutenant Kearny, you have gone and paralyzed my womanly reason."

"Miss Bullitt? You really should consider . . . *me*."

"Because you think I have no other choice? I will forgive you for the insult, Lieutenant, as I reckon even the Lord excuses us for bad training."

The lieutenant tried to soothe me, made his voice tender and soft and his eyes crinkled at the edges as he concentrated on his speech. He tapped out his words, touching his forefinger to my wrist as he said, "Miss Bullitt, you must hear what I have come to say. Nothing would afford me more pleasure than to devote my . . ." But then, Philip stopped as if waiting for the wind to finish his sentence. Reaching for his socks, he tugged them over his cold feet and then hurriedly donned his shoes. When he gave no sign of continuing, I thought to nudge him along.

"You wish to devote your . . . *what*?"

He paused and lowered himself onto the dock. Sitting down again, he leaned close to me. I could smell the laundry bluing in his shirt, the celery scent of his mouth, and see every line in his lips and the specks of green in his brown eyes. I speculated that the lieutenant knew how to kiss a girl slowly and sweetly. He touched the top of my hand with his forefinger and traced a circle there. I fought down the burning heat in my belly and the impulse to fling myself at him and pin his shoulders to the planking.

"Shame on me for finding you interesting, Lieutenant."

"And why are you interested in me, Miss Bullitt?"

"It is the natural pull of evil, I do believe."

I gazed up at him, but did not move or give him a hint. He let his mouth fall open the slightest bit, calculating, taut, and breathless, deciding what he might get away with. He cleared his throat, slid a finger under his collar, and turned his head slightly aside. "I wrote some verse about how we first met."

I sincerely doubted this, for he was not a poetic sort of fellow. But Lieutenant Kearny stared fiercely at the opposite bank and, unprompted by me, recited his poem, "In the autumn of the year the sunlight limned your face, and I told myself it was a trick of light that made me love you . . ."

Well, the pathos, the sheer awfulness of it—and his pride—won me over completely. In a fit of impulse, I touched his cheek and let my lips brush against his, hearing him exhale in a raggedy, involuntary sort of way. I kissed him on the mouth. Philip's beard stubble was bristly as a doormat. I had counted on him being gentlemanly and refined. I hadn't counted on him losing his self-restraint. But he threaded his fingers through my hair and began kissing me in earnest with his mouth open and pressing hard against mine. I felt a falling sensation in my stomach, and I wanted to tumble on top of him. *Keep kissing me until I say mercy.*

A shriek pierced the air. It was my mama.

"Diana Moore Gwathmey Bullitt! *Diana!* You, child! Diana! You, girl!"

I shoved the boy off. Dazed and bewildered, I sat up and looked around in a panic. Mama came running through the grass with her skirt knotted in her hands and her thin, fussy shoulders heaving with shock. Her fading gold spaniel curls bounced in rhythm with her step. An elegant fifty-nine-year-old Englishwoman from the Virginia Tidewater with fine features and tragic eyes, she dropped her skirt and let it trail in the mud as she gestured wildly at me, making a *Separate! Separate from that man!* motion with her hands.

Philip leapt to his feet and smoothed his hands over his hair. For a moment, he seemed not to know what to do. And then he stared across the water at my formidable mother, picturesquely indignant in her purple gown. He donned his coat, tapped his hat on his head, and pulled me to my feet.

When Philip spoke in his New York accent, my mama must have thought him devilishly foreign.

"Mrs. Bullitt, I am Lieutenant Philip Kearny."

"The Irish are not to be trusted!" Mama pointed at him and railed, "You are a scoundrel, sir! A blackguard! And for assaulting my daughter, I shall see you strung up by a rope around your neck and jerked heavenward to Jesus before the sun sets on this day."

"Mama! This is the young man who—"

But Philip cut me short. "Mrs. Bullitt! I'll have you know I am too much of a gentleman to let your daughter adopt such scandalous conduct without marrying her."

And turning to me, he said, "Miss Bullitt, nothing would afford me more pleasure than to devote the remainder of my life to you and to protect you and to provide for you."

"What are you saying over there? Take your hands off of my daughter, you vile Yankee!"

I toed a circle on the dock, thinking upon Philip's proposal before answering him.

"Well, all right then. I say yes. I do, Lieutenant Kearny. I shall marry you."

Philip called to Mama. "Mrs. Bullitt! Diana and I are going to be married."

Mama clasped one arm about her waist, pressed her fist to her mouth and thought a moment. "Do you love her, sir?"

"I think so. Yes . . . that is . . . as far as these things go . . . I think . . . Yes."

"Can you provide for her?" Mama asked.

I rose on my tiptoes as if it would improve my hearing.

"Why yes, of course," Philip said.

"And where shall you live, sir?"

"We shall divide our time between Washington City and New York."

"You are taking my baby girl into Satan's Empire?" Mama touched her forehead as if feeling for fever.

"Yes, yes. I shall give Diana a house in Washington City, where we shall live while I serve the War Department. Also a townhouse in Manhattan, a country house on the Hudson, the finest equipages and gowns from Paris . . ." And with a wink at me, Philip added, ". . . and Diana shall have all of the cake she cares to eat."

"My, that's pretentious enough for anybody," I said, but I was secretly pleased.

Mama squinted up at him. "Diana shall require an allowance."

I'd never heard Mama speak of money before now. My mother was so immensely dignified she could hardly add numbers in her head, and subtraction was too vulgar an act for a grand lady descended from one of the first families of the Virginia Tidewater.

I drummed my fingers against my ribs and paced the dock, thinking of my new life in the East. Now that I would marry, my life's ambition had been satisfied and no longer would I have to worry over dying a spinster in a dusty attic. At that instant, I promised myself that I would be the most compliant wife who ever lived. I would strive to excel at every domestic virtue, yet grace my new husband's life with the shining light of my spiritual loftiness and my faithfulness to all of his life's dreams.

Ah yes, ah well. If young ladies were wiser beings, marriage would not be a divine institution.

Emboldened by her successful bargaining, Mama stepped forward and put her hands upon her hips. "Can you provide for her mother, too?"

Philip lowered his lids in a smart affected way. "Must I?"

"Be assured, her mother will visit but occasionally. I'll be of no bother to you, sir."

"That is hardly true of most people's mothers," Philip said.

"Very well," Mama said, calming a little and smoothing the frizz of blonde curls away from her temples. "I can think of worse fates than being pitchforked into marriage with a perfect stranger."

Almost immediately, Philip left and went to buy passage on a steamer, then searched around Louisville for the Reverend Shaw, whom Mama had recommended to marry us. In Philip's absence, Mama and I packed my clothes into goatskin trunks. We tucked bracelets and perfumes into the leather pockets, layering fragile silks and airy muslins with white paper on top of my nightdresses and linens. When we finished, Mama sat back on her heels, pinched a few dill seeds from a small snuffbox, and slipped them into her mouth to sweeten her breath. A quizzing glass hung from a chain around her neck and made a clicking noise against the bones of her corset as she moved about the room.

Surveying the dozen trunks lined up before the door, she said, "I wish I could give you a few of our people as house servants but they are all pledged to Mr. Walker."

"Mr. Kearny wouldn't allow it anyway, Mama."

"Goodness gracious, Kearny isn't an abolitionist, is he?"

"Oh no, but he hires his own people. Besides, I am happy just to have the portrait of my sisters as a wedding present. It is enough for me."

Mama laid out fourteen cotton petticoat skirts, lifting them one by one as I tied the tapers around my waist. She said, "Kearny has peculiar Yankee ideas and an uncertain temper. I suspect he has difficult requirements of a wife."

But I did not want Mama to taint my perfect happiness with dire warnings about Philip. I balanced on one leg and pulled a silk stocking over my calf, fastening it with a garter above my knee. "Mama, will you come with us? I know you have many friends near Washington City. You could come with us and make small trips and visit your kin in the Tidewater."

"No, child." Mama began brushing my hair, following each stroke with a smoothing hand down my back to my waist. "I shall go to your sister and the general." She plucked the hair from the brush, wadded it into a ball, and pitched it into the china hair receiver. "I am a good judge of character. Lieutenant Kearny stands between light and darkness, and I sense he is trapped between his desire to be a good and honorable man, and . . . his unspoken appetites."

"Well, I admire his many qualities." I held my arms above my head as Mama carefully tugged the muslin gown over my petticoats. I tweaked the cascade of white silk violets tumbling from the waist to the hem as Mama laced me up.

Her eyes were red and moist.

"Mama? Don't cry; please try to be happy for me."

"Now hear me, Diana. Tell Philip *no* once in a while. Now and again, say, *no*. Really, it isn't so impossible. Tell him you are indisposed, when he persists, and he will, tell him you must decline the favor. Else you will have a baby every year until you are fifty." She fumbled in her skirt pocket for a handkerchief, dabbed at her nose. Mama planted teary kisses on my cheeks, and then pulled me away, saying, "I hear Mr. Kearny downstairs, and the reverend too. Let's not keep them waiting."

Philip met me at the foot of the stairs with a bouquet of single-bloom Virginia roses that he had gathered from our own yard and wrapped in a dinner napkin he had found in the pantry. "A bride deserves a bouquet," he said, placing the flowers in my hands, "and I thought Virginia roses suited you."

Philip hurried me out the back door where the Reverend Shaw waited under the grape arbor. We were married at four o'clock in the afternoon under the garden trees. Strangers still lingered in the house, so we could not marry in the parlor as Mama wished and no one in Louisville ever married in a church. Church weddings did not become fashionable for another ten years. The buyers in the house leaned over the windowsills and watched as Philip and I were declared man and wife. Throughout, I kept sneaking looks at my new husband, admiring his handsome profile and congratulating myself on my good fortune.

Mama muffled sobs into her handkerchief. She had loaned Philip her wedding ring and he slipped it over my finger, murmuring that he would buy a proper ring for me when we arrived in the East. But I preferred Mama's gold band, worn down by her gentle hand to a thread on the palm side.

When it was all over, I skipped through my house for the last time. Fired with youthful exuberance and excitement, I did not mourn my old life and all of my concerns about bankruptcy had vanished. Mama led us through the hall to the front while the strangers called out and cheered us on our way, wishing us good luck and Godspeed as if they were in the wedding party. Mama and I embraced in the shade of the porte cochere, murmuring wistfully to one another.

Philip had thoughtfully hired porters to load my trunks and all of the family paintings onto a wagon. He ordered them to be more careful as they hurled my luggage onto the wagon, tossing blankets over *The Bullitt Sisters as the Fates* and lashing the picture down with rope. Before paying them, Philip inspected their work, frowning as he checked the knots and wrappings. Satisfied that my things were secure, he told the men to form a line. The porters brushed the dust from their hands and pocketed the money Philip gave them.

Then, Philip helped me up the metal steps onto the seat of the hired hack. I arranged my skirts and made room for him. He hesitated, bending over, his hat in his hand and a strange and fiercely possessive look in his eyes. "This is not what I had intended, Diana, but it was the best I could do under the circumstances."

"Oh, there is no need to apologize," I began, and moving aside on the seat, gazed expectantly at him.

But he said, "I never ride in carriages. Carriages are for women and invalids."

"And you won't make an exception? Not even this once?" I asked.

"No," he said. And with that, Philip tossed a spare blanket over my lap, tucking it around my legs and feet to protect my white dress and nodding to himself as if satisfied that I would not be soiled by the trip to the waterfront. He withdrew from the carriage and swung up into the saddle. He would ride alongside like a squire and lead his spare horse to the levee.

Mama climbed inside the hack, straightened the bonnet on my head and reaching for my veil, unpinned it and lowered it over my face.

"Obey Mr. Kearny and do not vex him overmuch. Hold your temper. Understand his failings, forgive quickly, be mild and flatter him when he is in a bad humor and at all times, subordinate your will to his."

"But I thought you told me to decline the favor else I would have a baby every year? How can I decline him, yet obey him at all times?"

She glanced aside at my bridegroom waiting patiently on his horse and whispered urgently to me, "There is no contradiction in what I say. Husbands require a lot of help from their wives to make them behave like gentlemen."

"What sort of help?"

"You shall learn soon enough."

"But, Mama!"

"Tsk, now. Write as soon as you arrive in Washington." Her heliotrope cologne surrounded us, her blonde curls brushed my cheek as she kissed me, and her bones felt light and birdlike as she hugged me good-bye.

I leaned from the window and watched her as she climbed down and turned to Philip. Gazing sternly up at my new husband with a hand to the brim of her bonnet shielding her face from the afternoon sun, Mama said, "And as for you, Mr. Kearny, remember that marriage is meant to bring mutual solace, not bondage. Tyrannical husbands make women rebellious wives. If I ever hear that you have been cruel to my daughter, I shall pursue you like Death in the Apocalypse. I shall find you and whip you as if you were my own son."

Philip straightened in the saddle and blinked as he considered her threat. Then, he tipped his hat to my mother. "Be assured, Mrs. Bullitt, my wife shall reign sovereign in her household."

"Good-bye, Daughter!" Mama raised her arm, her handkerchief fluttering in the breeze, and I looked back over my shoulder as my home receded in the distance.

The steamer packets lined up along the Ohio River while the Negro laborers dumped barrels on the wharf. Whistles sounded and the air smelled of coal soot. A crowd of travelers swarmed aboard the boats. As we would soon travel into the free North, the mate of the *Cape Jessamine*—our honeymoon steamer—forced the Negro crew off the deck and onto the shore, stabbing at them with his barrel stave, ordering them away from the gangplank to allow the Irish and the German workers to take their place on the boat bound northeastward. No captain would risk losing a valuable slave crew to the abolitionists in the North, and so the mate ordered the Negroes down the riverbank to a side-wheeler bound for the sugar coast.

Philip's pair of white horses caused a sensation as they were led up the gangplank into the stern of the boat, the roustabouts having a morbid fear of any white animal bringing bad luck aboard. As the whistle blew and the engines churned, work-worn women and spindling children filed onto the deck. Sweaty men jostled by carrying armloads of wood for the boilers. A clerk came running up the wharf with paper and charcoal in hand to write down a list of our belongings.

Philip Kearny settled his hat upon his head, surveying the levee, a man who knew that his will must be done, on earth as it doubtless was in heaven. A man of boundless energy, he never stopped moving, tapping his walking stick on the wharf planking. I studied my new husband, memorizing every detail about him, from the flicking motion of his buff glove to the wave of auburn hair under his hat. Philip nodded to the steward as he tucked the walking stick under his arm and removed banknotes from his money clip.

As we boarded the *Cape Jessamine,* Philip put me in front of him, elbowing aside men who drew too close. Porters dragged my trunks across the boiler deck amid passengers clamoring at the rails, thick as chickens in a pen. I could smell their habits and their homes rising from their clothing—the tarry odor of coal smoke, geranium cologne, unwashed hair musky as pelts, and most prevalent, a top note of cam-

phor oil that smarted my nostrils. We climbed up to the hurricane deck
to a suite of cabins furnished with big cast-iron beds, tables, wash-
stands, and settees.

The porter ostentatiously swept aside a heavy blue canvas curtain as
we inspected our quarters. I hurried over to the portrait of my sisters
wrapped in a bit of oilcloth, secured with hemp twine. Peeking under its
cover, I was relieved to see it had not been damaged.

Philip gave the porter a withering look and shouted, "What? Where
is the door of this stateroom?"

"But I am holding it for you, sir," said the porter, of the blue curtain.

"That is no proper door! It is a rag. I won't have my wife sleeping
in an indefensible cabin!"

"No need to worry, sir, ain't nobody gonna trouble you. Ain't
nobody gonna hear nothin' neither." The porter leered at me.

Philip lost his temper. He shoved the startled porter up against the
wall. I gasped as my husband, with his forearm against the man's throat
said, "I want a damned door on this room. Let's you and I go find one,
shall we?"

And then, as calmly as if nothing had happened, Philip released the
terrified porter, who rushed out of the cabin. Though astounded by the
speed and violence of Philip's response, I was somewhat flattered, too.
Something in his nature, the contrast between his elegant gentlemanly
demeanor and the startling brutality of his response to such insults
appealed to me, but I was too young and infatuated to understand the
danger implicit in these contradictions.

He cleared his throat, rolled his shoulders, and then tugged at his
waistcoat as he said, "Why don't you make yourself comfortable, Mrs.
Kearny, until I return?"

With a bow, Philip left, and intent upon his purpose, stormed down
the stairs to the lower decks.

While I waited for him to return, I tried to think what a bride ought to do. I could not unpack, for where would I put my things? I dared not undress, or change from my muslin gown into traveling clothes for fear someone might come in. Besides, I couldn't unlace myself and I had no ladies' maid to do it for me, which meant Philip had to unlace me. Mortified at this prospect, I told myself that it was not a thing to be thought of. Still, I paced and thought about it anyway. My sisters and my friends said wedding nights were supposed to unfold with decorum. The bride in a prim nightgown waited under the blankets for her groom to come in the door wearing an ankle-length nightshirt and carrying a candle. Well, that meant Philip must wait half-naked outside on the deck. I couldn't envision him doing that. Needing something to do, I lit the candles in the wall cressets and the lamp on the table. Pacing the floor, I tapped my fingertips on my lips and listened to passengers shuffling by, small children whining to their mothers and the workers shouting at one another.

Soon, a small troop of smiling waiters bearing covered trays and wine followed Philip into the cabin. And miraculously, Philip had persuaded a clerk to fashion a door for us from the lid of an empty coffin he discovered in the hold.

Satisfied with his improved surroundings, Philip beckoned me onto the deck. As the afternoon dwindled away to twilight, wild plum trees bloomed on the riverbank, the coal smoke flagged over our heads, and the rear wheel churned ragged foamy webs in the water.

Resting his elbows on the railing, he asked me to name the homesteads we passed, and I did, telling him everything I knew about the farms and the people who lived on them, all the while feeling his gaze searching my face. He listened intently as if his life depended on my every word, but he was only trying to put me at ease. As darkness fell, all of the lights on board were extinguished and curtains drawn over the cabin windows, for the pilot was so particular about his navigating view of the Ohio being obscured by glare that no man dared even light a cigar.

Growing weary of the sound of my own voice and thinking to draw him out, I asked, "What did you think of North Africa?"

He feigned reluctance, but he was flattered by my interest and bowing his head with a smile said, "The fighting was elegant, but as for everything else, I most assuredly do not miss it."

"And the women in Africa?"

He raised his brows, clearly amused. "The women in Algiers are completely veiled but for one eye as they walk to the baths with their servants."

"Are they beautiful?"

"I am not an admirer of one-eyed women."

I tried again. "But the nomad women in the deserts who live in tents and herd goats? Did you see any of them?"

Philip did not answer my question, but took my arm and led me into our cabin.

I waited uncertainly by the iron footboard. It was hot in our room from the burning lamp oil and candles. I plucked at the pointed seam of my bodice as Philip removed his coat and hung it upon the back of a chair, then unfastened his cuff links and dropped them on the table. Taking my hand, he brought me over to the bed and there, he sat beside me. I dared not meet his eyes, but looked directly ahead at the mosquitoes clustering on the cotton shade.

Finally, he answered my question. "Why, Diana, there are so many different tribes. There are the green-eyed Berber girls kidnapped by their lovers and the lean aristocratic Taureg women who dress in indigo blue and nothing else, so that the dye rubs off on their skin."

"Did you . . ." I began pinching the feathers under the counterpane until I could feel the quills snap.

"Did I . . . what?" He leaned around to look at me, daring me to ask the question.

"Did you have carnal connections with any of those women?"

"No, of course not."

"I don't believe you."

But he just laughed. And reaching behind me, he lifted the modest silk scarf from my shoulders and pressed his mouth to the small bones under the coil of hair low on my neck. I felt the hair on my arms rise as he began whispering to me, telling me what he wished for us to do. He expertly loosened the braided strings on the back of my gown and my bodice and corset fell open like a pink shell in his hands. I closed my eyes and shivered as he slid his hands around me from behind and rested them on my hips. And turning me onto my back, he lowered his mouth onto the linen chemise, leaving the wet imprint of his lips over the cloth over my breasts. Reaching for my foot, he clasped my left ankle, pushed the fragile layers of my pale muslin skirt up to the middle of my shin and began unlacing the slipper.

Philip's cuff links tumbled off the table and went rolling over the plank floor. He spoke softly as he unwound the last ribbon and, cupping the slipper, removed it from my foot. "In the deserts of Africa, the unmarried Taureg girls take as many lovers as they please, and a lover learns her body at her ankles and explores the fine bones of her legs and upward until he reaches her mouth. What do you think of that?"

With a wickedly lascivious glance, his cheek at my knee, his mouth at the garter and then my bare leg above the stocking, he disappeared under the layers of skirt and feeling a gentle nudging, I flung my arms wide and fell back into the pillows. For the first time in my life, I understood the true meaning of my sisters' whispering about marital bliss. His body was lean and finely muscled, with auburn hair on his chest, speckles on his shoulders from sunburn, and the muscles of his back and his forearms were finely wrought from years of riding and fighting. The bones of his hips were sharp as the blade of a trowel, and his legs long and lean.

Afterward, Philip slept with my cheek pressed to his chest, my leg across his, my fingers tracing the line of hair on his flat belly, as I listened to his breathing. To lose myself in a man like this was the sort of pleasure that life and God rarely allow us, and as I had been allowed to enjoy him by the state of Kentucky and my Maker how much happier could a woman possibly be? Not happier than I.

∾ Washington ∾

Three

WHAT DID I KNOW about being married? My father died when I was so young that I did not remember him and my mama made her own decisions and lived alone. My sisters married before me, but then moved away and in their letters, made only vague allusions to the trouble their husbands caused them. I never observed the daily workings of a marriage and knew nothing about living with a man.

In the summer of 1841, Philip bought a red-brick colonial house with black shutters, five bays wide and three stories high located between Thirteenth and Fourteenth on K Street, very near the White House. Beautifully situated on cultivated grounds, surrounded by alder and dogwood trees, our private gardens and walking paths were protected by a brick wall. There, my husband and I passed every evening linked arm in arm, strolling after dinner while we discussed Philip's work at the War Department. We were virtually inseparable when he was at home, musing and planning for the future. Because he never hesitated to tell me what he thought and felt, I mistakenly believed there were no secrets between us.

Philip was a virtuoso ear-bender. He loved to talk, and after we attended parties, he kept me awake until the small hours of the night discussing everyone who had been there and what they had said and done. The following morning, he liked to read aloud at the breakfast table the flattering things the society columnists had written about him. And as he folded the papers, tucking them away, he'd watch me, resting his chin in hand and he'd tease me about my appetite. He said I ate like an Indian, whatever that meant. Without wondering at the cause, I had suddenly developed a mighty yearning for breakfast, for baked eggs on squares of ham with cream sauce, Maryland biscuits, deviled roast beef bones rolled in bread crumbs, and roasted potatoes; every morning, Philip gallantly yielded the last of the Boston apple pudding cut from puff paste at the bottom of a deep pie dish.

We could see Lafayette Park from our front stoop and as Philip shared the political gossip and scandal that he'd heard, I could not help but pity beleaguered President Tyler and his invalid wife. John Tyler of Virginia was the first vice president to assume office after the death of a sitting president. Many of Philip's friends at the War Department spoke scornfully of Tyler as *His Accidency.* They worried that having as our president a man who hadn't been elected meant certain ruin for our country. Some said Tyler ought to be impeached for daring to exercise the full powers of the presidency. Though I had no decided political leanings, I disliked hearing criticism of him, thinking it disrespectful.

Philip's commanding officer, General Winfield Scott, called upon us shortly after we had set up housekeeping, and having inspected the sprawling and lavishly furnished public rooms on the first floor of our house, declared that our parlors were the finest he had ever seen in the district. Since Philip was his aide-de-camp, the general delegated all of his party planning responsibilities to my husband.

But after the general took his leave, Philip closed the double doors to the first parlor and in a fury, shoved over a potted palm, railing that he was not a majordomo. He said that he needed to return to the field and complained that he hated desk duty in Washington. Worse yet, Philip thought hosting parties frivolous and beneath him.

Alarmed by his outburst, I retreated to the opposite end of the room. To his credit, Philip noticed that I had half-concealed myself behind a huge old colonial secretary and resting his hands on his hips, bowed his head, drew a deep breath, and stared down at his boots as he calmed himself.

"Diana," he finally said, extending a hand, "come out from there, I am sorry if I have frightened you."

But his mood did not improve until a few moments later when I volunteered to do his work for him.

Soon, I found myself hosting three dinner parties a week for one hundred eighty guests. In effect, I was operating a small restaurant in our home and entertaining the most powerful men in the district. I rose at five o'clock every morning and dressed. A little chambermaid carrying a basket of keys to the chests, cabinets, and closets followed me everywhere around the house. I met with Cook and my housekeeper to consult on the menu and seating arrangements, paid calls, ran errands, replied to queries, inspected the house, resolved disputes among the staff—there were always disputes—dressed for the nightly event, and by six o'clock the parties began. I did not fall into bed until all of the silver had been locked away and the staff had retired at one o'clock in the morning.

But then, in mid-August, in my third week as a Washington hostess, I accidentally very nearly almost killed Congress. In one fell swooping-cough, I almost launched into eternity every last man jack, the representatives of the people.

The trouble began when General Scott demanded I give a nighttime party aboard a boat on the Potomac River. On Thursday, August 12, 1841—a humid summer evening, the fireflies hovered in the tulip trees and curious pedestrians paused to admire the pretty sloop *Alhambra* lit by torches and adorned with garlands of flowers. A large crowd of men in military dress uniform, checked country jackets, straw hats, and spotted neckties slowly filed aboard as a string quartet played a Schottische.

I had only just begun to grasp the strange habits of my new city, but I was quickly becoming convinced that Washingtonians were a peculiar tribe of people. The prominent men of Washington dyed their hair and their beards with bizarre effect, for the lead dyes shone purple and green in the firelight. But the worst aspect of their behavior was their incessant spitting, for it seemed no man went anywhere without a quid of tobacco in his cheek.

Of the sixty-five guests sipping champagne on the *Alhambra*, there were only two women present, an elderly lady in a yellow silk turban with a peacock feather and me. We stood together in the center of the deck and commiserated. Wearing white lead face paint and a great deal of rouge, Mrs. Dolley Madison said lowly, "When my Madison was in office, there were married ladies at every levee and reception."

"I am not accustomed to these stag parties either," I replied, waving away a bee buzzing around the wreath of camellias upon my head. "When I was growing up in Louisville, married ladies attended dancing parties, but here in Washington, you never see young matrons after three o'clock in the afternoon. Girls attend parties until they marry and then vanish from the face of the earth. Why is that? No one at these parties but men and old—" Realizing my error, I stopped short and Dolley Madison cast a shrewd sidelong glance at me.

"You can say it in front of me, dear, I know I'm old." Mrs. Madison touched the edge of her tongue to her top lip. She sighed and pulled her shawl back over her arms. "I think married ladies stopped attending night-time parties during the Jackson administration and who could blame them? Who wanted to be out at night with that bullying lout holding sway? He was a remarkable idiot, Andrew Jackson."

And then she placed a hand to my cheek in such an intimate way that she startled me. "How lovely you are. Shame on that fat old buffoon Winfield Scott. It is unfair of him to burden you with such enormous responsibilities. Why *does* Kearny allow it?"

A white-coated waiter came by with a tray of raw oysters on the half shell.

"Mrs. Madison, will you take an oyster?"

She narrowed her eyes and flared her nostrils at the oysters glimmering on the tray. "I don't eat oysters in August. Where did you get those, my dear?" Mrs. Madison handed her empty champagne glass to a passing waiter, reached into her pocket, and opened a small ebony snuffbox.

"Benderleys. We don't eat oysters so I wasn't sure what to look for, but General Scott insisted upon them." Despite a vague queasiness, I began reaching for one but she slapped my hand briskly and I dropped it back on the tray.

"Don't eat raw oysters in August, child. Serve them only to your enemies." Her eyes skimmed the crowd as she pinched the snuff to her nose.

"Is there something wrong with the oysters?" I cried, leaning over the tray and sniffing.

But Dolley had fixed her attention across the deck. She crooked a finger and directed my attention to a balding man with a craggy face. "That is Senator Crittenden, from your home state of Kentucky, am I not correct? Sadly, liquor has washed every bit of sense out of poor Senator Crittenden. There are rumors he is leading an insurrection against the president. Be careful around him, for people are hinting that there will surely be violence in the streets."

"Violence?"

"Old Crittenden is a street fighter. He will lead men to riot on Pennsylvania Avenue."

"Over the annexation of Texas? About a war with Mexico?" I tried to guess.

"Hah, goodness no. About the one and only thing all of these politicians truly care about. *Money!* President Tyler wants a Second National Bank. Congress doesn't. Now, if you will pardon me, I think I shall hector Crittenden." She smiled. "And stop spoiling your young husband before he expects the impossible from you." With that, Mrs. Madison gave me a motherly peck on the forehead and drifted away.

The torchlight shimmered on the water while the violins played and the guests ate heartily, but I felt fatigued and vaguely nauseous. Unnoticed amid the general merriment, the roaring talk of men growing drunker with each passing minute, I sank into a chair and closed my eyes.

Philip came striding over to me, and fumbling in his pocket for his watch, opened it, asking, "What did Dolley Madison say?"

"She warned me off you."

He smiled rakishly as he moved the watch around to catch the light of the whale-oil lamps. "She did not."

"Did so." I slumped forward slightly and stroked my temples. When the orchestra struck up a polka, several of the congressmen turkey-stepped and linked arms and began swinging each other around and around.

Philip leaned near me, crossing one leg over the other, watching the politicians dancing their absurd dance. I could smell his cologne and hair pomade and the wool of his uniform coat. He wore his hair after the new style, curled forward over his ears and side-whiskers.

Peering behind him, I observed three of his army comrades boarding the sloop.

Lieutenants Henry Hunt and Richard Ewell crossed the deck toward us, stomping mud from their boots and laughing at some private joke among them, exuding as much charm and merriment as they did brandy fumes, the poor pickled devils. Both of them were hard-favored fellows, gaunt and sickly, both of them afflicted, oddly enough with lisps, but blessed with warm hearts and kindly souls. Following them was Captain Robert E. Lee, a sober army engineer, bearing a large basket tied with a bright red satin ribbon. I had known Lee in St. Louis, where he was a frequent guest of my sister Mary's.

While Philip and I greeted Hunt and Ewell, Captain Lee settled the lidded basket on the deck at my feet and removing his hat, combed his hair with his fingers. He wore it severely parted to one side and curling down the other, and cast a dismayed look at the mud puddle forming under his comrades' boots. Glancing askance, he nodded hello to the men he recognized on the crowded sloop.

"We have brought you and Phil a belated wedding gift, Mrs. Kearny," Lee explained. "Since you don't have children, the three of us figured you might practice on this little fellow." Lee smiled up at me as he opened the lid of the basket.

Philip and I peered over the rim at a sleeping Labrador wrapped in a flannel blanket. Captain Lee looked pleased as we made a fuss over the puppy. Lee explained, "Phil, you said you admired my dogs at Arlington and I thought you and Mrs. Kearny might want one of your own. My children love their dog so much that he comes to church with us on Sunday and sits between them on the pew."

Philip appeared pained and, scratching the back of his neck, asked no one in particular, "Where the devil are we going to keep a hound?"

I was delighted with the gift. Lee sat beside me and lifted the brown puppy onto my lap where it mewled and wobbled uncertainly as its sharp claws caught in the silk of my skirt. "He's beautiful, Captain!" I exclaimed, gathering it up and nuzzling it. The captain congratulated me on my recent successes as a Washington hostess. "You must call upon Mrs. Lee at your earliest opportunity. And when you do, please bring the dog."

As Lee, Hunt, and Ewell joined the party, Philip said to me, "Mrs. Lee is a crazy spoiled woman, little wonder she lets the children take a dog to church."

"I'll tell you who is crazy and spoiled—General Scott, that's who."

"My, my, Mrs. Kearny, who or what has put you in such a snit?"

I settled the puppy back into the basket, and muttered, "Philip, I feel unwell."

My husband knelt in front of me and peered into my face, his eyes earnest and full of worry. Dinner was announced and as the waiters began serving the soup course, my head reeled.

"Oh, I think I'm going to be sick," I said.

"You *look* unwell. Wait here. I'll make my excuses to Scott."

Now, just as Senator Crittenden began toasting General Scott's health with a raised glass, I heard a guttural heaving noise behind me. There, the congressman from North Carolina gripped one of the ship's ropes as if to counterbalance the bounding waves inside his own body and jerking around, he leaned over the rail and poured out into the Potomac all he had eaten that day. I will not recount the events consequent upon the oysters, but suffice it to say the ship smelled like a rending plant at low tide when the oysters worked their devastation. Within seconds the loftiest patriots in the land drooped over the rails, groaning and cursing. Trembling packs of congressmen lurched down the gangplank holding their stomachs.

Mrs. Madison called to me as she disembarked, "I think you shall have a great deal more leisure time from now on, Mrs. Kearny. Very clever solution with the oysters, after all."

Philip leapt over a prone man who seemed to be clawing the decking in agony. He checked on the puppy before lifting the basket and I slipped my arm in his as we followed the gravel path up to the road where our carriage waited. "They got what they deserved. How do you suppose the newspapers will style this little party? Republicide? Democracide? Whigicide?"

"You don't think the oysters made those men sick, do you?" I asked anxiously.

"If so, dearest love, you deserve a medal of valor from the president and the praise of a grateful nation."

The candles in the carriage lamp flickered, drawing moths. The driver hopped down and opened the door for us. Philip helped me up and then sat beside me. Now and again, the puppy made scratching and whining noises, but quickly settled into a deep sleep.

"I thought you didn't ride in carriages." I leaned against him but without waiting to hear his explanation, said, "I feel sick but I didn't eat the oysters. You didn't eat any oysters, did you?"

"Hell no, I'd never eat oysters in August, any fool knows that."

"Why didn't you tell me? I am terrified they are all going to die!"

"Those fellows are too corrupt to die. Blame it on the sickly country and the hot season. Call it a climate fever and deny everything."

I stroked my temples and moaned.

"Dearest love, don't fret. If General Scott is angry with you, maybe he'll punish us by sending me off on some field assignment, which is what I really want anyway." Stretching his legs, he slid down in the seat. "My father is arriving tomorrow afternoon. He's coming down from New York—St. Lawrence County."

"What! Why didn't you tell me sooner?"

"I didn't want you to spend days running about in a tearing hurry. And that's precisely what you would have done. Tear around in a panic fussing over his visit when there is no reason for it whatsoever."

"Oh, but your father!" The heat and humidity suddenly weighed upon me, the odor of violet talcum wafted up from my chemise, my hairpins dug into my scalp and my heavy skirts tangled around my legs.

"Not to worry. Tell Cook to prepare an ordinary family supper at our regular hour of three o'clock. Father doesn't eat anything. He subsists on spite and petty umbrages."

"What a horrid thing to say!"

"My father *is* horrid. You'll see."

At home, Philip retired to his dressing room to shave over the washbasin while I waited for him in my bedroom with the windows open. I could hear the muffled conversations of the pedestrians strolling on the street below. From upstairs came the sounds of the servants retiring to their rooms in the dormered third floor. The air in my room was oppressively still and damp. The flies and mosquitoes flew in with a marshy wind and the sheets twined around my legs until I kicked them off.

A quarter of an hour later, Philip crept into my bedroom, pushed aside the mosquito netting, climbed onto my bed, and slid his suspenders down his shoulders until they drooped over his arms. Hovering over me, propping himself up on his elbows, his hair falling long over his forehead, he said, "I have a new idea—something we haven't tried before. I'll be Genghis Khan and you, a trembling peasant girl in the steppes. I will roll you in the field, among the wheat stalks."

"Shh, Philip." I pressed my finger to his lips, "You must be quiet, the people outside will hear us."

He was peeling off his shirt and unlacing his trousers. "What do I care? Let them get their own damn wives. Ah! Too late for you, miss, Genghis Khan has come to town." He clamped a hand over my mouth, stifling my giggles as we tumbled off the bed and dropped to the floor.

An hour later, having exhausted his Mongol raider repertoire, my husband pulled me up onto the damp sheets and reaching aside, took a cigarette from a rosewood box. I sat cross-legged on the bed, flailing my arms at the mosquitoes.

"I hate fly season! Hate it!" I cried.

Philip lit his cigarette and drawing upon it, blew smoke around my head and the insects scattered. The tobacconist at the New York Hotel made them especially for him. He couldn't buy cigarettes anywhere else, as no one, save veterans from North Africa like himself, had ever heard of them.

I reached for the cigarette but he yanked it away, held it out over the floor.

"No. Ladies don't smoke. Not ever."

"Why not? I've seen plenty of the old colonial dames take snuff."

"That's different."

"Why?"

"Because I say so. And I am your lord and master and you must obey me."

"Wave it around, will you? The mosquitoes are growing bolder." I tried to snag the cigarette, but he was too quick and jerked it away.

Philip yawned, ran his hand over his face, plucked a bit of tobacco from his lower lip. I rolled onto my side, leaned on my elbow, and stroked circles in his auburn chest hair. "Why do you dislike your father?"

"I've always hated him. Ever since my unnurtured youth."

"Why, what has he done?"

"He was monstrously cruel to my mother." He placed the smoldering cigarette in a candy dish on my nightstand and rolled onto his stomach.

"When I was eight, he sent me away to boarding school. One day a servant appeared and took me home. It was raining by the time we arrived in Manhattan, at my father's house, Number 3, Broadway. We went inside and I could see the candles burning in the parlor. My father was slumped in a darkened corner, his face buried in his hands. I crept up to the table and stood on tiptoe, peering into the coffin. There was my mother sleeping in a box, her face white as linen. She wore her wedding gown, and there was a milk stain on her silk breast. She had this . . ." Philip spread his fingers, raised his hand in front of his face. "Her eyes were half closed, her mouth drawn against her front teeth in a hideous grin. And there was a baby lying on the crook of her arm. Father had gotten her with child even though the doctors had warned him that she shouldn't conceive again. He had had his selfish miserable way."

I whispered, "You mustn't blame him, it isn't fair. My father died when I was four, but I don't blame Mama."

This piqued his interest and he rolled onto his back and looked at me. "What killed him?"

"Mama said there was something amiss with his liver, an abscess or some such and that explained his bad temper and his terrible moods. I guess he was a real tyrant in his last sickness."

"Having a bad liver doesn't make a man angry, Diana."

"Oh, but it does. Mama said liver trouble makes you ill-tempered and that is why, when my father died I took on his bad temper."

Philip raised a brow, and couldn't hide his skepticism. "I don't quite understand."

"It makes perfect sense. If a ghost can haunt a house why can't my father's ghost haunt my liver? That would explain my temper, and far as anyone knows I never lost my temper until my father died and began haunting my liver."

"Lord, Diana, that is superstitious nonsense." He reached around me to the nightstand for jar of calomel pills made of mercury salts that he took in the morning with Turkish coffee, at noon with a glass of wine, and before bed, with a flute of absinthe. So much mercury coursed in his veins and permeated his skin, that when Philip perspired, he smelled like a bronze statue in the morning rain, and a mineral fragrance lingered over his clothing. I worried over the effects of too much calomel on my husband. I'd known men who'd gone mad from mercury poisoning.

"Say what you will, Philip, but I know what I know."

"Ah huh—come over here, why don't you?" After swallowing two pills, Philip reached drowsily for me, pulled me against him, and fell asleep with his face buried in my hair. When I was certain he was asleep, I pulled his arm from my waist, slid off the side of the bed, walked around to the nightstand, and lit a cigarette.

I stood by the window in my wrapper, smoking and exhaling smoke over the dark street, suspecting that Philip made rules for his father and that his father made rules for Philip, but neither had ever told the other what those rules might be. Watching Philip sleep, I vowed I would make things right; I would make everyone happy and all would be well again between father and son. What a naïve, tobacco-craving idealist I was!

The next day, my father-in-law arrived promptly at three o'clock in the afternoon.

Our butler opened the door and a hot blast of air and dirt from the street blew into the main hall. Philip's father—Philip Kearny, Sr., was a vigorous man of sixty-five, with stern and irritable little eyes and hair white as spun sugar. With his tongue, he poked at a licorice lozenge inside his cheek—an old habit, he later revealed, from his childhood when he practiced speaking with pebbles in his mouth to cure his stutter. He looked like the sort of fellow who wore a top hat and monocle to bed.

The elder Kearny removed his white silk scarf, gave it to Urban, then regarded Philip and me with a constrained smile such as a countinghouse merchant might give his clerks on a Monday morning.

Philip did not greet his father and Mr. Kearny locked eyes with my husband.

I brushed past Philip, and presented my hand to his father. "Welcome to our home. I hope your journey wasn't too taxing?"

"Oh no, no, the trip was no trouble."

I drew closer to him and smiled. "Will you take a glass of Madeira with me?"

"Oh yes. A glass or three." And when I slid my arm in his, I felt him trembling slightly and knowing he was nervous, I liked him a little better.

As I began ushering him into the second parlor, Father Kearny reached into his coat pocket and removed a packet of letters tied with string. He handed them off to Philip, who glanced at them, then tossed the packet to the butler to put on the hall stand.

Father Kearny said to Philip, "There are letters for you from your elderly uncles. I have also brought you some scandal, a pamphlet containing the full testimony in the Van Syckel divorce case. Her portrait is on the cover."

"Her portrait?" I asked.

"Mrs. Van Syckel's portrait," Philip said.

"A divorced woman?" Now, I had known of abandoned women and women who had quietly and discreetly separated from their husbands in Louisville, Kentucky. But I had never in all of my life met a divorced woman or yet, even heard of anyone who *knew* a divorcée. I wondered if Mrs. Van Syckel's portrait had a craven quality. She must be a sinister and fugitive sort of woman to be divorced. Even saying the word "divorce" gave me a morbid jolt.

Philip's father cast a sorrowful look in my direction. "My dear Diana, we knew Mrs. Van Syckel. What a tragedy to fall from such heights. But as the poet says, a woman once fallen must forever fall. Mrs. Van Syckel is outcast and ruined."

"How awful. What did she do?" I asked Kearny as I steered him into the parlor toward our old spindle-legged sofa.

Mr. Kearny flipped his coattails aside as he took his seat. "Mrs. Van Syckel sacrificed her right to her husband's protection and delicacy prevents me from saying more about the matter."

Ah, if *delicacy* prevented, then Mrs. Van Syckel's case had something to do with an illicit carnal connection. My curiosity had been piqued and I resolved to read the pamphlet on the sly tomorrow after Philip had gone to the War Department.

Philip sat opposite his father and reclined, lacing his fingers behind his head. I was vexed at him for plopping down on a fainting couch rather than comporting himself with the dignity due the occasion.

I hurriedly summoned the servants, who brought in the tea cart, the decanters clinking as the cart came to a stop. I poured a fine old Madeira redolent of marmalade and nuts and served my father-in-law, listening intently as he talked about the New York Stock Exchange—of which he was a founding member—and the family shipping business.

Philip held his wineglass upon his chest, staring through the crystal without comment.

We took our dinner in the third parlor. The disastrous evening began unraveling with the bouillon and the Hock. Philip snatched the decanter of Hock from our waiter and filled his own goblet. The old man drained his wineglass and the waiter filled it instantly. Glancing around at my husband and father, I sincerely hoped that I had not married into a family of surly drunkards.

My husband downed a tumbler of lemon shrub, and then overturned the glass until the lemon pulp slid onto the tablecloth. Reaching for his hand, I clasped it, and we exchanged a tense glance. Of late, his habit of overturning the china and crystal at table nearly drove me to nervous dejection. But when I released Philip's hand, he could not resist and overturned the empty waste bowl meant to catch the leafy dregs from our teacups.

"Philip?" I asked, "Why . . . why are you overturning all of the cups and glasses and bowls?"

Father Kearny tipped his chair back, and thumped the butt of his knife upon the table, murmuring, "I suspect my son's lunacy comes from his French grandmother. Philip's grandmother was a DeLancey, you know. The French are a nation of driveling lunatics."

But I ignored the old man as Philip leaned close to me and explained, "Things nest in upturned receptacles."

Trying to speak without being heard by Father Kearny, I asked quietly, "What sorts of things?"

"Insects. Vermin. *Djenoun*. Mice."

I leaned near him and whispered, "What was that you said? In between vermin and mice? Jay-noon? What pray, is a jay-noon?"

"*Djenoun* followed me home from French North Africa after a battle in an olive grove and they are in this house as surely as you and I are here. It's nothing to worry about as long as we take precautions. When I encamp, I am careful with my boots and my helmet, and I fasten my saddlebags." Philip turned his empty teacup upside down on the saucer.

The waiters carried a large covered tray. Father Kearny took a deep appreciative sniff of the lamb chops with sugared onions as the waiters served the course, then poured claret into the wineglasses.

"If that isn't my own Philip!" Father Kearny gulped the claret, his face flushing rosy with drink. "There's the gloomy boy I recognize. Young Hamlet! Young Hamlet, dost thou see specters?"

Philip drummed his spoon on the table. "Hamlet was luckier than I. He saw his father's ghost."

"Damn. Don't I hate it when the boy gets the upper hand?" Father Kearny cut the sugared onion into quarters and popped one into his mouth.

Philip suddenly looked tired. He closed his eyes, stroked a line down the high bridge of his nose.

Father Kearny cut into his lamb with undisguised enjoyment. "Diana, if I have not said so before, I am most pleased that my son has had the good sense to have married you. I could not be happier. The lamb is most excellent, only a wretched ingrate could find fault with this supper. Speaking of wretched ingrates—Philip, why don't you tell me about your work as aide-de-camp to General Winfield Scott?"

Philip drew circles on the tablecloth with the point of his knife and muttered sullenly, "I write the general's correspondence. I accompany him to inspect posts. I take him to St. John's Episcopal Church on Sunday mornings and as Mrs. Scott is unwell and living in Europe, Diana and I host the general's dinner parties on Monday, Tuesday, and Thursday evenings every week."

"My son is a glorified valet? A clerk-secretary? I envisioned something better for you. You studied law at Columbia. You ought to be a lawyer."

"Attorneys are poor creatures. A most inferior order of creation."

"Well, you are right about one thing, Philip; you were a dismal attorney. You were a poor student, a poor sickly weak specimen in your youth. Men like you are heaped like pebbles on the shores of oblivion. You may guess that I have two reasons for visiting you. The first is to meet your lovely bride. The second is to warn you against your old failings."

"Failings?" I asked, stiffening and leaning forward in my chair. "What failings?"

But while I waited for a response from my father-in-law the japonica roses in the center of the table slowly died of thirst. My husband regarded me with a thousand-rod stare, then reached across the table and slowly and deliberately overturned the kickshaw bowls.

Philip, morose, and surrounded by overturned cups, plates, and dishes, seemed to have gone deaf. Father Kearny ate his cake, clinking his fork against the plate, murmuring it was delicious.

I stood slowly, tossed my shawl over the back of my chair. "Pardon me," I said, and began to take my leave.

"Oh now." Father Kearny made a fist, and pounded upon his chest, making a rumbling noise. "You mustn't work yourself up, Diana. You will become accustomed to the way Philip and I talk to one another."

I folded my arms over my chest, pausing at the door. "I'd really rather not."

Philip tipped his chair back.

Father Kearny threw his hands up in the air. "My dear daughter, you are accustomed to your Southern *cavaliers* while we . . . we Yankees are coarse men of commerce and ill-mannered besides. As for me, I am nothing more than a pitiable Irishman descended of furry little tenant farmers and washerwomen. What do you expect of me? I am a congenital rabble-rouser."

"I really must go," I said.

"Oh, don't run away, Diana, wait for me," Father Kearny grumbled, pushing away from the table.

Philip seemed to come out of his trance. As we left the room, he raised his glass, his voice dripping acid, "To us, Father. May the suffering be equally divided."

"Pah, Philip, stop feeling sorry for yourself." Father Kearny hurried after me calling, "Wait, Diana! Wait for me, I must have a private word with you."

As angry as I was with him, I couldn't very well allow Father Kearny to fall up the stairs. Though it burned me to do it, I offered him my arm. He took it and to my astonishment, looked up at me with a roguish smile.

Reaching for the banister with his free hand, he shook his head, "Oh my, oh my. I fear that I have sinned against my liver."

"Mr. Kearny, I think you deserve the horse pond for the rotten things you say to Philip."

"Hah!" He recoiled comically as if he expected me to strike him. "But, Daughter, I like you very much. Indeed, I sense that you have iron bones."

"Iron bones? Why should I want iron bones?" I asked, growing more irritated with each passing moment. One of the candles in the silver wall cresset had blown out. I reached into the console drawer for a splinter and held it over one of the lit candles until it flamed.

"I loved my wife for her obedience. You are not obedient, are you? Oh now." The old man groaned and touched his hand to his temple. "I am being dishonest, for I was desperately bored by her, by Susan . . . my wife, and Philip's mother. Shh! Keep my confidence and don't tell Philip I said that. But his mother . . . Susan consulted my wishes far more than was pleasant."

I blew out the splinter and tossed it into an empty vase on the console table. "My husband's interests are my interests. I shall do everything in my power to help Philip achieve his dreams."

"Well, that makes me sick at heart." He scowled, dabbing at his mouth with his handkerchief. "So you will help Philip achieve his dreams, will you? Even if his dream means leaving you behind, alone and isolated for years while he fights in one paltry war after another?"

"Philip would never leave me."

"Yes, he would. He can't help it. My son is a dilettante."

I brushed past him, opened the door to his room, and observed approvingly that the chambermaid had turned down his sheets and had unpacked his trunk, neatly folding his nightshirt and nightcap on top of the counterpane. Father Kearny slumped on the side of the bed and unknotted his black cravat.

"I've even brought you a bribe of sorts."

"A bribe?" I asked, closing the curtains.

"A gift. I did not wish to give it to you until I first decided whether I could be fond of you, as this is very dear to my heart." He tottered over to his trunk, removed a long and heavy black walnut box. Bringing it over to the bed, he gently set it down.

He stepped back and grinned at me. "Go on then. Don't be shy. Open it."

I hesitated. "What is it?"

"Open it and you'll see."

With a suspicious glance at him, I opened the latch, lifted the heavy lid, and peered inside.

"It's a shotgun," I said flatly. "Are you having a joke at my expense? I have never heard of anyone giving a shotgun as a wedding present."

"Not just any shotgun, my dear, it's a Purdey, 1827. It belonged to my father and now it is yours. Philip boasted in his letter that you were quite the huntress and I could have given you some bauble, but if my son told the truth about you, I thought you might appreciate this. It's a fifteen-bore double shotgun that has been converted from flintlock to percussion cap ignition. This isn't just a fowling piece. Oh no, no, no. I have brought down deer and bear with this gun."

"It *is* magnificent," I said, touching the figured walnut stock and admiring the mirror-bright bores. "I do miss hunting. My brothers and I hunted in Kentucky and at White Sulphur Springs in Virginia. So, I thank you, Father Kearny, and I promise I shall take very good care of it." I gave him a peck on the cheek, closed the box, fastened the latch, and carried it to the door.

"But you must promise me, however he tempts you to it, do not shoot my son." The old man kicked off his shoes, fell back onto his pillows and murmured, "And don't you fret over Mrs. Van Syckel."

The gun box bumped against the door as I turned.

"Why should I fret over Mrs. Van Syckel?"

"The room is spinning. I shall put one foot on the floor," he muttered.

"What about Mrs. Van Syckel?" I persisted.

"Do not concern yourself about her. Philip abandoned her . . . oh, I'd say days, yes, yes, that's it, *days* before he traveled westward and then married you. I am sure he has quite forgotten her. He forgets all of his lovers with ruthless dispatch. Good night, my dear." He sighed and dropped off to sleep instantly snoring.

I shut the door behind me and leaned against the wall, closing my eyes. If what his father said was true, Philip's affair with Mrs. Van Syckel happened before we were married, before he came to Louisville, before we were reunited. I had to be practical. I reasoned that as a man of the world, Philip took lovers as it pleased him, but all of that was *before*. Before me. Before us. Before we were married. Even so, he had seduced a married woman; perhaps he had been responsible for her divorce! No, that was too terrible to believe.

For a long while, I stood in the hallway, letting the shock wear off.

Then, I looked for Philip. Coming down the stairs, I found him in the second parlor, asleep on the fainting couch, his knees drawn up, one of the tassel pillows from the sofa under his head. He slept hugging my shawl against his chest. I hushed the servants, drew the curtains, and let him sleep.

I went into the hall and, finding the packet of letters, took them into the library. I sliced the string with the letter opener and thumbed through the envelopes until I found the pamphlet. In bold print, the title said:

NEW YORK HERALD CERTIFIED EDITION

REPORT OF THE VAN SYCKEL DIVORCE CASE

Domestic Dissensions in Fashionable Life

I studied Mrs. Van Syckel's pen and ink portrait on the cover. She was fashionably dressed and looked about thirty—disastrously old—drooping helplessly under her bonnet, imploring the reader not to judge her too harshly.

Sinking into Philip's chair behind his desk, I scoured every paragraph of the pamphlet. My tongue stuck to the roof of my mouth and my muscles went rigid as I searched for Philip's name within the pamphlet's pages containing the printed testimony of the witnesses and the letters Mrs. Van Syckel wrote to her paramour.

Mrs. Van Syckel's servants had spied upon her, peeking through keyholes and telling the court that they had seen their mistress reclining on the sofa with her clothes above her knees and a man lying on top of her. Mr. Van Syckel had sued his wife for a divorce on the grounds of adultery—the only grounds for divorce in strict old New York. While testifying in court, Mrs. Van Syckel wept and trembled and fainted away with shame, but the men of the jury also wept with "manly emotion" as they read the verdict and found her guilty of adultery.

I would not believe Philip had ever been her lover. And to my immense relief, Philip's name didn't appear anywhere in the pages of the pamphlet. I read every line a dozen times and concluded that Father Kearny, being intoxicated, must have been rambling, or perhaps he did despise his son for no good reason, as Philip had intimated.

I decided that I would not mention Mrs. Van Syckel to Philip. He had suffered quite enough for one evening. Relieved beyond measure, I lit a match and burned the pamphlet to ashes in Philip's immaculate brass spittoon. Leaving the slumbering men to their wine-drenched dreams, I went outside and stood on the sunny stoop with my hands on my hips soaking up the late-afternoon sun.

I guessed that I had conceived a baby and the idea of my own fertility filled me with exhilarated self-regard. The street traffic rumbled past; ramshackle old nighthawks drawn by raw-boned horses, solitary gentlemen riders on glossy bay mounts, express wagons pitching and jolting over the ruts in front of our house. The wind spun cyclones in the dust and as I turned my head away, I heard someone humming. Sheltering my eyes with my hands, I saw a lanky red-haired girl of thirteen dancing in the midst of a small whirlwind, chasing the spun dust in a circle. Arms outstretched, braids flying, her shoddy skirts billowing above her pale legs as she went along leaping and shouting.

As I watched her, I hoped that my children were not redheads like Philip, for redheaded children were notoriously difficult. The child taunted an oncoming gig, and the driver whipped the horse and aimed for her. But she jumped up to safety on the brick curbstone in front of my house, defiantly chanting these words,

> *The Whigs is mad*
> *The Whigs is bad*
> *Worst enemies old Tyler's ever had*
> *They'll kick him out*

Without a pout
And burn the White House around his head

She followed the whirlwind down the street, pursuing the cyclone when she fell out of its embrace, her stockings sagging over the tops of her boots and her gangly limbs churning with wild exuberance.

I walked around to the back, past the Virginia creeper rustling on the brick, opened the arched wooden gate and entered our shaded garden. Taking a seat upon a bench under a chestnut tree, I contentedly watched the butterflies alighting on the ferns and the sweetbriar roses, knowing that in a few hours, the fireflies would glance through the air in the evening breeze.

God willing, my first child would be born in early April 1842. Let those surly men sleeping under my roof bicker and snipe at one another.

I had a grand mission. I was going to be a mother.

Four

FOUR DAYS LATER, on Monday morning, August 16, after waking, I heard a clamoring and shouting in the distance, and leaning from the window, strained to listen to the upraised voices of angry men. I asked my lady's maid if she heard the noises coming from the southwest, but she shrugged and said no, and then removing my hairbrushes from the bowl where they had been soaking in ammonia, she motioned me to have a seat before my dressing table.

Before leaving for the War Department that morning, Philip had instructed me to meet him at Quince's Daguerreotype Studio to have our wedding portrait taken, for he wished to preserve our images as bride and groom before I grew too large for my wedding dress and we lost the opportunity forever. My husband directed me to take the big black barouche, a ponderous and stately carriage. He said I must not use the open conveyances, neither the gig nor the curricle because a married woman should not parade about the city in plain view.

Though the hour was early, and the temperature approached eighty-six degrees, I donned kid gloves, wore a silk bonnet rimmed in pineapple brocatelle, and tugged a nose veil down over my face. With a shawl demurely draped over my shoulders and wearing nearly eight layers of finely embroidered lawn petticoats under my muslin gown, I climbed into my closed carriage, drew the curtains shut, and trundled through Washington. And then, in roasting misery, I gazed at the red-tufted leather upholstery of the bench opposite me. The carriage blacking, a mix of paraffin, grease, and tar, melted and dripped down the walls.

As we rounded the corner onto Pennsylvania Avenue, the carriage lurched to a halt. Around us, furious men shouted President Tyler's name. In the distance, someone shattered a glass window in what I could only presume was the White House and the gathering roared its approval. Gripping the leather loops dangling from the ceiling, I struggled to my feet, reached for the small knob, and then opened the hatch in the ceiling.

"Colburn? What is the matter?"

The driver's voice was shrill and panicked. "Now, ma'am stay put. There looks to be a fight brewing. Big crowd of rioting men, good gawd I don't know what they all in a fuss about but it don't look good. Like I say, you stay put."

I threw open the curtain upon a frightening scene. Beyond the Lombard poplars lining Pennsylvania Avenue, a tumbling sea of black silk hats and broadcloth suits mobbed the sparse and browning White House lawn. Men sitting in the trees waved banners, clenched their fists, and bawled insults at the president. Though it was late morning, some carried oil rag torches that smoldered and sent mirroring waves of heat into the hot summer air. The mob hurled rocks at the windows, breaking panes in the White House windows while roaring with malicious glee.

Many waved placards that read: IMPEACH TYLER! OUT WITH HIS ACCIDENCY!

A strange mob indeed: one with gold-tipped walking sticks, faces white as ivory beads under tall hats, round bellies bulging under waistcoats, and gold stickpins glinting in the sun.

Why, this rabble was made up of lawyers and statesmen, rich men and silky mongrels. Worse, I recognized many of them—they'd been guests at my parties and many had dined in my home!

"There!" someone shouted, and suddenly the crowd turned and looked at my carriage. "That's President Tyler's carriage. Look at that fine barouche right there. That's Tyler all right!"

"Look there, it's Tyler! Come outta there, you coward! Come out, you varmint!"

Colburn whipped the horses and urged them forward, which only made the protesters angrier.

"Tyler's trying to escape! Have at him, boys."

Colburn cried out as the mob surged, and the rioters surrounded us, panicking the horses. I shrieked and let the curtain fall. Colburn tried to calm the horses, begging the crowd to let us be. "Ain't nobody but a lady in this here carriage, just a young married lady who don't want no trouble. Go on!"

"Shut your trap, nigger. Hand over the president or we'll swing you by the reins from that oak tree!"

The mob rocked my carriage side to side. I grabbed the corner straps, looped my arms through them and prayed for my life. Back and forth the carriage swayed, the iron-clad wooden wheels coming down first on one side with a crash and then on the other. I pleaded with God not to let me die.

Suddenly, the door opened, admitting a shock of light and to my horror, a burly figure tumbled onto the floor, struggling to catch his balance in a way that made me think of a wild boar trapped in a pit. As the rascal rose on his knees, I reacted swiftly. Frightened out of my wits, I slid out of the shoulder straps, grabbed my King James Bible in both hands—I'd brought it with me for the portrait sitting—and swung with all of my might, hitting the thug squarely in the face. The man howled in pain, clutched his face, and blood gushed down his chin.

Outside, someone in the mob hollered, "It is President Tyler dressed in women's clothes! The coward is dressed as a woman!"

"Oh, I am killed entirely," the intruder groaned, rocking on his knees.

My temper was boiling and when I am angry, I do not think so clearly. I leaned from the carriage and lifting the veil from my bonnet and showing my face, I cried out to them, "I am Mrs. Philip Kearny and I am alone in this carriage except for this coward." I pointed at the pair of legs jutting out under the hem of my wedding dress. For effect I raised my Bible and said, "I broke this scoundrel's nose. Step up next if you wish to feel my vengeance and the Lord's as well."

A hush fell and then someone hollered, "Why, ain't she the gal who fed us tainted oysters a few days ago?"

And their furious shouting dissolved into raucous laughter.

Even in my agitated state, as I scanned the crowd, I recognized many of the guests. Why, these were senators and congressmen, our national leaders, and they were rioting on the White House lawn. Some fire-eater began speechifying and drew their attention away. I hopped down onto the dirt surface of Pennsylvania Avenue and searched for Colburn. He came around the horses with his slouch hat in his hand and asked, "Mrs. Kearny? You hurt, ma'am?"

"No," I said, brushing the soil from my skirt.

My victim, still groaning, rolled onto his back on the floor of my carriage. Slowly and agonizingly, he struggled to sit up. His nose was bleeding. His shirt was stained and he clutched a silk handkerchief to his nose and blinked at me, then squinted and ventured, "Miss Diana? Is that you?"

"Senator Crittenden of Kentucky?"

"Oh my Lord, what have I done to you?" he howled in misery. "I have insulted a Kentucky lady."

"You certainly did. You behaved most insultingly, Senator."

He examined his bloody handkerchief and grimaced. "Even so, Mrs. Kearny, you didn't have to hit me."

"Didn't have to hit you? After you came into my carriage! Well, sir, I redress my grievances myself and with all the force I can muster."

"What you mustered was impressive." The senator climbed wonderingly to his feet. I sat upon the seat, untied my bonnet strings and examined my dress for tears or dirt. With a cry and a violent jolt, the carriage raced away from the White House. Senator Crittenden fell back into the seat opposite me. "Where are we going? Am I your prisoner, Mrs. Kearny?" The old bon vivant asked jestingly, but I was in a bad humor.

"I was on my way to meet my husband, to sit for our wedding portrait. Do mop up that blood with your coat. I will not have stains on my best dress and slippers." I tugged off my gloves, one finger at a time. "My husband is going to call you out, and be assured he will make easy work of the likes of you."

Paling white as wool, the senator slumped against the seat. "Oh, Mrs. Kearny, you mustn't tell him what I have done. If Lieutenant Kearny insists on dueling me, I will end the day toes up."

"That, Senator," I snapped open my fan, "is your dilemma, not mine."

"You are a sensible woman, Mrs. Kearny. Let us make a bargain."

"What sort of bargain?"

I should have paused to consider that a bargain can ruin a woman and that a bad bargain is like a sharp-edged tool best left on the shelf.

"Don't tell Lieutenant Kearny what I have done. And I in turn, I . . ." Crittenden swabbed his brow with his hand and wiped it on his trouser leg. "I am a powerful man you know. Why, I am a member of the president's cabinet."

"You're in the president's cabinet, yet you assailed him on the White House lawn? You joined in that riot! I saw you!"

"Shhhh." He pressed a finger to his lips. "That was just harmless politics, you saw. I must please the president, but I must show solidarity with my friends in the Senate as well. Mrs. Kearny, I can do you and your husband favors. I am worth more to you alive than dead, now that is for sure."

I fanned myself more rapidly, feigning disinterest, but a plan was forming in my mind. "We are almost at the studio, sir."

"Have mercy on me, Mrs. Kearny."

I closed my fan with a sharp flick of my wrist and pointed it at the senator's chest. "Lieutenant Kearny deserves a promotion to Captain. Philip needs his own company of troopers. Won't you help him to secure a promotion? Perhaps post him to West Point? Or Carlisle Barracks in Pennsylvania? But assuredly, some place civilized, and any post in the East would suffice."

Relieved, the senator exhaled, crumpled his bloody handkerchief in his pocket. "That is a wholly achievable compromise, Mrs. Kearny."

"Then we are agreed, sir." I snapped open my fan and cooled my face. "And we shall not mention this incident again."

We stopped before the studio and Colburn helped me down but refused to aid the senator. Once inside, I let my eyes adjust to the gloom. Crittenden was still pinching his nostrils as the daguerreotypist beckoned us into the studio chamber.

Philip stroked his chin and eyed the senator shrewdly. "What the hell happened to you?"

The senator shot me a panicked look as I explained. "It was awful, Philip. There was a riot on the White House lawn and the hooligans overtook Senator Crittenden—he is a member of the president's cabinet after all—and just as the senator was about to be pummeled to death, I stopped the carriage and I gave him a ride. We made our escape in the nick of time."

The senator bowed so low he appeared to reverence the ground. "I am indebted to you and Mrs. Kearny. May I have the honor of a private audience with you tomorrow, Lieutenant Kearny? I wish to do you some favor to compensate your wife in some small measure for her"— he rubbed his nose and glanced at me—"kindness to me."

"Yes, of course," Philip said.

In the instant the portraitist distracted Philip, I glanced at Senator Crittenden, and suspected that he would never honor his bargain, for if he would betray the president, he would treat me similarly. What a nasty, cankered, deceitful wretch he was! I peered over my shoulder at Senator Crittenden as Philip took my arm and in a courtly manner, escorted me over to the mural backdrop of weeping willows and romantic crumbling castle ruins.

Quince, the daguerreotypist, positioned us so that I held a King James Bible in one gloved hand and rested my other hand on Philip's shoulder as he sat stiffly upon a chair.

I looked up. The portraitist told me to "hold" and I lifted my chin and showed the world my courage. The shutter blinked the instant I believed the future was infinite and I was ready for any challenge the years might throw down before me.

Five

TAKING UP RESIDENCE in a new city is like marrying a man; a woman never knows if she will truly love the city or the man until she has summered and wintered both. After three years of marriage and living in Washington, I had not followed Mama's advice. I rarely refused Philip or declined the favor and I did have a baby every year, or very nearly so. Susan was born in April of 1842 and our second daughter, Diana in January of 1844. On quiet evenings at home, Philip and I would bring the babies into the parlor and gather near the fire. Susan, now two years old, was ardently devoted to her father and mercilessly manipulated his affections. Every night, before putting her to bed, he held her on his lap, combing his fingers through her silky strawberry blonde hair while she chattered incessantly at him. Our daughter had inherited her father's talent for talking. Not a day went by that Philip didn't come home with some treat or bauble to delight her.

In April of 1844, as the wind stripped the blossoms from the cherry trees, I sat at the piano, holding a candle to the new sheet music Philip had brought home. My infant daughter, Little Di, slumbered in her basket at my side as I tried to play Philip's favorite songs, squinting as I plinked and then paused, scheming when I might slip away for five minutes to secretly enjoy a cigarette. Lately, my husband favored maudlin penny sheet music—the more mawkish, the more he liked it.

"A Tear Shall Tell Him All," "An Old Man Went A-Wooing." His new favorite was "The Minstrel Boy," an old Irish folk tune about a young boy dying in battle.

As I played, Philip read a book about cavalry warfare in the Indian Territory. Susan sat on his lap holding a glass globe he'd brought home for her filled with confetti and china figures, turning it over, frowning and muttering to herself. The burning candles in the hurricane lamp shone on their faces as Philip reached around Susan to turn the page of his book. Drawing his attention to the glass globe, Susan pointed at a figure and said, "Gog."

"No, Susan, that's not a dog, it's a little pony pulling a trap."

She lay back against his chest and smiled complacently at her treasure.

"Look. Goggy. Pretty."

"Um-hmm," he said.

Every afternoon at four o'clock, if the weather were mild, Susan and I would wait on the front walk for Philip to come home from the War Department. When Susan saw Philip's horse rounding the corner she'd leap to her feet and cry out, waving her arms in the air. He'd tie his horse to the post and bend down and lift Susan in his arms, swinging her in circles until she shrieked and laughed, her head falling back and her arms out like wings.

Little Di's official introduction to Washington society occurred during the first Marine Band concert of the season on the White House lawn in mid-April. Hundreds of people gathered under the trees enjoying cool breezes and military marches. There were tender green leaves on the trees and the spring shrubbery had started to bloom. Susan in her white pantalets and hair ribbons flew this way and that, running excitedly after the older girls on the White House lawn. Di napped in her pram as the children's nursemaid strolled after Susan, keeping close watch on her.

Philip and I stood under a blooming pear tree, exchanging pleasantries with his old friend from the First Dragoons, Lieutenant Richard Ewell.

"Have you heard there is a grippe that has stricken a dozen people last told?" Ewell asked. I had known Lieutenant Ewell since 1837. With his shrill lisping voice, gaunt, witchlike face, he had always impressed me as wildly eccentric, for he went everywhere accompanied by a barefoot Indian boy dressed in blue velvet livery and a white George Washington wig. "And what scandal—the plague is being called the Tyler grippe in honor of our much abused president! Everyone says no vice president ought to have the gall to exercise the full powers of the presidency, and that we ought to call for new elections."

While Philip spoke to Ewell, my husband kept glancing at a young woman in finch-green silk, a rice straw bonnet, and a violet parasol over her shoulder. She turned and looked pointedly at Philip, dropped her parasol, and then, acting out a flirtation pantomime, picked it up again, holding it across her waist, folded it carefully, one pleat at a time. The code of the parasol, the glove, and the handkerchief were well known to everyone in society.

Follow me, she was signaling Philip, *get rid of your company.*

How dare she! Barely controlling my temper, I asked, "Philip, what is that lady's name?"

Philip squinted in the sunlight as he looked off at group of young officers from the War Department and nodded hello to them.

"Which lady?" Ewell turned and searched the crowd.

"The lady who has been signaling Philip with her parasol."

"Fie, Diana, I have never heard of such nonsense. Parasol flirtations, indeed!" Philip scoffed, touching the brim of his hat and bowing slightly in greeting to a passing congressman and his lady.

"All the same, who is she?" I insisted.

"Oh, you mustn't acknowledge her, Mrs. Kearny. That is Minerva Speer. A notorious woman of the town," Ewell said.

"A courtesan, you mean to say!"

But when Philip gave Ewell a warning look, Ewell made his excuses and drifted away into the crowds as the Marine Band struck up "Hail, Columbia." People began clapping in rhythm. Susan and her new friends danced freely, hopping around in a circle.

Philip raised a hand and called, "Ah, good afternoon, Senator Crittenden, I received your kind letter and the good news by courier this morning."

"Good afternoon, Lieutenant." He tipped his hat, "Mrs. Kearny."

"Senator," I said. Though three years had flown by since the riot, he had not kept his bargain, and as far as I could discern had done nothing to help Philip win a promotion. I saw Senator Crittenden once a week at the various levees, receptions, and tea parties in Washington. He was unfailingly cordial, and though I never told a soul about the incident in the carriage, I suspected Crittenden never forgot his bad behavior during the riot but that he hoped *I* had.

Crittenden leaned into the pram and kissed little Di as she slept. "Such a beauty!"

"I am a man rich in daughters," Philip boasted, with a wink in my direction.

But I kept a guarded eye on Minerva Speer in her finch-green dress. She paused by the lilac shrubs to observe us, sunning herself like a lizard on a fence rail. Susan came running to Philip waving a milkweed she'd picked for him. He bent down to accept it and she looped her hands around his neck, planting a kiss on his cheek. He tucked the milkweed into his buttonhole and held Susan's hand.

Senator Crittenden punctured the damp green sod with the end of his walking stick. "Mrs. Kearny? Might I suppose you are eagerly anticipating your journey to the westward?"

Philip appeared alarmed by the senator's question. Turning slightly aside, he looked around my bonnet brim. I could smell the tobacco on his breath as he murmured in my ear, "The senator is speaking of the Kansas Territory."

"The Kansas Territory?" I tensed, placing my hand on Susan's head.

"Little Susan," the senator said, "what do you think of your father going far, far away to Kansas to fight the Indians, hmm?"

Philip stared censoriously at Crittenden. Susan popped her finger into her mouth and said nothing. I stiffened, and a smile froze on my face as I slipped my arm in Philip's. "I am pleased for my husband."

But the sudden ruddy color of Philip's cheeks belied my pretending that I knew Philip's secret. He gripped my elbow, and drawing me near, he met my eyes and whispered, "Diana, I have, these past few years, been urging Senator Crittenden to press my case with the War Department for an assignment to Fort Leavenworth. Though the senator kindly offered to secure a posting for me to Carlisle or West Point, I requested frontier duty, and he has been a most gracious ally in this respect."

Shaking my head in disbelief, I jerked my arm away from Philip, and observed malicious triumph in the senator's eyes. He said, "Mrs. Kearny, will you and the children be joining Lieutenant Kearny at Fort Leavenworth? Don't let the rumors of Indian wars and disease scare you. Fort Leavenworth, Kansas, is as civilized a place as any other large army garrison. Why you might come to love the wild, wild West!"

As if to remind me of breaking his nose, he placed his finger alongside his left nostril. Bowing, Crittenden said, "Ah, now there is Judge Taney. I must have a word with him. Good afternoon, Lieutenant. Mrs. Kearny. Enjoy the concert."

As I watched Crittenden disappear into the crowd, I murmured, "Why did you not tell me? Why did I hear it from him?"

Philip scowled and stared off in the distance. I remember his face so clearly, for I had become a scholar of my husband's moods. A cascade of light broke through the pear tree, and I knew that our luck had turned and nothing would ever be the same between us again. "I don't feel like listening to music anymore." And without waiting for his response, I turned and walked rapidly toward Pennsylvania Avenue, to our carriage.

Susan was sunburned and slept in Philip's arms. Her slippers had been polished with lampblack and the heels marked sooty little crescents on the legs of Philip's trousers. The nursemaid held Di and because the nurse was present, I could not speak to my husband. Tense with anxiety, Philip and I looked out of opposite windows of the carriage, riding along in silence and dreading the inevitable argument we'd have when we arrived home.

As the carriage pulled around through the back gates and came to a halt behind the house, Philip handed Susan off to the nursemaid and said briskly to me, "Diana, I shall speak with you shortly, but first, I must have a word with the stable hands." And then he leapt out of the carriage.

Once the nursemaid and I were in the house and the door closed behind us, I helped her bring the children up to their rooms. Then, I hurried down the stairs, removing my gloves, and untying my bonnet, tossed it on the hall stand. I raced out the back of the house in time to see Philip riding away from the stables, through the gate, slipping away because he would not confront me with his decision and its consequences.

Returning to the house, I dismissed the nursemaid, and grateful, she told me she'd return the next morning, but that she would visit her sick mother in Georgetown. When the clock chimed the quarter-hour, I went to the windows and looked for Philip. While Baby Di slept, I held Susan and read to her, fed her a snack of clabber and played a game of Chickamy Craney Crow with her in the parlor.

As the evening wore on, Susan grew more languid and kissing her forehead, I detected a slight fever. She refused to leave my arms, and would not let me put her to bed, and now and again she loosed a rattling old man's phlegmy cough that alarmed me beyond measure. I pulled the bell and summoning one of the kitchen maids, ordered her to boil brandy with a handful of cloves until the brandy was scorched, and to bring it up to me along with a soft cloth. Nothing cured a child's fever like a sponge bath in cooled brandy.

Susan's face brightened just once that evening, when our dog, Greeley, the one Captain Lee had given us, came trotting into the parlor. Leaning forward over my knees, she tried to snap her little fingers at him, scolding, and then laughing as the dog laid his massive brown head on my leg. At last, she fell into a fitful sleep. Greeley's nails clicked up the stairs as he followed me into the nursery, and I put Susan on her feather mattress.

At midnight, I told the servants to extinguish the candles and go to bed. I felt considerable anxiety over the possibility that Philip wished to leave me behind while he chased his dreams. Sitting alone before a low fire in the parlor, in my wrapper and my hair long over my shoulders, I cradled a cup of tea strong as lye and opened an atlas on the table. Desolate at the prospect of being left behind while Philip vanished into the Indian Territory for perhaps years, I turned the dusty pages, searching for a map of the Kansas Territory and Fort Leavenworth. But the atlas was an old one from the 1820s and at the western edge of Missouri the nation fell off in a shadowy land called "the Territory."

How primitive could Fort Leavenworth be? Philip's uncle, Colonel Stephen Watts Kearny, was commanding officer of the Army's 3rd Division. Colonel Kearny and his wife had lived at Fort Leavenworth for a time in the 1830s and they had survived, hadn't they? Well, so would I. In the army, there was a name for women left behind while the men were away on frontier duty: They called them grass widows. I had no intention of becoming a grass widow.

When the clock chimed two, I went to bed alone.

The next morning, I drew my dressing gown over my shoulders and watched out the window as men torched the piles of stone, one fire on every street corner as far as the eye could see. Noxious plumes of tarry smoke filled the morning air and a fog hung over the street. Emma, my lady's maid, worked in the anteroom clapping pearly white starch into my petticoats. She smiled at me through the powder.

"Yes, mum?"

"Have you seen the bonfires on the corners? What is the latest news about the fevers, do you know?"

"Tyler grippe, mum. That's what they're calling it. And that's all I know."

"Tyler . . ."

"On account of how ever'body dislikes President Tyler, they've named the grippe for him. Now then"—Emma looked around and tipped her head in the direction of my gray silk morning gown—"I was thinking of that gown? Will it suit you, mum?"

After dressing, I hurried down the hall and pushed aside the door to Philip's room. His bed had not been slept in. The clothes he'd worn last night were crumpled on the floor in front of his dressing chest. I bent to pick them up. The blue uniform coat and orange sash reeked of cigarette smoke; there, too, was his broadcloth shirt, his neck cloth, his braces, and his trousers. I gathered them in my arms, carried them to the bed, laying each piece out and then gave his coat a vigorous shaking. The contents of the inside pocket flew onto the carpet: a coin purse with a few twenty-dollar gold pieces, a house key, one of his button studs, which must have fallen from his shirt, and his own card, plainly engraved with his name. While placing these items on his table, I noticed writing in his hand, in pencil on the back of the card.

Minerva Speer at Mrs. Foster's—1 o'clock—248¹ᐟ² G Street.

I sat upon the bed and stared at the inscription, thinking of how Minerva Speer had looked at the Marine Band concert and the brash way she'd flirted with Philip, as though they knew one another so well that they had their own secret language. Though I tried not to believe my worst suspicions, I could not deny this damning evidence and felt as if I were suffocating with jealousy. If the other Washington matrons knew of Philip's affairs, they would say that as a wife I had been an appalling failure, for men were faithless only because their wives made them so. Philip required novelty in all things and I had somehow failed to please him. Though he had violated our marriage vows by spending the night with a prostitute, no one would call him to account for it. That Philip loved me, I did not doubt. But I was also learning that love is not enough to bind a man to a woman.

I left the card in his room and feeling numb and despondent, preoccupied with my fears, walked slowly down the hall. The nursemaid leaned from the children's bedroom, her white cap slightly askew on her head and her face shining with perspiration. "Mrs. Kearny! Our Susan ain't feeling so bright this morning."

Startled out of my mood, I followed the harried nursemaid into the room, but found Susan sitting upright on her bed smiling at me. She reached out her arms and clung to me, and then coughed a deep chesty cough. Looking over at the maid, I said, "Why, she looks much better this morning than she did last night."

"But, ma'am, she won't take no breakfast. I put her butter and hominy on the table but she pushed it away with both hands."

"Oh, I wouldn't worry so much about that," I said, trying to wrest free of Susan, for I intended to speak with my husband and demand an explanation before he bolted out of the house that morning. "Watch her carefully while I take breakfast," I instructed the nursemaid, "and if there is any change at all, come for me, will you?"

"Yes, ma'am, Mrs. Kearny, but maybe you ought to call the doctor?"

I tapped my fingers upon my lips and studied Susan. She had a firm grip on her china doll as she coughed at its painted face. "I don't wish to trouble the doctor just yet, as I believe she has a little cold and nothing more."

And then I went down to breakfast. We took our meals in the third parlor, overlooking the back lawn, and there, I heard Philip speaking to the serving girls. For a long while, I stood in the hall, steadying my nerves. Then, I took a deep breath and entered.

Upon seeing me, he folded his paper and rose to greet me. "Good morning, dearest love," he said, pecking my cheek and pulling out a chair for me. "Bring Mrs. Kearny's coffee and her breakfast."

"Yes, sir, Mr. Kearny," the maid said.

He sat at table, dressed for the day, but unshaved. Two serving girls in black dresses and starched aprons entered with trays, darting silently back and forth. One maid put the tray on the sideboard, lifting the covers one by one. She lowered a plate with a roasted calf's heart stuffed with forcemeat of bread crumbs and beef suet swimming in butter sauce in front of him. A plate of Boston brown bread, big as a Turk's fez, towered in the center of the table. Another servant placed a side plate of broiled lamb's kidneys, deviled mutton on toast, and a scotch tumbler of raw grated horseradish in front of me. I ate raw horseradish every day to keep my voice young and fresh.

I said in a light tone, "You did not come home last night."

Philip turned the page of his newspaper, but did not look up at me. "General Scott sent word that he needed me to write some reports for him and I didn't finish until so late that I was loathe to bother you, and I stayed at his house."

I picked bits of marjoram from my mutton and set them on the side of the plate. "Will you be leaving for Fort Leavenworth soon?"

The corner of his newspaper drooped and he cast a questioning look at me over it.

"Yes," he said quietly. "I leave this week."

"Ah," I said. "It's probably a good thing you're leaving. I hear there is a grippe in the city. That people have died of it. And that it is being known as the Tyler grippe."

Philip shrugged off my comment with a grunt.

"I have thought about it. The children and I are coming with you to Fort Leavenworth."

"No, you're not," he said, overturning his empty Sevres coffee cup and the gold-rimmed twifflers.

"Why not?" I persisted.

"Because I have decided it would be unwise." He drank a tumbler of water and placed it rim down on the cloth. Slinging his white napkin across his lap, he glanced my way. "Diana, your coffee cup is empty. Please turn it over if you will not fill it with coffee."

I stared defiantly at him and laced my fingers together as he reached for my cup and turned it over. Slowly and deliberately, I righted it. Exasperated, he sighed, reached over, and turned my coffee cup upside down on its saucer.

I had had enough. Locking eyes with him, I slipped my finger through the cup handle, and placed it firmly on the saucer, thinking vengefully, *I hope your damned North African* djenoun *spill out of every dish on this table and crawl all over you.*

Philip tossed his napkin onto the floor and placing his hands on the table, loomed over me as he reached for my coffee cup yet again.

But I snatched it and dropped it nonchalantly on the floor.

"What the hell, Diana?"

"So, when exactly are you departing for your little bachelor adventure in the Indian country?"

"Don't mock me. Your tone is offensive."

I cut into my mutton toast and asked, "Doesn't Minerva Speer mock you?"

He flinched and lowering himself into his chair, devoted all of his attention to his breakfast plate, but I caught the passing look of indignation and guilt. In that instant, I could see as clearly as if it had been engraved on his forehead that he had betrayed me. Such surprise and tensing around his eyes, for he never imagined I would discover his deception.

"Diana," he warned, sensing my outrage.

Jumping up, I sprinted toward the door, but he pursued me and caught me, dragging me back to the table, and holding me so tightly I began to choke. With terrifying force, he slammed me down into my chair and, gripping me tightly by the collar, shook me as if I were a misbehaving child. Then, he said in his harsh, cracked voice, "You are emotionally overwrought. You are high-strung and drawing conclusions that have no basis in fact. You need not concern yourself with my private interests."

I clenched my teeth, made fists of my hands and stared straight ahead. Surely and swiftly, the coil of my anger was tightening around me, but I would not relent.

"You are my wife and the mother of my children. I will not tolerate vulgar accusations from you about vulgar people. A lady never speaks of such things."

"But I am to tolerate Minerva Speer . . . and you?"

"Not another word, Diana. I have honored you, I treat you with respect, and I revere you because you are my wife. I have given you a life that every woman in Washington envies. I put you before all others. I have brought you fortune, and plenty, and I wish to live in peace with you. But unless you wish to destroy my deepest sentiments for you, be quiet and calm yourself. Calm your temper."

He hovered over me threateningly, so I nodded.

Fooled by my momentary complacency, he let me go.

I rose and with one quick and powerful thrust, overturned the entire table, shattering thousands of dollars of Sevres china and sending glass and French porcelain flying all over the room.

Philip threw up his hands and bellowed, "You poor devil bitch! Who do you think you are? Goddamned Attila the Hun?"

Susan's nursemaid joined the other servants rushing into the room and exclaiming at the destruction.

"Mrs. Kearny! I got to see you, ma'am, Mrs. Kearny?" the nursemaid tried, but Philip shouted at her, "Get back up to the nursery where you belong."

Our servants had come in just in time to see Philip clutch my wrists and pull me from the room, down the hall. I stumbled after him, writhing furiously. He shoved me into the library and then evicted the parlor maid who had been polishing the brass andirons. She skittered backward out of the room, her eyes enormous, her face pinched and white.

He locked the doors behind her and pocketed the key. I retreated, put myself by the window, girding myself against a brutish assault by him. But Philip sank into an armchair and crossed his legs. His hands fell to his sides and when he lifted his eyes to me, motioned at the sofa and said wearily, "Sit down, I am not going to hurt you."

Warily, I lurked back, caressing my throat and wrists.

In a voice infinitely gentle and infinitely suffering, my husband said, "I love you and I understand you as no one else does. You are so much like me that I cannot help but love you. Now come here and let us speak to one another. Let us be more than civil. Let us be kind."

His sudden equanimity, his stillness drew me in. I dropped onto the sofa and felt a brief interval of remorseful grief for both of us because I could not think what to do. I could weep like the wronged heroine in a melodrama, or let my heart turn to ice and follow the instructions of my minister and my church and try to change Philip through my righteous penitential suffering and martyrdom. But even in my distressed state, I couldn't imagine myself enduring martyrdom for more than five minutes without pummeling Philip to mush.

He tented his fingers, exhaled with a narrowed stare and a flat smile of reckoning. He resembled one of those stained-glass medieval knights of the Crusades with his fiercely hawklike features and his auburn imperial mustache and goatee; the incarnation of one of his damned haughty French ancestors who'd fathered babies by every female serf on his demesne. Philip was descended from centuries of libertines accustomed to having any woman they wanted, with no consequence whatsoever. Three hundred years in the aristocracy makes for a glut of privilege.

He leaned forward, placed his hand over his corrupt heart, and said, "I forgive you, Diana."

"You forgive me!"

"Yes, for destroying the china. And for your outburst."

"Oh, Philip, aren't you a sensitive soul?"

"I am, indeed."

"Well, you go on and bubble over with sensitivity for hours on end because I don't forgive you. Forgiving will only encourage you to be faithless once again."

He made his inconvenienced face and tried again. "Last night, I was at General's Scott's house, writing correspondence for him. Shall I ask him to call upon you and verify my story?"

I stared hard at him. "You do that."

"I shall."

Now I knew, and Philip knew, that it would have been disastrously self-destructive to verify his story with General Scott. The general would have excoriated him for failing to control his wife, and being an old wicked gossip, Scott would have spread terrible scandal around the city. Fatigue and excitement muddled my thinking. But there was something I wished to know, for my own sake.

"Did some woman make you sick? Is that the reason you take so much mercury salt? The calomel, I mean. Do you have syphilis?"

"Syphilis!" he exclaimed, crossing his legs and folding his arms. "Well now, this conversation is elaborately unrewarding, I must say."

"Philip, for the love of God, speak the truth. Were you with Minerva Speer last night?"

He did not skip a tick, but dismissed the question with a flick of his wrist. "I told you where I was and I will not answer another question about it. And so you know what you have done to me, I am devastated by your mistrust."

"I mistrust your recklessness. How many have there been?"

He came over and sat beside me on the sofa, touched my hair with the crook of his finger, and said, "I have loved one woman."

I leaned away from him. Resting my chin in my hand, I tipped my head and searched the ceiling, anything to avoid his face. The pins holding the small veil over my chignon had come loose and I reached up and tucked them back in along the crown of my head. My brain was a wellspring of rage and profanity. I was thinking words I'd never thought before. *You lying bastard. You whoremonger.*

"I have had in my life but one love. I have known these many years but one grand passion. A beautiful dark-eyed girl from Kentucky," he said, scooting closer. "Who wantonly destroyed a fortune in china and Baccarat crystal with no provocation. But in the spirit of reconciliation, I forgive you. Diana, you must believe me. I have never lied to you."

Oh, how I desperately wanted to believe him.

"Philip, if you told the truth your cock would fall off."

My unexpectedly profane outburst had aroused him. He laughed softly, traced the line of my jaw with his forefinger until I pushed him away. He whispered, "There is something I must know."

I glanced aside at him. "What?"

"Something I ardently wish to know." He slid down the sofa until his cheek was resting in the skirt over my thigh, his head heavy as a stone indenting the silk folds of the fabric. He pressed a kiss into my leg, which I could not feel for all of the petticoats layered there. "You cannot deny me anything. By law and by right, you cannot deny me anything."

I began to wrest away from him, but he pushed my shoulders back onto the sofa. "You have dressed so carefully, you always do, and I know it takes so much time and effort that I wouldn't want to destroy your lovely morning gown. What I have in mind, you need not remove a single item of clothing." He was already reaching under my skirts, fluffing through the layers until he felt the warmth of my skin and his eyes brightened and he whispered, "Our own sweet invention. You know that you must let me do as I please or else I shall have you unwillingly."

We were both thinking with the blood. I tried to push him away but he was so much stronger, his eyes keen and lustful, and he intended to do as he wished.

Why were Philip and I a little angry at one another all of the time? Why couldn't we simply be at ease with one another? But as the old story tells us, even the gods are not angry forever. Our clothes were strewn from one end of the room to the other. Despite his brutishness and my violent outbursts of temper, he had never forced himself on me. I stretched out under him, moved slowly against him. "Not yet," he said and guided me up so that I was astride him, shuddering toward ecstasy. "Not yet," he said again, urging me onto my knees, whispering into my shoulder as he touched me so that I cried out with agonized desire.

When I think of all the trouble I caused myself over the years by desiring to lie down beside that man . . . well, it never fails to astonish me.

Six

MRS. KEARNY? Mrs. Kearny! Come out here, Mrs. Kearny, our Susan is real sick and I don't know what to do!" The nursemaid pounded furiously on the library doors and called again, "Mrs. Kearny, I can't put it off any longer, in the name of mercy, come out of there, will you?"

Philip and I woke from our lovemaking stupor on the library floor, and sitting up slowly, blinked in bewilderment at one another. He leaned on the sofa and pulled himself up, then offered me a hand and brought me to my feet. Searching around for my layers and layers of clothing, I began grabbing for petticoats while Philip crow-hopped into his trousers.

"A moment," Philip called but the nursemaid would not be deterred.

"You got to call for the doctor, Mrs. Kearny. She is sicker than I ever seen her in her whole life."

"I'm coming, right this minute."

"Come faster, ma'am. Please!"

I ducked into my gown and without bothering to lace it, unlocked the doors, and throwing them open, met the nursemaid, who looked to have been weeping in panic.

"Take me to her," I said and raced up the stairs behind the nurse to the first landing and thence down the hall to the nursery. She opened the door and we were met with a rush of heat from the English coal grate. I was stricken at the sight of my daughter Susan, standing on her bed, holding tight to one of the bedposts, stooping as she gasped for air. When she lifted her face to me, her lips were bluish and her eyes brimmed with fear.

"Philip!" I shouted as I ran to my daughter and lifted her in my arms.

Philip came running into the room, bare-chested and breathless. "What's the matter with her?"

"It's the croup, Captain, she got the croup and she's choking for want of air," said the nursemaid.

"She's suffocating!" Philip yelled at her. "Don't just stand there, go for the doctor, now! Go, goddamn you!"

The nursemaid rushed out the door and down the hall, calling for Colburn to bring the wagon.

Susan pressed her hands to my cheeks, dug her fingers into my flesh, and scratched with all her might, drawing blood from my face and making harsh noises as she struggled, fighting whatever it was that blocked the air to her lungs. Sweat covered her body and her whole face took on a bluish cast.

"Well, damn it, do something, Diana!"

I tried a mustard plaster, I dosed her with a little nitrate smoke, which the doctor recommended for asthmatics, but aside from these remedies, I could not think what to do. I bathed her in vinegar, cooled and warmed her, prayed and pleaded with her, all the while bargaining with God, that if He made her well, I would never lose my temper again, and I would endure every hardship without complaint.

After a time, Philip carried her over to the bed, speaking to her in a gentle voice, "Calm yourself, Susan, there's my girl, calmly now, can you be calm for me, darling girl?"

She grasped at my hands as I joined Philip at her bedside, she sat up as he banked pillows behind her and removed a knife from his trouser pocket and then opened it so that the blade gleamed in the spring sunlight streaming in the windows. The child scratched at the bedcovers, clawing like a small animal being strangled.

"What are you doing?"

"I think she has a false membrane in her throat. I think she has the diphtheria. This is something I saw done by the French surgeons in Algiers when men were dying of croup and suffocation. I would need a sort of tube." He looked around for something that might suffice.

"No, I won't let you do it."

"It may be her only hope. I would make a small cut right there." He pointed at a spot above the collar of her nightgown. "And we'd insert the tube into her throat and she would breathe through it."

Susan had very little time left. I knew this without a doubt, for she was shuddering and yet heaving at the same time as if she would vomit. I gathered her off the bed, held her in my arms upon my lap, but she trembled so violently, and her eyes strained forward.

"Philip, I will hold her for you." And glancing aside at the breakfast table with its green oilcloth and bowls of uneaten hominy grits with butter, I removed a glass straw from a tumbler of untouched cider and tapping it on the rim, held it out to him. A spot of brown cider dripped from the straw and stained the white bed linen.

"Would this work for the tube?"

"I . . . don't know. I don't know what we need."

"It must work. We have no choice! Tell me what to do and I will help you."

Susan had fallen limp in my arms, and this alarmed me even more than her struggling. Philip sat forward on the bedside, staring at the place on Susan's neck where he would press the blade. I embraced Susan, my forearm across her chest, the skin over her collarbones beginning to blister from the mustard plaster I'd applied an hour before. I cupped her chin up high with my other hand so that her throat was taut, and said, "I'll help you. Go on then. I won't flinch."

Susan's face had turned dark blue, and her eyes were dim and unseeing. She was so still that she frightened me.

But as Philip regarded our daughter, an expression of utter hopelessness crossed his face, and the knife in his hand wavered. Susan's feverish chin felt damp and fragile in my palm. I knew then that Philip could not cut into our child any more than I could have.

"Please," I begged him, but to no avail. Defeated by his own want of nerve, he let the knife fall on the floor, and resting his elbows on his knees, hid his face in his hands.

I carried Susan over to the same rocking chair where I had nursed her as an infant and tucked a pillow under her head. I rocked her, pressed my feet to the old boards, heel to toe and heel to toe, humming her favorite bedtime lullaby and looking down at her face, all pinched and blue, her eyes half closed.

I bent and kissed her forehead.

She opened her eyes then, raised a hand, and clutched my hair in her small fist and whispered, "Mama, help me."

And then she passed out of this world. She wore a shocked expression, her brown eyes wide open as if asking why I had failed her so terribly.

Still holding her in my arms, I rose from the chair. The mantel clock ticked loudly until I opened the glass case and stopped the pendulum marking the time of her death at half-past three in the afternoon.

I put her upon the bed without disturbing her sleep. Philip and I sat on either side of her, keeping silent vigil, for what could we say when we knew the truth in our hearts? Both of us were to blame. We blamed each other and we blamed ourselves. If only we hadn't wasted precious hours bickering and fighting, if only we hadn't ignored the nursemaid's plea for help at breakfast rather than lock ourselves away in the library, if only Philip had had the courage to risk the unthinkable, if only I had been a good mother and not a selfish, jealous, petty wretch. We stared down at Susan, numb, guilty, locked in our own hellish misery, avoiding each other's eyes.

The doctor arrived an hour later and after making a pretense of examining our daughter, turned to Philip and announced that Susan was with God now.

Philip said, "She doesn't belong with God. Susan belongs with me. My little girl belongs with her mother." And then he fled the room. Where he went, I know not, but I did not see him again all that day.

The doctor left without collecting his fee.

I took Di's baby blanket from her crib and draped it over the mirror so that Susan's soul would not be trapped in its reflective surface. On the table beside her uneaten breakfast was an overturned basket with handfuls of grass she'd torn from the lawn, wilting strands of lady's-smock and pale anemones shriveling in the sunlight; a bouquet frail as a spider's leg.

On the day of her funeral, I fussed over Susan, intent upon making her look her best. She had a scab on her knee because she had fallen a few days before while chasing the dog down the bricked footpaths behind our house. The palms of her hands were scraped, and though I had tried to tweeze the dirt and gravel from her wounds, I could not pry them loose. So, I poured herbed vinegar into the basin and dipped the cloth into it. The aroma of rue, lavender, and sage wafted around me as I squeezed out the rag.

Little Di lay in her crib, dressed in a white gown trimmed in black mourning ribbons stitched in my hand. In those days, we honored a child's death by wearing white mourning bands over our black clothing, white gloves on our cold hands, and we interred the young in white coffins.

After writing Susan's death certificate, the doctor had alerted the district coroner that our family ought to be quarantined. The coroner had sent a gravedigger to the house with a cart, and had insisted that Susan's body be disposed of according to the president's orders; he had demanded that Philip bring her downstairs. He said that the coroner was tarring and smoking the bodies before burying them in a distant mass grave.

Philip, pale, haggard, and tense as wire, had wordlessly opened the front door and then had lifted the man up and had thrown him out onto the front walk. Then, he paid a ruinous bribe to the Reverend Alexander Marbury of St. John's Episcopal Church in Georgetown and arranged a funeral worthy of a princess and burial for Susan in the old Episcopal cemetery. No daughter of Philip Kearny's would lie for eternity in a pauper's grave.

We buried Susan in the morning on a soft spring day as the long winds blew off the Potomac and the horses pulling the white hearse tossed their heads, and made the white plumes between their ears dance elegantly.

I felt that I had died with my daughter and returned to my house as somebody else. The morning after Susan's funeral, I dressed and forced myself down the stairs. My head was stony, my heart felt gangrenous in my chest, and I descended the stairs, uncomprehending. The only thing I could feel was my own blank hopelessness. I wished to understand something about it, but could not, only a scattered sensation as if my house had been hit with a mortar shell and the rubble of my life had been strewn about me.

I stepped out into the back, under the trees, and looked up through the branches moving in the strong wind. Greeley ran by me with his nose to the ground, weaving through the shrubbery and bounding over the low border fences. Pulling my shawl tighter about my shoulders, I listened to the carriage traffic on the dusty streets.

Philip stood beside me, and for lack of anything better to do, we both contemplated the dog. My husband looked disastrously unwell, nervous and distressed as if he were on the verge of crying. But Philip would never cry in front of me or anyone else. He came from that generation of men who did not cry in the presence of other people, not even a bereaved wife. Yet he could not hide his despair; sorrow lined his face and darkened his eyes. The strain of sleepless nights and his self-imposed fast showed in his noble face.

Finally, he said, "I have orders to leave today."

"Yes. Yes, I know."

His eyes reddened, and he turned crisply on his heel and began to walk off toward the stables.

"Philip?"

He turned and met my gaze.

"Philip? Please." My throat felt dry and tight.

He stepped toward me, the graveled drive crunching underfoot. "What is it?"

"Don't go."

"I must go." He disappeared into the stables, where he began speaking of his travel arrangements to his valet, Rinnah June, who would accompany him and remain at Fort Leavenworth.

That evening, Philip departed Washington City for the frontier. Our windows and our door had been draped in black and white crepe to let everyone know Susan had died. The servants lined the walk in starched aprons and velvet livery wearing white mourning armbands but they could not resist the gallant figure Philip presented, and though tradition and decorum deplored it, they broke into a cheer as Philip mounted his horse.

I held my daughter Di in my arms and watched my husband with a growing sense of panic. Surely he wouldn't really go. He couldn't leave me alone, not now.

Rinnah June, Philip's valet, sat upon a mule behind Philip, fidgeting with his armband, mutely begging me to save him from the unthinkable horrors of the West. The old servant, dignified in his cutaway coat and salt and pepper trousers said, "Mrs. Kearny, if I had my druthers, you know I wouldn't be leaving."

"I know, Rinnah," I said, squeezing his hand.

Philip swept off his dress helmet, flourishing a black plume big enough to cover a hearse as the servants broke into even louder cheers.

As there are wild creatures that never venture too far from their habitats, then there are those that wander the land. After Philip left me, I carried Di on my hip as I walked alone in our garden. Last year's leaves disintegrated under my feet. All of my crying wouldn't make them green again.

The Territory

Seven

THE RUMORS IN 1844 of Indian hostilities against immigrant wagon trains were a bloody myth. After months spent ossifying at that two-penny outpost called Fort Leavenworth, drilling my troopers, engrossed in meaningless garrison detail under a bullying sun, I feared my wonderful instincts and elegant training as the foremost man in this cavalry were rusting.

What can I say of Kansas? As for the climate, it is windier than Washington City in election season. Kansas wants only good society and clean water to make it habitable, but then, that's all hell needs, too. Excepting the red-armed laundresses and dirty squaws, there were no women at Fort Leavenworth and the men became so crazed for the sight of the fair sex, that they contrived ridiculous practices. Our hunting expeditions became such putridly sentimental affairs, that none of the troopers or officers would bring themselves to shoot female animals— not doe, not buffalo cows and their calves, not elk cows, not even damned quail hens if they could help it.

Our martinet of a commanding officer picked the worst recruits for my allotment, a company of fifty Illi-nuisances from Chicago who'd never been on a horse nor fired a weapon, and arms so thin they could not lift a light sword. But ever the patriot, I resolved to make Company "F" the finest troop in the army. I bought the best tack for my men out of my own treasure. I purchased ninety of the finest chestnut horses to be found in the country and paid for them out of my own pocket. This, even though my paltry salary as a lieutenant was $1,400 a year! Why, in Washington City, I spent that much alone on one overcoat. Clearly, the army needed someone of my high tone and prestige.

My troopers woke to reveille at four in the morning. At five-thirty, the buglers sounded "boots and saddles"—the signal to march. I trained my men in horsemanship and tactics, made them shoot until they could hit a four-inch bull's-eye at seventy-five yards, and taught them every dirty trick about hand-to-hand combat with various weapons. I made a fine example for the army, selflessly and tirelessly devoting myself to my profession while other officers squandered their time drinking, whoring, and gambling.

I became disgusted by the petty discord and lack of discipline at the post in mid-July of 1844 upon returning from a three-day patrol with my troopers to find the post nearly deserted.

Peering around the empty parade grounds, I found my comrades, Lieutenants Richard Ewell and Henry Hunt, sipping rye whiskey, wearing broad-brimmed straw hats, and barefooted. Ewell and Hunt had pinned back the flaps of their tent, passing the long dull hours playing cards and smoking cigars. Hunt was trying to learn phrenology, believing that the bumps in a man's skull told him everything he needed to know about a man's nature.

Ewell removed his hat and Hunt thumped Ewell on the brow, above his left eye.

"That, you old bugger, is where your amativeness is."

"Amativeness? What the hell is that?" Ewell asked. He was a pupsy-looking fellow with a squeaking voice.

"Your capacity to love and be loved," Hunt said.

I interrupted their nonsense. "Where is everyone? Have there been orders to march that I don't know about?"

"Nope," Hunt said, scratching his beard. "The troops got themselves in a peck of trouble."

Ewell said, "Last night, all the men broke into the sutler's. Drank themselves sick. Drank with a slat-hound vengeance, I tell you what. Then the whole camp brawled on the parade grounds. Half the command is jailed in the guardhouse. If I am lying, you can write me down an ass."

"But that ain't the best of it," Hunt said, studying the cards in his hand. "Every damn officer in this whole damn garrison has preferred charges against every other damn officer."

"The end effect being," Ewell laughed his shrill laugh, "that me, you, and Hunt are the only officers in this hellhole who aren't going to be court-martialed. Rest of the officer corps is up on charges!"

Hunt and Ewell thought this howlingly funny.

But the next morning, a Sunday, our commanding officer ordered every man—jailed or no—and every lug-jawed laundress to attend church services as penance.

The entire camp assembled in rows under the broiling sun. The circuit preacher must have despaired as he surveyed the congregation of profligates, whores, and drunkards.

Crossing my boots, I leaned back in my camp chair letting the sun warm my face while the preacher droned on about those vile and lecherous idiots Adam and Eve.

What a frivolous vixen was Eve! Diana would have beaten that snake to death with a stick and saved the world the trouble. When the minister fell silent, I opened my eyes to a sea of smirking faces and realized that I had spoken aloud.

Eight

THE MORNING WE WERE to baptize baby Di I received a letter from Philip.

Dearest love,

Of late I feel most lukewarmly about Fort Leavenworth, a place that is breaking down my spirits. My talent is going to the devil. My so-called "superior" officers are indifferent, lazy, and worthless. Indeed, they are envious of me and treat me shabbily.

What I wouldn't give for a few moments with you, but the rivers are running too low and my wishes cannot possibly be achieved. Though I dream nightly of enfolding you in my arms, it cannot be, as you could never come West without a gentleman escort and besides, I would never put you at risk in the Indian country.

Whenever I lead an escort detail of immigrants on these wagon trails, I am under orders to shoot the white women rather than let them be taken by the Indians. This would doubtless please some of their henpecked husbands.

But the Indians are despicably peaceable, except for
a troublesome sniper who has been shooting up the camp
and so far eludes capture. The Indian sniper took a bead
on me yesterday as I was watering my horse, and though
the bullet hissed by my ear like a pronged serpent's fang,
I did not wince a particle.

Kissing the lines he had penned, I folded the note and tucked it into my bodice over my heart. In September of 1844, Di was eight months old. Bathed in the white light of the vestry at St. John's Episcopal, with Mama and Philip's father standing witness, the Reverend Alexander Marbury sprinkled holy water over my baby girl as her long white baptismal gown reached to the floor. And to think, that not so very long ago, I had stood in this very spot with Susan in my arms.

Having been in mourning these many months, we had delayed the baptism, but fearing for her granddaughter's soul, Mama would not tolerate further delay. After intense, exclusive preoccupation with Susan's death, I emerged at last from my room, where I had hidden like a sick recluse.

I held a hyssop branch over Di, a blessing to protect her from sin and the wickedness of the world. Philip had said that baptizing a baby was the surest proof I believed in the immediate presence of the devil, for otherwise, why not let the child go unsprinkled and surrender her to God's mercy? Perhaps a darker influence took hold of me during the baptism, for I decided to join Philip and no force of nature could have changed my mind. I touched the lace cap on my infant daughter's head, stroked the silk ribbons and the soft curve of her cheek with the crook of my finger. Irritable from teething, Di clutched my finger and gnawed upon it.

After the ceremony, friends and family who had come for this auspicious occasion conversed on the walk before a long line of gleaming black carriages. Soon, we would all depart for a luncheon hosted by Father Kearny at the club in honor of the baby. The guests bestowed marvelously inappropriate gifts upon my daughter; lace gowns, silver rattles, gold bracelets (jewelry for children was quite the thing), and bank bonds. They pledged Di's health with champagne until everyone suffered headaches and the party dispersed in a benevolent fog around mid-afternoon.

My daughter loved riding in the carriage, indeed, she thought it a most dignified form of recreation and as we returned home, she sat upon my mother's lap, solemn as a judge, staring around at us as she tried to understand our conversation.

I said to Mama and Father Kearny, "Philip has written to me. He is lonely and he needs me. And so, I have decided that little Di and I are going to Fort Leavenworth to be with him."

Mama and Father Kearny both gave me a long pitying look as if discovering I suffered from a want of common sense.

"You simply can't go." My mother sighed and shook her head. "A lady can't travel without a gentleman escort and no one will accompany you to Kansas. No one even knows where Kansas is."

Father Kearny squinted at the small print on the church bulletin. "I think Kansas is somewhere west of Trenton."

"Ah. There now, you see? As the old hymn goes, you may reach Kansas only through distant worlds and regions of the dead. Oh, come now, don't pout."

"A lady traveling alone is a lady in danger." Father Kearny opened a tin of peppermint lozenges, put one on his tongue, and tucked the tin into his pocket.

"Then come with me. We can make the trip together!"

Neither of them said a word in reply. Mama talked to the baby. "Such red cheeks and eyes bright as jet buttons. Why, you're an Indian papoose, aren't you? Yes, you are. Let Grandmamma kiss those fat cheeks." Di returned her kisses with hands to Mama's face and her mouth open wide. Mama wiped the infant spittle from her cheek with her handkerchief.

I sat forward on the seat and gripping the wing cushions, tapped my father-in-law's boot with the toe of my slipper to get his attention. "Father Kearny, come with me. Be my traveling companion."

Philip's father smiled, turned the page of the church bulletin, and pretended to scan the pages. "Dear child, I have never been west of Philadelphia. I am a drowsy, lazy city man with no interest in horizons beyond the Jersey shore."

"I have no choice but to go alone, then."

"Nonsense! What a silly idea," Father Kearny said. "Without a gentleman traveling companion, you might be assaulted."

"Who shall pay the steward?" Mama joined in. "If you haven't a gentleman along, who shall shout at the porters?"

"Who shall guard you from rude and jostling crowds?" Father Kearny rolled the church bulletin and pointed it at me. "And thieves, rogues, scoundrels, and murderers who lurk on the wharves?"

Mama reached across and patted my knee for emphasis. "None but mill workers and needlewomen travel alone. Why, Diana, if word spread in Washington that you were traveling alone, your reputation would be like a spoiled egg. I forbid it," Mama said, as the baby gripped her finger. "Really, how could you put your baby girl in such peril?"

"Do abide your mother's counsel," Father Kearny said, chewing his lozenge.

When we arrived at home, the old people retreated to their rooms for an afternoon nap. Thinking despondently of Philip, feeling his letter under my bodice and against my skin, I climbed the stairs to my bedroom with little Di on my hip. I stood at the window soothing my girl and rocking her side to side as I gazed down at the broad dirt streets, grieving over Susan and yearning for Philip. The air in my silent house was warm, rich, and hazy. A pack of stray dogs lay under the shade trees, too hot to chase the water cart as it rolled by, spraying and settling the dust.

My lady's maid came in silently and undressed me. I looked down at my ribs and belly, vigorously rubbed the long red marks left by my steel corset stays as the maid shook out my silk dress. A bowl of potato liquor in the anteroom drew flies as she soaked a rag in the liquor to wipe dust from my gown, but I asked her for privacy and sent her away.

I went over to the chest and removed a bundle of Philip's clothes, the last civilian clothes he had worn before leaving in April. I had squirreled away his whole outfit, from his socks to his braces, and even his cravat. Inhaling his scent from his shirt, I imagined that I could feel him close to me. Lifting Di into my arms, I tossed Philip's shirt over my shoulder and sat in the rocking chair, then brought Di to my nipple and she clamped it greedily. I slipped my arm into Philip's sleeve and wiped my runny nose on the cuff.

There, over the fireplace, hung *The Bullitt Sisters as the Fates*. I liked to open the curtains as the light moved across the painting, illuminating us one at a time, and in moments like this, when I felt despondent, I imagined returning to a distant place when my sisters and I were young and without care. Looking up at the painting, I asked my sisters, "What would you have me do?" And then, I sopped the briny outflow of my shameless self-pity with Philip's shirt. My daughter, a sympathetic little soul, wept too, and so we loosed a chorus of ill-repressed feminine sobbing. It was quite exceptionally priceless, both of us bawling and rocking.

Sniffling, I put the baby into her bed, then slipped my arms into the sleeves of Philip's shirt, and searched for his trousers. I wanted to be as close to him as I possibly could. The trousers were tight around my hips and my thighs strained the seams, but the length was perfect, for I was nearly as tall as he. His black broadcloth suit-coat flared slightly at the waist and fell to my knees. Tugging on his fine calfskin boots, I reached for Philip's rolled-brim stovepipe silk hat and shuffled over to the full-length mirror and peered into the glass. Why, I looked immensely dignified, if I did say so myself, and the solution came upon me sudden as sheet lightning. I would go to Philip and take my chances with the world. I felt a rising sense of exhilaration and my blues vanished instantly.

Donning my black mourning dress, and leaving the baby with my lady's maid, I went to the ticket office of the Baltimore & Ohio Railroad on Second and Pennsylvania Avenue Northwest where I purchased one ticket to Baltimore. Then, I flew around the city, gathering everything I would need and preparing for every possible contingency.

Returning home around six o'clock, I hid my purchases in my room. Before leaving for Fort Leavenworth, Philip had left me four hundred dollars in gold coin that I sewed into a belt worn under my clothes, and thus armored in money, I could clip coins as I needed them during my travels. From Philip's gun case, I took a pistol that I would carry in a leather pouch. Into the bottom of my trunk, I packed the Purdey shotgun in its wooden box, then neatly folded Philip's fine broadcloth suit and placed it on the gun box lid—he might be yearning to wear civilian clothes again. Lastly, I put a pair of green sun-spectacles in the built-in jewelry box on the inner wall of the trunk.

That night, while the old people slept, indeed, while the whole house slept, I packed one trunk with gowns that laced up the front, as I would not have a maid to dress me. All of our servants except my lady's maid were free colored people and while Philip was fully capable of protecting Rinnah June from harm, I could not risk taking a servant down the Ohio River into the slave states. Placing our wedding portrait on top of my clothing, I slid the lock into the trunk's latch and pocketed the key.

As I was still in mourning for Susan, and would be for an entire year, I wore a black bombazine dress and a long black veil that fell to my knees. Then, I sat at my desk, dipped my pen into the inkwell, and wrote Mama a letter by candlelight.

> *Dearest Mama,*
> *I have gone to be with Philip. I would rather die*
> *and drop beneath the sod unpitied than spend another*
> *day without him. I have taken the baby with me.*
> *Your loving daughter, Diana.*

I shook sand from a pewter can onto the page to dry the ink, and then blew the sand off the paper, folded the note, and heated the stamp over the candle flame, melting the edges of the wax wafer, and sealing the letter. I crept down the stairs into the main hall, and placed the letter on the receiving tray upon the hall stand where Mama was sure to find it.

I paced the floor while staring at the clock, tiptoeing now and again down to the darkened kitchen, where, out of sheer nervousness, I smoked six cigarettes. At four o'clock that morning, I sat upon the lid of the goatskin trunk waiting by the light of one candle for the sun to rise. Shortly before dawn, the hired hack appeared at the door and I scurried down the steps to greet him. I directed him up to the second-floor landing and gently lowered the baby into her traveling bassinet.

Mama rang the servant's bell in her room, summoning the chambermaid for her morning tea. I clutched the baby's bassinet by the sturdy handle and with my free hand grabbed our smaller cases, too. As I tottered down the stairs toward the main hall, Mama impatiently rang the servant's bell again, grumbling as she opened the door of her room. "Who is out there? Diana, is that you, my dear?"

I ran out the front door and across the stoop. The hack driver had strapped my trunks onto the back of the carriage and tossing the small cases inside, removed a tiny ladder from under his seat. Taking his sweet time, he carefully opened the door and positioned the ladder just so.

Mercifully the baby slept through it all. "Hurry!" I cried as I scrambled up into the hack and, grabbing the inside handle, slammed the door shut.

Mama blearily poked her head out the front door, holding my unopened letter in her hand. "Diana, you come back here at once, child! Come back or you'll be ruined!"

I banged on the thick roof with the metal point of my parasol, heard the whip cracking above the horses as the carriage trundled off, swaying side to side. I would not turn back now, not when my daughter and I were launched on the high road to adventure.

As we made our way to the station, I threw back the curtains and smiled upon the city. The sun began to rise, filling the air with humid breezes and birdsong, milkmen stooped under wooden yokes and pails went house to house, peddling their wares. Colored women singing the praises of their fruit pushed carts heaped high with pears and apples. As we pulled into the Baltimore & Ohio station, my spirits soared for I had finally been released from a tether that had bound me to a narrow perch and held me captive. Excited passengers filled the platform, milling about and chattering on a balmy summer morning. The hack driver hailed a porter, who loaded my luggage on a cart and then pushed it over to the baggage car.

So far, this was easy enough. Burdened with a hamper of food, I carefully balanced Di in her bassinet and walked down the line searching for the first-class car amid shouting porters and clanging bells signaling the train's departure. The train chuffed, clouds of steam and black-coal soot drifted over the platform.

Above the loud gabbling of the passengers the porters shouted, "Mrs. Philip Kearny! Mrs. Philip Kearny!"

There, by the station, my father-in-law sat on his horse scanning the crowd with his opera glasses. I ducked my head and trembling with apprehension, accidentally dropped the hamper of food. I had a hard time of it, trying to hold baby Di, while scrambling for the hamper around the legs of running passengers.

Meanwhile, the porters came closer, pressing through the crowd and shouting, "Mrs. Philip Kearny! Return to the platform, please!"

Seeing my distress, a lady in a blue traveling suit stopped in my path and smiled compassionately at me. She told her husband to assist me with my hamper. The gentleman graciously motioned me to precede him up the steps and so my daughter and I boarded the first-class car.

"Mrs. Philip Kearny! Mrs. Kearny!" The porters shouted, running along the line.

Outside, I thought I heard Father Kearny's harshly distinctive voice. "First class, I said. She's going to be in first class, damn you, up ahead. Hurry!"

I took the window seat and settled the baby in her basket on my lap, whispering and praying, *Go away, go away, oh, Lord, please don't let him find me.* A shadow fell over the window as a porter searched the car for a young woman in mourning clothes traveling with an infant.

Doubling over so that I could not be seen from outside, I rested Di's basket on the tops of my boots, and pretended to fuss with her clothes. The elegant woman in blue took the seat beside mine and settled my hamper of eatables at my feet. "Thank you so very much," I whispered, turning my face aside but not rising for fear of being seen.

The lady rapped the glass with her gloved hand and scolded the porter looking in the window. "Go away, you!"

The porter vanished. Under my veil, I whispered a prayer of thanks and explained to my traveling companion, "My mother is terribly ill, and I had to go to her immediately, with no time to wait. I am meeting my husband once we arrive at Havre de Grace."

"But where is your lady's maid? And this baby's nursemaid?"

"In the baggage car," I lied. "In the Negro car."

"Ah."

At the back of the car, the door was squeaking shut as I heard Father Kearny ranting, "Let me aboard. My daughter is on this car and I insist upon speaking with her."

My traveling companion leaned aside and asked, "Is that angry gentleman a white man or a Yankee?"

"A Yankee," I answered.

The lady made a face.

"Let me aboard or I shall—" Father Kearny sputtered, banging on the doors.

The porter shouted back, "Sorry, sir, I can't let you board without a ticket and this train is departing. Please step away."

When the train lurched forward Father Kearny hollered, "Diana! Diana, come out of the car this instant!"

"Sir! Step away or you will be crushed under the wheels," the porter warned.

But when the train began to move, Father Kearny thrust his walking stick into the door and raged, "I'll show you, you odious reptile! I'll buy this paltry railroad tomorrow and put you out of a job."

"You do that, sir."

The door slammed shut, the bolt slid into place, and I turned in my seat looking for my father-in-law. I felt bad, but I also knew I could not obey his rules and my heart as well. Kearny leapt nimbly onto the platform, whipped his hat from his head, and threw it down, cursing as the train pulled away.

"What a horrible man," the lady in blue murmured, buttoning her glove at her wrist.

"Perhaps he is only searching for someone who doesn't exist."

"Even so, if there is one thing I can't tolerate it's a vinegar-faced Yankee."

The lady's husband settled into a seat on the opposite side of the aisle, opened a newspaper, tented it over his face, and then dropped off to sleep, snoring like a buffalo. Di yawned and stretched in her basket lined with cotton batting, sheepskin, and my softest cashmere shawl. When I lifted Di and held her, she smelled milk and began rooting at my bodice, searching for my breasts. I felt milk leaking into the padding under my chemise. Di clenched the buttons on my bodice and grumbled at me in frustration. "Ma, ma, ma, ma."

A man behind me leaned over the seat and hissed, "Silence that brat or I'll do it for you."

I must have appeared stricken for the lady in blue placed a gloved hand on my sleeve and lifting her veil showed a smoothly pleasant face and shining blue eyes. And then she said, "Why don't you let me hold your child while you settle your things and find her bottle in your hamper? I am mother to five and thus, know *a little* about babies."

She sat my baby upon the soft billowing skirts over her lap. Di struggled to stand, bouncing on her legs and smiling as she reached for the lady's ringlets, but the woman was too wise and quick for my daughter. I rummaged in the hamper, fumbled with the unfamiliar India rubber nipple and series of interlocking rings, spilling condensed milk onto my skirt hem. Taking the bottle from me, the lady assembled it and began feeding Di. The baby made sucking and gulping noises, and astonished by the ease with which she extracted milk from a bottle as opposed to my breast, drank so greedily that milk spilled down the sides of her fat cheeks.

When we arrived at Havre de Grace, I slipped away unnoticed. Concealed amid a banked cloud of men in black capes and hats and umbrellas, I boarded a ferry across the Susquehanna and thence took another train to Pittsburgh where I bought passage on the steamboat *Mentoria*. Mama's warnings had been wrong thus far. No one had taken much notice of me, a woman in mourning weeds, a long black veil that fell over my shoulders, and a babe in my arms.

Nine

THE THREE-DAY JOURNEY from Pittsburgh to Louisville was uneventful, but while I waited to board another steamer at the Louisville levee to proceed on to St. Louis, a storm gathered and dull shaking thunder drawled into the distance, gusty winds caught my skirts, and someone's umbrella tumbled over the quay. The gangplank grew slippery with manure and mud. I huddled under my umbrella with my hired porter, shielding the baby, and waiting while teams of mules, braying like old squeaking pumps, were led to the boat's stern. The fires flared in the furnaces, steam hissed, and the whistle blew as I hastened aboard the *Mentoria* with Di. A porter followed behind with my luggage.

I stomped my feet and shivered, hunched my shoulders up to my ears. But just then, I heard a splash and a shout from the rousters.

"Man overboard!" the mate hollered.

While carrying cargo aboard, an Irish rouster had slipped off the muddy plank and fallen into the river. Unable to swim, he flailed in the oily black water, crying out for help. The captain leaned over the rail and peered into the water. Rain streamed from the leather bill of his cap. "Aw, it's only an Irishman. Let him sink."

"Sorr, ye can't just let him drown," a rouster pleaded.

"See if I can't. Now if it were an eight-hundred-dollar nigger, I'd fish him out."

The crew hauled the boy out of the water and hung him upside down by his ankles. The mate drubbed him on the chest until his lungs poured forth all of the water he had swallowed. No older than fifteen, the boy looked like a blonde St. Paul hanging upside down on his cross with a linen shirt falling over his face. When the mate was satisfied that he would live, he cut him down, and the boy fell onto the deck like a sack of grain. As the boy rose weakly to his feet, the captain punched him in the face for causing him so much trouble.

I tiptoed around the puddles on the deck and asked, "Boy? Are you badly hurt?"

"Are ye badly hurt? Are ye badly hurt, ye mama's suckling?" the rousters mocked. "Are ye hurt?"

I tried to help him up with my one free hand, but he cringed away from me, ashamed by my fussing. With a flinty glance around, the boy wiped his face with his wet shirt and bowing his head, hurried back to work.

The *Mentoria* was one of the finest boats running the Ohio River in the 1840s, which meant my first-class cabin boasted sham elegance, garish furnishings, and a level of filth that my children would have thought shocking when, twenty years later, they traveled aboard the legendary opulent floating palaces on this very same river. Rain leaked through the ceiling of my cabin and formed a stream through the center of the room so that the carpets squished underfoot. Stained with tobacco spit, the flocked velvet walls looked to have been sprayed with a hose. Beneath the gilt acorn posts of my berth, I slept on a straw mattress, a pillow stuffed with moldy cornstalks and gray, threadbare sheets.

The rainy air smelled of burning oil from the engines. Long streaks of mud caked over the deck as I hurried with the baby down along the row of cabins toward the single ladies' washroom shared by the first-class passengers. On the washroom counter were a long row of wash-basins, one toothbrush on a chain, and a big block of brown soap. Holding Di's basket, I turned a circle. Flies buzzed in the stall over the rustic toilet. One stiff, soiled towel was crumpled on the counter.

A woman squinted at her reflection in the long sheet of polished tin above the washbasins. Her silk dress had a dirt-blackened hem, and her bonnet flourished an ostrich feather. Removing her glove, she dragged her nail between her teeth and then squeezed an atomizer of rosewater cologne at her face.

"Good morning," I said as I settled Di in her basket on the wooden counter.

"Good morning. I am Mrs. Myrtle Shunk. And who are you?"

"Mrs. Philip Kearny," I answered, but did not meet her eyes for I had no desire to converse with her. Myrtle Shunk looked me over from head to toe and sensed something was wrong. As she scrutinized me, I could hear the alarm bells clanging inside her head. Only a lady could afford the wildly expensive mourning dress I wore, but a lady would never, under any circumstances change her own child's diaper in a washroom. A lady traveled with a retinue of servants, including a nurse and an undernurse.

In an icy tone, she asked, "Where is your child's nurse? Or the under-nurse for that matter?"

"Pardon?"

"Where is this child's father?" Myrtle pointed at the baby. "Where is . . . *Mr.* Kearny?"

When I darted a withering look in her direction, Myrtle Shunk huffed out of the room, muttering, "I thought as much. I know your kind."

"Now there goes a specked peach," I said to the baby as I changed her diaper. Exiting the washroom, I tossed Di's dirty diaper overboard into the river.

Every night before falling into bed I put Philip's boots outside my door so that any one strolling by on the deck would think that inside my cabin, my husband and protector slept. At sunset on the first evening as little Di was blissfully asleep, rocking gently in her basket suspended from the ceiling hook by strong ropes, I slipped outside onto the deck, hoping for a breeze. Leaning over the rail and looking down at the boiler deck, I saw boys carrying large buckets of food to the rousters, and then slopping the contents directly onto the deck. "Grub pile," they cried as the rousters clambered atop one another, fighting for handfuls of bread and broken meat.

The trip from Louisville to St. Louis took just three days and on the second night, I stood alone, staring wistfully at the water sliding away, listening for Di crying or whimpering in her sleep, pretending not to hear Myrtle Shunk's ceaseless tirade against me. I could not imagine what I had done to offend that woman. I guessed that Myrtle believed the world owed her something that life had failed to deliver, perhaps she had wanted children and had none, or maybe she had hoped to marry better. Whatever the cause, her failures had made her bitter as the papery husk around a walnut.

Sitting beside her husband in a canvas chair, Myrtle whispered, "There she is. There is the woman I told you about."

"Now, Myrtle, you are imagining things."

"If you don't speak to the captain, I will. She looks love into the eyes of every man who passes her."

"Don't be ridiculous. She's a poor widow with a baby. Besides, how can she look love at anyone through that thick black veil? I can't even make out her face under it."

"Oh, you'd like to try, wouldn't you?"

Mr. Shunk sighed and rose from his camp chair. "I'm going to the gentleman's saloon to partake of a little Monongahela Rye."

"Mr. Shunk, you come back here," she scolded after him, but he waved her away and lumbered down the deck.

I retreated to my room, thinking, so this is what it meant to be hated by a perfect stranger and for no reason but her suspicion that I somehow didn't measure up to her standards, which, by the look of her, couldn't be too lofty. Alone in my cabin, I disrobed, dressed in my white nightgown and lay abed on the straw mattress. Around midnight, Myrtle hectored Mr. Shunk so loudly her voice pierced the thin walls, as did his weary replies.

I studied my wedding portrait on the nightstand, the one Philip and I had taken on the day of the riot. Reaching aside, I smeared a circle in the dusty glass. Whenever I looked at the picture, Philip's image appeared more shadowy and distant, a trick of light and fade of time, and all because he had been too restless to sit still for the daguerreotypist for a few minutes. Dressed in his cavalry uniform, a hussar jacket draped loosely over his shoulders, Philip leaned forward, his eyes sharp on the middle distance as if he was about to sprint out of the frame. Unable to hold a pose, my husband had roamed the daguerreotype studio despite the portraitist's objections. And in the intervening years, Philip's image had faded during the long exposure time so that only his phantom could be seen in the glass: a ghost limned in silver.

Things went from bad to worse the next day. It seemed Myrtle Shunk occupied all of her time marshaling her forces against me. In profile, I could see her nose pointing beyond her bonnet brim. She may even have been a reasonably attractive woman, but her mean-spiritedness made her ugly as a hedge fence in winter.

At any hour of the day dozens of passengers crowded the deck, the women sitting side by side, fanning themselves and sewing or reading, the gentlemen playing cards and drinking ardent spirits from morning till night. I could not exit my cabin door without bumping into someone, and thanks to Myrtle Shunk, conversation would cease as, with head down, I scurried through the gauntlet to the washroom with the baby and back again to my cabin. The row of bonneted heads would follow my progress, and Myrtle and her friends made sure that I could hear them.

When I walked by those women, I felt like a grasshopper darting across a chicken pen under twelve pairs of seedy eyes and twelve pecking beaks. Mr. Shunk sat on a camp chair beside his wife, reading his newspaper and to his credit, he pointedly ignored her slanderous gossip.

"She is dressed finely enough. Those are mighty expensive widow's weeds she's wearing. At table her manners are impeccable."

"With a certain class of women, manners are fine, if you know what I mean."

"No, Mrs. Shunk, I don't. What do you mean?" asked another traveler.

"She can't very well earn top dollar if she swills at the trough, can she?"

The women gasped in horror, but then broke into laughter. "Oh, Myrtle, you're a card. Aren't you a card?"

"I asked my Horace to complain to the captain. But he is a noodle, and none but noodles have the world in charge. So you see we must suffer indignity and slights when women like her are allowed to take first-class cabins."

"What Myrtle says makes sense, doesn't it? For it would make sense if that widow woman was a lady of the town, being able to afford fine things, yet no one to accompany her, not a servant, not a gentleman escort besides."

"But what about her baby?"

Myrtle continued. "Of course, *the baby*. She is an abandoned woman. I asked her to her face who was the father and she turned up her nose and would not answer me. Mrs. Philip Kearny, she says, an arrogant hussy, I says."

"We cannot tolerate the insult, having her sleep next door and engaging in shocking depravity. Every night there is a different pair of men's shoes outside her door. She is engaging in trade right under our noses!"

"We must put her off the boat. We must insist the captain stop the boat and leave her stranded on the shore. Leave her on a sandbar, if need be. I have been on boats where thieves were put on sandbars wearing nothing but their underdrawers. She deserves no better."

Whereupon Mr. Shunk interrupted, "Oh, fie, now you are jumping to conclusions, don't you think? She may be an honest widow, fallen upon misfortune. Hardly Christian of you to slander her without knowing the truth."

But Myrtle was fired with pious zeal. "The Christian thing would be for us to refuse to tolerate sin in our midst. The Christian thing to do would be to put her off the boat and let the Lord decide her fate."

Mr. Shunk grunted. "Seems to me, Myrtle, you are playing the role of Lord Almighty well enough as it is."

"If she is a depraved woman, she must be put off the boat."

Outraged, I yearned to confront her, but that would only give her more reason to carry through her plans. And so, with my baby's well-being foremost in my thoughts, I stayed close to my cabin.

Suddenly, the boat ground to a halt, stopping mid-current with a horrifying grinding and groaning noise from the engines. I heard the engineer raging as he ran across the deck. "The damned boilers is gonna burst. The tubes is clogged."

"Clogged with mud?" asked the stoker.

"Clogged with goddamned diapers. Who got a baby on this boat?"

I winced upon hearing this, remembering the numerous diapers that I'd tossed overboard over the past two days. Little Di's diaper cloths must have been sucked up into the ship's boiler engines.

"I guess there's lots a babies on this boat," the stoker called to the engineer.

"You find them. You find every baby on this boat."

"And then what, sir?"

"Then I'm gonna slap every baby I see, don't you doubt it."

Outside my door the women lowered their voices and one said, "Now would be the perfect time to evict that trollop. There are nothing but woods for miles around. That would teach her, wouldn't it?"

Well, things were looking mixed and I felt truly afraid. Evicting passengers for offenses real or imagined was a common practice on the Ohio River steamers, and I knew the baby and I were in real danger. For a quarter of an hour, I hid away in my cabin, thinking what I ought to do. Then, I loaded the pistol and tucked it into my skirt pocket. Collecting my wedding portrait and a packet of Philip's letters from my trunk and carrying the baby, I slipped outside as the women on the deck muttered vicious things about me.

I went looking for the captain and found him leaning over the rail observing the argument between the stoker and engineer about the clogged boiler. The captain wore a broad-rimmed straw hat and black vest. His job on this boat was to be a business manager and to host the first-class passengers. He did not pilot the boat, nor did he supervise the crew. Nearing fifty, a slightly built man, the captain smoked a cigar with about four inches of ash at the end, tipped like a telescope to keep the long ash from scattering. Seeing me, he plucked the cigar from his mouth and the ash showered sparks down his coat.

Brushing the ash away, he grinned and said, "Good evening, madam."

"Sir, I wish to speak to you about an urgent matter. I am Mrs. Philip Kearny and I have taken the first-class cabin nearest the camphene lamp."

"Ah yes, Mrs. Kearny, is it? I was just coming to have some private talk with you. Several of the passengers have expressed concerns and though I intend no insult, madam, they are speculating about your motives."

"Yes, I've heard their slander."

"A few of the ladies have insisted I put you off the boat." He leaned on his elbows on the rail. "The gentlemen, however, have not voiced any opposition to you whatsoever."

I disliked his oily tone but handed him my wedding portrait and Philip's letters. "That is a picture of my husband and myself. And these are his letters, bearing his address at Fort Leavenworth. He is a lieutenant in the First Dragoons and I am traveling with our daughter to meet him at the fort."

The captain squinted and tilted the wedding picture to catch the light from the lantern. He scratched his temple. "I ain't even certain I can see a feller in this picture. I only see you in this picture and a blurry ghost." He lifted his shoulder as if to let me know he was helpless in this matter. "There is talk a different man leaves his shoes outside your door every night. Is that true?"

"That is one pair of shoes, my husband's shoes, and I put them there thinking it would silence such speculation. What are the names of the people who have said these vile things about me?"

"Mrs. Myrtle Shunk." The captain leaned back against the rails on his elbows and regarded me with a friendly smile. "Don't you worry, Mrs. Kearny, I won't let any harm come to you. Why don't you go get some rest? We arrive in Louisville early tomorrow." He returned the letters and portrait and said, "One more matter, ma'am. Did you buy passage through to St. Louis?"

I turned, "Yes, I did."

"Then I look forward to being your protector for the remainder of the week." And he tucked the cigar between his lips, leering disgracefully at me.

That night, I locked the door, bolted the shutters over my window and placed the pistol under my pillow. My door had a keyhole and a camphene lantern burning on the post outside sent a thin beam of light onto the floor.

At one o'clock in the morning, someone crouched in front of the keyhole, blocking the light. Slipping the pistol out from under my pillow, I crawled to the end of the bed. A key turned in the lock and instantly, I knew the intruder. No one but the captain had keys to the first-class cabins.

The captain tiptoed through the door, but lust had muddled his thinking and he left it slightly ajar. Seeing my shadow on the end of the bed, he whispered hoarsely, "You're waiting for me. I knew you would be. Now I'm gonna give you what you want."

"You're going to give me a cabin that isn't moldy and filthy?" Holding the pistol behind my back, I stepped aside toward the shuttered window.

"Take off your nightdress. Then lay down and do as I say." The captain dropped his trousers down around his ankles and stood in the middle of the room in his shirttails, touching himself.

I dared not shoot in the dark for fear of hitting the baby in her suspended bassinet.

"Stay there, Captain. I am coming over to you," I whispered. With the pistol in one hand, I reached up and unbolted the shutters, letting light into the room. The light through the window shone upon the captain. If it is true that you can judge the size of a man's empire by the scepter he wields, then the captain's empire was very small indeed.

The barrel of my pistol gleamed in the light of the camphene lantern. When he saw the pistol aimed at him, the captain's aspirations wilted. He stopped ministering to himself and raised his hands in a placating gesture. "Now, Mrs. Kearny, put the gun down."

"Put your pants on."

"You'd better not get into a row with me or you'll go to the wall. Is that what you want?"

"I can shoot a four-inch target at seventy-five yards. Believe me, I could destroy *that* four-inch target from here."

Cursing and hurling the most profane invectives at me, he hopped around, struggling to pull up his trousers. And as I held the pistol on him, I could see him remembering the baby, and seizing upon the idea that he could threaten her and so make me do whatever he wanted. In the instant he looked down to lace his trousers, I struck him hard upon the temple with the butt of the pistol.

For a moment I stood there, staring at the captain face down on the floor. His injuries looked severe and blood matted his greasy hair.

The next five hours were the most nerve-wracking I had ever experienced in my life. I stuffed the captain's big red handkerchief into his mouth and tied his shirt around his head. He did not wake or stir and I worried if I'd killed him. Using the ropes suspending the baby's bassinet from the ceiling, I tied his hands and his feet. Peeking out the door and seeing all was clear, I grabbed the captain under his arms and dragged him down the deck into the ladies' washroom.

Then I ran full speed back to my cabin and locked the door. The enormity of what I had done sank in. It occurred to me, pacing in my nightdress, sick with anxiety, that I might put Philip's broadcloth suit to good use. The steamer would dock at the St. Louis levee in a few hours, at dawn, and when it did, I intended to escape the *Mentoria* in disguise.

Ten

IN THE DIM LIGHT before dawn, I, Joseph Hartwell, resembled any other prosperous merchant waiting to disembark the *Mentoria* in my black knee-coat and trousers. Unnoticed in the large crowd pushing to get off the boat, I had pulled a hat low over my ears, green eyeglasses sat upon my nose, and a fashionably high-pointing parricide collar concealed my face from jaw to cheekbone. I carried Di on my hip as the mate rang the bell summoning the first-class passengers to disembark and soon, the gangplank was lowered and the hawsers went up.

On the deck above me, the captain was shouting at the St. Louis constabulary. His head had been bandaged and he gestured wildly, reenacting his great ordeal with himself playing the central role of the heroic warrior. And then it occurred to me that the captain was probably lying about who had attacked him, for it would damage his pride too much and spark suspicion if he said that a lady had been responsible for his injuries. Any man with sense would guess that a female assailant had been defending herself against the captain's unwelcome advances.

I smoked and watched him and suspected I was right on point.

With a courteous nod and touching the brim of my hat with a gloved hand, I walked past the constables on the deck. A hired porter pushed my trunk in a handcart up the levee to the row of countinghouses overlooking the river. Di squirmed restlessly on my hip, but I could not set her down on the levee.

Walking around lumpy ridges of wholesale merchandise and rows of grain barrels, I read the swinging signboards and found my destination: WILLIAM GLASGOW, IMPORTER OF FINE WINE. The building was dark and the door was locked. I peered up at the mansard roof of Glasgow's countinghouse, at the iron balcony shedding long ribbons of rust and cautiously carried little Di around a pulley wheel. Holding her in my lap, I sat upon the steps and observed the rousters heaving hogsheads of molasses and rum onto the levee. Before me gleamed the great river, but when I looked left and right, as far as I could see there stood a row of warehouses, some with wind-tattered green and white awnings, some with signs advertising wholesalers and cotton factors and grain merchants.

While I waited for William Glasgow, I looked through the windows at the dim outlines of box-lined aisles and floors thick with slut's wool. Dust caught in my nose and dried on the back of my tongue and though I had tried to stave off thirst, I could hold out no longer. Holding Di on my hip, I walked down the sloping levee to the communal water bucket. She wanted a drink too, but I would not risk it. Dipping the ladle in the Mississippi's bounty, I sipped it through clenched teeth to filter out the slimy river sediment. We returned to the steps where we sat between a keg of shingling nails and a huge gunnysack of fragrant cedar and oak chips.

At half-past six in the morning, an open carriage rolled toward me bearing William Glasgow, an elegantly dressed man of forty with a broad face and deep-set blue eyes. Beside him sat a familiar figure, my dearest friend Anne Lane, a short but slender lady who stepped from the carriage leaning on her parasol. She had hair the color of old brass, wore a rose-colored gown and a bonnet with a pink ribbon.

As I had hoped, Anne Ewing Lane accompanied her brother-in-law, William Glasgow, to his countinghouse today as she often did. She calculated his accounts for him. I had known Anne Lane since we were both fifteen years old. We'd met at school and in the first week of classes, had exchanged bracelets made of our own hair, wearing them around our wrists until they disintegrated.

Anne's back was knotty as puddingstone, her left leg shorter than her right, her spine curved like an "S" and when she was eleven, her father had sent her to Lexington, Kentucky, to live with a doctor who specialized in diseases of the spine. The doctor had said that Anne must lie on the floor until her backbone straightened. So for a year, Anne Lane had put herself on the ground, using her elbows to flipper and wiggle around the house. In school, Anne had too much energy and smartness to appear like a perfect lady so our teachers marked her for spinsterhood from a tender age. I wish I had been more like her, but while at the academy, I was mostly a refugee from deep thought.

Anne's eyes widened as she approached me and saw a strange, bespectacled man with a baby, sitting on the steps of William's business establishment. I stood and was about to introduce myself when Glasgow muttered under his breath and took Anne's arm protectively. "Come around to my other side, Sister. That swarthy man has the wandering eye of a libertine."

Well, it stung me to be called a libertine. Not to mention swarthy.

Di gurgled and shrieked, then reached up and snatched my spectacles from my face. While I tried to wrest them away from her, I met Anne Lane's eyes.

Glasgow touched the brim of his hat. "Good morning, sir, may I help you?"

Anne paled and her mouth fell open, she stared at me as if I were a frog in a bottle. When I tried to smile, she pursed her lips and shook her head. "Diana Bullitt Kearny, you are the pet child of calamity!"

"Oh, Anne, you must help me!" I pleaded, shifting Di from one hip to the other. The baby popped my green spectacles into her mouth and gummed the lenses.

Married to Anne's sister Sarah, an invalid with rheumatoid arthritis and a deadly morphine habit, William Glasgow had always treated me as if I were a rambunctious younger sister. A muscular man with a ruddy Scottish complexion, he lifted his gaze to my face and blinked in bewilderment as he fished for the key in his pocket. "I have never seen a woman so dressed in all of my life. Diana, I cannot bring myself to look away."

"Please try your best, Will. You're making yourself conspicuous," Anne said, taking the key from him and inserting it into the lock.

Turning to me, Glasgow cleared his throat, and blushing darkly, whispered, "You are a most compelling woman."

"What do you mean by that?"

"Inside with all of you!" Anne said, slamming the door shut behind us. "Diana, why are you dressed like a Wall Street lawyer?"

"Now, Annie, it is a sign of maturity not to be scandalized, but to try to find explanations in charity."

"You are not a very convincing man."

"Not a convincing man at all. You may take Mrs. Kearny into my office, Anne," Glasgow offered, licking his thumb, flipping through a stack of invoices as Anne and I wound through towers of wooden crates filled with Malaga and Hock and Burgundy wines.

Once inside Glasgow's office, I sat behind his desk and removed my shirt studs and cuff links. Anne threw her arms around me and squeezed me hard, the brim of her bonnet bumping my cheek. "You wild girl, why have you come out here all by yourself? Surely, your mama did not allow it. And where is your escort? Why have you no traveling companion?"

"Scold all you wish, Anne, I don't care a whit about other people's opinions anymore and it is mighty freeing. The truth is, traveling alone has made a man out of me." I took off the tall silk hat and my braids sprang out around my head like the snakes of the furies. Anne clucked her tongue against the roof of her mouth as she took my hat and then tugged the masculine neck cloth from my shoulders, balling it into the hat. "But, Diana, why would you risk this sweet baby's life by being so foolish? Why would you jeopardize your own life by traveling alone?"

Di had reached the end of her patience, and she gripped my hair in her hands, wailing for her breakfast.

"Oh, I'll tell you soon enough. But first, I really must feed this child."

"I received your letter about your little Susan. I am so sorry," Anne said, watching me closely. At the mention of Susan's name, I felt my heart seize with familiar grief and for a moment, I could not meet my old friend's gaze. Instead, I continued shedding Philip's clothes, threw the shirt aside, and asked Anne to help me unwind the binding that flattened my breasts.

"I can't speak of her," I said finally.

Anne merely nodded as she rolled the long gauze bandage into a neat ball. "You ought to wean that child and fill her bottle with river water. River water is most fortifying. Besides I don't know of any respectable lady who nurses her own children. It will weaken your constitution, Diana."

My daughter gave me a saucy look and pinched the skin on my neck with her fat hand.

When I did not reply, Anne continued, "How was your journey? What was it like, coming downriver all alone? Did you see anyone we know? Did you meet any notorious people?"

As the baby nursed, I told Anne my tale. Her eyes shone with shrewd amusement as I recounted my troubles and related my hopes for the future. I asked, "What do you think I ought to do?"

"Hold still," Anne said when I'd fallen silent, and licking her thumb, she wiped something from my cheekbone. Anne was one of those people you might call a "groomer." She'd groom you spotless whether you wanted her to or not. She couldn't bear to see an unraveling string on a sleeve, lint on a lapel, or a hair on a white collar. "Don't move," she'd say, "Let me get that for you," and she'd brush a fleck of dust off my skirt flounce. I didn't know whether to be gratified or insulted. Unfortunately, her eyesight wasn't so good and her dexterity not much to speak of, so while saving me from a stray lash she'd jab her thumb into my eye, and while tucking a loose hairpin into place her rings caught in my stiff hair, mussing it so that it spiked off crazily to one side. When Anne groomed me and I let her, we resembled the idiot and her keeper.

I burped the baby and then Anne said, "Give her to me, let me hold her. Now, this baby looks like you. She has Kearny's eyes and your hair. But where did she get her sweet temper?" Then, she added, rather nonchalantly, "By the by? I am going with you to Fort Leavenworth."

"Oh, but I was hoping Glasgow would accompany me."

"Pardon my gallantry, insipid thing. You refuse me outright?"

"Anne, don't take offense, but what good can you do? I need a gentleman escort."

"Glasgow *can't* escort you to Fort Leavenworth. My sister Sarah is in a very bad way; her arthritis has crippled her to such a degree that she is tied to her chair and wholly dependent upon poor Will and he is devoted to her care. He will not be persuaded to leave her even for a day. Others have tried."

"Then I shall continue on alone. I am so close to Fort Leavenworth now, I simply can't turn back. Not now." I drummed my fingers on the leather blotter. Di crawled up on the desk and reached for the Will's feather pen, but I took it from her and jabbed the pen into the inkwell.

Anne sat on the edge of the desk and argued on her own behalf. "Listen to me, Diana. You will keep your disguise and I'll go with you as your wife and no one will be the wiser." And as if daring me to say no, she peered at her reflection in the window behind me. "I have always wanted to travel without Glasgow. When we board the steamer in St. Louis, I will dance the fandango in a red silk dress with gold beads around my neck. I will gamble a fortune at the whist table and eat a rasher of bacon and one whole pie at every meal. Yes, indeed. You stay here, I'm going to tell Glasgow and he'll rant and rail but he's only my brother-in-law, after all."

Well, I could hardly say no. That I did not discourage Anne was the surest proof I had become a scoundrel of extraordinary magnitude. Anne rushed home to pack a trunk and at noon that very day, we bade farewell to Glasgow on the levee, but not without first listening to his stern lecture and admonishments.

But Anne interrupted him, straightened her bonnet, and looped her arm in mine saying, "This was my idea, William. I am on the wrong side of twenty-five, emancipated, and financially independent. Why shouldn't I have a little fun?"

"Don't worry, I'll look after her, Will," I assured him, handing the baby off to Anne. Glasgow forgot himself and grabbed me by the shoulders, kissing me on both cheeks above my starched collar, provoking odd looks from passersby.

The trip from St. Louis to Fort Leavenworth took one week aboard the *Hatchee Eagle*. As we steamed toward the Indian Territory on the Missouri River, Anne and I lounged on the deck chairs and played with the baby. We gossiped with the other passengers, including a sutler in a fur hat who carried all of his worldly belongings in a "possibles bag" slung around his neck by a leather cord. The bag held every possible thing he owned. After supper, he valiantly tried to play a Brahms concerto for us on his accordion.

We arrived at Fort Leavenworth at dusk on a Thursday and discovered that it wasn't much of a fort at all. Though in later years a city by this name would rise near this very spot, my first impression of the encampment was of an open sort of place, with a fine jumble of stone and log buildings perched on a steep river bluff. A few weathered clapboard shacks clustered on the muddy river landing and on the opposite shore grew a thickly wooded rush bottom a mile wide.

We disembarked in a bustling wagon yard and supply depot. As far as I could discern, the muleteers were all Mexican men and a half dozen of them rushed at the passengers, offering their services. The muleteers threw our luggage onto a baggage cart. Holding the baby, I took a seat on the bench in a blue Dougherty wagon with the canvas sides rolled up. Anne sat beside me, steadying herself with her parasol pointed into the wood floor of the wagon.

The Mexican teamster snapped the thick leather strap over the lead mule. We climbed the bluff and were thrown around like potatoes in a wheelbarrow. Teams of mules hauled the wagons up a steeply winding road all the way to the top of a high ridge rising from the edge of the Missouri River. Pack mules and heavy wheels had ground the dirt road's surface to a fine ankle-deep powder.

Anne opened her parasol and shaded us from the setting sun. But as we neared the crest of the hill and Fort Leavenworth came into view, our driver shouted to us in broken English, "Heads down. Heads down. Down, down, down. Shooter! Shooter!" And then, most disconcertingly, the muleteer reclined upon the driver's box until he was lying flat on his back, squinting out from under the broad brim of his hat as he whipped the mules.

"What in the world can he mean? Did you understand what he said?" Anne frowned.

And then, to my immense alarm, I heard the sibilant hiss of a bullet passing by my ear. I shrieked and with Di in my arms, slid off the bench seat, down onto the blue wagon bed.

Reaching up, I jerked Anne down to safety beside me.

"What in the name of God?" Anne cried as she bumped onto the floor.

The muleteer shook his fist at a dense stand of cottonwood trees on the bluff and throwing his head back, crowed, "You Injuns bad shot. Too bad for you!"

"That settles it," Anne said, stretching her legs across the wagon bed and primly tucking her hands into her skirt pockets. "I wouldn't take Fort Leavenworth if the United States Army gave it to me. I have done my duty by you and as soon as Kearny can arrange it, I'm returning to civilization and St. Louis."

Another bullet pinged harmlessly against the iron rim of the wagon wheel. "You'd think the sniper would at least be able to hit one of the mules," I wondered aloud as we rolled into the fort.

Once we crested the grassy plain I saw a village of frame buildings and dirt streets with a broad green parade ground and a dry goods store. On the main parade ground by the flagpole and the powder magazine, a military band played tunes and the enlisted men danced with laundresses. I saw very few women aside from the laundresses who lived in the line of shacks called Soapsuds Row and who boiled uniforms in huge copper kettles over fires. Though, in two years time, by 1846, the post would be populated by hundreds of families, in 1844, Fort Leavenworth was a sleepy paradise of soldiers and washwomen. But the enlisted barracks were grand; two-story frame longhouses with deep porches, and there were limestone quarters for the more senior officers.

As the mule wagon rumbled down the dusty road between the old buildings, the driver shouted, "Soldier's Quarters Left Wing! Kitchens, Right Wing!"

I had no idea where to begin looking for Philip. The baby whimpered and squirmed in my arms. Anne clucked her tongue as she climbed back up onto the bench seat and looked around.

The muleteer turned to me. "Where?"

"Will you stop a moment and let me inquire?" I asked the muleteer, handing the baby off to Anne. Leaping down from the wagon, holding my hat down on my head, I ran across the grass to the soldier standing guard before the powder magazine.

"I am looking for Lieutenant Philip Kearny, First Dragoons, Company "F." Do you know where I might find him?"

The sentry stared at me with an odd expression, reminding me that I must look a poor specimen of a man, but then he rolled his shoulders and hefted his musket from one hand to the other, pointing to the west. "This time of day he usually takes a swimming bath at three-mile creek. Go three miles west from this here flagpole. Follow that wagon trail until you reach the tall grass prairie and the mossy creek under the cottonwood trees."

I told the muleteer to drive us to the officer's mess hall, an unpainted two-story building with a covered porch crammed full of furniture and sunburned young men leaning curiously over the railing. Introducing ourselves as guests of Lieutenant Kearny, we were heartily welcomed. Upon seeing Anne and my little daughter, the men instantly stopped playing faro, extinguished their cigars, and hid their flasks of hunter's rye whiskey, begging her for news from St. Louis.

Anne settled with the baby on a comfortable wicker sofa. "We were shot at as we came up the road!"

The officers chorused their dismay. "We have been trying to capture that sniper for months now, but he is a sneaky cuss!"

"We have pursued that sniper with a slathound vengeance but he will not be caught."

"Luckily, he's a terrible shot. He hasn't killed anybody."

"Hasn't even wounded anybody!"

While I stared impatiently at the trace that the sentry had pointed out for me, lonely, talkative young officers besieged Anne. She conversed with them, sipped lemon shrub and bounced the baby on her lap in time with the military band concert.

Bidding her good-bye, and assuring her that I would return shortly,

I started down the westerly road hoping for the sight of Philip. Following the picket's directions, I walked west of camp on hard trampled footpaths. I saw the man I loved bathing in a frog pond as I approached a stand of cottonwood trees and willows. He stood with his back to me, staring into the distance at the tall grass prairie, his fingertips on the surface, his back glistening and the water circling his waist.

Silently, I came upon the muddy shore where his clothes, his carbine and brace of pistols, and his light cavalry sword were piled atop a tumbled swath of grass. I stood under the cottonwood tree, the wind blew the leaves, and the grass ran and fled off into the distance.

"Who are you?" Philip turned lazily. "And what are you staring at? State your business and be gone," he muttered with a dismissive slash of his hand in the water. "If you have nothing to say, then go on. Get out of here."

But I sat in the mud and pulled off the boots and wiggled my toes. "No, I think not, as I rather enjoy the view."

"I don't like being gawked at by a craven dandy, and I'll show you I mean business."

"Go on then, show me you mean business." I slipped out of the black knee coat and threw it on top of his firearms.

"I hope you've made peace with your maker as I intend to put you to sleep for good." He slicked his hair off of his brow and glared at me.

"As long as I can sleep in your arms, dear." I tickled the air with my fingers.

He splashed toward me, the water swirling around his knees.

I reached for his cavalry sword, and brandishing it in the air, laughed, "Are you looking for this? What would you call this thing? A potato masher?"

"Why, you insolent puppy! You'd run if you knew what's good for you."

"I am only trying to be helpful."

Philip's eyes fired with rage as he tore the sword out of my hand, but he was wet and he fumbled the grip. I plucked at my shirt buttons and grinned slyly at him. "Seeing you in your natural state causes me a delightful but strange agitation."

"That is enough from you. You better leave or I'll cut your onions off, see if I won't." He charged after me in all of his naked glory, and having prolonged the joke too long, I was well and truly frightened. I fled, with my knees churning high and my arms spinning. He rushed up behind me. I heard the sword whooshing above my ears and the top of my tall hat was cut away and went flying across the grass.

"Stop, Philip, it's me! It's me." But my fierce and brilliant talent for self-preservation kept me running as fast as I was able and then I heard him close upon me. I felt a painful blow to the backs of my knees and fell hard into the grass, scraping my chin in the dirt.

He grabbed at the back of my head, the wig came away in his hands, and my hair tumbled out in a snarly mess. "What the devil do we have here?" Rolling me over, he sat upon my legs and for a moment, he was aggressively mystified.

"Hello, Philip." I propped myself up on my elbows and shook my hair out, imagining that I looked very fetching indeed, but then, I tend to surrender to vanity at every opportunity.

"Jesus Dandified Christ!"

"Aren't you happy to see me?"

"Diana! What the hell do you think you're doing?" The hair on his legs and chest streamed with water and the tops of my pant legs were soaked.

"I have been lonely without you; aren't you glad I'm here, Philip?"

He stroked his chin a moment, lowered his weight onto me, placing his hands on my shoulders. "I don't believe you are my wife. The only way I can know is to see what you have hidden under your chemise." He began tearing open the shirt so that the button studs popped like corn. "Now, let me see what you have hidden under there. I am afraid I must remove this troublesome thing to complete my inspection," and without waiting for my response, he tore the garment asunder. "Ah yes," he bent his head and whispered, "but I cannot be sure unless we have a look under these trousers." Whereupon, he reached down, kissing me in a line between my ribs to my stomach, unlaced my trousers, and lifted my hips so that he could tug them down to my knees. He pretended to be baffled by my white belly and hips until I laughed and covered my eyes with the crook of my arm.

Philip leaned over me. "Could it be? Is it you? There is one more test, and I can't be sure until I try." And pulling me up, he rolled over and sat upright with his back against a cottonwood tree and brought me on top of him, and taking my face in his hands, my hair falling around us both, he said with mock seriousness, "Young lady, I command you to entertain me, no, no, dearest love, leave the trousers on and around your knees."

As I took him at my pleasure, I smelled the scent of musty soil, opened by the recent rains, and I heard his blood's drowsy humming.

But after I thought I'd exhausted his energies he flew into a coarse passion and began to hold forth, angrily scolding me. He scrutinized me with such disdain that I felt resentful. And then we argued all the way back to camp. This wasn't how I had imagined our reunion.

"Why the hell did you come all the way out here?"

"Because you wrote that you were despondent and that you missed me—"

"I wrote no such thing," he snapped.

I sat in the saddle while he walked and led the horse down the trail ranting, "Disgraceful. Disgusting and abhorrent, my wife going around dressed like . . . like—"

"You didn't find me so abhorrent fifteen minutes ago."

"Did anyone see you?"

Sullenly, I refused to answer him. I hadn't come all of this way to be yelled at for my troubles.

"Where's the baby?"

"With Anne Lane at the officer's mess," I murmured, not daring to meet his eyes.

"Did Richard Ewell see you?"

"No, but the other fellows met your foppish cousin Joseph Hartwell."

"I don't have a cousin named Joseph Hartwell."

"I am Joseph Hartwell."

"Just, goddamn it, when we get back to the fort, don't say a word, let me explain it."

"Fine, you explain it."

"How shall I explain it?"

"The baby is yours. Hartwell and Anne Lane were my traveling escorts. Wishing to surprise you, I sent them into camp first. I shall appear tomorrow morning, dressed like a proper wife, beaming upon your friends with ladylike grace and benevolence."

"That's good. That's quite good, Diana."

"So you see, I can be just as great a liar as you."

"I have never lied."

"You are an expert at concealing the truth without telling a lie."

He straightened his shoulders and nodded smugly. "Exactly."

Realizing with a start that I'd gotten the best of him, he scowled. "Wipe that smug grin from your face, Mrs. Kearny. And ride like a respectable cavalry trooper. Light hands, and a tight seat."

"But I'm not a cavalry trooper, and we're only walking."

"Don't argue with me."

Eleven

PHILIP EXPLAINED that no married housing was available at Fort Leavenworth and that I would be quartered in his tent as long as I stayed. He preferred sleeping in a tent to the overcrowded officer's barracks. When we returned to camp he told me to wait for him by the log stables where the horses were standing at the hayrack while he fetched Anne and our baby. I could not fault his warmth and courtesy to Anne. Attentive and charming, he arranged to have a pair of troopers leaving on furlough escort her back to St. Louis and insisted on accompanying her down to the landing and paying her passage. But that same night, after having returned from the steamboat landing, his mood changed for the worse.

He directed me into a tent pitched on the farthest edge of the grounds, held the fly aside and motioned me in, then lit the lamp in the center of a round table. I could see my reflection in the full-length mirror. Shelves laden with his hair tonic, soap, and cologne hung from the tent poles. Philip's mess chest overflowed with Sevres china and crystal and in the corner was a whiskey barrel heaped with ice, wine, champagne, Congress Water, lemons, and a bowl of bellflower apples.

"What do you think of our campsite?" Philip asked his daughter. But Di regarded her father sternly, holding him at a distance, her fat little arms stiffly outstretched and her hands flat against his chest. If our baby's guarded response made Philip unhappy, proximity to her father made her more so. She wiggled out of his arms as she reached for me.

"What the devil is wrong with her?"

"She doesn't know you. She hasn't seen you in six months!"

"All the same, you'd think she could muster a little affection for her poor father," Philip yawned, and I noticed he'd lost one of his back teeth. His face had new lines from exposure to sun and wind, there were deep creases under his eyes and his hair had turned much lighter, almost blonde, though his mustache looked a darker red.

Outside, in a little tent slept his valet, old Rinnah June.

"Is Uncle Stephen Kearny here?" I asked, meaning Colonel Stephen Watts Kearny, hoping the answer would be yes, for I intended to appeal to him directly and ask about housing. I expected nothing fancy, simply the sort of spare, regulation married housing I'd seen at Jefferson Barracks. But as if reading my thoughts, Philip turned his back to me, picked through the basket of lemons, inspecting them one by one. "No, the colonel isn't here, and won't return for a while. We don't anticipate seeing him until the spring."

Somewhat crestfallen, I put the baby on a blanket atop the rug and asked, "What would you be doing right now if I were not here?"

"Thinking of you," he smiled, tossing one of the lemons into the air.

A bushel of lemons out of season must have cost a fortune to ship up here, but then Philip wrote boastful letters to me about the lavish entertainments he hosted for his fellow officers. He'd even purchased a billiards table for the officer's mess. Philip quartered the lemon and offered me a piece. When I declined, he said, "By sundown, I'm usually in bed. Reveille is at 4 A.M. You will join me tomorrow morning for a hunting detail."

"A hunting detail? But what about the baby?"

"Rinnah is an old hand with babies; she'll be well looked after. You'd best undress and get some sleep."

Tossing the uneaten lemon quarters upon the table he wiped his hands upon a small towel. I undressed as Philip talked. He paced, unbuttoning his shirt, beginning one of his monologues that required no participation from me. "This late in the year, when we come upon those oxen-pulled prairie schooners, I urge the immigrants to winter at Fort Laramie or Cheyenne, but under no circumstances to continue into the mountains."

I pulled my nightgown over my head and noticed that my arms and legs were white and soft as unrolled dough. When had those spidery purple veins sprouted behind my knee? Having the babies had eliminated all vestiges of my girlish grace and lissome figure. I had faded red lines and faint rippling stretch marks from my ribs to my legs and my breasts felt ponderously heavy. Holy Jerusalem, no more pie for me! Also, I would follow a strict smoking regime to regain my health. I was twenty-four years old and falling apart; positively disgraceful.

Philip continued, "Next spring, the First Dragoons will follow the Oregon Trail to Fort Laramie, from there, along the Arkansas River to Bent's Fort and our mission will be historic, one that will be remembered and studied at military colleges for centuries to come . . ."

I felt exhausted and unable to concentrate. Why was I having a hard time following his talk? I bounced Di on my lap and gave her a string of big wooden beads. She crammed them into her mouth, and they hung down both sides of her chin.

"My father has not written once to me and my own uncle, commander of this division, does nothing to advance my cause, even though I have proved by spending my own treasure, giving my own—"

But I interrupted him. "Did you really find dead immigrants along the trail?"

"Diana, I spoke of the immigrants five minutes ago. Do keep up." He sat on the chair and pulled off his boots, wearing a sour expression. "I think you should be more sympathetic."

"Oh, but I am sympathetic."

"If you say so," he replied, emptying his pockets and placing the contents on the table.

I slid between the covers on the side of the bed closest to the tent wall, with Di beside me on her back, her legs and arms in the air as she held the beads up and inspected them with rapt interest. He hadn't asked a single question about the house, our family, our friends or—me, for that matter.

Philip extinguished the lamp and joined us in the bed. Outside, I could hear the pickets talking and the dogs barking. We stared up at the canvas ceiling. He was so obviously uncomfortable that I tried not to move or breathe or distract him further. He stretched his legs, kicked out in frustration, and sat upright rolling his head as if his neck were bothering him.

"The baby and I can sleep on your bedroll on the carpet. Really, I don't mind." And I began crawling out of the cot. But Philip spread his bedroll on the carpet, reached for his pillow, and stretched out on the floor.

"You shouldn't have come," he said, tossing, rolling over, and punching his pillow. Soon, his breathing steadied and he fell asleep.

Throughout that night I suffered a bad bout of anxiousness, and sat up in bed staring at him as he slept on the floor. At four o'clock the next morning, a bugler sounded reveille so piercingly he must have been right outside our tent. The baby jolted awake and began crying. Philip groaned, rubbing his eyes and blearing around the room, startled at the sight of us on the cot.

"Oh yes, right," he muttered, rising stiffly off the floor.

I opened my trunk, pulled out my black mourning gown, shook it a few times and laying it upon the bed, brushed the dust from the pleats.

"No, not that. It is time to pack away your mourning clothes, Diana. Wear something showy and fine. It has been too long since I have seen you turned out in finery."

"But I have been in mourning only six months. I can't wear color for two years."

"Even so. Pack away your mourning weeds. Did you bring a riding habit?

"Yes, but it is black, too."

"You would raise the morale of every man at this post if you dressed in something colorful and festive."

"I haven't brought anything showy and festive with me, Philip." I did not say that wearing even the riding habit with its bright pearled buttons felt as if I were breaking faith with Susan. Of late, whenever I found myself smiling upon a beautiful day, or laughing at something Di had done, I would sink into morose gloom, feeling guilty for having enjoyed myself even for a few moments.

As I searched around in the trunk I asked, "Do you ever think about her?"

Philip, standing naked in the middle of the floor with his back to me, brushed his hair with a small round flat brush in each hand. He turned, and raising his brows asked, "Think about whom?"

I took a small anxious breath and reminded him. "Susan."

"Yes. Yes, of course I do." Said as casually as if our daughter were a distant acquaintance but he hid his true feelings because he could not bear to speak of them in my presence. A few weeks after his departure from Washington, he had written at the bottom of a letter that Susan was the only child he could ever love, as if caring for Di or any baby we might have in the future would put him at too great a risk of heartache. He put the hairbrushes down and ran his thumb and forefinger over his mustache. By his abrupt reply I knew Philip wished me to put away my grieving and not speak of Susan to spare him, as if he wished to pretend that she had never lived.

Rinnah June, impeccable in his swallowtail coat and white vest, ducked into the tent and lit the table lamp. A slow smile broke across his face and he kept trying to hide it, pressing his lips together.

"Good morning, Rinnah June," I said.

"Morning, Mrs. Kearny. Very fine to see you and the baby."

"Why, thank you. Very fine to see you, too."

"How is everybody back in the district?" Rinnah asked as he opened a footlocker and removed my husband's fatigues. I gave him the news.

Philip stood before the glass with his arms out at his sides as Rinnah dressed him in flannel trousers and a blue flannel shirt. Philip buckled hunting knives in a holster around his waist, and before ducking out of the tent clapped a broad-brimmed, low-crowned hat upon his head. "My dear, meet me at the Company "F" stables promptly at five o'clock. Rinnah, help Mrs. Kearny with whatever she needs and get my Hawken rifle for her."

Rinnah followed him outside carrying the rifles, a short barrel carbine, and a brace of pistols. I dressed in the trailing velvet skirt of my riding habit, tied my white throat stock, and thrust a pin into the knot of the stock. With hundreds of fretful instructions that doubtless annoyed long-suffering Rinnah, I left my daughter in his competent care, but not before kissing her a dozen times.

Hurrying through a ruddy daybreak across the grove of cottonwoods, I met Philip at the stables. The troopers of Company "F" rode chestnut horses that Philip had personally selected and paid for, as he believed the government allowance was insufficient. The cavalry companies in the First Dragoons were distinguished by the color of the horses they rode: black for Companies "A" and "K," gray for Company "G," and company "C" rode bay mounts. My husband had picked six troopers for a hunting detail to supplement the monotonous army diet of salt pork and bacon.

Philip introduced me to his men with a proud expression. Most of the young officers were penniless, second-born sons from the South and New England and as the men tacked up, they peppered me for news from the East. I rode out with Philip and on that perfect fall morning, I decided that the baby and I would stay here and that I would somehow manage to secure married housing for us even without his uncle's help.

As we went along, Philip pointed out the wagon trails leading out of the fort. The horses, oxen, and livestock had eaten all of the forage along the trail, but as we rode farther, we came upon the high prairie, a mix of lush grasses tall and short but most striking were the wine-red patches and dark gold forbs. I never saw a group of men who enjoyed themselves more than those cavalry troopers. They joked, bragged, and poked fun at one another, until Philip leaned aside, smiling under the brim of his hat so that his eyes were shadowed and said, "They are showing off for you."

"It doesn't seem right exactly, hunting buffalo."

"We have to eat something, Diana."

"Yes but, they're so—"

Philip rolled his eyes and interrupted me. "Romantic? Noble? Diana, they're herd beasts and we only kill what we eat. If you wish to disparage someone, criticize the Osage. I've seen them slaughter the buffalo recklessly and leave a hundred fifty pounds of good meat on a carcass—a feast for the gray wolves that follow the herds. And don't think it's only the white sports hunters who hunt buffalo just for the tongue or the hides . . . the Indians do it, too. I've seen them do it."

"But I thought the Indians never wasted what they killed."

"Pah. All men are alike, red and white. They waste and slaughter when it pleases them to do so."

We kept on for nearly three hours, pausing to water the horses at a nameless creek where the grasslands stretched infinitely in all directions. Though the men talked loudly to one another, I fell silent, sensing a change in the temper of the landscape, certain I felt something, but so did my horse, for his ears cupped and turned and his breathing changed. The grasshoppers clicked and whirred, took flight snapping their wings and landing; the meadow birds called to one another from their wavering perches on the goldenrod. Moisture and heat seemed to rise out of the broom weed and the grasses rolling away from us, the heat creating its own weather, an ominously heavy cloud rising, growing with unnatural speed over the distant horizon, a brown and gray cloud rising broadly and long, making a dull grumbling thunder that grew louder and still louder until I felt the trembling of the earth inside my bones. My horse sidestepped nervously, his eyes shining whitely, and the cloud billowed until it loomed and spread not only heavenward but following the slopes and deeps of the landscape, the ground shaking beneath us.

Inside the cloud coming over the long bent crest of the hill, illuminated like shadows as the sun filtered through the dust, we saw the enormous humped silhouettes of the buffalo running in our direction. I felt as if I had descended into a place of awe and thunder slowly filling with shadow, a shadow siphoning toward us, a pulsing tide of dark brown so that the very ground trembled underfoot.

The troopers, unable to contain their excitement whooped and hollered as they took in the scene. Though a hunter all of my life, from game birds to deer, I had never ridden herd with buffalo and could not have known that a buffalo can easily outrun the fastest horse. What fearless beasts, thick of bone, bellowing their guttural roars with great blue tongues, digging their horns in the sod and tossing up chunks of grass, dripping froth in long white ropes from their mouths, the thick mat of their shoulder cloaks speckled with burrs and prickly seed pods.

I brought my horse around sharply and, removing a pair of field glasses from the saddlebag, scanned the herd. The calves, light red in the coat, shouldered down the hill beside the cows, stampeding toward us with tails uplifted and whisking.

The men dispersed with joyous shouts, spreading out on both sides of the approaching herd. Philip brought his horse up beside mine and shouted as he pointed at a hill behind us, "Listen to me, Diana, you must ride parallel to them, don't let yourself get caught in their midst. And when you pick your mark, shoot as low as you can behind the fore shoulder to hit the heart, and if you can't do that, hit him in the lights, I mean to say, his lungs and he'll keep running, but we'll follow him."

I nodded and surprised him by spurring my horse and galloping away without awaiting further instruction.

"Be cautious!" he shouted above the thundering noise. "They have poor eyesight, so don't get yourself in front of them. Do you hear me?"

"Yes!" I called back and turned for the hill, a long low ridge cut with ravines, clustered with blackjack oak and reaching a point where I felt I had an advantage, peered through Philip's field glasses at the grand spectacle unfolding below. My husband and his men rode down the hill at a diagonal to the herd, each man picking his bison and separating it out. I was decently scared, yet thrilled by the sight, watching Philip and the soldiers riding alongside the great animals into the tall grass.

The blowing clouds of dust burned my nose and throat, my eyes wept, and I felt nearly blinded by tears and dirt when, as a precaution, I loaded the Hawken rifle. Philip and the men had isolated several buffalo cows with the intent of bringing them down. I could smell the animals, the musky dense odor of their bodies as they came near me. Seeing something out of the corner of my eye, I turned sharply aside, and peered at a dark figure rushing up the incline in my direction.

A bull had separated from the herd and came snorting up the hill; he was six and a half feet tall at the shoulder, two thousand pounds of muscle and fury hurtling in a direct line at me.

Alarmed, I dropped the field glasses, dismounted the sidesaddle, and yanked the rifle from the holster. The bison tossed his massive woolly head and heavy curved horns, the air gritty and blowing, resounding with his rage, for I had trespassed into his domain and he would have none of it. "God help me," I whispered to myself and steadied the butt of the rifle against the muscle of my shoulder.

Lowering his head, he stopped and charged at me so that I could see the curly thick hair on his convex forehead and the massive bone below his brow. No bullet could penetrate that thick skull. As the bull came into range, it looked at me and I saw fear and anger mingled in his small eyes. But then, he wheeled as if feinting the charge and turned his body away so that he was parallel to me. I aimed, pulled the trigger with a catch in my throat and a pain I felt deep in my soul, and I fired into that noble animal's heart. My supposedly troop-trained cavalry horse bolted, the rifle went flying out of my hands, I hit the ground flat on my back, and all was darkness.

When I woke, I thought, *Well, here is a pretty picture of heaven.* The sun haloed a circle of bronzed faces, handsome strong young men leaning over me, but carrying a whole graveyard of melancholy in their expressions. I tell you true, I hope on the day I die, I am lifted into heaven by the angels of young soldiers in blue coats.

Philip clamped my hand to his breast. "You were very brave, Diana. It was an elegant kill, right through the heart."

I groaned and rubbed my aching head. "Oh, I wish I had missed him. Why did he have to run up on me like that? I didn't want to kill him."

"Well, we're grateful to you for our supper, Mrs. Kearny, as you are the only one who brought a bison down!" One of the young troopers laughed, swatting his hat against his leg.

Sitting up with Philip's help and looking around at the men, I asked, "Is that true?"

"Rest of the herd is halfway to California Territory by now," another soldier said.

"She's suffering a shock to her nerves," Philip explained, kissing the back of my hand.

"No, I'm not," I protested, struggling to my feet. But Philip ignored my comment and said to his men, "Best butcher him, the wolves will be sniffing around here, soon."

As a sign of their respect, the troopers cut the buffalo's tongue out and gave it to me with great flourish and ceremony. Though I thanked them, I handed the gruesome thing off to Philip when they weren't looking.

That night, the regiment hosted an impromptu dancing party in the officer's mess. As my friend Richard Ewell described it, the dancing party was a pretty unique affair given there were so few women at the post. The regimental flags hung from the rafters, candles lit the high-ceilinged room, and the camp cook, standing behind a long banquet table, drove his knife with fine expert cuts into rancid old rations of salt pork. There would be no feasting on the bison I'd shot until he'd been hung and aged for a week. In his freshly dead state, he was much too tough to eat.

During a pause in the dancing, Philip introduced me to Colonel Stries.

"Aha, is this the young lady who shot the patriarch of the prairie?" The colonel laughed. "Perhaps we ought to set Mrs. Kearny after our Indian sniper. Goodness knows none of my regulars have been able to bring the shooter down; perhaps you will have better luck!"

"Has the sniper been about again?"

"Oh yes, Mrs. Kearny, with most damaging consequences. The sniper ruined a tierce of brandy and shot holes in barrels of whiskey coming up the trace." After exchanging pleasantries and more compliments on the day's hunt, I watched the colonel go and tugged my husband's sleeve. "Philip, why can't I talk to Colonel Stries about obtaining quarters for us? There is no reason for me to stay in Washington while you are here. We could live here together, we could be a family, again."

"Have you any idea how unspeakably damaging that would be to my career? Sneaking around, begging for special favors!"

"But I wouldn't be sneaking around. I'd walk right through Colonel Stries's front door. You make it sound as if I was going to scale the wall and tumble through an open window in his office."

"Now be quiet, woman, I will hear no more on the subject."

Sometimes, looking back on my life, I wish I had been able to accept my husband's authority without question. Had I possessed a far more gentle temperament my life probably would have been so much easier. But whenever Philip insulted me, or spoke hard words, it only made me more determined to have my way.

Alas, I could not turn the other cheek unless my tongue was in it.

Twelve

W IIEN THE AUTUMN rains came, toadstools grew on our dirt floor and I swept them out of the tent with a broom. Having finished the task and finding myself dusted in soil, I asked Rinnah to heat water in the pot over a fire for my bath. Philip had been sent north on yet another routine three-day patrol where he would meet with the Osage and the Kickapoo who were encamped in the far reaches of the territory. Though three days had passed, he had not returned, and I cast a worried glance at the loaded pistol resting upon a stack of my letters to him. He'd left it for me, for my own protection, he said.

In the dim yellow light of the tent, I sat with my knees drawn up to my chest, bathing in a whiskey barrel that had been seared inside to remove the odor. Even so, as I ladled water over my skin, I could still smell the liquor. When I leaned back and looked up, I could see enormous black blotches of mold forming around the tent poles on the canvas. We desperately needed a proper shelter.

As I bathed, I composed a letter to Anne in my head, responding to her alarming missive about the recent attentions of an elderly suitor.

> *My dearest Anne,*
> *You must not abandon your aspirations and marry*
> *this balding man without eyebrows and his fingernails*

falling off. I should hate to have a new husband with his nails falling off. In an old one, it would not be so bad. Do not surrender! Only say the word, and I shall send for you and you may live here at the fort where you can marry any soldier you wish, all of them with fingernails intact.

Di sat upright on a grain sack spread over the ground, and I smiled down at her as I slipped a finger over her bottom lip. She scrunched up her face at me, motioning with her hands like a bird. Her two bottom teeth had come in and I could feel the bump of yet another. Soon, I would have to wean her. I climbed out of the barrel and wrapping a woolen blanket about myself, pinched one piece of dry rice left upon a plate and fed it to her. My daughter's eyes crinkled at the corners and forcing her tongue over her lip, she spat out the rice. Like her mother, she was very decided in her preferences for people and food.

Hearing men shouting excitedly from the parade ground and the frantic keening of a woman, I hopped over Di and clutching the blanket around my wet body, peered cautiously around the tent flap, holding it like a shield against the scene unfolding before me.

Colonel Stries rode past the flagpole and the stone powder magazine in the center of the parade ground as a company of infantrymen cheered him on. The colonel wore a panama hat with an oiled silk cover. I squinted in the bright autumn sunlight and tried to see who followed him. A rope stretched tautly from Stries's saddle.

Stumbling behind Stries, her wrists bound with rope, was a captive Pawnee woman. Stries carried her rifle in his left hand. Furiously inconvenienced by the mayhem she'd caused the camp and himself, Colonel Stries gave the rope a vindictive tug, causing the Pawnee woman to stumble and fall. And when she fell, he halted his horse, and turned in his saddle to berate her as she climbed to her feet.

The soldiers gathered to watch and called to Colonel Stries, "That the sniper? You got the sniper, Colonel?"

Behind Colonel Stries, another trooper carried an infant bound to a papoose board. The baby cried piteously. Even as she was being dragged forward, the woman called assurances over her shoulder to her child in her native language. When they reached the west end of the parade ground, she fell again but despite Colonel Stries's hectoring and the taunts of the soldiers, she did not try to stand.

Stries dismounted, and ordering a soldier to hold the reins of his horse, walked back to the woman, where she lay prone on her belly, her face buried in the grass. Stries stood over her; frustrated, he stared off angrily in the distance, resting his hands on his hips. After a few moments he cursed and he kicked her in the ribs.

I think the young mother startled Colonel Stries with the speed and ferocity of her response, leaping all of one motion to her feet. Before he had a chance to react, nay even to blink, she had stolen the Bowie knife from the sheath on his belt.

Startled, he stepped back. Hands protectively over his face, Colonel Stries loosed a cry, and in that instant I do not doubt that he feared for his life.

But she was made of sterner stuff than Colonel Stries. She made no sound as she thrust the Bowie knife into a vein in the side of her neck spraying blood all over her captor. And so, without asking leave of the United States Army, the Pawnee woman set herself free.

I let the tent flap drop and sank to my knees in despair, unable to quash my own sorrow for her. Outside, the men celebrated Colonel Stries's conquest with big war cries, but he ordered them to bury the Pawnee woman immediately. I gathered Di in my arms and held her as I sat upon the cot, rocking her and covering her ears so that she would not hear the brutal talk among the men about what might be done with the Indian infant.

"Leave it outside for the wolves."

"Let it die of starvation, as it surely will."

But Colonel Stries ordered the infant to be taken to the infirmary until a decision could be made about its future.

"Oh, Philip, come back," I fretted, pacing back and forth in the tent, wishing for his counsel. I could hear the baby wailing as the troops carried it into the hospital.

Dressing quickly, I hurried across the camp to Colonel Stries's office. His aide greeted me in the anteroom and presented me to the old man, who was gloating over his victory with a bottle of Schiedam. I offered to take charge of the Pawnee child.

But the colonel interrupted me in mid-sentence with a harsh rebuke. "Mrs. Kearny, I won't hear of it! An officer's wife playing nurse to a little savage? It is unthinkable and Kearny would never approve. No, madam, I cannot allow it."

The colonel escorted me to the door and shut it behind me. How could anyone be so unfeeling? I wondered. But thinking of Philip, I suppressed my gathering emotions and did not hold forth with him.

At nine o'clock that evening the bugler stood on the parade ground under the flagpole and played tattoo, signaling the end of the day. In the silent watches of the night, with Di at my side and Rinnah June slumbering on the floor, I could hear the orphaned infant crying. The thin and distant sound brought my milk forth and my breasts felt heavy.

Certain that the child was starving and growing weaker by the hour, I could hesitate no longer. Glancing warily at Rinnah June, I slipped into my wrapper, tying it around my waist. My daughter, under a blanket on the cot, slept on her back with her arms outflung and her hands balled in fists.

"Rinnah," I whispered, touching his shoulder. His eyes flew open and he sat up.

"What is it, Missus Kearny?"

"I am going over to the infirmary. Will you watch the baby for me?"

"Why are you going over there?"

"Stay here and look after Di will you? I shall be back shortly."

"He ain't going to like that. He ain't going to like you wandering about all by yourself at night."

"My husband isn't here." I put my finger to my lips to hush him and before he could protest again, I slipped out into the chilly dark air. Hurrying along the footpath, my head down, I was grateful for the overcast night, for in my white wrapper, I would have been conspicuous in the moonlight.

The hospital, a two-story log building on a stone foundation, loomed darkly as I approached and darted up the wooden steps. It was a rickety place where the cottonwood log posts sprouted leaves and the wind blew through the gaps in the chinking. The air reeked of caustic medicines; mustard plasters, oil of turpentine, and camphor.

A sleeping sentry sat perfectly upright behind a desk, his eyes tightly shut, chin tucked against his chest, his arms crossed, and a single candle burning over his ledger book.

The floors creaked underfoot. I paused, listening for some clue as to where I might find the baby. As if answering my silent query, I heard it whimpering up on the second story and rushing up the staircase in the candlelight, I ran down the hall.

I followed its cries and found the poor little thing naked on its back in a soapbox on the floor. It was a boy-child and until today he appeared to have been well nourished. I guessed him to be about a month old. A shock of black hair crowned his head and a tiny bracelet of blue beads ringed his fat little wrist. Indignant at having been starved and neglected, he kicked out his legs and thrust his arms above his head and wept.

With a furtive look around, I lifted the baby from the rough and wet sacking and scurried unnoticed by the sleeping sentry out the front door. Sprinting around the hospital, I clutched the baby against me and ran toward my tent, adding "kidnapper" to my list of crimes since venturing West.

I ducked into my tent with my young ward, feeling breathlessly triumphant. Rinnah June did not even rise from his pallet but shook his head, covered his eyes with his hands, and moaned. "I ain't seeing what I'm seeing."

"Rinnah, would you please step outside while I tend to this child?"

"Don't even want to know about that baby or why you got it here," he grumbled, rubbing his lower back, his knees popping as he crossed the floor.

The infant's crying woke baby Di. She was curious about the little stranger and I put her on the floor, but she quickly crawled over to me and clung to my robe and asked, "Be-be-be?" I brought the Pawnee boy over to the washbasin and gave him a bath. Di, furious over being ignored in favor of this new stranger, howled. The water calmed the baby boy, and drying him, I pinned one of Di's diaper cloths around his hips and dressed him in one of her muslin gowns. But the baby was hungry. With both children squalling, I sat on the side of the cot and opened my nightdress.

The Pawnee boy clamped hungrily on the nipple and riveted his bright black eyes upon mine. But Di had no interest in sharing her mother. She put her hands on my knees and pulled herself up, wavering unsteadily on her feet. Scolding me and yammering, Di was determined to assert her rights; as she would not be appeased, I slid my hand under her, and cupping her bottom in my hand, brought her to my other breast. And so I sat by the light of one candle, as both babies took nourishment, feeling like a milk cow and wondering what would become of this boy.

"You've been born under a trying star, haven't you? What will become of you?" I said to the baby. Having burped both children, I fell asleep on the cot with my daughter on one side and the Pawnee baby in the bassinet.

The following morning when the surgeon discovered the Indian infant missing, all of the camp supposed his kin had skulked into the hospital and had stolen him. I overheard the troopers strolling past my tent say that the surgeon was more outraged at the imagined trespass than he was over the missing infant.

I hid in the tent with the two babies until the following afternoon. But surely, the pickets must have heard *two* infants wailing for their lunch. When finally, Philip returned to camp, I overheard a muffled conversation between him and Rinnah. He cursed under his breath and blustered into the tent, regarding the babies and me as if he had discovered fleas in his bed. Unbuckling his holsters, he put his guns on the table. "Have you any idea how unspeakably damaging your folly may be to my career? Have you lost your mind, Diana?"

"What would you have me do, Philip? They intended to starve him to death."

A dawning look crept over him and he clapped his hand to his forehead. "Good God, tell me you didn't—"

I bore it all with my usual magnificent fortitude. Lifting my chin defiantly, I said, "I most certainly did."

"It could have the pox! It could be afflicted with consumption or the measles!"

"Not *it. He!* The babe is a little boy!"

Philip sank onto a chair with elbows on his knees. "Do you care so little for your own reputation and for Di's health that you would expose her and yourself to diseases from that little savage?"

"Don't you ever say that to me again," I said, shaking with anger. "No one loves my daughter more than I. No one, not you, not anyone."

"Do you wish to be the cause of discord at this post, Mrs. Kearny? Do you wish to earn me the hatred and enmity of every trooper here, notwithstanding all of my hard work?"

"I—I—only thought—"

"Woman, the more you talk, the less clearly you think."

No one could frame an insult like Philip. The Pawnee baby blinked up at our loud voices, and Di, still fascinated by him, clung to the side of the cot. Standing on tiptoe, she reached up and poked the boy in the cheek with her forefinger. "Be-be-be-be."

Philip spoke with quiet fury. "I have tolerated your presence here, against my better judgment, in the hope that you would quickly tire of the wilds, but you have proved more tenacious than I ever imagined. If I'd wanted you to come West, I would have sent for you. As it is, you have intruded where you are not welcome."

"Intruded! Because I wished to be with you?"

He pointed at the clean swept dirt surface under his feet. "This is my sphere. Not yours. You belong at home with our children, not out here shooting buffalo and kidnapping little red children and interfering with my duties."

"I thought you were proud of my hunting!"

He dragged his hand over the back of his head and down his neck. "Did you have to go and kill the biggest bull on the plains?"

When I did not answer, but felt my face burning as I stared down at my hands, Philip tried again in a gentler tone, "Dearest love, you belong at home in the East with our daughter, not out here, in a forlorn and infinite wilderness that will never be settled. Surely, you agree with me?"

I swallowed a half-spoken word that tasted bitter as it went down. "Rinnah, I am going for a walk. Kindly look after the children for a few moments." I turned on my heel and exited the tent.

"Yes, ma'am."

I strode past the officer's mess hall under the gold cottonwood trees toward the muddy creek. Philip pursued me, ordering me to stop but when I would not obey him, I heard panic creeping into his voice. "The sun is setting and these prairies are swarming with wolves."

"I'd prefer their company to yours."

"Stop this instant. I can hear them in the distance and they will tear you apart before you know it."

"Such a death would be less painful than your arrogance." With my thoughts in a muddle, I ran a circle around the log stables and sprinted all the way back to the tent.

Once there, I began packing my trunks. Rinnah June rose from the chair with the Pawnee baby in his arms and asked, "Where are you going?"

"I'm going home, Rinnah." I flung clothes into the open trunk.

"Can I come with you?" Rinnah asked.

"Yes, you may."

"No, you will not!" Philip bellowed, slapping away the canvas tent flies in frustration as he came in after me. And then in a more conciliatory tone, he said, "Diana, I think you are very wise to go back East. I'd rather you be in a city with your friends and family, and when my tour here is finished, I'd like to come home to a pretty, welcoming house in New York City."

I shook my head in disgust and threw one of my slippers into the trunk. "You've even forgotten where we live and it's not New York! And just so you know, I am taking that baby boy with me. I dare not leave him in this place surrounded by . . . what was your word? Oh yes, surrounded by all of these white *savages* in blue coats with their rattling drums and blaring bugles and guns and knives."

Rinnah made a face and slowly began backing to the tent's entrance.

"Diana, go back East and sell our Washington house. We have no reason to live there any longer and I want my children to grow up in my native city. Go and build a new house in New York on the land I own on the north side of Twenty-second Street. You may build any sort of house that suits your fancy."

"I don't want a new house. I want a husband and an ordinary life. I am sick of living like a widow. You may as well be dead for all I see you."

Philip's face flushed and his eyes shone with fury. "You'd like it if I were dead, wouldn't you?"

"Yes, perhaps I would."

"How gratifying to know my tender spouse wishes to finish me off with an ax."

"No ax, I'd use the shotgun your own father gave me."

"You'd like nothing better than to play the merry widow, with my fortune and your incessant flirting I have no doubt you'd—"

I struck him across the face so swiftly it stunned him.

But Philip raised his hand and slapped me, in turn.

I cried out in pain and turned a few circles with my hands clasped to my cheek. "Oh, how could you? Now I'm going to have a bruise." And with great dramatic aplomb, I collapsed on the floor and wept.

He sputtered nervously as he sank onto the floor beside me. "What would you have me do? You flew at me! After seeing how you dispatched that buffalo, no one would fault me for defending myself."

"Wretched excuses."

"You know damn well I have never struck a lady in my life, Diana."

"Well, you have now." And tugging a handkerchief from my sleeve I sobbed into it while he patted my shoulder helplessly.

"Don't cry. Dearest love, please don't cry."

I hiccupped miserably. "And you diminish me, and yourself, by thinking you can make me forget how alone I am by showering me with baubles and houses and wardrobes and carriages. It is how we began our lives together, isn't it? And I was dazzled by it and by you. But not anymore—I wanted to make a home for you and the baby."

He slid his arm around my shoulders and prying the handkerchief from my hands, dabbed at my eyes, "There, there. As a sign of my devotion to you, I shall deny your allowance, let you dress in rags, and you can sell matches on the street corners. Would that make you feel better?"

I had not yet replied to him when we were both summoned outside by Rinnah June. My husband and I exchanged sullen glances as we met Colonel Stries on the parade ground. The colonel introduced us to the Indian agent for the Pawnee people, a white man of middling years in a frock coat, and with him, a tall and lean Indian woman, whom I guessed to be in her late thirties, wearing a cambric tunic over deerskin leggings. She must have combed ocher through her hair, for it was stiff and clotted with dark red paint and black hieroglyphics had been tattooed upon her forehead and weathered cheeks. Had I met her under other circumstances, perhaps outside of the safe confines of the fort, I would have been frightened of her; but now, she met my eyes and scrutinized me so keenly, I felt as if I had been weighed and in the balance, found wanting.

The agent explained, "This is the mother of the dead woman. She has come to take her grandson back to the village."

I admit that I felt crestfallen. In less than a day, I had already fashioned a whole life for the boy and had fancied rearing him as one of my own.

"Colonel Stries, you will pardon me, but I must see to my men." Philip saluted his commanding officer and strode off toward the officer's mess.

"Do you speak her language?" I asked the Indian agent

"Indeed I do." The agent turned to the old woman and said something.

I motioned them both into the tent and the old woman's face shone with joy upon seeing her grandson again. She stripped the muslin gown from the child's limbs and unbuttoning her tunic, put him inside her clothing, close to her heart.

"He has been fed and should not need to eat for two hours," I said.

The agent translated this and the old woman nodded and asked, "Who fed him?"

"I did."

And with a slow wary smile, the old woman said, "Heh," which I took to mean she was either amused by the idea or grateful for my kindness.

After an awkward silence, I said, "Your daughter was very courageous."

The old woman listened to the translator and nodded mournfully in agreement.

"What . . . what was your daughter's name?"

"Nic-an-ansa," the translator explained. "She wishes me to tell you that the blue coats shot her daughter's husband—the father of this child—while he was out hunting for his family."

And then the old woman reached into the pocket of her tunic and removed a small leather bag, placed it into my hand, and met my eyes with her penetrating glance before taking her leave with the agent.

"What is that, Missus Kearny?" Rinnah asked, peering over my shoulder.

I opened the bag and, bewildered by her gift, showed it to him. "A silver dollar. I didn't know Indians carried coin money."

"Course they do," Rinnah said, sitting on a bench and picking up a polishing rag, then rubbing blacking into Philip's boots. "Carry it like anybody else when they come to the sutler's store and the trading posts up here."

"But what do you suppose she meant by giving this to me?"

"She probably don't much like charity," Rinnah said as I gathered Di in my arms and tied her little bonnet under her chin.

"What complicated people," I wondered aloud. "The daughter shot at me, the infant took nourishment from me, and the grandmother paid me with a coin, as though I were a common wet nurse."

A few days later, in keeping with Philip's wishes, Di and I boarded a steamer. Lieutenant Richard Ewell had generously consented, on his furlough, to accompany me all the way to Washington City. The sky was heavy with snow, a cold wind blew Philip's cape sidelong as he stood on the shore, watching us go. What a sad day it was and soon, we would spend our first Christmas apart. Notwithstanding a lowering snowstorm, I stayed on deck with our daughter, holding her wrist and urging her to wave good-bye to her father.

I couldn't stop looking back at Philip, standing on the shore, where he remained until the steamer rounded a bend and I could see him no more.

Thirteen

I N ST. LOUIS, when Ewell and I changed boats, I rescued Anne
Lane, for as she was twenty-five and as yet unmarried, her family
had taken to treating her as a sort of servant. Her father was pres-
suring her to marry an old man who wanted a nurse-housekeeper without the nuisance of wages. There is little worse in my mind than a good
woman marrying an invalid, let alone a tightfisted old invalid, so I persuaded Anne to come with me to New York.

After May 1, 1845, and during that entire summer, I did not
receive a letter from Philip. I felt certain that he had died in a skir-
mish somewhere in the western reaches of the Nebraska Territory
between Chimney Rock and Scottsbluff. I had nightmares and woke
sobbing in my sleep, crying out so despondently in my dreams that
Mama would rush into the room and hold me in her arms and rock
me as she had when I was a little girl. Whenever I thought of my experiences in the West, it all felt like half memory and half dream. I often
wondered about the Pawnee boy, speculating that one day, when he
was grown, I might see him again. During those short months in the
territory I had been so keenly alive, tearing through years of numbness
that I think I gained an understanding why Philip sought adventures
all over the world.

And though Anne and Mama and I explored the myriad excitements and amusements in New York City, I often grew wistful for my freedom and the wild beauty of that strange place. Suffocated by the narrow streets and confined by the crowds, I would sometimes baffle Anne by escaping outside in the hope that if I looked up at the narrow sliver of sky between the tall buildings, I might see a hawk circling overhead. That I might, through some trick of time and place, enjoy a far-seeing view of rolling hills and a quartering wind and a herd of bison grazing along a broad and untamed river.

One spring afternoon, having toured the art collection at the Lyceum Building, we stopped at Contoits on Broadway and, taking a seat under the arbor, sampled their specialty: soft-boiled eggs sprinkled with brown sugar served with heavy iron spoons in tall dessert glasses. Having finished mine, without thinking, I upended the fluted dessert glass on the marble table. While Mama and Anne discussed the merits of Titian's *Martyrdom of St. Lawrence* and the other paintings we'd just seen, I fell into a daydream, wondering if I'd ever see my husband again, and fearing he'd never return.

Then too, I was heavy with my third child and by the summer of 1845, lethargy wound around me like a serpent. I would sit in my walled garden wearing little more than a white muslin shift and my hair in one long heavy braid down my back while Anne read the newspapers to me and Mama sewed baby clothes. I must have conceived in Fort Leavenworth, on the cot in our tent.

I hired architect Jemmy Renwick to design a brownstone house on the north side of Twenty-second Street. Down the block to the east, the new Gramercy Park neighborhood was an incomplete dusty mess. The park itself was pretty but the square was impassable, being constantly clogged with building materials piled high on the cobbles, not to mention the busy and loud commercial marble yard. Philip owned the vacant lot where Calvary Church would be built, but in 1845, he was as yet undecided what to do with it. This part of the city was still looked upon as the northern hinterlands, a wilderness occupied by vaguely eccentric people.

In any event, our house was fine enough, with acanthus leaves curling out of the cornices and medallions in the ceiling hung with gasoliers. Down the main hall on the right of the staircase, three sets of double mahogany doors opened onto spacious public rooms. I installed all of the modern conveniences, including gaslight and two boiler furnaces in the basement. But best of all, we had running water in all of the bathrooms. Hot and cold water came gushing out of the lead pipes thanks to the glory of the Croton reservoir. That I had lived to see such miracles! The house was four stories tall, not counting the cellar and basement, where the servants slept. In the rear was a carriage house and stables to shelter seven horses and a milk cow.

Nearing one o'clock in the morning on Friday, July 25, 1845, I sat up in bed, put a hand upon my enormous belly, and called for my mother. She came stumbling into the room, tying her wrapper. I stood in the middle of the room with my nightgown plastered to my legs and the carpet beneath me soaked. Quicksilver lightning shot above the house as a violent thunderstorm broke over the city. Believing fresh air would encourage a healthy birth, Mama threw open all of the windows and the rain poured over the wood floors; raindrops as big as eggs blew into the room.

Anne Lane sat at my side, swabbing my brow with a wet cloth. In between contractions, she rubbed my shoulders. I sat upright on the mattress, my nightdress over my knees, holding onto the headboard with both hands, staring at the painting of my sisters over the fireplace mantel. I asked my departed sister, Anne Bullitt Alexander, to watch over me and to give me strength to live through the very thing that killed her. She had died at eighteen in childbed and even now as I looked up at her, she seemed to take pity on me, her expression changing in the gaslight.

That night, I gave birth to the largest baby ever in the history of the known world. Shouting at the top of my compass as a child came fighting out, Mama shoved Anne out of the way, and lifting the baby in a towel said, "Oh, Diana, you have yourself a son! A big old baby boy!"

Mama followed the old rules of childbed, which meant that I wore only red nightdresses, for it was a proven fact that red silk prevented childbed fever. I was not to rise from the bed for nine days. I drank eight cups of pine-top tea every day while trying to keep my outlook bright because a mother's moods were transmitted to her infant through her breast milk.

One sultry afternoon, Mama and Anne sat in cane rockers on either side of my bed, while from the street below, I heard the vendors singing about their damson plums. A sparrow scratched for his supper on the sill.

Anne was reading the New York *Tribune* out loud. "Diana, we now own Texas!

I laughed at her bright expression. "You say it as if we've just bought a pair of shoes."

"Texas has voted to be annexed by the United States." Anne folded the paper back and jabbed the headline with her finger as she showed it to me.

Mama put a porcelain thimble on her thumb, licked the end of a strand of thread, and slid it through the eye of a needle. "Not so quick, Miss Lane, Mexico may have something to say about that. Mark my words, we have just bought ourselves a war."

Anne put the paper down and reaching for a straw fan, folded the sheets over my hips. She began fanning me with slow lazy motions. "What do you think, Diana? Do you think the Mexicans will fight to keep Texas?"

I reached aside for a glass of water and drank. "It is all about slavery. Making Texas safe for slavery. But even so, Philip will surely go if there is a war. He may go to Mexico from Fort Leavenworth and it will be years before I see him again. If I see him again."

Anne, worrying that she had upset me, tried to keep the subject away from Philip and back on slavery. "Nothing worse than hiring these Irish and Dutch. It is a wonder you aren't poisoned every day by your staff. God save me from living in a free state."

But my mind wandered back to Philip. He had gone off and left me the caretaker of our family and our marriage as if it were some sort of specimen plant that would always be healthy and ready to bloom and to bear fruit in proper season as long as I stayed behind to prune it and water it and place it in the sun.

Mama was hemming a white gown for the baby. "I read in the papers that the Mexican ruling classes keep peons, sometimes fifty or more on a farm. I am sure the better sort of Mexican will welcome Southern planters as brethren. Aleck writes that half the farmers in Louisiana are thinking of buying land in Mexico and raising sugar or cotton down there."

Anne took the water glass from me, and sighing, sat in her rocker, and picked up the newspaper once again. "Well, the abolitionists are sure to be opposed to this war. We have six Negroes back in St. Louis. What would they do, if not for my family? Where would they go? How would they live? The abolitionists never think that far, do they?"

I felt as if I were floating, trying to anchor myself to the arguments and not drift off again. "Philip is opposed to slavery. So is his father. But they are not abolitionists."

Anne interjected, "I can't imagine any decent family receiving an abolitionist or being seen on the streets with one."

Mama made a derisive noise as she held the gown up and inspected her work. She snipped a thread and smoothed the gown across her lap. "And you, Diana?"

"I adopt my husband's opinions as my own."

Mama and Anne exchanged a skeptical look. A wave of fatigue came over me and I closed my eyes, knotted the sheets in my hands, and tried not to feel the dull aching pain. Mama rose, folded the baby gown, and coming over to my side, took my hand. "Enough of this dark talk," she said. "Let's discuss something cheerful. Now Anne, you go over to the writing desk. Let us make a list of names for the caudle party."

Anne leapt up, tossed the newspaper aside, "Yes! A caudle party! We'll make it an elegant affair!" She ran over to the desk, and pulling out the chair, arranged her skirts. Taking pen in hand, she dipped it into the glazed jar of ink and looked up expectantly at Mama.

"All twenty-eight of Philip's aunts and uncles to begin with . . . Father Kearny—"

"A caudle party?" I asked.

"An old-fashioned caudle party to introduce my grandson to all of our friends and family."

During the party, a weekday in mid-September 1845, I sat enthroned in the bright front parlor, in a sunny window. I received guests with apologies for sitting in a queenly manner with my feet upon a footstool, but I was yet too weak and unsteady to stand for long periods of time. How I disliked the front parlor! There was nothing worse than the fatiguing stuffiness of a hot city room crammed from floorboard to ceiling with gilt-framed paintings of ruddy generals on rearing horses, flat-chested colonial dames in towering wigs, and dour statesmen in black cravats. Try as I might, I could not escape the disapproving regard of our illustrious dead.

I kept glancing aside at the window, wishing I could run away. So many rules for such a simple little party. Afternoon teas were passé, and so my servants treated the guests to plain cake and tiny glasses of Madeira. We dared not serve an iced cake before five in the evening for it would have been as outrageous as wearing a spangled ball gown to church. Wire-stiffened ladies praised my gigantic baby while the gentlemen in furzy gray sideburns and yellow gloves muttered over rumors of a war with Mexico. Father Kearny gave my son a gift of one hundred acres in St. Lawrence County and one hundred shares in his shipping company. Admiral Archibald Kearny, my boy's great-uncle, presented him with the deed to a warehouse on the Hudson.

Midway through the tea service, everyone turned at once toward the door but I could not see beyond the flounced skirts blocking my view. The old men pressed toward the entrance, shouting exuberantly over one another, "There he is! Hurrah, old boy! Welcome home to you!" The ladies turned as if one, moist-eyed and sighing down at me. With a rustle of taffeta and silk, they parted and I looked up and saw him.

Philip knelt beside my chair and I threw my arms over his shoulders and held him. Still wearing his dragoon uniform, he smelled like sun-bleached grass. He had grown a full beard and his skin was brown.

"I hardly recognize you. You've changed so much!" I exclaimed, and giving his beard a playful tug, I added, "Husband? You look like an old sailor."

"Now, now, Diana, I am home, no need to worry any longer."

The guests murmured as Anne and Mama shooed them out of the parlor and closed the heavy doors, leaving us alone together for the first time in ages.

Philip brushed the hair from my face. His hands were scuffed and veined with chalky lines and he kissed my mouth and he said, "You gave me a boy. What a fine mother you are to have given me a son."

"I named him John Watts, after your grandfather."

"Why did you not name him Philip?"

"I liked the name John."

"Don't worry, we can change it easy enough."

"But I don't wish to change it. John is his name."

"Dearest love, his name must be Philip. Every firstborn boy in our family has been named Philip for three hundred years. You can't possibly think of breaking tradition." He lifted the baby out of his bassinet, put his small finger to John's curled hand, but the baby turned his head aside and brushed Philip's finger away.

"I brought him a gift," he said, and with the baby in the crook of his arm, he walked over to his saddlebags and removed a sealed jar. Coming over to me, he placed it in my hands.

"It is full of muddy water."

"This water is from the South Platte River from the Rocky Mountains."

"Will you drink it or bathe in it?"

"I intend to baptize my son with it. I had a dream you see, while camping one night near Courthouse Rock. I knew the baby would be a boy and he will be baptized in this water so that he will be a true Westerner, a man of the future and the nation's glorious march to the westward. Little Philip," he said, kissing the baby's forehead.

"John," I said firmly.

Outside on the street below, I could hear the newsboys running over the bricked walks, crying, "Here's the *Herald* and news of Texas! General Taylor's army is in Corpus Christi!"

Their cries echoed against the brownstone and the shining carriages parked on both sides of the street; their cries cut me to the heart for I knew what would come.

Philip, with the baby in his arms, stepped behind me and closed the windows and mercifully, silenced the news of war.

❧ Mexico ❧

Fourteen

I SOMETIMES WISH the war in Mexico had lasted twenty years. I loved the country and the people and the excitement of that conflict. I thrived in the desert clime, but our horses suffered immensely as we pursued Santa Anna across blue salt fields, forests of chaparral, plains of prickly pear, and the volcanic wasteland of the Pedregal. How invigorating it was to ride at the front of the column, leaning back in the saddle, my boots white with brine and the horse's hooves caked with salt. The horses chewed the air as if disbelieving the dryness. There was so little forage that they were weakened and died at an alarming rate.

I often think of the little ranching villages, like Camargo, near the mouth of the Río San Juan in northern Mexico, where the native palm tree, *sabal texana*, lined the river in forests twenty miles deep. The Mexican señoritas were not to be touched, but the married women were eager for sport and it was a running joke among the troops that there would be many blonde babies born in Mexico in 1848.

Diana wrote every day and the letters, delivered months later by steamer packet, arrived in twenty-pound bundles tied with jute string. When the "Northers" blew the tent flaps and sank the temperatures, I burned her witty and amusing letters in my little camp stove, grateful for the warmth she supplied, even indirectly. I'd pour myself a bumper of sugarcane brandy and the air in my tent was redolent with burning lilies of the valley—the fragrance my wife sprayed onto the pages of her letters.

At Churubusco, a little village of sun-hardened brick farmhouses roofed with cane, I did things no man ought to do, and then my luck ran out. In August of 1847, General Scott had nearly surrounded Mexico City, and we had crowded the three plazas in Churubusco with crates, boxes, and barrels of supplies. Girls in red *rebozos* sold sugarcane brandy and dried tamarinds in the plaza. Old men in white shirts and immaculate loose white trousers sat around the fountain in the center of the plaza, fiddling Mexican dancing tunes with the American army bandsmen bleating along on serpentines and French horns.

Thousands of white army tents lined the ridges and we chopped down the thick stands of chaparral and mesquite trees for fuel. The metallic roll of the bugle sounded incessantly, troops and mules and wagons crowded the dusty streets.

The main road through Churubusco crosses a bridge, passes a church, and stretches through one of the gates of Mexico City—the Garita San Antonio. At those gates, General Santa Anna's lancers crowded the ramparts, a glittering line of gold breastplates and shining helmets, all of them dressed as if going to a costume ball.

On August 20, 1847, in the afternoon, I waited with my dragoons on the road outside of Churubusco for the order to charge. General Scott held Company "F" in reserve for most of the day. Ewell and I sat our mounts until our calves cramped. He read a two-penny edition of *King Lear,* moving his lips and laughing to himself.

Looking through my field glasses, I saw the Mexican conscripts milling on the road as our twelve-pound guns exploded and the shells fell harmlessly around them. The Mexican boys closest to the gate were throwing rocks and clods of dirt at one another, ducking and laughing. The standard bearer, a tall skinny child in a straw hat, jousted the wall with a blue streaming pennon. It was the goddamnest thing I had ever seen starving, shoeless little boys, armed with clubs and slingshots. A few of them had ancient Prussian flintlocks.

Santa Anna was a contemptible malignant dog.

I had been eating a handful of red peppers from my saddlebag. The peppers were about the size of a rifle bullet and they grew wild all over the country. I ate them slowly, leaning aside to spit out the stems, then drained the last of the sugarcane brandy from my flask. The Sixth Infantry waded through the muddy cornfields carrying a torn blue regimental flag, climbed the embankment up the road and fell into columns, walking along, unconcerned by the artillery fire. White webbing across their chests held their cartridge boxes as they dug around the cartridges for quids of tobacco. When they came to a halt, the Sixth did not dump their packs, but moved their walking sticks around behind them and propped them like tent poles to ease the weight of the sacks on their shoulders.

At four o'clock in the afternoon, the fighting began in earnest. Our howitzer lobbed shells at the road and half the bridge calved into the water. A cloud of debris fell, pelting me with scorched stone and a wall of choking smoke blew over us. The skirmishers from the Sixth Infantry shouted and then charged down the road, vanishing in a coiling veil of smoke.

Colonel Harney sent a courier galloping over. The courier reined his horse sharply and gave me the order to charge.

The bugle sounded, a thin wavering noise penetrating the bombardment of musketry and grapeshot. I led one hundred fifty men down that road with sabers drawn, though I couldn't see a thing. We charged through rolling black clouds of smoke. The Mexicans had set fire to artillery wagons; there were dead mules hanging in the harnesses off the side of the bridge and columns of smoke spewing from carts of burning supplies. We went by instinct, the pounding hooves of the horses and the men and sabers appearing out of the smoke.

Two miles down the road, we slammed into the Mexican conscripts, who threw down their worthless old muskets and ran in a bawling scramble toward the gates of Mexico City. I remember tasting smoke on the back of my tongue from the Mexican cannons.

The soldiers I cut with the saber died curling up in agony. The ones I shot died on their backs or bellies with limbs flung out.

At one point, I turned and looked over my shoulder, but the dirt and smoke was so thick I couldn't see anything, not even the rider behind me.

I thought I heard a bugle sounding the recall, but it was too thin and distant a noise. So I rode on, chasing those poor miserable barefoot bastards to the gates of the city.

I pulled up sharply when the road fell off in a defensive pit and trenches. The wind blew and the air cleared and I saw hundreds of those child-conscripts climbing the gates, screaming for mercy, begging the gold-clad Mexican lancers and officers on the ramparts to let them in. Some of those boys had fallen into the trenches, and were trying to hide themselves in the dirt.

My horse, weakened by poor forage and the deprivations of campaign, was used up. It hobbled forward, tumbled sidelong. I recall half jumping and half falling, wrenching my feet free of the stirrups and hitting the ground with arms outstretched so that my teeth cracked together.

I stumbled to my feet and those conscripts clinging to the city gate quieted. One by one, they jumped down from the fence and the mob of them stared my way. I heard a furious uproar of shouting, and they fell upon me in a heap, ripped off my baldric and scabbard, slugging and thumping at me with their bare hands. There I was, at the bottom of the pile, on my belly, unable to move or breathe.

Above my head, on the gate's pinnacle, the Mexican artillerymen lit the cannon fuse and fired into the brawling mob of their own troops.

The road buckled as the concussive force of the grapeshot cut into the men on top of me, spraying flesh, burning cloth, and a fountain of blood. It felt as if someone had emptied a kettle of hot gumbo over me. A boy's thighbone had broken in two and the force of the blast staked the bone into the dirt. I clawed out from under the dead, wobbled to my feet, stood and tried to see through the filthy black air, but could not get my bearings, could not decide which way was the gate and which way led back down the road to my troops.

An explosion split the air and grapeshot shredded a stand of palm trees. Palm splinters fine as needles shot through my coat, lodged in my chest like arrows, blowing a hurricane wind right through me. I felt lead searing through my body and wheeled in shock as if swung around by some invisible force wishing to have a look at me from another angle.

And when I looked down at myself, I saw that my left arm was gone below the elbow, the bone a sharp splinter surrounded by a sloppy meaty fringe of muscle; the brachial artery dangling out like a wire and jetting blood into the sand.

Hearing men shouting in Spanish behind me, I turned my back to the gate and began dragging the cold length of myself down the Via San Antonio, sweating and puking and stumbling through the dust. I searched the smoke-blackened road for Ewell but did not see him or any of my troopers. I could not see and I could hardly breathe. I had lost my sword and my revolver and expected to be decapitated from behind with my own sword at any minute.

For one merciful moment, the wind blew, clearing the air.

I fumbled in my pocket and the gold case tumbled from my hand in the hot August light—the daguerreotype of Diana, a spinning gold miracle falling and I watched it fall, mesmerized by the gleam as it tumbled into the dust at my feet. I had neither the strength nor the presence of mind to unlatch it, but I was certain I was dying and I wanted the comfort of holding it in my hand. It was a way of being close to my wife in that final moment, I suppose.

I saw Ewell, then. He came galloping through the black cloud of gunpowder with his sword drawn, coming toward me through a shabby black curtain of smoke as if he were being created whole out of the mist.

I wavered there a moment looking up at him.

"Phil," Ewell shouted as he dismounted and ran toward me. "You got to help me, friend. Stay awake, don't go falling asleep on me." And then Ewell and a few men helped me—at great peril to themselves—mount a spare horse before escorting me back to our line.

Somehow, the orderlies responsible for getting me to the infirmary, lost me instead. I woke at dusk in an open coffin, my mouth and eyelids covered with flies. A fly thrummed over my bottom lip, indeed my whole face tickled with stiff and glittering wings. A flock of boat-tail grackle hovered in the chaparral tree above my head, staring down with an ominously hungry look.

Someone tugged at my coat. An American orderly in a forage cap yanked the watch out of my coat pocket and ran off with it. My jacket and trousers were stiff as canvas from dried, clotted blood.

A vast shimmering flock of parrots crossed the twilight sky, a rainbow of violet and pink and green parrots.

A trooper ran back and forth along the row, peering into each box. Following him, a man dressed head to toe in black moved slowly and deliberately down the row of corpses and dying men. At first, I thought he was a minister, but then I recognized the black army surgeon's uniform. A shadow fell over me and I heard Ewell shouting in a panicked pitch. "I found him, Doctor! I found him and goddamn it if he isn't alive!"

Nearing midnight I lay upon a wooden table and stared up at the sky over Churubusco, Mexico.

Surgeon Franklin Pierce clasped my cheek and jaw. "Be still," he said.

I could see the yellow shadow of the bonfire through a canvas drape

Surgeon Pierce had raised to keep the men from watching. A Mexican boy, carrying a bucket from the cistern, splashed cold water on my left arm.

"Close your eyes," Surgeon Pierce said, "and I will hold you."

But I would not close my eyes because darkness was the same as death. The surgeon strapped me to the table, pressed a wet rag over my face, and I inhaled chloroform smelling of mint fragrant as the wild green meadows around my father's house in St. Lawrence County. Wielding a long gleaming knife, he sliced into my flesh just below the shoulder and stopped upon meeting a gritty resistance. Then, his surgical saw scraped at the bone of my left arm, scraping to the shoulder, a relentless drag, back and forth. I heard the ailanthus trees on Fourth Avenue cracking in an ice storm, the snap of branches excruciatingly painful as the remnant of my arm tumbled into the dust.

I tried to remember how autumn felt in New York City, the leaves brown as wrapping paper, and welcomed a vision of Diana slipping a sprig of chrysanthemum into my lapel, standing on tiptoe to kiss my cheek, and whispering, "Come home safely to me, come home soon." My hallucination of her summoned such grief and longing for the cool gentleness of her hands upon my face and the scent of her skin that I felt a parched soreness in my throat and thought to weep but could not.

Surgeon Pierce spilled nitric acid over my bleeding stump, the chemical smoke drifting up to the black sky, a shred of my muscle clinging to the table's edge. He capped the bottle of nitric and set it on the table.

The orderlies carried me away, past a soldier swinging a lantern, the light smearing a ghostly arc through the night. The troops conversed in hushed tones and the pickets paced the perimeter and talked about the cavalry charge.

I heard Ewell asking, "How is Kearny doing? Did they take his arm up to the shoulder?"

Two days later, I woke in an infirmary tent, and sitting at my bedside was Ewell, reading a penny edition of *Troilus and Cressida*. He looked like a haughty schoolmaster reading along as a student declaimed his lesson. Ewell put his thumb in the book to hold his place and glanced sidelong at me.

He fished in his pocket and placed the case containing Diana's portrait on my chest. "I'm always picking up after you," he said, and turned the page.

Fifteen

PHILIP'S WARS invariably started with parades and ended with funerals, and while I endured my husband's long absences, he enjoyed all of the exhilaration of battle. I gave birth to our fourth child, Anne De Lancey Kearny (we called her Nannie) while vacationing with my family at White Sulphur Springs in West Virginia in June of 1847. Mama, the children, and I had passed the summer in the springs to escape the fever troubles in the city. Since Susan's death, I took no risks with my family's health but as autumn approached, it was time to return home to Manhattan. Anne Lane went home to her family but promised she would visit in the spring of 1848, if I would send for her.

We had been traveling in a cramped carriage for three days. By the time we took the ferry from New Jersey to Manhattan all of us were tired, travel-worn, and disheveled. Two-year-old Johnny rode the entire trip making ominous burping noises and gasping for air. Three-year-old Di sat on the floor at my knee reading a children's book. Baby Anne, just three months, slept in a basket on the seat beside Mama.

I rested my chin in my hand and read the swinging sign boards above the stores while men paced the footways wearing sandwich boards advertising UPHAM'S ELECUTORY and BUCHAN'S BALSAM OF LIFE. The city felt closed in, heat rising from the paving stones, rubbish and manure fouling the streets from curb to curb. I snapped open my fan, tugged my collar out as far as it would go and tried to cool myself as I leaned on the window ledge. Noticing a most curious sight, I urged Mama to come look.

Coming down the street, we watched the progress of a giant black pasteboard hat, nearly nine feet tall and pulled by a team of horses. A brass orchestra played the quickstep from "The Arab Maiden." The musicians sawed away at their instruments while perched on chairs all around the hat rim under a hatband proclaiming, REVOLT OF THE HAREM—CONCERT TONIGHT AT THE BOWERY THEATRE. We watched the hat go by and a mob of rowdy boys tossing papers of lit gunpowder at the horses to frighten them. And then, as we began our journey uptown on Broadway, Mama and I both saw the terrible display at the same time.

In the long plate-glass windows of Plumbe's Daguerrotype Studio, swathed in red, white, and blue bunting hung ten imperials—large portraits of Philip, all in a row, with a banner slung above proclaiming in bold letters,

NEW YORK CITY'S OWN SON

CAPTAIN PHILIP KEARNY
—*America's Beau Sabreur*—
THE HERO OF CHURUBUSCO.

Aghast, Mama and I slowly turned and stared into each other's eyes. The only time a man's portrait was swathed in bunting and put on public display was when he had been killed in the midst of a heroic act. I leapt forward and clutched the carriage window, staring in horror at Plumbe's shop.

And then Mama said a perfectly sensible thing. "Now, Diana, do you see the color of the bunting?"

"Red, white, and blue."

"It isn't *black* bunting."

"What could possibly have happened to him? It sets me crazy not to know!"

Though I wrote to Philip at the last address I had for him in Mexico and sent pleading letters to his commanding officer and the War Department, I learned only that he had been somehow wounded in a cavalry charge. Weeks passed without a word. Then, a month after the battle, I received a brief letter from a surgeon saying that after Philip had recuperated sufficiently, he would be sent home.

On Monday evening, December 13, 1847, with the windows of the nursery slightly open, I could hear the lamplighter cursing the cold weather from under the brim of his bent and rusty hat. Carrying his ladder and a smoldering punk on a long hooked stave, he paused in front of our house on Twenty-second Street, tilted the ladder against the lamppost, slid the pane aside, and lit the wick. He whistled as he lumbered off in a fine misting rain.

It is a medical fact that warm rooms made cold coffins; and so the nursery windows were always open and in this way, the children became hardened against the cold. If given the chance, little Di would romp in the snow naked as a picked chicken. On that night, I was upstairs in the nursery with Nannie, Di, and John reading them *The Pilgrim's Progress*. The pilgrim had just arrived at the wicket gate. Di sat cross-legged and alert, her eyes wide, silently repeating words that captured her fancy. John lifted our dog Greeley's ear and examined the gruesome bits of wax, small parasites, and burrs lodged in there. Nannie sat on my lap.

"'The turnings and twistings belong not to the road, but to the devious paths that lead out of it; and these are not narrow, but wide; not straight, but crooked,'" I read.

"Turnings and twistings," Di echoed, affecting a wondering expression and motioning in the air with her hands. The child gave dramatic emphasis to every element of her day, whether it was eating her toast or having her hair set in curling papers.

The icy rain wrinkled and poured over the windows.

"Mama?" Di asked, tapping my wrist. "Read, Mama. Read!"

"Weed," John said, scratching the dog's belly.

"That is enough for this evening, it is time to sleep," I said to the children, lowering Nan into her bed, and folding the blankets over Di and John. I reached for the daguerreotype portrait of Philip on the nightstand and gave it to Di. In it, her father wore his uniform, staring grimly at the greater world, a hand on the scabbard of his sword, the other holding his dress helmet with the plume.

"Kiss Daddy good night," I said, and the children did. The glassy surface of Philip's portrait was smeared with oatmeal, blackberry jam, and infant spittle.

"When is he coming home?" Di asked plaintively.

"Do you miss him, Di?"

"Does he miss me?"

"He misses you every minute of the day." I kissed the children on their cheeks, while the dog curled up at the foot of the bed. Turning the lights low, I shut the door.

Downstairs in the library, a room that spoke of my husband, I sat at his desk with a glass of Madeira and a cigarette smoldering between my fingers. Philip's souvenirs from Algeria cluttered the bookshelves. Before leaving for the war in Mexico, he had stacked military reports atop his black walnut desk. However, he had not taken the picture of Susan with him. I could see my likeness in the frame cradling Susan at an awkward angle, holding her up so that the daguerreotypist could capture her face. Though everyone had consoled me that time would ease my grief, I missed Susan more with each day; as if I were thirsty for a drink of water that I could never have, not for the rest of my life.

After plucking a bit of tobacco off my lower lip, I began reviewing the ledger of household accounts and ciphering the bills. It was hard to believe that a scant few years ago, the idea of handling money was entirely foreign to me and Philip forbade it. But with him away on duty, we had no choice, and I had become quite adept at managing our finances.

Tomorrow, I would accompany the housekeeper to the markets. A woman who let her housekeeper shop unsupervised was setting herself up to be robbed. Since the war started, some old customs had changed, yet others hadn't. The master of the house still had to establish all of the household accounts, then give his written consent and advance approval before his wife could purchase anything from the local merchants. But of late, the old tradition of men doing all of the household marketing had changed. In years past, no lady of any rank would dare be seen in the Northern markets, but with the men at war in Mexico, none but women with baskets slung over their arms crowded Packer and Knapp's poultry store.

I tamped out the cigarette and began the task of filling out my lie-bill; a list of destinations for my driver including the ladies I wished to call upon, and the shops I intended to visit; Stewart's, Lyman's Ribbons, and the chemist's on Broadway.

Mrs. Neatly, my housekeeper, knocked discreetly upon the door and peering around at me, pushed her spectacles over the bridge of her nose. I beckoned her in. Looking smart and crisp in her black dress, white collar and cuffs, she said, "Mrs. Kearny, ma'am? Oddest thing, a baggage wagon has come through the back gate and the grooms are unloading it as we speak."

I rose to my feet and my pulse felt heavy. "Philip?"

"No, ma'am. Only a baggage wagon."

"Oh my lord, if not my husband, then who else would send a baggage wagon to our house, Mrs. Neatly!"

I lifted my skirts and sped down the main hall where the gasolier had been lowered so that the light was a dull bronze. Reaching for Philip's cape, I pulled it over my shoulders and opened the front door. Then I stepped into the darkness, out onto the wet stoop, looking up the street and down, yet I saw nothing.

Sleet fell like bridal rice upon my shoulders. Gripping the cloak at my throat, I lifted my chin at the clopping sound of hoof falls and the clattering of iron wheels. Snow gusted down from the pitched roofs of neighboring houses.

A hack dragged to a halt before the curbstone. The driver sat up high and straight, staring directly ahead, gathering the reins in one hand as he tucked his whip into the whip socket with the other. His beaver hat was tied to his head with a black wool scarf and a blanket shawl hung over his long black coat.

Trembling with cold and apprehension, I observed the slow progress of the passenger emerging from the carriage. He huddled under a heavy buffalo robe, steadying himself over his walking stick. I did not recognize this old man and my hopes sank. His face was incised with starvation, he resembled a vine withered and gone black in the snow. He had a heavy auburn beard and mustache, wore a sealskin coat, and a fur cap with broad ear tabs. As he glanced up, his gaze flickered over the front of the house.

"Philip?" I cried, running down the stoop. "You're home, my God, you've come home to me."

Halting and infirm, he said nothing as I slid my arm around his waist.

"Come inside, come with me, and I'll look after you." I kicked open the front door and kicked it again to close it. The dog barked and the servants came running upstairs in their nightclothes asking what was happening.

"Urban!" I called. "Urban, you go and fetch Dr. Robert Watts at the Union Club. Tell him Kearny has come home. And you, Daniel, take the bright bay, ride for Colonnade Row and ring Mr. Kearny's bell until someone answers and tell him that his son is home from the war. Go, now, hurry."

"Ma'am!" Mrs. Neatly cried, "What can I do?"

"Make him some beeftea and bring up my medicine box. Let Mama know he is home. But tell her I don't want anyone else to disturb us. Not the children, not the servants, not anyone except the doctor and Philip's father."

"Yes, ma'am."

Slowly, with his weight on me, his walking stick thumping on each riser, I brought him up to his room.

Opening his bedroom door, I patted along the wall, feeling for the gas sconce. With Philip leaning against me, I turned the key, listening for the pop and hiss of the wick, shielding the flame with my free hand until it flickered low. His bedroom was heavily curtained and papered in dark green and brown velvet, the walls adorned with his own charcoal sketches of military parades, dragoons sitting horses before a Rocky Mountain backdrop and chasseurs, lounging around campfires in French North Africa.

Two long windows on each side of the fireplace overlooked Twenty-second Street and the air in his room smelled of cold and linseed oil. I dashed over to the fireplace, tipped the coal bucket with one foot, shoveled a scoop into the English grate, and lit a fire.

"I'm weak as water," he mumbled. Kneeling in front of him, I put my hands on his legs. "I don't want to undress you until it is warmer in here."

His eyes watered but from fever or emotion, I could not tell, and he stared at me in a nervous way, unsteady from fatigue and illness.

"There now," I murmured out of habit—I suppose from calming the children when they were frantic. I pulled the sealskin hat off his head and brushed the hair from his eyes.

"I need a bath. I haven't had a bath in months."

"I'll run a bath for you. I'll start the geyser; it takes a few minutes for the water to heat up. Will you be all right here for a moment?"

"Yes."

I struggled to hide my shock at his condition, but my fears pained me acutely; the blood tingled in my face and a light fever swirled in my head. I had prepared myself for every contingency except that my husband might have come home to die. In the bathroom, I lit the gasolier and the sconces on both sides of the mirror over the sink. Every noise echoed loudly against the marble floor and tiled walls. Keeping an eye on him as I sat on the edge of the tub, I twisted the brass wheels above the spigot and tested the temperature as the geyser gushed scalding water. The tub resembled a giant teacup sitting flush with the floor, situated near radiators hissing forced air from two coal-burning furnaces in the cellar. I dragged a wooden hoop and cheesecloth net along the surface of the water scooping out the leaves and grasses, insects and tadpoles and small fish hurtling out of the tap. Turning the tap off, I let the water cool to bathing temperature.

He hadn't moved, but sat exactly where I'd left him. Unhooking his sealskin coat, I asked, "Are you able to stand?"

He rose, unsteady as a lamb. Tossing the fur coat aside, I unbuttoned his dragoon uniform coat and threw it on the floor, and then reaching around him, unfastened his braces, trying to hold my breath and not smell the odor of death and Mexican mud and dirty bandages that clung to him. Mealy ropes of lice hung in his chest hair, groin, and under his arms, but he seemed not to care and made no sound as I cut his bandages and cast handfuls of crumbling poultice and fabric onto the floor.

"What has happened to you?" I clasped my hand over my mouth and tried not to meet his eyes, for his arm had been amputated above the elbow. He had about four inches of upper arm left below the shoulder muscle. The end of the stump resembled the top of a bag gathered with string but at least the wound was not infected; the rippling scar extending from the end of the incision to his shoulder was a healthy pink.

I slid my hands under the stump, his ruined limb felt heavy and dead as if God were taking him away, piece by piece.

When I touched his face, he turned his head aside to feel my palm against his cheek.

"Come beside me, Diana. Come here and kiss me."

He saw me hesitate and I felt ashamed for it. My courage had plummeted, but even so, he leaned close to me and I felt his rough lips on mine. To kiss him was like sliding a copper penny under the tongue; a corrosive flavor lingered in my mouth, this flavor owing to daily doses of mercury salts prescribed by his doctor. An underlying mineral fragrance lingered over him.

"It is a sin upon my memory that I have not been kinder to you, Diana."

"Don't speak of such things, not now. I am so happy you are home, you mustn't think of anything else, but that you are home now, and safe," I said, gripping the bootstraps on the hem of his trousers and tugging them off.

His hipbones jutted at a starving angle, his legs thinned to tendon, his torso sunk at the seam of his ribs. The auburn hair on his chest and groin had begun to turn gray.

He insisted on climbing into the tub without help, but lost his grip and his footing, and tumbled into the water. He clutched the side of the tub with one hand, sliding on his left side until I helped him upright. Sputtering angrily, water streamed over his face, as he thrust out his jaw, dragged his hand over his beard.

I sat on a three-legged stool, rolled a big block of brown soap over a piece of suede, and began to scrub him.

"Are you using lye soap? Why lye soap, Diana? Goddamn, it burns!"

"Now, that's the irascible man I remember marrying," I smiled, deciding not to mention the lice.

"It burns, Diana! Wipe it away, it's burning me!" He sucked air through his lower teeth.

"John never complains about it. Does it really hurt that badly?" This was a little white lie—I'd never use this soap on our baby—it would have skinned him like a grape. Even so, my words had the intended effect for Philip was thinking that if his two-year-old son could tolerate the harsh soap, he ought to as well.

"John? What sort of boy is he now?"

"John is fearless and reckless. Yesterday afternoon, he poked a millet broom into the coal embers and held it there until it sparked. He marched around the nursery with a flaming broom over his head, shouting his own name. Little Di put the fire out. She grabbed the broom from him and plunged it into the water bucket." Lifting one of Philip's feet, I scraped at a strange fungus growing on his heels and between his toes. "He is a very small version of you."

"And our girls?"

Deciding not to tell him that his daughter had used his shaving brush as a hearth broom, I emphasized her brighter qualities. "Di rules the nursery and bosses John around. Baby Nan is so quiet, Philip, we have never had a more serene child, why she has angel blonde hair and the bluest eyes."

I submerged my arms in the bathwater and the blue dye from the wet sleeves of my gown trickled over my wrists. Switching to a soapy soft bristle brush, I scoured under his arms and across his chest.

"A damned orderly stole my watch." He inhaled sharply as I scrubbed his belly and his skin turned scarlet from the harsh soap. "I liked that watch."

"We shall buy you another." I pinched the soapsuds from his earlobe.

It suddenly dawned on me that Rinnah June was not with him. "Where is Rinnah? Why did he not come home with you?"

"Rinnah is dead. Shot to death at a mountain pass called Cerro Gordo."

"Oh! Not Rinnah."

"Yes, Rinnah." Philip climbed out of the tub and sat on the edge with a towel over his lap. Without a left hand he couldn't wrap a towel around his waist. I helped him with this, walked him over to the sink, and sprinkled lime powder onto the toothbrush with a little tin spoon.

Philip craned at his reflection in the mirror, poked a finger in his mouth and jiggled a loose molar. "I'm thirty-two years old and my teeth are turning black as apple seeds."

While he brushed his teeth, I stepped over the puddles on the floor and returned to the bedroom. He came into the room drying his hair with a towel as I turned back the blankets, removed an old colonial bed warmer from under the bed and plucking a few coals from the fire, filled the pan and ran it back and forth across the sheets.

"Would you like something to eat? Or drink?" I asked.

"I can't drink. When the liquor reaches my heart, it pumps into my blood and makes my wound throb. But I will take a little laudanum."

"How much?"

"Fifteen drops laudanum in two fingers of water and no more." He reclined on the bed. "I need pillows under my left side. I can't sleep on my left side or turn over. I might drown in the fluids in my lungs."

Covering him with the blankets, I turned the gas down in the sconces.

"Don't leave me, Diana. Not now."

"I won't leave you."

"Will you sleep here? Rather than your own room?"

"Yes." Lying beside him and looking at him across the pillow, it occurred to me that I had never seen him so still in all of his life. Fearing he might be dead after all, I bent low and was relieved to feel his breath on my ear. He had always been such a vital and restless soul, fiddling with his silverware and mangling his napkin at table, drumming his fingers on any surface and lacking a surface, drumming them on himself. When at home, he rode for hours a day and when not riding, he walked to the Hudson River, strolling along the shoreline, admiring the views of New Jersey until his feet blistered.

While watching him sleep, dangerous truths about the both of us came wafting up in the coal-heated air. Philip's ardent temperament, his habitual craving for excitement, this craving void of his could only be satisfied by wandering and by bloodshed, however patriotic, ill-conceived, or purposeless. None of the smaller aspects of our lives seemed enough to placate him even for a short time. Our children, our home, and our marriage could not console him and I couldn't help but wonder what inner torments my husband hoped to escape while on campaign.

An hour later, Philip's father arrived. He pounded on our bedroom door, trying to catch his breath. Rushing to greet him, I threw open the door and taking his hand, led him into the room. "Father Kearny, I am so glad you have come."

"My dear girl, how bad off is he?"

"He is tired, Father. He is weak, but he is not feverish and his wound is clean. Come, come in."

Kearny stood at the bedside and looked down at his son. Though staid and severe of aspect, the old man tensed against his despair. He moved the lozenge around in his mouth, trying to think of the appropriate thing to say. Slowly, he lowered himself into the chair I brought over for him.

The two of us perched on the edge of our seats, stiff as pins in a row.

"I've sent for Dr. Robert Watts," I whispered.

"That was a wise thing to do." After a long silence, Kearny spoke.

"Philip once told me that men live forever in the desert. Perhaps that is why he has always chosen to fight in deserts. Perhaps he believed he was immortal in Mexico, in the Southwest territories, and in the Atlas Mountains of North Africa. He must have known something of the truth for he is alive despite all. But to see my boy like this?" The old man touched his temple with a tremoring hand. "To see my boy ruined has put me completely out of heart."

Sixteen

PHILIP SLEPT through most of December. And when he woke I helped him to the bathroom, fed him bouillon, and then, he slept again. When the incision smelled and began suppurating, I brought him a basin of ice and he sat upright, staring across the room at the window, soaking his stump for as long as he could stand it. Sometimes, while soaking his limb, he did not wish to speak, but fixed his gaze on me, yet did not see me, for in those moments, he relived his war in Mexico. I kept a workbasket of darning and sewing by my chair for those times, my head bowed over my own busy hands clicking the knitting needles, whip stitching a hem, or replacing a button.

"What do you think of being married to a lame devil, Diana?"

Putting the knitting needles down in my lap, I tried to tease him out of his self-pitying mood. "What is this you are trying to tell me, Philip? Now you are *le diable boiteux*? You have the mark of Satan because you have lost part of your arm? Surely, it can't mean you've misplaced your soul as well?" I joined him on the bed, took his hand in mine, and kissed his roughened knuckles.

"Do I repulse you?" His eyes shifted over me.

"No, I love you even more." Reaching for the work I'd left on the chair seat, I lifted the needles, fingering the yarn around the tambour.

"Because I think sometimes that I am cursed, almost"—he licked his top lip and narrowed his eyes at me, testing the impact of his words—"as if I'm predestined to evil."

A small laugh escaped me and I leveled a look on him, held his eyes steadily with mine as I resumed knitting. "Would you really like to hear my opinion, Philip?"

"Yes."

"Thinking you've been handpicked by Satan is about as grandiose an idea as saying you're God's chosen child."

"Good Lord, woman, where do you gather these ideas? I only meant to say I require a little more tenderness and affection now that I am lame . . . now that I'm a poor lame devil."

"My dear husband, you are not lame. You are momentarily indisposed, but you are constitutionally incapable of ever being lame. As for you being devilish, that I will not dispute."

This answer seemed to satisfy him, and he grew calm. Soon, he wearied, but before falling back to sleep, he murmured, "You aren't leaving, are you? Don't go away, even if I sleep."

"I shall be here when you wake," I assured him.

One sunny afternoon before Christmas 1847, Father Kearny took John outside and the two of them sat upon the back stoop with a small pile of beech and willow kindling. Taking a break from Philip's bedside, I joined them, sitting with chin in hand, and could not help smiling as the old man tried to keep John's attention while he whittled a slingshot. My boy was as restless as his father.

"Where did a city fellow like you learn to whittle?" I nudged Father Kearny with my shoulder.

He brushed away curly wood shavings as he worked. "I was a boy once, don't you know?"

"No, I didn't know."

"Don't sass me, Miss Diana. How is Philip?"

"The same, still sleeping." I lifted my face in the cold sunshine and drew my shawl closer around my shoulders.

John hopped on the path, bent down for a pebble, and threw it with all of his might. Father Kearny held the wishbone up and examined his work. "John! Go find a good rock for Grandpa."

Kearny wiped the blade on the leg of his trouser and lifted a sanding block and began smoothing the grain. "I've been thinking about Philip. Losing an arm like that . . ." The old man stopped sanding and watched my boy crouching and filling his pockets with rocks. "Philip might have troubles. He had troubles the year he came home from North Africa."

I thought about Philip's rules forbidding lamb and his preoccupation with *djenoun*. Squinting in the sunlight, I asked, "What kind of troubles?"

Father Kearny appeared to think a moment, then ran the back of his hand under his nose and went back to his sanding. "He'd disappear for days at a time. He'd come home looking gray and worn out, but he'd never say where he'd been or what he'd been doing. The French massacred whole villages of Arabs outside of Algiers, you know?"

"Yes, I remember you speaking of that at dinner a long time ago."

Father Kearny rested his elbows on his knees and peered across the walled garden at John. "I have a bad feeling about Mexico."

Hugging myself, I straightened my legs and stared at the bows on my slippers. "But the newspaper accounts were all about . . ."

The old man grunted in disgust. "Pah, the newspapers!" He leaned back on the stairs, resting on his elbows. "I fear that your burdens shall only increase with time."

"Here! Here, Grandpa!" John came running over with a handful of pea gravel. The old man put the boy's hands on the slingshot and showed him how to pinch the stone in the band and pull it back. They let it go, the stone thwacked the tree trunk and my son bellowed with glee. "I do it! I do it, Grandpa!"

"A norther is coming on." Father Kearny slapped his legs, and sighing, rose to his feet. "Diana, let's you and I go inside and take a glass of Madeira by the fire. I have a gift for you."

"A gift!" I held Johnny's hand as we climbed the stairs.

"I am going to astonish and delight you by reading to you from a new book I bought at Formby's."

"Something scandalous, I hope!"

"No, this is a new novel called *Wuthering Heights*." He held the door for me and gave the slingshot to Johnny as he darted down the hall. "There is this gloomy fellow named Heathcliff."

I groaned as I brushed by him. "Let's play euchre instead."

The next morning, hushing and shushing, I brought Di into Philip's room to keep me company. While Philip slept fitfully, I opened the children's magazine on my lap and began tearing out the pictures that gave her nightmares. My daughter despised elves and dwarfs, expressing fear she might turn into one. Where she got this idea, I knew not, but still, I humored her, removing a story about pygmies and a cross-hatch sketch of a phantom, and handed the offending pages to Di, who crumpled them up and tossed them one by one into the fire.

"Through." I flipped the magazine pages one last time. "I think those are the last of the bad pages."

Di wore an Irish poplin pinafore and a green ribbon held her chin-length hair neatly off her face. She slid colored glass panels into a magic lantern she held in her lap, and gripped the slides by the wooden handles, scowling as she made a tock-tock noise, pushing them in and drawing them out again. Her feet jutted out straight from the chair seat.

"When is he . . . going to wake up?" Di asked, looking up from her magic lantern.

"He is sick, Di. When you are sick, you sleep, don't you?"

"No. And I am stronger than John."

What she said was true. She devised mischief like jumping on the beds until the rope webbing sagged, but when she heard a doorknob turning, she'd stop jumping, run over to a chair, and sit with a book in her lap gazing with grave disapproval at my boy, who continued flopping wildly.

I sorted through a basket containing more than fifty pairs of Philip's gloves, most of which he hadn't even worn. A gentleman needed gloves for every occasion; driving into the city, and attending theater, dining, and business. Di outstretched each pair of gloves like butterfly wings while I snipped the binding ribbons. I stacked the right gloves in one pile and the left in another, and as we worked, snow sputtered against the windows.

"It seems such a waste to throw all of these left-hand gloves away," I said.

"Oh yes, a terrible waste." Di mimicked my forlorn manner.

And then, growing weary of our work, Di picked up her magic lantern and her magazine and silently left the room.

Philip gasped and sat up ramrod straight. Perspiring, he looked bewildered when he met my gaze.

"How do you feel?"

He made dry smacking noises with his mouth. He swung his legs over the bed, hunching there a moment and said, "I feel . . .as if I might take my wife for a stroll."

Two hours later, we descended the stoop. Philip, dapper in a broad-cloth suit and overcoat and a beaver hat, leaned heavily on his walking stick. The left sleeve of his coat I had neatly sewn, tacking it up at an angle so that it would not flap about when he moved.

"Now, Diana, why are you on my right side? You know a lady never walks street-side. Come around here."

I refused to budge, smiled at him around the brim of my bonnet and tucked my hands into my fur sleeves. "I am your guardian, don't you see?"

He made a face and waved the walking stick. "Get on this side of me or I shall go no farther. How insulting to be protected by a woman!"

We walked toward Gramercy Park, pausing on the crossway to survey the street. I opened my parasol and the frame made a soft popping sound as the dark fabric swelled above my head. An omnibus came to a stop and the passengers riveted upon Philip, staring at his amputated arm. I could read their lips and there was no doubt about their comments. In those days, people thought nothing of staring at and ridiculing the crippled and the lame. The map colorists and ribbon clerks turned about on the benches, but mercifully, their comments were drowned by a clattering onrush of shouting drivers and clanging horse bells, and if Philip had noticed them, he gave no sign of it. For this, I was grateful and relieved.

He craned forward at the sight of Calvary Church with its two awkward steeples ornamented with wooden crosses. "What do you call that abomination? A double-horned church?"

"You signed the deed, Philip."

"What trembling pack of parvenus designed that piece of malinquity?"

"Mind the horse car rails in the middle of the street," I said, tucking my hand around his back.

"I lost an arm, not my sight. Now I wish I had lost my sight. What an ugly church! Scratch a Presbyterian, you'll find a parvenu with garish taste."

We strolled by the church as boy choristers in black robes played caps on the steps. One of the boys stared at Philip's left side and exclaimed, "Hang me, if that fella ain't got no arm! Look there, that fellow ain't got an arm."

Philip stiffened but pretended he hadn't heard. He didn't see when

I swung my parasol around and discreetly jabbed the little urchin in the leg with the metal point.

"Ow! Hang me if she didn't stab me! She stabbed me!"

Philip raised an eyebrow at me. "What did you do, Diana?"

I blinked innocently at him. "Whatever can you mean?"

The clouds lowered, a blustering darkness erased the light as the snow began falling thickly. He held the brim of his hat. "Ailanthus trees have sprouted everywhere. So many new houses being started. I count at least six excavated foundations and two new houses on the south side of Gramercy Square."

"Ailanthus?"

"That is an ailanthus." He pointed at a spindly tree growing outside the park gate. "The Amboinese people call it the tree of heaven and they believe that the roots of that tree reach the center of the earth and if you could somehow follow the roots you would reach the center of paradise."

"What a lovely legend."

Philip touched the corner of his mustache with his gloved fingertip. "Ah, but every inch of that tree is poison. From the sap to its seeds; it is pure poison and it thrives here."

"Kindly tell me what you mean?"

"Only that the ailanthus tree is a little like marriage, don't you think? All newlyweds begin life on the crown of the tree and the tree is a tangled maze of branches. But if man and wife could see clear to get to the root of why they love one another, they would enjoy a paradise of sorts."

"And us?" I asked, ducking away from the freezing wind.

He regarded me so tenderly that he took me aback. "I cannot tell, Mrs. Kearny. Are we to be blinded by a thicket of leafy twigs and branches?"

"Never."

He looked away from me then, up at Calvary's offensive double towers. "Sometimes it astonishes me, how much alike we are. I've told you that you are so much like me that I cannot help but love you."

"And how are we alike?"

"Each of us is certain we possess the fiercer heart."

"Oh, is that all?" I sighed and Philip, laughing at my response, let me take his arm as we turned and retraced our steps.

Nearing our house, we stepped off the walk and into the street to avoid a ragpicker scavenging through the ash cans. He resembled one of the desert fathers with hair long as Absalom's blowing in the breeze. Shoving the sleeve of his filthy robe up over his elbow, he plunged his rag hook into the ash can shooting a silver plume into the air. He shouted at Philip, "You! Know this! I hear the thunder of the captains and the shouting. Hear me! Before He heals with Eternal Grace, the warriors of God strike down His enemies with the sword He came to bring!"

"Amen, brother!" Philip called, glancing back over his shoulder as I urged him up the stairs to our house.

"What an awful man."

"Probably a veteran, and navy most likely."

"Really?"

He raised a brow at me and shook his head at my gullibility.

We dressed for dinner that night. Mama, Father Kearny, and I waited in the parlor for Philip to come down the stairs. But at table, Philip could not wield both knife and fork. When the roast was served, the butler silently took his plate over to the sideboard and cut his meat for him. Philip was visibly embarrassed and made his excuses and left the table before we'd finished our meal. I think too much stimulation all at once had a negative effect. After Father Kearny had bid us good night, Philip looked gaunt and pale, and I urged him to bed. When I thought he was asleep, I went to bed too. But around two o'clock in the morning, he woke, and taking a lantern in hand, opened the bedroom door and went into the hallway.

"Philip," I said, following him and taking his elbow. "Philip?"

He lifted the lantern and peered down the hall and spoke calmly and authoritatively. "Take a detail to the river and rebury those men. This time, cover the graves with rocks and stones. Tell Corporal Aultman to poison a calf carcass with strychnine and set it well away from the perimeter."

"And then what?"

"That ought to keep the wolves from digging up and eating our dead."

"Yes sir," I said, and gently led him back into the bedroom.

The next morning, Sunday, December 19, 1847, Father Kearny, Mama, the children, and I walked down the block to attend service at Calvary Church. Philip, suffering a relapse, remained in bed. I wrapped myself in a sealskin cape, pinning my veil down over my bonnet. The morning snapped cold and bitterly bright and all along our street, the ailanthus trees were gemmed with frost. A cold wind blew, spinning dust around dust.

"Good morning!" Mr. Gerard called from across the street, striding along with his hand to the brim of his stovepipe hat and his black knee-coat whipping in the wind.

"Good morning to you, sir," we called back.

The children made a game of balancing on the curbstone. Johnny's stiff tartan skirt blew up around his waist, showing off his fat knees but Di modestly flattened her skirt with her gloved hands. Both children were dressed in red wool mittens and woolen scarves and capes.

A carriage rumbled by and I called, "John, come away from the curb." As we ducked into the newly built church, Father Kearny removed his hat. Down the aisle to the second pew from the front, I sat between Mama and Father Kearny. The children climbed up, scraping their boots against the seat and took their places beside Mama.

Father Kearny cleared his throat and sniffed. "The distemper paint is still wet and the plaster looks damp."

Mama fidgeted with the ribbons marking pages in her Bible, peering through her quizzing glass at the scripture. "Diana, Mrs. Maxwell is trying to get your attention."

I was reaching around to remove Di's hat and mittens and looking up, I waved to Mrs. Maxwell. Plump as a red bird and of nervous temperament, she struck me as the sort of woman who'd spent so much of her life trying to please other people that she'd never bothered to form her own opinions.

"I dislike her," Mama said. "I don't trust her. She is ambitious."

Father Kearny rolled his eyes. "Everyone in New York is ambitious. Men and women must assert themselves or sink into oblivion. It isn't enough here—as it would be in Virginia, merely to be first family."

"Yes, but Mrs. Maxwell speaks of other people not being comme il faut as if she were quite certain she was."

"She simply doesn't know better," I said, tying Di's mitten strings to the frog of her cape. "She has a benevolent heart if not the clearest head."

Mama, unconvinced, leaned across me and tapped Father Kearny on the back of his hand with her gloved finger. "She is a climber. A vulgar climber."

Father Kearny blocked my view so I saw nothing but his bushy white side-whiskers and ruddy cheek. "Mrs. Bullitt, I beg you, please be civil to them. Hugh Maxwell is director of the New York Port Authority and as I earn my daily bread by way of a shipping company, I would be most obliged if you could summon a little Christian sentiment for Mrs. Maxwell."

My elders squabbled and so did my children. As the organ music intoned somberly, John leaned close to Di and blew an enormous spit bubble. It popped, splattering Di's cheek. Di primly wiped the spit from her cheek with her velvet sleeve, tucked her chin-length hair behind her ears, and slapped John across the face—a loud cracking noise that drew the attention of everyone in the front pew.

Johnny threw his head back, kicking and screaming, "Mama!"

I rose, shuffled around my mother and the children, gripping their hands tightly and giving them a shake whenever they so much as looked at one another.

Reverend Southard stepped up behind the pulpit and delivered the sermon with a muslin bandage around his head for his toothache.

When the service ended, a dark parade of men in beaver hats and women in horsehair crinolines shuffled down the aisle. We stepped out, the winds of heaven whirled around our ankles and blew our skirts side to side like bells. Father Kearny held my children by the hand. I was thanking the reverend for the sermon and taking Mama's elbow to help her down the steps when Mrs. Maxwell and Hugh Maxwell and their thirteen-year-old daughter greeted us.

Mrs. Maxwell, in a black velvet bonnet festooned with green silk roses, said, "Mrs. Kearny, I just wanted to thank you for the church."

"For the church?" Mama echoed.

I gave Mama's elbow a hard squeeze. "Mrs. Maxwell, forgive me, but I don't quite understand."

"Hugh is a trustee and he tells me that you and Captain Kearny donated the land for Calvary, and those magnificent engraved gold chalices for the altar and—"

"You are too kind, Mrs. Maxwell." And I meant it, because we hadn't *donated* the land, but had sold it at fair market value to the trustees. "Who is this lovely child?"

The girl had been hiding shyly behind her mother, but now she peered around at me, and Mrs. Maxwell pulled her out from her hiding place and said, "This is my daughter, Agnes Maxwell."

Agnes, in gray scarf with long red hair tumbling down her back, blushed deeply and bobbed a curtsy. The girl had her mother's wide, thin mouth and square, blocky chin, deep-set gray eyes, and a complexion so pale, she looked as if she had been fed her whole life on blush roses and milk.

On the walk home, Mama muttered, "Too bad about the Maxwell girl."

My son trailed behind Di, tugging at her cape. I called, "John, if you touch your sister one more time, I shall lock you in a dark closet."

"She touched me first."

"I did not." Di flounced off ahead of us.

"Both of you keep an arm's distance from one another. Don't think about each other, and don't even look at each other. Now, Mama, what can you mean about the Maxwell girl?"

"She has a face that reminds me of a wooden puppet, with that awful square chin," Mama said.

"Why are you picking on that poor child? I thought she was quite pretty."

Mama gripped her cape, put her head down, and charged into the brisk wind. Father Kearny, striding along with his hands to the brim of his hat said, "I asked Hugh Maxwell to call upon us. He wishes to pay his respects to Philip."

"You say it as if Philip were some sort of public monument," I said.

"Well, now that he's a hero, Philip is a public figure, isn't he?"

"Why, Father Kearny!" I smiled, sliding my hand around his elbow as we climbed the stairs, "Can it be that you are actually proud of your son?"

"Is that such a peculiar thing, Mrs. Kearny?"

"It's about time," Mama grumped at him.

I hurried up the stairs to check on Philip, and opening the door, found him standing naked in the center of his bedroom, staring at his reflection in the full-length cheval mirror. In his right hand, he held a yataghan, a short broad sword he'd brought home from North Africa, and strewn on the carpet all around him were his weapons: flintlock muskets, a dagger, his army-issued carbines, light swords and heavy sabers, and a hunting knife.

"Philip, what are you doing?"

He didn't answer me.

"Philip?"

Turning his wrist, he pointed the sword at the mirror. "Most people don't understand that if you are going to hit the torso, you have to turn the saber sideways or it won't penetrate the ribs."

I lifted my bonnet from my head and placed it on his nightstand. "I didn't know that."

"A trooper can easily dislocate a shoulder during a cavalry charge if he isn't careful."

I grew tense as he regarded my reflection and then his own in the mirror. Carelessly tossing the sword aside, he padded by me to the door and locked it. Walking over to an ornate little chest filled with tiny drawers, he opened one of them and removed a paper with some sort of powder. I was astonished when, despite his illness, he swiftly caught my hand and whispered, "Don't make noise. I don't want them to hear you . . ."

There was something terribly wrong with him beyond his obvious wounds; something troubled his mind and he had a look, all keen, glazed, and precarious, as if anything might prompt him to violence. And in that instant, as he pushed me back on the bed with an icy expression, his eyes empty as if he did not see me at all, I realized that if I did not do as he said, he would think me his enemy. If I were Philip's enemy, he would retaliate against me, he would hurt me, or in his deranged state of mind, perhaps even kill me. With one arm, he could not manage alone, but he terrified me by pressing his hand hard upon my chest just below my throat as he whispered instructions to me, "Lift your skirts, no, no, I want you on your stomach." With my face buried in the pillows, I could hear him breathing behind me as he slid his arm under my hips, demanding gratification as his due. I clutched the pillows, I tried to numb myself, tried not to think what I knew to be the truth—that this was his way of showing his victory over me, and his sense of superiority by asserting violently all of his outrage in the wrongs he believed he had suffered in Mexico. As he shuddered, he pressed his mouth to my ear and whispered, "You satisfy all of my hungers, don't you?" And rolling off me, he tumbled back, tucking a pillow under his amputated limb. Without so much as a glance my way, he fell into a deep sleep.

Trembling uncontrollably, I climbed off the bed, arranged my clothing, and peering into the mirror, tried to fix my hair. Wanting to be out of that room, I descended the stairs shakily, holding tight to the banister, trying to steady my nerves, confused and horrified about what had just transpired.

A burst of light and noise and merry voices surged up the staircase from the public rooms where I had decorated the parlors for Christmas. But I went through the motions of entertaining my guests as if I had only just awakened from a nightmare—as if moving through the cottony fog of my own nightmare, I conversed with my relatives but did not hear their replies, served tea, but could not taste it when I brought the cup to my lips, embraced my children when they crawled into my lap, but my daughter Di stared at my red-rimmed eyes and pale face and clasped my cheeks in her hands and asked, "What's wrong, Mama?"

Garlands of greenery twined around the banisters, holly and mistletoe swagged over the mantels, and bayberry candles burned on the tables. The children danced and ran wildly up and down the halls every time the front bell rang and another guest was announced. I had invited all of the Kearnys for a family Christmas dinner but as they began arriving, I could not stop thinking about what happened in the bedroom. Though my family chattered happily, I did not speak a word. Mama ushered Philip's relatives into the music room, where Philip's Uncle Archibald and some of his elderly aunts gathered around the piano singing Christmas carols while the servants brought in cocoa and toddies.

Thereafter, I slept in my own bedroom with the door locked, but if Philip suffered some remorse, indeed, if he had memory at all of what he'd done, he gave no sign of it. The next morning, he woke and greeted me brightly as if nothing had happened, didn't seem to notice that I winced and shied away from his kiss. Over the next few days, Philip seemed to improve and he developed a routine. He'd have breakfast with me and then he'd rest, rising around noon, he'd read his correspondence as I wrote replies to letters for him.

But every afternoon, he insisted I join him in the bedroom, and even though I did not wish to, I quickly learned that obliging him was the only way to keep the peace. One day, I tried to refuse him. Philip responded by smashing a gas lamp, and reaching onto his desk, threw a heavy marble ashtray at my head and mercifully missed. Mama and the children hid in the nursery; the servants cowed and ducked away under the staircase. His rage did not subside all that night, and so, the next day, I did as he asked.

On Christmas Eve, Philip dictated a letter of thanks to General Winfield Scott for having been brevetted major for his bravery on the Via San Antonio. But the next letter from the Secretary of War agitated him extremely. As I sat at the writing desk, Philip opened a small rosewood box, put two black peas of hashish into a pipe and lighting it, began cursing so loudly that I leapt up and shut the library doors.

"I don't want the children to hear such language."

Philip, in a fury, kicked the ottoman and stormed around the room. "How dare they deny me my brevet rank on the grounds of recklessness?"

"They will not deny your brevet, Philip, I know they won't."

He waved the letter at me. "The Secretary of War says I endangered my company by failing to retreat! By failing to retreat when the recall was sounded!"

As I tried to coax Philip into a better mood, the doors opened and there was my son John, bleeding from the knees and palms, wailing at the top of his lungs that Di had pushed him down while the two of them were stealing sugar out of the sugar box in the basement kitchen.

Philip gritted his teeth and glared at me. "Can't you shut him up?"

Blood trickled down John's shins into his sagging socks. I bent and picked him up. The slingshot Father Kearny had carved for him tumbled out of his skirt pocket and I tossed it onto the seat of the armchair. "I shall be back shortly, Philip, and I'll help you to finish your correspondence," I said, rushing out of the room.

But Philip did not answer me. Looking up from his letter, he seemed to contemplate our boy's slingshot with great interest. I gave the matter no further thought until late in the evening.

That night, after the house was dark, realizing that I had run out of cigarettes, I thought to pilfer a few from Philip's humidor in the library. Tying my wrapper around my waist, I darted out of my bedroom with a lit candle in my hand. As I came into the darkened main hall I saw light coming from the library. Nearing the room, the double doors slightly parted, I reached for the knob. Peering between the doors, I saw Philip, apparently asleep, his head against the back of the old wing chair. A fire burned in the fireplace and the gaslights had been turned down to their lowest setting until only a dull bronze glow filled the room. Intending to extinguish the lights, I set the candle down on a table in the hall and silently entered. Turning the key on the sconce nearest the door, I heard a muffled noise and then Philip's head moved slightly and he groaned.

I smelled hashish smoke, tarry and dense. A pipe smoldered on the little table beside the wing chair. I came closer and saw one of the chambermaids naked to the waist, her pale shoulders and back starkly pale in the light, still wearing her white cap, her cheeks hollowing and her head moving up and down over my husband's lap. Philip's eyes were shut, his hand on the back of the chambermaid's head.

The maid saw me from the corner of her eye and jumped up, struggled into her clothes. "Mrs. Kearny! I didn't want . . . I didn't . . . he told me what to do," she bawled, thrusting her arms into her blouse.

"Get out of here," I said.

"Yes, go," Philip slurred.

I tried to think, tried to tell myself he was sick and not in his right mind, and that this was unlike him. And yet, buffeted by alternating currents of rage and despair, I wanted to kill him. He reached for the pipe on the table. "I have been smoking hashish. Took a little cocaine and sniffing chloroform the surgeon gave me."

"Is that all? May I bring you a drink? Yes, why not have a little bourbon as well?"

"It isn't you. Isn't you, Diana. Don't blame yourself."

"How could you do that? In our own house? How could you?"

"Doesn't matter who it is," he muttered. "Any woman. Ugly. Fat. Stupid. Helps me not to think for a few minutes is all. But I do wish you would have let her finish me off."

"I'll finish you off." I reached for the fireplace poker and I jabbed the sharp end to his chest.

Numbed by the drugs, his lids heavy, he slowly raised his head. "You'd need to push harder. So, you see, you don't hate me as much as you ought."

I stood there holding the iron, feeling miserably old and bitter, duped into loving a man who cared so little for me and our family that he'd seduce a housemaid right under our own roof and not even bother closing the door when he did it.

He drew upon the pipe and then dropped it carelessly on the table.

"I should have told you long ago. I should have explained what happened to me in Mexico . . ." he began, his voice thick with smoke.

"I don't give a goddamn about Mexico, Philip. Because of Mexico, you seem to have formed the idea that you can do whatever you please, with no regard for other people or the consequences of your actions." I hurled the fire iron across the room hitting his desk before it thudded onto the carpet.

"I don't wish to be insulted. You are behaving in an insulting manner, cutting me short," Philip said.

He stood and leaned against the fireplace mantel, his forehead against his arm and his voice sullen and gruff. "I've tried to tell you that I'm a different man."

"Even you don't believe yourself anymore."

"You had to bring that slingshot into the room, didn't you?"

"Johnny's slingshot?"

He came around the chair, shuffling like an old man. I stood by the door with my hand on the knob, and I didn't want to hear his confession.

"I couldn't see. There was so much smoke and dust in the air. I couldn't see. This boy, I think he was eight or nine, in torn pants and barefoot and a shred of a shirt was running away from me."

"Philip, I don't wish to hear it."

"I cut right into him between the ribs. I don't think he weighed sixty pounds. He was so small. He shouldn't have been on that road. A little boy like that."

I opened the doors and ran out into the hall. But he pursued me, gripped my robe as I climbed the stairs, catching me on the middle step.

"The boy had a slingshot in his back pocket and it fell out when my saber cut between his ribs. I had to kick him off the blade. He didn't die, he was calling for his mama and the slingshot fell in the road right under my horse's front hooves."

"You are sick, Philip. You're not well, you don't know what you're saying."

"No, I am confessing to you, don't you see?"

"No."

"Long as I live there won't be any mercy for me. Nor any peace either."

"Listen to me—calm yourself and listen—"

"You're the only one who understands me, we are so much alike, you have to help me."

"I want to help you, I have tried, but I don't know what it is that you need from me. What is it that you need? What, Philip?"

He closed his eyes, released me, and leaned the back of his head against the wall.

Mama, on the landing in her nightdress and wrapper, called down to us, "Why do you fight so?"

But I stumbled past her, ran down the hall to the nursery, and once inside, bolted the door, too ashamed to let my mother know what I had seen and heard.

When she knocked and called to me through the door, I would not admit her.

The next morning, I woke in Di's bed to find my two older children sitting on both sides of me, playing with my hair, poking their fingers in my ears and in my nose and chattering to one another.

My daughter said, "Let's make Mommy pretty. Let's paint her face with my paints. We'll paint her lips blue and her cheeks green."

John curled back his lips and pointed to his mouth. "Her teefs. Paint her teefs."

They were opening the lids on little pots of paint as Nannie the baby stood in her crib babbling at us. John stuck the paintbrush handle in his mouth and watched me curiously.

Mama knocked on the door and my daughter unbolted it. Dressed in a rich London smoke silk morning gown, a crisp net house cap over her silvering hair, Mama bustled into the room, going around opening the curtains with a rustle of her taffeta petticoats and the heels of her slippers clicking on the wood floor.

"John, put those paints away. What are you thinking, child?"

"Aw," John whined.

"Now, daughter, are you going to tell me what that terrible row was about last night?"

I rolled onto my side, gripping a pillow against my abdomen and drawing my knees up. "Mama, will you tell Mrs. Neatly to fire the older parlormaid? Violet is her name. Tell her to find a new one."

Mama glanced at the children and sat opposite me on Johnny's bed. "So that is the reason the two of you were arguing last night? Not one of the maids?" She tapped her fingers on her lips and said, "It infuriates me when a man is too lazy to get himself to a brothel."

"Mama!"

"I mean what I say. There are ten thousand daughters of joy in New York City, three brothels on every block, and Philip has trifled with a chambermaid in your house. That is outright lazy if you ask me. Not to mention disrespectful to you. By the by, he at least had the decency to leave. He's gone. Philip left before dawn this morning."

"But it's Christmas morning!" I kicked out my legs and covered my face with my arms. "Where did he go?"

"Perhaps to his club, to the Union Club." She lifted a shoulder. "I don't know."

My mouth felt cottony and my head ached, my stomach felt like a nutmeg grater had roughed it. I rolled onto my stomach and buried my face in the sheet. The linens smelled like my baby girl. I screamed into the mattress and threw a temper tantrum, flailing and letting out all of my anger and frustration.

"What's wrong, Mommy?" Di asked.

Mama picked my daughter up and held her in her lap, stroking her hair. John squatted in front of a tower of wooden blocks he'd built, contemplating his own genius. "Enough of this shilly-shallying, children, you must dress in your Sunday best for the church processional. We don't want to be late," Mama said.

Seventeen

ON WEDNESDAY, January 17, 1848, snow fell brightly out of a slate sky in a blinding swirl of pinfeathers. The weather had snapped so cold that the Hudson froze and snow curved in soft banks over the footways, frosting the ailanthus trees. Cornices of snow hung from the roof of our house threatening to fall upon the wood boys trudging through the snowdrifts, carrying saws over their shoulders, hollering into the wind, "Cut your wood to fit your fireplace! Cut your wood and split it, too!" Our coal boy bantered with them as he shoveled the footway and the stone porch, scraping the blade against the stone stoop.

Black smoke billowed from the chimney pots for though we stoked the coal fires and both furnaces, the temperature in the house was only thirty-eight degrees. I dressed warmly in a dark red velvet gown, pinned a veil to the crown of my head and donned half mittens to keep my hands warm as I went about my work. Now and again, I smoothed my hands over a waist thickened from bearing four children in seven years, but my domed skirt was so full and flounced that the black velvet belt at the bodice still appeared narrow by comparison.

I sat at my desk, penning a letter to Anne Lane, breathing frosty clouds above the page as our winter circle gathered before the fire. Mama taught Di her letters and John lay on his belly eyeing a battlefield array of lead soldiers, knocking them over with a flick of his thumb and forefinger.

I had not seen Philip in three weeks. On Christmas Day, he'd sent me a note saying he would not be coming home for a while; but since then, I'd heard nothing and did not know if he was dead or alive. Sometimes I wished he were dead so that I could get on with my life. Other times, I became anxious about him, wanted him to come home so badly I made myself sick. Having had a great deal of time to think about Philip's transgressions, I'd concluded that he truly believed his injuries in Mexico had given him some sort of divine—or wicked—right to indulge all of his irrational passions, and that the moral rules of our world no longer applied to him. I sensed that he was fighting not just his lustful impulses, but the repugnance he sometimes inspired in women who were visibly shocked by the sight of his amputated limb. Doubtless, Philip felt he had to prove that being an amputee did not make him less of a man, but more. He took pride in the lunacy that he was somehow cursed, haunted by gods or demons, I knew not what, but it wasn't enough for him to be a war hero, charging forth where other men quailed, nor was his aristocratic birthright sufficient. Philip took whatever pleased him, when it pleased him. And he expected *me* to save him from his excesses.

I crumpled the letter I was writing to Anne, a fearful tissue of complaints about my thoughts of perhaps separating from Philip. I had even gone so far as to look up divorce lawyers in the city directory, but divorce meant social exclusion—and no one in our circle ever divorced. The mere idea frightened me.

I remembered the Van Syckel divorce pamphlet from so many years ago and now I was certain my husband had ruined that poor woman, but that Father Kearny had bribed her lawyer to keep the fact away from the newspapers. I did not wish to have my domestic miseries printed in a booklet and sold at newsstands all over the city, or to have my marriage be the object of speculation by thousands of strangers. Divorces in New York City were rare and squalid. As the only ground for divorce in New York was adultery, the scandal and public humiliation would have been too great to bear. I'd have to testify before a crowded courtroom about Philip's indiscretions. I'd be sketched and every word reported and read eagerly by scandalmongers. And so I was thinking of a quiet, discreet solution—perhaps a separation from bed and board, wherein Philip would support the children and me even though we lived apart.

I raised my head, put my pen down, and listened, for I thought I heard a disturbance in the back courtyard, and the gate bell ringing as the stable boys greeted someone. But then, the clock chimed four and Mama took the slate, the chalk, and the chapbook away from little Di and pulling the bell, summoned Mrs. Neatly to look after the children. After they'd gone, Mama sat on the arm of the sofa and folding her hands in her lap said, "Diana, I have had a letter from your sister in St. Louis. I am going to visit her awhile."

I put the pen down and looked up in alarm. "Mary is in trouble?"

"She is forty-four years old this year and she is widowed and alone."

"Don't leave me, Mama. I don't know what I shall do without you. For all I know, Philip has abandoned me."

"Philip has not abandoned you. But he is terribly sick, I fear." Mama clutched her quizzing glass in her hand and turned it over and thought. Finally, she said, "I remember the men coming home from the second war against Britain in 1812, and hearing tales from their wives that they suffered similarly. Until your husband recovers his senses, you could come with me. You and the children could take a house in St. Louis and start a new life."

"St. Louis?" I dipped the pen in the inkwell and drew spirals on a blank piece of paper as I considered Mama's proposition. Anne lived in St. Louis, as did my sister, and my extended family lived not so far away in Kentucky.

"St. Louis is the third largest city in the country. Why not come with me?" Mama came up beside me and put her hand between my shoulder bones.

"The more I think about what you say, the more I like the idea."

"You will let me know by tomorrow morning, then?"

"Yes, Mama, of course I will."

Left alone in the library, I gave up writing a letter, and sealed the lid on the ink bottle. I shuffled and stacked the writing paper, thinking about Mama's suggestion.

I heard her saying hello to Philip in the hall, letting him know I was in the parlor, but by her tone, it was clear she resented his presence. I quickly checked my reflection in the mirror over the mantel and fought the prickling apprehension sharp as thorns all over my skin.

Hurrying back to the desk, I pretended to be engrossed in my correspondence as Philip silently entered the room and closed the doors behind him. Snow lay thickly on his black coat, he brushed it off his shoulders and his hat; his cheeks and the end of his nose shone red from cold. I stuck the pen in the rest and closing the paper box asked quietly, "Why have you been away for so long?"

I asked the question even though Philip would never explain or apologize. It was my duty to tolerate his absences and infidelities, to listen to his unstoppable reminiscences. I felt no greater suffering than my own doubts when I desperately wanted to believe in him and in both of us.

"I've been staying at the Union Club." He reached for me, pulled me against him, pressed his mouth to my hair, and then kissed my forehead. I could feel the cold on his coat, the smoke and smells of the city in the wool, and I pushed him away, wiping a streak of melted snow from my cheek.

He reached into his coat pocket and removed a robin's egg blue box. But I refused it and went over to the window, gazing out at the snowscape, thinking how I despised his glittering bribes. I couldn't bear the sight of those damned blue boxes. They were such a cheap consolation prize from a rich man who thought he could make everything right with an expensive bit of metal and stone. I always tossed the gift boxes unopened into one of my trunks, saving them for a rainy day when I'd have to sell trinkets and baubles to support myself.

When I didn't react in the way he'd hoped, he put the box on my writing desk and grunted. "Well, then," he said, stroking the back of his head and raising his eyebrows. And sitting, he crossed his legs, unbuttoned his coat, and stretched his arm over the back of the sofa.

I said in a measured tone, "I am going to St. Louis with the children. My mother and sister need me."

He tipped his head back slightly and looked down his nose at me. "No, I forbid it."

Turning my back to him, I put my hands to the doors but he called sharply, "Diana, where do you think you're going?"

"To help my mother pack her things."

"We have servants for that. Come here."

I opened the doors and hurried out into the hall.

"Diana!" he shouted.

I rushed up the stairs.

"Diana, stop!"

I leaned over the banister. "I do not wish to speak to you."

His eyes brimmed with warmth and he gazed up admiringly, his mouth open and tremulous as if he were contemplating a smile. He was playing with me and I despised him for it. I hadn't seen him for three weeks, and he was merry as a grig, bringing gifts as if nothing had happened.

"Go upstairs and dress or we'll be late," he said.

"Late?"

"Teresa Truffi is singing *Lucrezia Borgia* tonight at the Astor Place Opera House."

"I am not going with you. I need to pack my things because I am leaving tomorrow morning."

But he was enjoying this little game and he darted up after me. "Your face is all rosy, Diana, which is the surest sign you wish to hold forth with me. So go on, I'll be a gentleman." And with a glance over his shoulder looking around for servants, he put his hand on my hip. "Give me a good tongue lashing."

After everything else, it was too much; seducing the chambermaid, an absence without so much as a word of explanation, and now an innuendo. My anger took on unholy dimensions, "I am not going to the opera. I am not going anywhere with you."

"You'll go and you'll enjoy it. And if you are civil, I shall let you go to St. Louis."

I put my hands on the banister and took his measure. Philip smiled, "Come with me this evening and tomorrow, I'll buy passage for you and your mother."

Thinking to appease him, I went to my room and dressed.

At the appointed hour, we huddled under blankets and pelts piled deep in the sleigh and off we went, down Fourth Avenue to the Astor Place Opera House. I sat low so only my nose was visible, listening to the thin sound of harness bells. The forward motion of the sleigh blurred the snowfall. Taking my hand in his under the blankets, he said, "Gold has been discovered in California. I am thinking of investing in some claims there."

"So, when are you leaving for California?" I asked hopefully.

But he grinned and squeezed my hand. "I wouldn't think of leaving you again."

I tried to hide my disappointment, and yet, I felt as though I were dancing atop a powder magazine. Tomorrow, I would be free of him, no more nights spent wondering whether he was betraying me or endangering his own life. How I envied the happy couples in the sleighs we

passed with their jags of laughter and spatters of talk, but it was so cold
that voices sounded glazed in ice.

We arrived at the opera house, a Greek temple at the convergence of
the Bowery and Fourth with Lafayette and Eighth Streets. Once
inside, we entered a necropolis of diamond-bedecked dowagers and
ruddy old tycoons in white waistcoats. Despite the weather, two thousand people had turned out in tailcoats, white kid gloves, and satin ball
gowns to hear *Lucrezia Borgia* and to sit on the purple velvet sofas in
their boxes and peer through their glasses at one another. Through the
lobby, up the stairs and past the retiring rooms, we paused to greet
friends and acquaintances, and then Mrs. Maxwell, in an extravagantly
fringed and flounced blue gown, caught my eye. She moved deter-
minedly through the crowd, with her husband, Hugh Maxwell in tow.

"Mrs. Kearny!" she exclaimed.

But Philip had spied someone he knew. A look of joyous astonishment crossed his face and he said, "Diana, one of my closest friends
from Mexico is here and I'd like you to meet him. Don't go drifting off,
I'll bring him around to you." And then Philip disappeared from my
side.

"Mrs. Kearny, how good to see you!" Mrs. Maxwell bubbled.

Hugh Maxwell looked put out at having been dragged across the
lobby.

"Mrs. Maxwell, good evening. Is Agnes with you?"

At the mention of his daughter, Hugh Maxwell made a rubbery
noise with his lips. "That frivolous slip. What a waste of petticoats."

Shocked by his mean-spiritedness, I protested, "That was certainly
not my impression of Agnes, Mr. Maxwell."

"You don't know her, do you? She is a delicate girl with a weak
heart. I wished for a third son, but there you are. I can't imagine anyone
wanting a plain little thing like her. She'll be a burden on me forever,
mark my words, the romantic little flibbertigibbet."

I said, "I should be delighted if I were blessed with a daughter like Agnes. She is a pure spirit. You must promise me that we shall see more of her. There is nothing better for a delicate heart than long walks on mild days. You and Agnes must call upon me, Mrs. Maxwell."

Hugh Maxwell stared around impatiently and fidgeted as Mrs. Maxwell and I finished our conversation.

The bells chimed and it was time to go in, and though Philip came searching for me, it seemed he had forgotten to introduce me to his friend from Mexico. Not that it mattered to me. Philip had never been to this particular opera house. Astor was still so new the walls were wet and thus the acoustics poor, but so fashionable a venue that no one attended the opera elsewhere in the winter of 1847. At his request, I explained the significance of the various balconies to him.

"Why is no one sitting under the chandelier?" he asked.

"There is a rumor that it might come loose and fall upon the spectators. Now there, across the way, that is the Dowager's Shelf, where it is rumored that the old ladies are wearing modesty scarves for fear gentlemen in the boxes above will try to peer down their décolletages," I whispered, and he leaned close to me so that I felt his mustache tickling my cheek. "And those are the Approachables, the girls who are ready to marry. Any fellow who wants an introduction must slay the old dragons in the back of the boxes."

"Ah, yes, yes, I see," he said, his lips skimming my bare shoulder, looking love into my eyes. The enormous gas-lit chandelier dimmed and the footlights came on.

"There is Fop's Terrace." I pointed with my closed fan. He nuzzled under my ear but I continued, "and that area crowded with old people is known as Apoplexy Row. Down on the parquet is the Bachelor's Pit."

In the fifty-cent seats, the young toughs stomped and thumped their walking sticks on the floor. When the curtain rose, Philip abandoned all pretense of watching the opera. Sliding closer to me on the sofa, he whispered, "I have missed you, Diana. You must understand that nothing has been decided. We can do anything we please, you and I, as if we only just met."

I moved forward on the sofa, peered through my glasses at the basso profundo on stage, but I dared not reply to Philip. He had said these words to me before and betrayed me not long after. At the very moment I thought it was safe to entrust my heart to him, Philip inevitably uprooted it to see how it was growing.

He whispered pretty compliments in my ear throughout the first act. Despite all, I felt cautiously lustful. He was so attentive that I enjoyed a light fever of anxious pride and I felt that finally, perhaps he might be his old self again, and wishing it were true, I felt my hopes soaring.

We left before the second act, our sleepy driver hunched down in the collar of his coat as he whipped the horses to hurry us home.

It seemed a time of quiet rejoicing, so I held my husband close while his breath tickled the ringlets over my ear, and around us the snow softened, flattened upon itself, and took on the chimney smoke. The next morning, I woke in his bed to the sounds of the butcher's cart, the milkman, and the penny dainty men braving the snow. Gathering a blanket around me while he slept, I parted the curtains and looked out into the gray morning light. Twenty-second Street was a mud canal and all the pristine snowy beauty of the previous evening had vanished.

Eighteen

THE VERY NEXT DAY, Philip's father fell ill and appeared on our doorstep suffering a bad case of the yellows. Plagued by a series of debilitating symptoms, his illness made it impossible for him to live alone and as we were uncertain of his malady I insisted he come and live with us. Having reconciled with Philip and being preoccupied with nursing Father Kearny through the last year of his life, my plans for escaping to St. Louis were postponed and then ultimately forgotten.

His illness played ugly tricks upon the old man. He thought he was living at the Astor Place Hotel. Philip arrived home in the evening at five o'clock after a day of recruiting duty and long hours spent trying to persuade young men to devote themselves to a military career and there'd be Father Kearny in his chair, surrounded by those enormous three-foot-long and three-foot-wide newspapers that were so popular with readers in the late 1840s. Glancing up from his reading and upon seeing Philip, the invalid would shout, "Bellhop! Stop your loafing and take my trunks up to my room. Here is a shilling for you."

"I'm no goddamned bellhop," Philip said, throwing his cape at the butler.

"Bellhop! I am paying four dollars a day for this hotel and I expect decent service. Harrumph."

A month later, finding myself once again pregnant, I told my husband and Philip reacted with tender regard for my condition. Overnight, Philip's wicked habits and vile appetites appeared to have vanished. I rejoiced in his company and my good fortune and tried to forget the past.

Our fourth daughter, Elizabeth Watts Kearny, came into this world on October 7, 1848, a night when the city of New York honored Philip's heroism in Mexico with a spectacular illumination. A military band serenaded us, playing marches under our window as I writhed with labor pains. On the street below, boys darted over the footways crushing chestnuts underfoot and brandishing sparklers. Brilliant clusters of candles burned in every plate-glass window on Broadway, candlelight wreathed our neighbor's houses on Twenty-second Street, and hurricane lamps glowed atop the roofs. Despite the chill, thousands of people strolled in front of our home, staring in wonderment at the beautiful shimmering pools and columns of light, pausing to shout up at my window as I struggled to bring our baby girl into the world. They cried, "Huzzah for Major Kearny! Huzzah for the Hero of Churubusco!"

In late March, on an unseasonably balmy spring night, I sat at Father Kearny's bedside with Elizabeth in my arms. Fixing his rheumy eyes upon me, he said, "Let me see that baby." Kearny, desiccated and sinewy, fingered the blanket away from the infant's pink face. He made a clucking noise with his tongue and sighed, "This one will amount to nothing. I sense too much religiosity in her nature."

The opium in his system had muddled his thinking, so I did not bother refuting his observation. I rose and stood at the window, rocking side to side, cradling Elizabeth in my arms. The gaslight had overheated the room, the air smelled heavily of burning fuel and melting candles. Philip, wearing a midnight blue silk vest, his right shirt sleeve rolled up and the left pinned neatly, sat directly across from his father, his legs crossed, drumming the fingers of his right hand upon the carved wooden chair arm. Even now, he played the scowling and unregenerate son.

Lowering myself onto the bed with the baby resting on my lap, I reached for the basin of water on the nightstand, wrung the cloth, and dabbed Father Kearny's brow.

Kearny began gasping for air. Turning his head aside, he said to Philip, "Stop your whining, son, and grow up and be a man else you shall lose everything."

"I haven't said a word yet you accuse me of whining!" Philip retorted.

"You shall have my entire fortune. What will become of you, I wonder?"

"Don't add to my woes by making me the second richest man in America, Father. I, above anyone, would have relished the challenge of making my own way, so don't go cursing me with your filthy millions. As if I needed your money in the first place."

"You hate my money, do you?"

"I don't need it. And I don't want it."

The old man croaked a dry laugh, "That is precisely why you shall have it."

Philip's heart was hard as Hudson brick. When his father died, I came down the stairs and found him in the library, reading.

As I broke the news, Philip reached for the floral arrangement on the table, took a rose from the vase, shredded the flower into his coffee, and then sipped. "I suppose we'll bury him at Trinity," he said, "and once we do, I won't give him another thought."

Father Kearny's body reposed in our dining room in a rosewood coffin filled with ice, surrounded by hothouse bouquets of white japonica. Two liveried footmen kept a round the clock vigil over his corpse. All of elderly New York filed through the dining room, leaving in their wake the odor of underarms, opium, and sarcophagus breath.

After the burial in Trinity Churchyard, Philip turned to me, touched the brim of his tall silk hat with the big black mourning band and the black crepe scarf fluttering long over his shoulders, and he said, "Thank God I never again have to look at his sour old phiz over the dinner table." This was a ruse, but I didn't grasp the full impact his father's death had upon him until much later. Slowly, invidiously, Philip's control over his self-destructive impulses began unraveling. At first, I hadn't realized just how fragile he was because he didn't have any more of his "episodes." No, this was different. Indeed, he kept busy with recruiting duty in the poor and working-class neighborhoods in Lower Manhattan, and he came home promptly every evening.

In some ways, our married life was far more normal than it had ever been and Philip didn't speak of Mexico at all. And then Philip lost interest in loving me. Perhaps he felt ashamed of the frightening memories he had when we were intimate, perhaps when he pulled me close, my husband could not put aside memories of his sins in Mexico. After his father's death, Philip kept me at a distance. One evening, after the children and the servants were asleep, I knocked discreetly on his bedroom door. "Philip? Are you asleep?"

Philip opened the door, but stood on the threshold in the dark.

"May I come in?" I asked.

After a long silence that made me feel self-conscious, he said quietly, "I'd rather you didn't." Without another word, he closed the door, leaving me alone in the hallway. And he never welcomed me into his bed again that year.

In the spring of 1849, the cholera arrived with the immigrant ships. The Irish immigrants had been sick with it and the ships were quarantined in the harbor, but the cholera spread onto the island, nonetheless. Hundreds had taken sick in the Five Points. The unburied dead lay on the footways of Mulberry Street and doctors projected that tens of thousands would die in New York City before the epidemic subsided. A panicked exodus of people in wagons, carriages, and on horseback clogged the streets and the ferries were filled to capacity. All over the island, the footways and streets were nearly impassable; fathers packed their families while butlers and footmen armed with pitchforks or sometimes nothing more than scowling looks chased off the scavengers and thieves who tried to steal a valuable or two from the heaping wagon carts.

Philip and I were caught up in the frantic desire to get our four children out of the city before any of us fell ill. I sped around the house directing the servants and packing trunks while he sternly instructed the grooms and drivers about the proper care of the horses during the long overland journey to Virginia. Outside my window, I could hear neighbors shouting at their maids as they filled carts with furniture and baggage.

The weather was overcast and sultry; a drizzling rain fell and laid the dust.

Philip had not gone to the army recruiting office in the first week of May. Since his father's death he had expressed a need for intense, prolonged periods of peace and quiet and I kept the children out of his way, doing my best not to provoke him.

On the fifth of May as I flurried down the hall, I paused and found Philip in the library. He sat in the wing chair, brooding over ledgers containing an accounting of his father's estate.

"Philip?"

Glancing up, he said, "I want you and the children to leave immediately without me. Go to White Sulphur Springs and don't return until this plague lifts. We can't expose the babies to the cholera."

"We can't expose *you* to the cholera! I won't leave without you."

"I have responsibilities here and I have a recruiting quota to meet this month. And then there is the matter of my father's estate . . . so much real property that must be sold and so many expenses."

Crossing the room, I stood beside his chair and looking down at him, asked, "Philip, why not join us in the Virginia mountains? You know how much you love the woods there and the horse races and the hunting and the parties? All of your friends from Mexico are going. John Magruder will be there and the Lees and Dick Ewell, too. Why not come? You will regain your strength and you always sleep so well at White Sulphur."

"I can't ask for a furlough now. Not when the War Department regards me as an invalid. I have to prove that I am well enough for active duty."

But you're not well enough, I thought. *You haven't been well in nearly two years.* Just when we thought he had recovered his vigor, he'd be incapacitated by the grippe or the ague. He had a persistent rasping cough. In his weakened state, he would be susceptible to the cholera and I felt a rising sense of panic and foreboding the more I thought about our summer arrangements.

"I insist you come with me. I will not leave without you."

"If you insist, Mrs. Kearny—"

But the next day, he stood on the stoop, watching the children clamber into our two carriages with my ladies' maid, a nurse, and an undernurse. Looking wan and pale as he came down onto the footway, he instructed the drivers of the two carriages and the baggage wagon, walked around our little caravan inspecting the equipages and horses and then, trying to appear jaunty and vigorous, hopped up the step into my carriage and sat beside me on the seat.

He said, "I shall see you in mid-September, but do not risk your health by returning earlier. I shall write to you every day. You have money, and you know where to draw if you need more?"

"Yes." I looked at him and felt remorseful about the impending distance between us. "Come with me and let me look after you. You can relax on the piazza and feel the sun on your face and breathe the mountain air and you'll grow strong as you were before Mexico."

"No, I have work to do." Then, Philip clasped my chin in his hand and murmured, "Whatever you do, promise that you won't fall in love with any of those Southern boys in Virginia."

And as we drove away, I leaned from the window like a smitten schoolgirl, waving all the way down the street as he stayed on the curb-stone watching us go. Despite the excitement of the children, I could not shake my melancholy all the way to Virginia.

Upon arriving at White Sulphur Springs, I found Mama, my broth-ers and sisters, their spouses and children in the cabins at Paradise Row. Our cousins had penciled messages to one another upon the painted wooden columns of the piazzas. The row consisted of one-story brick cabins with a long shared piazza crowded with my julep-sipping, card-playing relatives, who, like the other Southern families here, came to heal in the spring waters. The resort was teaming with people, and the proprietor was forced to turn away hundreds every day.

Every morning at six-thirty, Anne Lane and I hurried out of our cabins with our maids following behind bearing large pitchers, blankets, and parasols. So happy to see one another, we chatted and giggled like girls, holding hands and whispering and sharing secrets about our joys and failures.

We'd walk over the graveled path to the Ladies' Spring, a domed pavilion surrounding a bathing pool that emitted the most noxious odors on account of the healing sulfur in the water. When we drank the spring water we held our noses and grimaced, but after a time, grew accus-tomed to the taste. Anything that bad had to be good for us, we rea-soned.

Huge black spiders lived in the springs. A bath keeper scooped the spiders out before we climbed in. After taking our baths, we'd walk arm-in-arm under the elm trees down to breakfast in the huge ballroom in the center of the resort.

After three months of near perfect bliss in those green woods, long walks on the dense laurel paths, and long talks with my family, I began to feel like myself again. And so many amusements to pass the time! Why, a traveling pair of lacquered red wagons appeared in mid-summer, charging us a penny a person to view the mysterious wonders on its wooden shelves. Anne and Mama, the children, and I moved slowly through the narrow and musty wagon, gaping in disbelief at the bold labels on the jars and their dubious treasures: A feather from the Archangel Gabriel's wing. A sliver of wood from the True Cross and there—glaring reproachfully at us through murky yellow chloroform—was St. Jerome's left eye.

My children flourished at White Sulphur, playing nine-pins and hide-and-seek in the woods with their numerous cousins. Di, five, got covered with mosquito bites; John, a wild four-year-old, had scabs all over his knees; and Nannie, now two, toddled after her older brother and sister everywhere they went. Elizabeth was ten months old and had just begun walking.

On a mild afternoon, on the twentieth of August 1849, I relaxed in the elm grove looking over some ribbon I'd purchased at the little store on the corner of Virginia Row. Anne Lane and I had decided to try to make laurel wreathes for the musicians who came by to serenade us every night.

We sat amid a pile of branches and ribbons, while in the gazebo behind us, young people gathered with guitars and flutes and were arguing over the sheet music. Anne wore a straw hat with a yellow band and a brim so wide that all I could see of her face was her nose and chin. I showed her the work I'd done so far. Using my knees to hold the laurel wreath, I tied the two ends together to make a circle and then covered the hemp twine with pale blue ribbon and held it up for her to see.

"Nicely done," Anne said, lifting her chin high to see out from under her huge hat.

I snapped off a wayward twig and frowned down at my project, poking stems of ambrosia and mignonette flowers into the laurel.

Behind us, a loud party of Carolinians on horseback returned from a successful deer hunt preceded by sixty baying hounds trotting in the advance, a man blowing upon a hunting horn, and colored servants driving a wagon carrying the carcass of a stag.

"Have you heard from Philip?" my old friend asked lightly, but I detected the worry in her voice.

We had been at White Sulphur for two months. I put the wreath on the grass and began a new one, selecting my first branch. "No, I have not had a letter since June and then he wrote that he'd seen cholera victims vomiting in public places, having seizures, and turning inky blue right before his eyes."

Anne plucked leaves from one of the twigs and said, "Miss Emily Mason, do you know her? She's staying in Spring Row. Well, Miss Mason says that there are five thousand dead in New York City and that the bodies are rotting in the streets."

Mama, sitting above us in a camp chair with a basket of sewing on her lap, leaned over. "Miss Emily Mason is my cousin and she told *me* the Board of Health is dumping the corpses on Randalls Island and letting the rats eat them because they can't hire gravediggers. No one will do it and can you blame them?"

Anne waved a branch in the air and said, "It is the Irish. They brought the cholera to New York. First thing New York must do is sweep out the Irish and all of those feral pigs living in the cellars and garrets."

I squared my shoulders, "My servants are Irish, my husband's ancestry is partly Irish, and I will thank you not to disparage those poor unfortunate people."

But Mama said, "Cholera is God's retribution for sin against New York generally and the Irish particularly. Only sinners die of cholera."

"Mama, that is superstitious nonsense. Plenty of respectable people have died of the cholera, too."

"For once, I agree with your mama," Anne said.

"Di! You, John. Anne De Lancey! You children put on your hats!" I called and then turning to Anne, said, "My children were all born poets and geniuses until they ran around without hats and their brains dried up in the sun."

The children stopped a moment and stared at me, and then shot off squealing down the hill with their hands above their heads.

A cake man slowly crossed the elm grove carrying a big wooden tray suspended by leather straps over his shoulders. His voice resounded over the green. "Warm pound cake! Apple fritters. Maple sugar taffy. Sweet biscuits, three fo' a penny." Upon spying him, my excited children came flying back up the hill and jumped around me, begging for pennies.

Anne puffed air over her bottom lip, then removed her hat and fanned herself with it. After the children had shrieked away with their pennies to besiege the cake man, she said, "You really must come to the dancing party tonight. You haven't been to any of the cotillions so far and quite a few of your gentlemen friends have inquired after you."

"I am an aged married lady, too far gone for dancing." I brushed bits of leaves and wood from my skirt and looked at the children, gravely selecting their treats from the cake man as if their lives depended on it. I tucked a bit of ambrosia behind my ear.

"Nonsense, you're only thirty years old!" Anne swatted me with her big hat and then tugged it onto her head.

I picked up a twig and twirled it between my fingers, feeling myself sinking into a gloomy mood. "Besides, it is nearing the second anniversary of the day Philip lost his arm. I cannot be dancing while he is all alone back in New York in that empty house with nothing to think of but that terrible day. Anniversary days are very difficult for him."

"Philip Kearny is quite capable of taking care of himself," Anne said.

"You'd be surprised."

"Nothing he does would surprise me."

"I won't hear him disparaged, Anne. I'll thank you to stop criticizing my husband."

"Never you worry, Mrs. Kearny, I shan't say another word about him."

"Fine."

"Good."

"All right then."

Now that very same evening, as my family danced the Virginia reel in the grand ballroom, I left my children in the care of their nurses and wrote a note to Mama and Anne, explaining that I was slipping back into New York City for a few days to look in on Philip, but that I would return to White Sulphur in a week. I would not expose my children to the cholera until I knew that the epidemic had subsided.

Three days later, on Friday, August 24, 1849, at twilight, I arrived in New York where a thick low cloud of tarry smoke snaked over the paving stones. Wagons loaded high with coffins and driven by elderly black men in low slouch hats crowded the streets. The city was draped in black bunting. Hearses plodded slowly to the cemeteries. A foul and sweet odor of decaying bodies penetrated the cabin of my carriage. Hordes of the gaunt and dusty poor crouched up against the counting-houses and darkened storefronts, staring with desolate resignation as we passed. A boy in short pants slumped against an ash barrel, legs relaxed, eyes open, his trousers stained with piss. He had wet himself as he lay dying.

Packs of starving stray dogs attacked our horses but the driver whipped at them, and then, I heard a pistol shot and the dogs yelped and dispersed.

On Fourth Avenue, a dead woman sprawled in the doorway of a music store. Her jaw hung slack and her hands were upturned as if she were waiting to receive the word. A young mother ambled past her wearing a chamois mask over her face with holes cut out for her nose and eyes, carrying a limp child with dark blue feet and hands sticking out of a winding sheet. Men pushing carts laden with stolen things wore handkerchiefs bank-robber style over their faces. Lean bristle back hogs trotted in the gutters and lorded down the footways. I couldn't bear to see any more and terrified, I lowered the curtain, praying that Philip was still alive.

By the time I arrived at home, it was nearly dark, but the lamplighter was nowhere to be seen. Twenty-second Street was silent and ghostly. Iron shutters had been tightly bolted over the windows of the houses on the south side.

The driver pulled up in front of my home and I felt a rising sense of panic. The large windows in the library were broken. The front door stood ajar. The cans had been knocked over and piles of ash, charred wood, and charcoal blew over the paving stones.

When I spoke, my voice echoed in the empty street. "I am afraid to go in."

The driver, a stocky young Irishman, said, "Don't you worry, Mrs. Kearny, I'll go in first." And taking his whip from the socket, he climbed down and preceded me into the house.

Removing a pistol from my skirt pocket—after the steamer incident I never traveled unarmed—I loaded the chamber, and then concealed it in my skirt band.

The driver pushed the door aside and peered around into the main hall. Newspapers blew across the floor. Empty lager bottles glittered at the foot of the steps and the house smelled like rotting garbage and cigar smoke and liquor. He and I peeked fearfully into the public rooms and I was relieved to see they were undisturbed. The library was undamaged except for the broken windows.

"Where have the servants gone?" I wondered and called up the staircase, "Philip? Philip! Are you here?"

The driver climbed the stairs and I followed, turning the keys on the

gas sconces and lighting the way as we went. As we neared my husband's room, I smelled hashish smoke. The driver pushed the door
open with the butt of his whip and we both squinted into the darkness.
I ran across the room, opening the heavy velvet curtains to find Philip
lying face down on his bed, shirtless and barefoot but wearing his
trousers.

The driver touched the whip handle to his temple. "Ma'am, I'm
going to look in the other rooms on this floor and the next one up."

"Thank you," I said, feeling Philip's damp face. "Philip. Philip,
wake up. I hope the seeds of fever are not in you!" But I could not rouse
him, and smelled the stale almond odor of laudanum. On the table, a
brown glass vial of laudanum stood empty. Lifting Philip's hand, I
inspected his fingernails for blueness—a sure symptom of the cholera,
but observed with great relief that his nails were healthy and pink.

The Irishman leaned out of my bedroom and called to me. "Mrs.
Kearny? You been robbed, ma'am."

In my bedroom, my jewelry chest had been overturned and all of the
Tiffany boxes Philip had given me were gone. Someone had ransacked
my wardrobe. Tissue paper, hosiery, and slippers were strewn all over
the floor. I peered into my anteroom and saw that any summer gowns I
had not taken to Virginia had vanished. Gripping the driver's forearm,
I said, "Our family doctor and Major Kearny's cousin, Dr. Robert
Watts lives on Washington Square. Will you bring him here? Will you
tell him that it is urgent?"

"Yes, ma'am!"

I tapped my fingers to my brow, thinking how I might revive Philip.
What was the cure for too much laudanum? Calomel? Magnesium
powder or a bath in oil of turpentine? Or maybe stimulants like coffee
and tea?

Unnerved by the robbery and desecration of my home, I could not
recall the answer and descending the back servants' stairs to the base-

ment kitchen for my medicine box, stepped around pudding bags suspended from tripods and pots and pans littering the brick floor. It looked as if a hurricane had blown through the kitchen. Cook and the maids were nowhere in sight.

Women's voices pierced the silence from the servants' dining parlor. I pushed aside the swinging door and for a few seconds, my eyes adjusted to the gloom. Sitting around the servants' table were three young prostitutes wearing my summer dresses.

Overwhelmed by mingled anxiety and outrage, I observed that my Tiffany jewelry was stacked on the table and that the prostitutes were untying the white ribbons, opening the boxes, then dividing the loot among themselves.

Upon seeing me, the whores seemed not in the least surprised. The brunette, with brown spots of decay on her front teeth and her arm laden with gold bracelets said, "Mrs. Lindabury send a second shift in, now did she? Ain't you prim? Look at her, girls. Ain't she prim and fine for a chippy? You ain't goin' to turn two bits dressed so prim."

The other women at the table laughed, and a blonde with ax-pick scars all over her cheeks grabbed at a sapphire necklace as it spilled off the jeweler's cotton onto the table. "Ooh, will you look at this? What sort of woman don't open these boxes, Althalia?"

"Who cares?" The smallest one, a mousy girl with lank hair, held her hands out to admire the rings on her fingers. "This will buy me rum for a year."

"For a year! For your life is more like!" the leader said. And taking another look at me, she sneered, "Go on then, he's upstairs and he ain't a bad sort. Smells good. Dead in the eyes is all."

"'At's the only part of him what's dead!" The blonde snorted and they all laughed again.

"And don't get all titivated up; there's still the silver cabinet and plenty of booty upstairs. The fellow upstairs is so far gone, he was tossin' all manner of things through the front windows this mornin'. Breaking windows and speaking in tongues, Spanish names of places or some such. Not that I care."

"Whad he toss through the front winders?" the blonde asked, holding an earring up to the table lamp and watching the diamonds sparkle.

The brunette whore grinned up at me, "Go on, lass. Have a look around and help yourself to whatever pleases ye. There's more where this came from."

A heavy silence fell as the whores exchanged sly smiles, waiting for me to leave and when I did not, the old brunette growled, "What are you looking at?"

Trying to control my shaking voice and shakier nerves, I removed the pistol from my skirts and pointed it at her. "You had better leave. That is my jewelry and you aren't taking it with you."

They exchanged glances and then cackled, but fell silent as they looked at my pistol, gauging whether I'd really shoot them.

"We ain't going. We was invited here!" the blonde protested. "And you cain't shoot all of us, now, can you?"

"No, and that is why I intend to shoot only you," I said to the brunette. "That ought to satisfy my womanly outrage, don't you think?"

They jumped up, knocking chairs over as they fled the basement and scurried up the stairs, but I followed them all the way out the door. They stumbled, cursing and half naked, down the stoop, bickering with one another, squabbling all the way down the street over the few pieces of jewelry they'd managed to steal as they made their escape.

I locked the door and exhaling in relief, slumped against it. Even in my agitated state of mind, I knew without a doubt that Philip had desecrated our home, had violated our house as well my trust and our marriage; he had brought those filthy whores here and had possibly exposed all of us to the cholera.

I knew what I had to do. I hurried up to the nursery and threw all of my children's clothes, books, and toys into one trunk, then pulled it into the hallway and secured the latch with a lock, pocketing the small key. Then, darting down the stairs to my bedroom, I dragged a chair to the fireplace mantel and standing upon it, carefully lifted the portrait of the *Bullitt Sisters as the Fates* down from its hanger in the crown molding and set the painting beside the trunk.

The driver returned within an hour with Dr. Robert Watts. The good doctor rode up on his own mount behind the carriage. Looking aghast, he met me in the hall. Watts was a tall and ruddy fellow with deep blue eyes and a kindly, scientific manner. He took my hand. "Diana, what has happened? Shall I summon the police?"

"No, please don't," I said, and then I looked around him and spoke to the driver. "There is a trunk and a painting on the third floor in the hall. I should like you to strap those items onto the carriage. My things from Virginia, I trust, are still tied to the back?"

"Yes, ma'am," the driver said.

"Are you too tired to begin the journey back to White Sulphur?" I asked the driver.

A dawning look came over him and he said, "No, ma'am. I'm not tired at all. Let me go around back, and tend to the horses and I'll be ready in a quarter hour."

"Thank you. And you will find my Labrador retriever in the stables. He answers to Greeley. Will you be so kind as to bring the dog around, too? Philip won't look after a dog."

Feeling the overwhelming weight of shock and sorrow at what I was about to do, I watched the driver go upstairs for the children's trunk and the painting. Robert Watts followed me into the library where I sat at the desk and dipping the pen into the inkwell, wrote my husband a one-line note. He moved his medical bag from his right hand to his left and observed me with consternation. I finished my letter, sealed it with a wax wafer, and handed it to him.

"Diana, please tell me what is wrong."

I took a deep breath. "Philip is upstairs in his room. I think he has taken laudanum, a little too much, but not enough to kill him. I suspect he did this because he is struggling to reconcile himself to the second anniversary of losing his arm. In the basement, in the servant's dining room, you will find a pile of my jewelry. Three prostitutes Philip hired and brought into our house had been dividing it up among themselves when I discovered them. I don't want it. I will not wear jewelry that Philip's whores have worn. Now, Robert, please give my note to my husband. Tell him that I shall contact him via correspondence to arrange for support of the children and myself."

I felt sorry for having involved Robert Watts in this. I felt sorry for myself, sorry for Philip, and sorry for my children. Watts looked about frantically as if searching for a solution to our problem.

"Diana, I know Philip has behaved outrageously but I urge you, for your sake, for the children's future—don't be hasty. I cannot put it strongly enough, Diana, you will be ruined. Your name will be the talk of the city and you will never be allowed to enter the very houses where you and Philip have been celebrated. Think before you go! You will be shunned. You will be the object of derision and pity by all who have known you."

"I don't know why, as I shall never divorce Philip. We have many mutual acquaintances who are separated and they are not shunned or ostracized." Seeing the portrait of Susan on Philip's desk, I snapped the case shut and slipped it into my reticule, then slid the silken cord over my wrist and headed for the door.

The doctor's eyes were wide as he followed me out onto the stoop and pleaded, "My dear woman, please consider what may befall you if you leave Major Kearny. It is sheer folly to think you might reconstruct your broken union if you leave. Stay, and try to reform him, why don't you?"

"Oh, Watts," I untied my bonnet, letting the strings fall over my shoulders.

"Diana, all of society will spurn you."

"Then spare me the desolating company of society. I am not so worried about what I shall become, I am mostly dismayed by who I have been."

The carriage pulled around and as I climbed into the carriage, Watts stood on the step and leaned through the window, still trying to reason with me. "If this becomes a scandal, if your circle in New York learns of this, Diana, you and Philip will both be excluded from polite society."

I looked down at my hands and nodded. "I will not divorce him, and so I don't understand your warning, Robert."

"For God's sake, what shall I tell Philip?"

"Explain by giving him my note," I said.

Watts squeezed my hand and said, "You may rely upon me, Diana. I shall help you to the extent I am able."

"I thank you for that," I said and rapped the ceiling with the point of my parasol. Greeley jumped into the carriage, ran to the opposite side, sat up on his hind legs, and poked his head through the curtain and out the window. I heard the box rattle, the iron horseshoes striking the cobbles as the driver cracked his whip and the horses pulled away. I was thinking of the words I had penned and wondering how Philip would react when he read them.

You do not love me, thus I leave you without regret.

Nineteen

I RETURNED TO White Sulphur Springs, so afraid of my own decision that while traveling at night, I lit a candle in the coach, held it in my hands, and did naught but stare at the flame. In the daylight hours, I knitted railroad stitch stockings for my children. When food was offered to me, I did not eat. I was filled with fearful apprehensions and greatly distressed over Philip, pitying him and missing him, wondering if I was just one more person who had betrayed and abandoned him. The shock of having run away made me feel like a guilty fugitive. After all, it was Eve's boldness that brought down mankind.

I returned to my family with my face grimed in coal soot, my fingernails ringed in dirt, bringing scandal and disgrace and a drooling Labrador retriever with me. Feeling torn and battered, I had not changed my clothes in days. Wearily, I climbed down from the coach, and when my whole family came out onto the piazza to greet me, I was too ashamed to look at them. Instantly, they knew something was wrong. Though my brothers called my name I stood with my back to them, refusing to answer, numbly staring at my trunks and valises lashed onto the coach.

The sugar maple boy, seeing a crowd gather and hoping to make a little money, came scrambling over with his basket of syrup and candies.

He smiled around at us, held his basket of candy at arm's length with one hand, and clasped his big straw hat atop his head with the other.

"Go away, boy. You are not wanted here," my brother Aleck said.

"Daughter? What news from the city?" Mama asked. "Does the cholera abate?"

Brother Aleck shouted at the servants to unstrap my trunks and carry them into the cabin, while my family gathered like God's jury, awaiting an explanation.

"Daughter, what have you done?" Mama asked in a frightened voice.

"I have," I began, raising my hands and then letting them fall. My bonnet was crooked on my head.

Aleck cleared his throat. Someone scuffed a boot on the piazza.

"I have left my husband's house," I said, finally. Reflexively, I hunched up my shoulders and squeezed my eyes shut, expecting Mama to pull out a switch and thrash me about the head and shoulders. You could hear the crickets chirping in the valley. "I can't submit anymore. I am lost, Mama. I am so lost, most days Philip makes me believe that I am not in my right mind."

My brother Aleck cleared his throat and called, "Well, all right then. Diana, why don't you come in and have some pie?"

But Mama came up behind me, her voice trembling with emotion. "Did he beat you? Did he hurt one of the children?"

"No," I admitted.

"Mama," my sister Mary said gently, "let her be. Can't you see she is tired and sick at heart?"

But Mama asked, "Is it his old affliction? The same trouble he suffered with the parlormaid?"

Nodding, I bent at the waist and began vomiting into dust sent whirling by a sharp westerly wind. I shall always be grateful to my sister Mary, for the strong and warm bracing of her hands upon my shoulders. Wiping my mouth, I muttered, "I am so tired of being a living sacrifice."

"Then do not hide your face. Ease your worries and look into Mama's eyes. You won't turn to salt. It might raise your spirits some," Mary said.

My brother Aleck spoke up. "Mama, would you go inside and instruct the servants as to our supper plans? Tell them to bring out the pie, why don't you?"

I blew my nose and then crumpled the handkerchief in my hand. Coming down the steps, my brother Aleck stroked his chin and made a face. "Is that all you brought with you, sister? Two trunks? That can't be all you have."

"I took nothing from Philip," I whispered.

"Why not?" Mary smoothed her hands on her bodice, and squinting down the road murmured, "You have always suffered from a want of appreciation for yourself, Sister, putting up with Philip's bad behavior and worse temper."

"Yes, Diana, why didn't you clean house? Why didn't you take all but the curtains? After eight years of marriage you are surely entitled to more than clothing," Aleck said as he opened the carriage door.

My dog bolted out onto the dirt road and ran over to an oak tree.

Why couldn't I be happy now that I was free? Philip had been an unfaithful husband, icy and remote not to mention callously neglectful of the children since returning from the Mexican War. Yet, I suppose you don't love a man a thousand times and give birth to his children and nurse him through his injuries without it leaving a scar upon you.

The cabin where I slept had a gray-painted floor and the brick walls had been whitewashed but were always cold and shiny with damp. In the quiet of my bedroom, I opened the drawer in the rickety beech nightstand and removed my small leather calendar book.

After we parted in August of 1849, after that incident with the three prostitutes, I had recorded the days Philip and I spent together. I needed to see the days in ink, written in my own hand. I pressed my fingertip to the times when Philip had been with me. Eight years had come and gone and yet, during the short season of our marriage, we had been together only four years. Four years broken into bits and scattered through the pages of my calendar book.

I glanced at an empty bowl of soup on the nightstand, reached for it, and turned it over. The rim of the bowl clinked onto the plate. And it came to me then; I hadn't been able to fulfill my husband's needs, and he had been unable to satisfy my love hunger, both of us trying to get something from an empty bowl.

St. Louis

Twenty

C AN A WORSE FATE befall a man than being abandoned in the most cowardly and ignominious fashion by the woman he loves? Diana committed a far more violent act than anything I had ever done on a battlefield by leaving me and taking our four small children. It is a violent thing to end a marriage, and more particularly a love affair, as I believed my marriage to have been. All of a sudden, with no reason, she had changed against me!

And her craven little note; salt in the wound, salt torture, because it was a lie compounding her betrayal, so then, we lived without love? What was she thinking? That she could somehow unlove me? That she could erase the years of devoted and tender passion? I would show her how wrong she had been.

Once I recovered my lost health, I locked up the house on Twenty-second Street and set off for St. Louis. After little more than a month's separation from Diana, I arrived by the first of October 1849, one of those golden apple-picking days on the prairie. It seemed my wife had taken a house on Lucas Place, a fashionable address in a garden spot. But to find Diana, I hadn't even needed to call there. Riding over the limestone pavestones, raising yellow dust like a pestilential cloud, I rounded a corner and there was a beautifully watered park, with streams and a pond and willow trees. As if sensing me watching her, she lifted her parasol slowly and looked at me. Diana wore a gown the color of bittersweet, the same color as the light in the autumn maple leaves, her bonnet far back on her black hair, her lovely face radiant.

I brought her to a bench, and sitting beside her, said most earnestly, "Dearest love, you must come home."

And as she took my hand, I saw that she was tortured with sorrow, uncertainty, and regret as she said in the sweetest voice imaginable, "Why, Philip, you have broken my heart so thoroughly I cannot share your home until I am certain your character is changed."

"There is no one I love more than you. How can you doubt me?"

Turning aside to glance at me, her eyes damp and embittered, she replied, "It is your unhappy lot to have thought of me as worthless when I lived with you. Now that you no longer have me, you suddenly find me irresistible?"

"You're my wife, damn you. I have the right to expect that you and my children will come home—"

"You say that as if I am some base animal in whom you have a right of property." She rose imperiously, closed her parasol, and clasping her hands over the cane handle, said, "God help me, I still love you, Philip. I suspect I always shall. But until you pledge that you will never betray me again, I cannot live with you."

I took her by the shoulders and said, "If you think I am going to allow you to live in a grand style separate from me, you are sorely mistaken. You have a duty to me. As my wife, you owe me your presence and your devotion. I have every right to claim you and to take you home and make you understand your responsibilities."

A nurse in a striped apron pushed a pram by us. Diana held her opinion and watched her go, then lifted her face to me. "Philip, what you say may be true as far the law sees things. But my heart understands a different story all together."

"The difficulty is entirely yours . . . you don't seem to—"

But she cut me short, walking off. "The difficulty is ours, Philip. It is ours."

Thereafter, I sought her out every day for two weeks but she was not at all straightforward and refused to hear the reason in my pleas. I applied myself assiduously to the delicate but hopeless task of winning Diana's heart. Yet whenever I met with her, she was remotely inaccessible. Time was running short.

Fearfully disappointed at having failed to win her over, I told her I had been ordered to Oregon to put down an insurrection of the Rogue River Indians. Diana wished me well and with my emotions in disarray, I kissed her good bye, promising her that I would send for her, telling her I would allow her time to think and to miss me and to realize her brutal error in thinking that the two of us would ever be happy apart.

And then, I went to Oregon. I was certain that true to our habits and history, when this military campaign ended, Diana would welcome me home from the territories and we would resume our lives together.

In Oregon, the Rogue River Indians made a stand on a promontory. My men and I surrounded the tribe, took captive the Indian wives and children. It was a tawdry business and put me in a black mood.

From Portland, I wrote to Diana: *I am coming back. You are my wife and I long for you. I shall meet your conditions if you agree to come home with me to New York.*

But she never replied.

Stricken to the heart's core by Diana's coldness, by her refusal to write to me, I suffered extremely. Made a nuisance of myself at a nasty little watering hole in Portland, where I paid an Irish tenor twenty dollars to sing for hours on end. Yes, well, the tenor sang and I brooded over my whiskey, occasionally bellowing my goddamned traitorous wife's name until the proprietor invited me to leave and never return.

Perplexed and distressed by her cruelty, I alternated between resigned misery and angry obstinacy. My wife had been taken away from me, and now surely, I faced public humiliation because of it. For months, I wrote furiously pathetic letters accusing Diana of slaying me with neglect but she never answered a one.

She never answered me.

Twenty-one

PHILIP WROTE to me until 1853 and then he stopped writing. Every morning, I sent my servant to the post office to ask for letters, but none came. My letters to Philip were returned unopened. An ink slash through his address let me know my husband no longer lived in New York, nor could he be located anywhere in the Oregon Territory. And looking back, I think it was for the best. In half of my letters I had shamelessly begged him to come back to me under any circumstances that might satisfy him and in the other half, I wrote that I never wished to see him again.

Donning a veil of oblivion, I retreated with Mama and Anne Lane to St. Louis, Missouri, banishing myself from a city I loved, from the house I built, and the man I had married, as if I were a murderess or a traitor to my country. I vacillated between relief and cautious pride having finally escaped my nightmare and yet, every morning, flung myself face down on my narrow little bed and moaned into the feather mattress.

Until I began receiving support checks from Philip twice a year, in August and in February, I borrowed money from my brother Aleck to live and to feed the children.

Some days, I walked around as if benumbed. Other days it was all I could do not to celebrate by dancing through the house and gardens and rejoicing that at last I owned my days and answered to no man.

Philip had never once written to the children, nor had he ever attempted to visit them. I couldn't understand how a man could have children and not care to see them. Even so, I devoted myself to educating my four little children—with mixed results. Being a truly superb mother requires an executive ability that I lacked. The St. Louis schools did not admit children until they were eight years old, and so, every day, I brought them into the little schoolroom I'd made and I taught them to read and write, to cipher, and to speak French. I taught them Latin and music and astronomy and we memorized our scriptures. The children soon found their favorites, particularly the Old Testament prophets who called down doom upon sinners. Nothing thrills children more than the idea of adults simmering in lava soup over the devil's fires.

My eldest daughter, Di, would sit upon my feet to keep them warm. With a charcoal, she traced a pattern on onionskin paper that I would later use upon my embroidery hoop. One day in 1857 when Di was thirteen years old, she said, "Men are wicked from the waist down. But women are wicked from head to toe."

"Where did you hear that?" I asked.

"Our teacher, Mr. Blaine."

"Mr. Blaine has some very primitive ideas."

"Mr. Blaine is a royal twit," said Nannie, now ten years old, as she propped an abacus on her knees. She bent her silvery blonde head in concentration, tocking the beads from one metal spool to the next as she rapidly finished her arithmetic. A few years ago, when I had taken my children on a family holiday to see Niagara Falls, Nannie had observed that except for their height and volume of water, the falls were hardly worth seeing.

Di, ever the family peacekeeper and mother's helper, would change the subject whenever anyone criticized me. "Mama, tell us about when you lived with . . . with our father." I suppose she wanted a memory of a long ago time when her family was like any other, and the neighbor children didn't taunt her, and accuse her of being disreputable because her mother and father had broken their vows to one another.

I'd glance around at my children, looping yarn about my forefinger, my knitting needles clicking like insects in the night. And crossing the needles in a downward motion, I'd tell the familiar tale. "Once upon a time, a girl from Louisville, Kentucky, went to live among the aborigines of Manhattan; a Southern girl in a Northern city where the men of the tribe wore lemon-colored gloves and grew furzy sideburns, and expectorated into spittoons. The girl endured the rigors of life in New York purely out of love for a Yankee war chief and soon, children were born, and the magi from Union Square and Lafayette Park came bearing gifts. One day, you will understand that the North is the habitat of a warlike and barbarian people."

"Are Yankees really barbarians?" Di asked.

John gasped and poked Nannie in the shoulder. "Sister, you and me . . . why all of us are half-Yankee."

"No, we're not!" Elizabeth cried. "You might be half-Yankee, Johnny, but we girls aren't."

"The Bible says Yankees are the devil and all his imps," I said, picking up my work. This was a favorite ruse to occupy the children. "Now go find the prophet who said it."

"Where does it say that? The Bible doesn't say that!" Nannie tossed the abacus aside and ran over to the bookstand. Di jumped to her feet and stood shoulder to shoulder with her younger sister, a dark head bent beside the bright one. The pages fluttered, the girls moved the marker ribbons and murmured to one another, and then Di cried out and ran over with her discovery, propping the book on her knees as her sisters gathered around her.

Nannie pointed her finger to the passage. "Out of the North," she paused for dramatic effect, lowered her voice, and narrowed her eyes. "Jeremiah."

"What does it say?" John asked. "Read it, Nannie."

"'Out of the North, an evil shall break forth upon all the inhabitants of the land. And they shall fight against thee; but they shall not prevail against thee; for I am with thee saith the Lord to deliver thee.'"

Johnny, sitting nearest the fire, writing a paper for one of his classes, looked around and said, "You know *who* that means."

"Who?" Di asked, frowning at him over her shoulder.

"You know. Our Yankee father and the armies he'll march into St. Louis."

"He'll kill us all!" Elizabeth shrieked, and chewed on the end of one braided pigtail.

"Oh, your father isn't going to kill his own son and daughters," I sighed, but the children didn't believe a word I said.

Philip, in their minds, was mysterious and slightly sinister.

Every morning, I walked the children to school through Lucas Place. The girls wore their school bonnets, shawls, and carried satchels on their arms. They bowed their heads and closed their eyes, clapped gloved hands over their mouths so as not to breathe the crushed limestone dust blowing yellow clouds down the streets. Di carried the umbrella, but Nannie tried to wrest control of the handle away from her big sister. Elizabeth, my dreamer, always lagged behind. When it rained, the girls' white lisle stockings turned muddy brown. Wagons rumbled by, wet spokes and axles spraying water on us as they passed. John, a spindling and nearsighted boy of twelve, carried his schoolbooks in a green canvas bag that left streaks of green dye down the back of his coat.

On such days our big limestone house never seemed more welcoming. I opened the gate for the children upon their return and ran under the arching trellis of roses. John bumped Di out of the way and bolted up the steps first, threw the book bag carelessly onto the floor, and roared into the kitchen searching for sugar jumbles and orange tea.

One afternoon, John came home from school with his clothes torn, the side of his face bruised from fighting.

"What happened?" I asked, swabbing his wounds with orange iodine.

John answered me by folding his arms over his chest. He would not speak of it, out of shame; but he cried himself to sleep. I slipped into his room, set the candle on the nightstand, and held him as I had when he was a baby, his head in the crook of my shoulder. Safe in the dark, my son spoke his mind. The other boys said he had no father. Said the stories he told about Philip being a great soldier were all lies.

"Why doesn't he want to see me? Does he hate me?"

"He doesn't hate you. He is careless."

"But you said he was coming home. He never came home. I trusted you, Mama, and you lied. You lied to me."

What the boy said was true, for I had believed that after a brief separation, after the Oregon campaign against the Rogue River Indians, Philip and I would have been reconciled and that the children would have their father back again. Plainly, while in the Northwest, Philip had been distracted, his initial ardor and his declarations of love in the park must have cooled as something or someone else captured his interest. And then I knew that I had been right all along and that he had never truly loved me or the children, at least, not enough to devote himself to us the way other husbands and fathers devoted themselves to their marriages and families.

"I am sorry, John, I had thought he was coming home years ago. I am sorry you're sad. I just didn't know what would happen. But we must learn to forgive those who have hurt us." I brushed the hair out of his eyes. "For our own sakes, if not theirs."

"Forgiving only leads people to do wrong again. That's what you always say, Mama."

"But you can forgive your father and you'll feel better if you do."

"What is the point in forgiving someone who doesn't even know I exist?" John asked, throwing up his hands. "I hate him. I hate him, I hate him."

"You can hate him if you wish, John. I won't think less of you for it."

Every morning at eight o'clock, my sister Mary arrived to have breakfast with Mama and me. Mary walked three city squares from her house carrying the newspaper rolled in her gloved hand, and through the open window, I could hear the swish-swish of her petticoats as she came up the steps and rapped on the door knocker. She embraced me and I breathed in her bergamot perfume, and then Mary tossed her shawl carelessly onto the console table. She glanced around and complained, "How can you breathe amid all of this clutter, these statues, ferns, and frippery; a tangle and a frizzle-frazzle of finery, if you ask me. And that wallpaper is poison."

"Clutter," I said, "makes me feel less lonely."

"But poisonous wallpaper hangs in the halls." It fascinated her that the new aniline dyes were made of arsenic.

"I've told you before, it is the new copper arsenate green. But I trust you shan't be licking it."

"No, but your children might."

"Sister, I shall whip them if I catch them with their tongues on the walls. Besides, they're too old for that sort of nonsense."

A courier banged on the front door, and without waiting for a servant to hurry down the hall, I greeted him, took the letter from his hand, and tipped him.

Mama, now in her seventy-fifth year, came down the stairs clutching her swansdown mantel over her shoulders. Of late, Mama had a skeletal look; her eyes were sunken, her hands covered with spots, and her limbs were all sticks and knots. "What do you have there, Diana? Have you a letter?"

As I read the return address on the envelope, I felt the blood draining from my face. "It is from Philip, addressed from Bellegrove, New

Jersey. I didn't know Philip lived in New Jersey." I turned the envelope over slowly as if it might burn up in my hands.

I glanced at my sister. Her wavy dark hair was threaded with gray, and a sapphire pendant earring dangled against her white throat. At fifty-three, being sixteen years older than I, Mary was more like a second mother than a sibling.

"Would you like me to open it for you?" Mary asked.

"No, I can do it." I tore it asunder, scattering the wax seal over the floor.

> Diana,
>   We must meet, soon. Shall I come to St. Louis or
> would you prefer to visit New York? I shall pay for
> your passage, of course. Philip.

"Philip is sending for you! Your husband wishes to resume relations. Oh, this does my heart good. Diana, you might be able to atone for your sins against God and your husband yet!" Mama effused, taking the letter from me, reading it through her quizzing glass. She gave the letter to Mary, who scrutinized it skeptically before folding the paper carefully and returning it to me.

"I don't trust him," Mary said. "I suspect Philip's motives, indeed I do."

The maid summoned us for breakfast, and we went into the dining parlor. Mama, Mary, and I divided up the morning papers and read to one another over our coffee. Mary pointed to an advertisement in the upper-left-hand corner of the newspaper page. "Diana, I am thinking of buying one of these new sewing machines for you. They cost one hundred dollars, but think of how much time and effort you would save sewing the children's clothing."

"One hundred dollars is a great deal to invest in an uncertainty," I answered quietly, for I wasn't concerned with sewing machines. In truth, I couldn't stop thinking of Philip. I found myself fidgeting nervously, thinking obsessively about him as the color rushed into my cheeks. It flattered me to receive a letter from him, and yet, my thoughts were tinged with anxiety because he did not hint of his reasons and I did not trust him or our shared history enough to dare to hope that he might wish to reconcile and reunite.

Two parlormaids entered with trays, giggling as they darted back and forth between the sideboard and table. Mary folded the paper, filled her empty coffee cup with cream and sugar and a splash of coffee, and declared, "Don't go back to him, Diana." She fingered the brooch pinned to her lace collar. "I think you should sue Philip for a divorce."

Mama choked on her cruller, brought her napkin up over her face. "Stop, Mary. Stop this talk at once," she said, then drank water to clear her throat. "Turn away, Diana. For the sake of your soul, turn away from Mary's advice."

I put my elbows on the table and rubbed my temples. "Philip and I haven't lived together since 1849, not for eight long years. What would you have me do, Mama?"

"You knew what Philip Kearny was when you married him. You made your bargain, Diana. Didn't we speak of this very matter on your wedding day? If not for your temper, you might not be in this fix now."

"Mama," Mary warned, pushing her chair away from the table. "Let us speak of other things."

"A woman has her sphere and a man his, but mix up the natural order of the world and the world shall cease to exist, mark my words," my mother insisted.

Staring down at my plate, I asked, "What is the sphere of a woman who finds three prostitutes in her house, wearing her clothes and jewelry?"

"All men are sinners, Daughter."

Mary held up her napkin like a curtain in front of her face and said out of the corner of her mouth, "Philip Kearny, a man with a piston fired by locomotive power."

I laughed, but Mama scowled at us. "Philip's sinful behavior is God's punishment. You must accept His judgment with an open and uplifted heart."

My sister raised her brows, and after cutting into her breakfast sausage, lifted the fork and the link to eye level and grinned at me. "Tell me, Diana, does Kearny suffer the Irish curse?"

"What is the Irish curse?"

Casting a wickedly defiant look at Mama, Mary said, "I hear it said that Irishmen are cursed with tragically small sausages."

When we burst into giggles, Mama, outraged by our conduct, said, "Mary Ann Bullitt! I will not tolerate street talk from any daughter of mine. God's nightgown, where did you learn such language?"

"Oh, I don't know, Mama. Perhaps living at a military post for sixteen years had something to do with it."

In the past year, my mother seemed irritable about everything. Now and again, she acted crazy as a street corner preacher. I'd find her sleepwalking out the front door in her nightdress, her hair spooled up in rags all around her head, wandering like a dyspeptic ghost, wearing nothing but gray yarn socks. She would stir magnesium into a tumbler of gin, arguing with her memories of my father. Sometimes, to make her happy, I'd take Thom Bullitt's role and I'd play him. I'd thicken my Southern accent and I'd grump about the price of hemp, the ruinous cost of shipping two hundred demijohns of sherry to a remote outpost on the frontier. Whenever I did this, Mama brightened. She'd kiss my cheek, finish her gin, and retire contentedly to her bed.

Mary took bacon from the dish and leveled her cool blue gaze upon our mother. "Mama, a new tract has come from the Presbytery. I have seen it on the hall stand. Why don't you go take it up to your room and read it so that you may instruct us in the Word this evening?"

"I shall. I shall do it." Mama waved her hands around her ears as if brushing away flies and tottered out of the room.

"I thought she'd never leave," Mary sighed, buttering her toast. "Philip's business agent, Ravaud Kearny, writes your support checks, doesn't he?"

"Yes, and the checks are never late, and they come in August and February," I said, salting my crispy brown smelts with cream sauce.

"We must go to New York." Mary crooked her finger and the parlormaid lifted the silver lid over the veal chops.

This was not the advice I would have expected from her.

"Why the sudden interest in these matters?" I asked, feeling the letter where I'd tucked it under my napkin in my lap.

Mary leaned over the table, her form starkly severe against the white tablecloth. "What is it you want, Diana?"

I want Philip to come home. I want my husband back.

"I try not to think about it. I get melancholy when I think about what I want."

"Well, you ought to think about what you want." Mary sat back in her chair, crumpled her napkin, and tossed it on the table. Clasping her hands together, she made a steeple with her forefingers and pointed it at me. A large pearl ring on her finger gleamed in the morning light. "I have heard rumors that might jeopardize all of this, and your life here, and the well-being of your children."

I froze, staring numbly at her with my mouthful of smelts.

"What? What have you heard?"

"To begin with, there may be a financial panic in New York City."

"How can you be sure?"

"The banks are suspending payments and are no longer trustworthy." Mary pushed away from the table, and sweeping her skirt clear, rose and stood at the door. "You must be practical about your situation."

"Practical?" I asked, rising from my chair and holding my sister's gaze. "Haven't I managed well enough? Aren't I a practical woman?"

"No, Sister, you are not practical, because a practical woman is very emotional about her money." Offering me her arm, Mary said, "Come, let us walk and talk and plan for you in practical ways. While we are away in New York, Anne Lane can watch the children for us."

That night, alone in my room, I lit the oil lamp on my nightstand and reread Philip's letter a hundred times, searching for some nuance that might give me a clue into his thoughts. I plumped pillows up against the headboard and smoked, flicking ash into a teacup. Daring to hope and to be optimistic, I wondered if my time of trial, of the unshared burden of raising our children, was about to come to an end. Easing into a daydream, I formed clear and happy views of our reunion. Would I appear old to him? Probably, and he might be so shocked by me that he might not want me. I felt a painful tug in my belly and curled onto my side. But surely, his appearance had changed, too. I brought his letter to my lips thinking I might smell him on the paper, but it smelled of nothing. Over the past eight years, I had yearned for Philip, had prayed that he would return to me a changed man. Truth be told, I ached for him. I wished he would come for me and we would live together and take pleasure in raising our children. I had always believed we would someday live together again and care for each other in our old age.

Turning the key of the lamp, extinguishing the light, I drew the blanket over my shoulder, whispering like a maniac in the darkness, "What a fool you are, Diana Moore Gwathmey Bullitt Kearny."

I suppose saying *all* of my names in a string made my self-disdain even more chastising.

Twenty-two

AFTER WRENCHING MYSELF away from the children, who clung to me and begged me not to go, relenting only when greed eclipsed their mother-want and they each supplied me with a long shopping list. Not long after, Mary and I were on our way to New York by railway car. We arrived in the city in early October of 1857 and took rooms at the Metropolitan Hotel at 580 Broadway. While the bellhops took our luggage inside, I stood on the footways in the light that shined off the plate-glass windows of the shops on the first floor.

The lobby of the Metropolitan thrummed with polite conversation from the marble floors to the gilt capitals under the frescoed ceiling. A perpetual murmur pulsed around us. Laughter and cigar smoke from the gentleman's parlor on my left mingled with the pauses and bursts of feminine conversation from women perched on the settees in the hall. Guests and hotel employees flew about in all directions, into the hotel bar, the reading room, and up the grand staircase.

Mary and I followed the bellhop down miles of hallway, under a golden canopy of branching chandeliers and past the brocade ladies parlor. While our maids unpacked our trunks, Mary and I retired to the parlor for tea. There, I composed a note to my husband and arranged to have it sent to him via Philip's business agent and cousin, Ravaud Kearny.

Philip,

> *You may call upon me at the Metropolitan Hotel*
> *in New York. I shall be here for a few weeks. Diana.*

In the corner of the parlor, a girl sat at the grand piano, battering a Brahms sonata from the keyboard. I put the pen down and admitted to Mary, "I would take Philip back if he came home to me."

Mary shook her head and put her cup and saucer on the table. "You must not."

"But I think I might still love him."

"Of course you do, but remember, the warriors God sends to wreak vengeance upon His enemies don't make good husbands."

"Are you going to eat the cucumber sandwiches?" I asked and when she said no, I took all nine of them, stacked them on my plate and bit into a bland little white triangle. "You're making me miss him even more."

"Philip is a romantic memory, Diana."

"That isn't true."

"Oh, but it is. Come now, Sister, think about the first time you discovered he'd been with another woman."

"There are worse things than faithless men. Vulgar and ugly men are harder on a woman's nerves than a faithless husband."

"You hurt only yourself with this thinking, Diana. Do yourself the favor of remembering Philip's indiscretions clearly."

"He provided for us. He still provides for us. It must mean something."

"Listen to you, Sister. You've revised Philip into a rescuing prince."

A courier came into the parlor and took the note I'd written.

"Tonight, we celebrate." Mary leaned over and patted my knee. "I've taken a box for us at the Academy to see *Don Giovanni*."

I didn't want to attend the opera, but I dare not disappoint my sister, who had come all of this way to advance my interests. Now, Mary gazed out at the traffic on Broadway as I took a slice of almond cake from the tiered dessert tray and thought about Philip's telegram and allowed myself to enjoy the fantasy of the two of us reuniting and courting again and then falling into bed and staying there for a week, making love and voicing our regrets and promising to be kind to one another. I had not been with a man in eight years, and had grown weary of the feeling of my own hands upon my body.

At seven o'clock in the evening we were on our way to the Academy of Music on Fourteenth Street at Irving Place. Dressed in steel hoops, Mary and I rode standing up in a hired carriage, lurching and clinging to the ceiling straps, for we couldn't sit down without bending our hoops out of shape.

When we arrived at the Academy, Mary gracefully exited and walked up to the imposing brick building as if she didn't even feel the needling cold rain. She waited for me under the marquee. From inside the carriage, I called to her, "It is lightning and I am wearing twenty pounds of steel around my hips. What if I am struck dead?"

"Oh, come out of there, you little coward!"

I tented my shawl over my head, hopped over a small river in the street, past the gas lamps haloed in rain, and up the curbstone to the door. How exciting it was to be in the city again, the streets echoing with the noise of iron wheels and uplifted voices and the astonishing wave of light reflecting on the rain-wet paving stones.

A thousand people filled the Academy from pit to dome. The gaslights unevenly illuminated the chalky white and gold interior, throwing deep shadows over the draped boxes that flanked the stage. Surrounded by a sparkling and perfumed crowd, I felt my spirits soaring with excitement. Philip would soon receive my response, and within the week, I might see him. And then . . . and then, who knew what could happen? I tried to think how the children might react upon learning that we might have their father with us again. Before leaving, I hadn't told them why I had come—only that this was a necessary trip.

Mary and I found our box on the second level directly to the left of the stage. In the dark box, we found the back sofa occupied by Maria Lydig Daly, one of our social circle. I had known Maria when Philip and I lived on Twenty-second Street. With her this evening was her new husband, Judge Daly, a man twenty years older than Maria. My old acquaintance did not introduce me to him for the overture had started. Doubtless Maria and everyone else in New York knew that Philip and I had separated, but she was too polite to mention the fact. After greeting Maria and nodding hello to Judge Daly, whom I'd never met before, my sister and I sat forward upon the front crimson sofa.

We leaned around the heavy drapery trying to spy people we knew and whispering comments to one another.

Mary scanned the crowd through her lorgnette. She regarded someone who interested her for a rather long while and then abruptly tucked the glasses into a case. Mary folded her hands in her lap, biting her lower lip. "Diana, give me your opera glasses."

Assuming she thought mine sharper than hers and thus wished to borrow them, I put the opera glasses into her elegantly gloved hands.

"You have no need of these," Mary said and dropped my glasses into her purse.

"Mary, I should like to have my glasses. Give them back."

"No." Mary stared at the stage with steely resolve.

"What is the point of going to the opera if I can't look at people?" I complained, and leaning aside, grabbed her purse from the floor, removed my glasses, and surveyed the other side of the theater. Many of the boxes were vacant. I drew my glasses from the top row to the bottom, and then adjusted my sights slightly and did the same with the vertical row closest to the stage.

I focused the lenses on a lean, knifelike figure of a man with a military bearing, who wore a black tailcoat, white cravat, and white waistcoat.

"Philip?"

The woman at his side waved at someone on the parquet. Philip brooded, bowed his head, and appeared to be reading his program as the woman smiled and chattered in his ear.

"Oh, it can't be," I whispered, my hands trembling around the nickel casing. "No, I can't believe it. Philip is here. Look, Sister, my husband is here. And he is with a woman so very young and pretty."

Mary made a disgusted noise and yanked her opera glasses from the pouch and peered alongside me. "Nonsense, Diana. She isn't pretty in the least. That woman is pretty in the way a big white cow is pretty. She's got beef cheeks."

I couldn't help whimpering like a child, I hurt so badly. Pain lodged in my bones and seared me from my ankles to my skull. I fixed upon them, riveted with apprehension and yet, feared that if I looked away, Philip might vanish.

Mary turned in her seat and asked Judge Daly and Mrs. Daly, sitting behind us, "Who is that woman with Major Kearny?"

Maria Daly squeezed her husband's arm, but though she tried to silence him, the old judge blurted, "Why, that woman over there is Mrs. Philip Kearny."

"Shh," Mrs. Daly said to her husband with an apologetic glance at me.

Mary frowned and redirected his attention with her fan. "No, *that* woman. The young woman sitting beside Major Kearny, wearing the cherry silk dress."

Judge Daly grumped at us. "As I said, that woman is Mrs. Philip Kearny, ma'am. I have just left the major and he introduced her to me as his wife. His second wife."

"His wife!" My voice broke and I clapped a hand over my mouth. "His wife?"

Mrs. Daly shook her head. "You mustn't listen to such gossip."

"Philip is a lecher," Mary hissed. "A blithering lunatic."

"Oh, Mary, what shall I do? I don't know what to do."

Judge Daly, bewildered by my comments, shot a panicked look at Mrs. Daly, who twirled her finger at her temple to let me know her husband had his facts wrong. Being a scrappy Irishman from the Lower East Side, Daly could not have known the particulars of our personal scandal, and as he had not traveled in the same circles as we, did not have an inkling of how mistaken he was. But Maria knew, and the glittering hundreds who'd dined in our home and danced in our ballroom, the very same people sitting in their boxes all around me and across from me, surely knew.

"The major introduced that woman as his wife," the judge insisted. "Damn it, Maria, I know what Kearny told me not a quarter of an hour ago."

I put the opera glasses to my eyes and focused on my husband and his little grisette. The red-haired woman lifted her opera glasses and returned my scrutiny. I thought she looked vaguely familiar. She reached aside and touched Philip's arm, pointed me out, and then handed the glasses to him.

I leapt to my feet and leaned over the box like a witness identifying a murderer for the court. Bending perilously over the rail, over the frothy gulf of evening gowns and the dark trough of black evening coats in the pit, I wanted Philip to see me. I needed to prove to him and to his mistress that I was not dead, that I would not be diminished by his lie.

Below me, upturned faces watched our squalid drama unfolding on opposite sides of the stage. A sparkling wave of opera glasses reflected the gaslight, a shining current of silvery fish swimming from my box and back again to Philip's box. As the stringed instruments resounded from the orchestra pit, I agonized with jealousy.

Judge Daly asked his wife, "What is that woman doing?"

"She has been wronged."

"Who *is* she?"

"The real Mrs. Philip Kearny! The only Mrs. Philip Kearny."

"So Kearny is a bigamist?"

"He is a wicked, wicked man," Mrs. Daly said. "The most wicked man who ever lived."

"Diana, you must sit down," Mary said, grabbing my hips and pulling back with all of her might. "My God, have a little dignity, Sister."

I peered at him again through the glasses. Philip had exited the box. Pausing at the door, he motioned to his agitated companion to remain in her seat. There was a disagreement between them and sullenly, she obeyed him, lifting the opera glasses my way.

I lifted my left hand and pointed to my wedding ring.

The girl slowly lowered the opera glasses, her mouth dropping open slightly and then she disappeared from view entirely, fainting sideways onto the sofa. The people sitting on the parquet burst into soft laughter at the sight of her toppling sideways like a felled tree.

"Come out into the hall with me," Mary said. "Take my hand, Diana. Now, breathe and calm yourself, you have done nothing wrong. You certainly have no reason to be ashamed. We'll walk out of here with our heads high." Mary gripped my wrist and pulled me up the stairs, opening the door and shoving me out into the quiet and deserted hall.

I covered my face with my hands. "What did I do to make him stop loving me, Mary?"

"He's a brute and everyone knows it. A monumentally selfish brute."

"He calls her his wife. He's introducing her to everyone as his wife."

"No one in New York but that feeble old Irishman believes Philip's lies." Mary was pulling me down the hallway, to the stairs, saying, "We shall return to the hotel, we'll draw a hot bath and pour you a toddy, and you will feel much better, but we must leave." Mary rushed me down the stairs, carrying our wraps and silk purses in her free hand, but then, she halted abruptly on the landing and putting an arm out in front of me as if to keep me from falling down the steps, said, "Diana, wait. Think before you act, think before you speak."

At first, I noticed only the dark figures slipping in and out of pools of gaslight in the lobby; saw the gleam of a silk hat and the flick of a cape disappearing in the hollows. The lights and shadows were so changeful that I doubted my own eyes.

And then he approached slowly, his shoulders slightly stooped, and I met Philip on the landing. He bowed as if I were a stranger, as if we were strangers meeting for the first time in a hotel and strange indeed, he looked. Why, there was white in his hair and in his beard. When he met my eyes, I thought, *who is this old graying man, a narrow face pitted with smallpox scars, an imperial goatee, his eyes bitterly red and moist?*

He stood on the step below me looking pale and haunted.

"Good evening, Philip," I said, filled with sad foreboding.

When finally he spoke, he lifted his hand and let it fall at his side, saying, "Diana, I did not want this."

I had almost forgotten how nasal, harsh, and staccato his voice could be.

"What do you want?"

"I think you will agree that our marriage was a failure."

"Well, I do admit, it left a terrible impress upon my spirits." I was trying to be flip and casual, but my voice broke at the end, destroying the entire intended effect. Now, I felt like a fool, and I wanted to leave, but Philip came closer, put his hand on the banister, and stared ferociously at me. I wondered who had sewn his empty left coat sleeve to his jacket. Surely, not her. She didn't look old enough to ply a needle.

"Even so, Diana, I have wanted you. All of those years, the only one I ever wanted was you. Don't you remember how I came for you in October of 1849, and wrote for you, sending for you in 1851, but whenever I tried, you turned me away. My family has savagely attacked poor little Agnes. She is—she sacrificed her reputation and risked everything to be with me. If nothing else, I feel loyal to her for having put her in this situation."

"Loyalty to her? Am I supposed to admire you for feeling loyal to her? And what situation are you talking about? Who is this Agnes you speak of?"

"Agnes Maxwell."

"Agnes Maxwell is thirteen years old. She wears a beret and her father is wretched to her."

"Agnes deserves my protection. I cannot bear to think of her feeling her own degradation."

"Because she tumbled into bed with a randy millionaire? What was she giving up? A dreary life as a clerk's wife in Brooklyn?"

"New York won't accept her. The society women make the most violent assaults upon her character!"

"Sleeping with another woman's husband *will* provoke gossip."

"Give me a divorce, Diana." He lowered his chin and said this forcefully, as if issuing an order to his troops.

I stepped back and up a stair, felt the hair on my arms prickling and a cold breeze in the hallway. "No. I shall never divorce you. You belong to me and I belong to you."

He made a fist and hit the banister with his white kid glove. "For eight years, you have absented yourself from my bed and my society."

"Because you . . ." I stammered.

"Yes, yes, I know, I did terrible things, but is that not the perfect reason to dissolve our attachments? Diana, I freely admit destroying our marriage, and it was unfair to you. We were . . . well, think about it, we were a bad match from the beginning. You said so yourself in the letter you wrote when you left me. What was it you said? As we lived without love—"

But I turned away from him, clamping my hands over my ears. "Don't be so cruel."

"She . . . Agnes . . . has given me two children. We have two little girls."

"You have children by her!" Being isolated and far away from the city, I had not heard any hint of this, and doubtless, Philip's family had been so shocked and shamed, suffering ridicule from society, that they were loathe to break the bad news to me.

As I was out of sight, I had been out of mind.

Philip may as well have punched me in the stomach. I hid my face in my hands, heard myself moaning as if I had been wounded, and though I told myself to stop, to summon my pride and walk away with my head high, I couldn't. I felt Mary's hands on my back, and until now, I had almost forgotten her. She said not a word.

Philip kept talking, his words mercilessly cutting into me.

"Agnes is gentle. She is obedient. We never argue, she and I. Please don't cry. Diana, don't cry. Here, take my handkerchief." Philip thrust the handkerchief into my hand but I threw it over the banister and it fluttered down and down onto the marble floor of the lobby.

"I don't want your damned handkerchief, I want you to come home. We have *five* children, doesn't that count for anything? Where is your loyalty to them?"

"Four . . . children." He narrowed his eyes as if I had worried him by miscounting.

"*Five* children. I bore you five children. Susan was with us once or have you forgotten her, too? Oh, you have forgotten her." Sinking upon the step, I hid my face in the satin flounce of my ball gown.

"Don't be ridiculous. How could I forget the only child I ever loved?

No, I have not forgotten our Susan. Indeed, didn't I name my firstborn girl by Agnes, Susan?"

When he said this, I was so horrified by his callous disregard for me and for the memory of our lost child that I could not speak, but stared whitely at him, thinking him the cruelest man who ever walked the earth.

"Diana, I have always felt that I have had to . . . to live up to you. It has always been so damnably hard living up to you and I . . . I'm getting old and I can't do it anymore. I don't wish to do it anymore. Agnes doesn't challenge me, she is compliant and sweet." He said this with a flinch of his armless shoulder.

We were both silent, locked in our own misery.

He leaned against the stairwell, avoiding my gaze. "I could forgive you anything, Diana. I could forgive you but I haven't been able to forgive the women who've failed to replace you. Including Agnes. You could have stopped me from suffering public humiliation if only you had taken me back, if only you had listened to reason."

Not this old complaint again. Having seized for himself the starring role of fallen angel, now came his ridiculous pleas that I work for his salvation, followed by accusations that I had somehow been responsible for his descent into immorality.

"If only you had not been so hardhearted, I should never have met Agnes. I would still be your protector."

"You're the only man I need protecting against, Philip."

"I shall settle a significant sum upon you and the children. You shan't want for anything."

Firmly in the grip of my own distress and perplexity, I could think of nothing else to say to my husband.

"Here, let me recommend a lawyer for you." He reached into his pocket, pulled out a small pencil, and balancing the little book on his thigh, he wrote something. He tore out the page, holding the pencil and book in his fingers, and offered it to me. "There is a fine law firm on

Liberty Street called Miller and Devlin. You must make an appointment to see them. We could end this in a matter of weeks and both of us will be free to start new lives. Think of it, Diana, a fresh start for both of us, without these old ties and old sorrows."

I felt so sick and lost, as if I were plunging downward into hopeless despair that I shed all of my self-regard and began to beg. "Whatever I've done, I'm sorry for it. Whatever you've done, I forgive you. Come home to us."

"I can't, Diana. I can't come home." Looking beyond me at Mary, Philip pinched the bridge of his nose as if he were stopping a sneeze, but then he made a harsh and ragged sound because he was trying not to cry in front of us. He couldn't speak, and so turned his back and started down the stairs.

"Philip?"

He stopped and turned and looked up at me with red eyes. Tears streamed down his jaws, spotting the immaculate white points of his collar and shirtfront.

"Philip, I shall give you your divorce."

He fixed his gaze on me, and there was a bitter downturn in his mouth. He walked away, leaving me once again for another woman. I had not anticipated how violent this would feel when the day finally came, this final act of violence rending apart my illusions and hopes, my past and my future.

Mary put her arm around me and I leaned upon her as we walked out the door, with people staring and talking about us. As we went, she put her lips to my ear and whispered, "Sweet girl, it is time to wish peace on the ashes of your marriage."

Twenty-three

I T SNOWED the following day, and the filth in the streets turned the snow dark as burned butter. In the carriage, Mary held my hand as we drove down to Liberty Street. I wish I could brag that I had been stoic, but my situation was so bewildering I couldn't even begin to fathom a new life for myself, and sat with a handkerchief pressed to my raw red nose, staring in abject gloom at my own feet. Marriage to Philip had shaped my life. From marriage, I had taken my strength, benefited from the prestige of being married to him; my whole life had been formed around being Mrs. Philip Kearny. Well, what now? What would I be without it?

Mary patted my hand and said, "You listen to me, Sister. I intend to write a letter to that Agnes. *Dear Miss Agnes, one day Philip Kearny will think of you as a burden. Snakes are not burden carrying animals.*"

When we arrived in the bricked canyon of three- and four-story office buildings on Liberty Street, Mary pushed the driver away and helped me into Miller and Devlin's plush office. It was a sort of temple to mahogany and overstuffed leather. The clerk, a thin fellow with a hooked nose and balding pate, greeted us, looking up as his steel nib scratched across pages of documents. A cat sat on the desk, reaching out and batting at the pen now and again. The clerk laughed indulgently, "Now, Buchanan, you're going to make me foul up."

My sister and I sat side by side on a leather sofa and held hands. She said, "You will be fine. You'll see. You will walk away from this a happier woman, Diana. I know it is hard to believe now, but it must be true. If there is any justice in the world, it must be true."

Another woman came in and walked up to the desk. The clerk smiled up at her and said, "Miss Winslow, thank you for being so prompt!"

Miss Winslow wore a demure charcoal-colored dress with violet piping, jet earrings, and a pert little hat and veil that covered her nose. She looked like a banker's daughter dressed in mourning weeds.

Mary and I whispered to each other. Why would a "Miss" see a divorce lawyer? But there were odder things in New York City. After an eternity, I heard a bell jingle. The clerk rose from behind the desk, lifted the cat, put it onto the floor, and then opened a door onto a long narrow hall.

"Mrs. Kearny? The attorney will see you now."

I heard an animal rasping noise and realized it had come from me. I felt as if I were being dragged down to the Tombs, where I'd be locked in a cell with a dirt floor and a view of the workingmen building my scaffold. My hands fluttered up around my collar by my neck, and like a condemned woman, I kept assuring myself it would be over soon and that I wouldn't feel much pain.

Mary stood too, but the clerk wagged a finger at her. "No, no, madam. Attorney-client privilege must not be breached by a third party's eavesdropping."

"But I need her!" I protested.

"I am her sister." Mary squared her shoulders with the authority and grandeur one would expect from the Grand Duchess of St. Louis.

"The divorce statutes make no exceptions for sisters."

Miss Winslow lifted her veil and showing a genteel face and a fine mouth of white teeth smiled. "Where are you from? I hear the South in your voice."

Mary sat stiffly. "St. Louis."

"Never been there," Miss Winslow fluffed her skirts and leaned back into the sofa. "The farthest west I've been is Louisville."

"I'm from Louisville, originally!"

I followed the clerk down the hall as the sounds of my sister and Miss Winslow conversing trailed off. My horsehair crinolines had flattened under me and stuck out so that I resembled a squished tea cozy with legs. I tried to smash my skirt back into a proper dome shape and yet keep pace with the law clerk as I walked down the narrow hall between high bookcases impressively filled with dusty law books. The clerk brought me into a high-ceilinged office furnished with two chairs, a heavy desk, and a marble fireplace, the fender heaped with coal. Behind the desk, a slender bearded man with spectacles came around and took my hand, directing me to one of the chairs.

Miller, my attorney, thanked his clerk and removed his spectacles. He blew upon them, wiped them with a handkerchief, and tugging the handles over his ears, squared a set of papers over his blotter and looked up at me.

"Mrs. Kearny, do you wish to divorce your husband?"

I felt as if I had a sponge in my throat, and I coughed, avoiding his eyes.

"No," I said, lacing my fingers tightly. I could feel the bump of my wedding ring under my glove. Philip had designed it himself, he'd slid it over my finger as I lay in childbed, having just given birth to Susan. He put that ring on my finger and clasped his hand to my cheek, and promised that he would love me forever.

"No?" Miller leaned back in his chair, staring at me as if contemplating a messy and protracted contested divorce trial.

"I mean to say, yes."

"Good, good. Ah, good. Major Kearny came to see me last week. He proposes to pay you eighty thousand dollars secured by a debt of indenture. Major Kearny made it clear he wishes to provide generously for you and the children. And to secure his promise, he is deeding land and buildings on Twenty-second Street and Broadway to you."

"Will I have to testify in court? In front of reporters? Will I be required to tell a judge about Philip's women?"

The lawyer sat forward, put his elbows on the desk. "No. You will petition the court for a divorce on the grounds of adultery. It is the only grounds for divorce in our Superior Court."

I could feel him parceling out information in tiny servings as if he doubted my ability to absorb too much at one time. "What will Philip do if I accuse him of adultery?"

"Major Kearny will admit to adultery."

"With Agnes?"

Miller frowned slightly as he reached for a coffee cup, sipped, and then put it down. "With a witness who will swear out an affidavit admitting that she committed adultery with Major Kearny."

"Agnes will swear out an affidavit?"

The lawyer stroked his beard and said, "No. The condition for Major Kearny paying you a generous settlement is that you sue him for divorce for having committed adultery with Miss Jane Winslow."

"I don't understand. Miss Winslow?" I began to rise out of my chair. "Philip slept with," I began, but Miller patted the air as if to calm me and explained. "No, no, no, Major Kearny has never seen Miss Winslow in his life." He stepped around his desk, went over to the washstand, poured a glass of water, and brought it over to me. "Miss Winslow swears out affidavits in most of my divorce cases."

"So, she doesn't know Philip?"

"No. Major Kearny will pay Miss Winslow fifty dollars in gold to say that she had carnal connections with him in 1851 to protect your reputation, his reputation, and to protect Agnes Maxwell's reputation.

If you agree to this, Major Kearny will pay you a generous settlement not to mention Agnes Maxwell's name in these divorce proceedings."

Lawyer Miller repeatedly jabbed his pen into the inkwell, clenching his jaw as he did it, glancing up only to look at the clock on the fireplace mantel. "Miss Winslow owns a profitable brothel at 73 Mercer Street."

"She is a madam!" I cried.

"She supplements her income by helping me with these cases."

What was I going to say to my children? How would I tell them this news?

"If you refuse to agree to these conditions, if you insist on naming Miss Agnes Maxwell, Major Kearny will contest the settlement and alimony. Your divorce will become a public spectacle. You don't want that, do you? The courts typically grant innocent female plaintiffs one third of the husband's holdings as if he had died intestate—meaning without a will.

"But if you contest it, the divorce will take a long time. It will be costly. You will have to pay my fees. Your every move, action, and word will be dissected in the press and talked about by everyone in New York. We may go through all of these horrors only to find Major Kearny's assets so diminished by the current economic depression that you would have received eighty thousand anyway."

"But you're asking me to perjure myself."

"It is how we handle these matters, Mrs. Kearny." The lawyer continued, "My fee is eight hundred dollars. Major Kearny will pay my fee and your court costs. He is the most generous defendant I've ever met in the course of my career."

"Yes, my husband is a great man," I said, with silky contempt.

"Now, as a routine matter, there will be a clause in the divorce decree freeing you to remarry as soon as the decree is issued."

I had never thought of marrying anyone else.

Attorney Miller continued, "But Major Philip Kearny will be prohibited by New York law from remarrying in New York State as long as *you* live."

"While I am alive, Philip cannot remarry?" My hopeful expression must have been evident, for the attorney leaned forward and couldn't help smiling.

"Mrs. Kearny, the State of New York requires this clause. It is meaningless boilerplate. For reasons of public policy, the state doesn't wish to reward a defendant's bad behavior by allowing Major Kearny to remarry. But Major Kearny will probably marry Miss Maxwell in New Jersey the day after the divorce decree is granted in New York. Ah, don't be glum, Mrs. Kearny. You will not only take this huge settlement free and clear of any strings, but you will be able to remarry anyone you choose, anywhere you choose. You will be rich and free."

"When will the decree be issued?"

"Three weeks. Then you will be a free woman, Mrs. Kearny. A free woman with a lot of money in the bank." He came around the desk, reached for a quire of paper and his pen, and dipping it into the well, handed it to me.

At first, my hand shook, showering ink drops on the page as if a spider had gone running over my signature. But then, Miller began asking me the dullest questions as a matter of formality. I signed and answered his queries. Yes, the North River Bank was suitable. Yes, I knew the property securing the debt. Yes, I trusted Ravaud Kearny to manage the payments.

After we'd finished, Miller ushered me into the lobby.

Mary leapt to her feet, regarding me brightly. "Diana, have you met Miss Jane Winslow? She is the most extraordinary woman! Why, she knows everyone in New York! We've been talking about the mayor and the governor and all of the Astors, not to mention Philip's cousins, the De Peysters. Miss Winslow knows all of Philip's people! Well, most of the gentlemen anyway."

Miss Winslow rose slowly and locked eyes with me. She smiled kindly and said, "Mrs. Kearny, do not grieve so. If I have learned one thing in this life, it is the nature of men. And believe me, any man worth your tears will never make you cry."

My sister and I returned to the hotel. As I wearily climbed the grand staircase to our rooms, a desk clerk came running after me, waving a telegram and calling my name. I let Mary open it, but the news shook her so badly that she steadied herself against the stair rail. "Oh surely we are now in affliction," she cried, handing the telegram to me.

It was from St. Louis.

YOUR MOTHER DIED IN HER SLEEP STOP
I WILL AWAIT WORD FROM YOU STOP MY
HEART IS WITH BOTH OF YOU STOP
ANNE LANE

Affidavit of Jane Winslow

Jane Winslow being duly sworn says that she resides in the city of New York and has resided therein for sixteen years and upward, has been a housekeeper in said city for thirteen years past, is thirty years of age and upward.

Q. Do you know Philip Kearny, formerly an officer in the United States Army and if you do how long have you known him?

A. I do know him and have since 1850. The person I refer to has lost an arm. I think it was the left arm. He was called Captain and Major Kearny.

Q. Was Major Philip Kearny in the habit of visiting your house and if so, in what years?

A. He was. He visited there in the winter of 1850 and in the summer and fall of 1850. Thereafter, he came to my house to visit me.

Q. Do you know of Major Philip Kearny having carnal connexion with any woman and if so, with whom, when and where.

A. Yes, I do know he had with myself in the spring of 1850, in the city of New York. I also know that in the fall of 1850, he visited a lady by the name of Elizabeth Byron, and he had carnal intercourse with her about that time in the city of New York.

Subscribed and sworn to before me this 31st day of December 1857, Philip Reynolds, Referee.

(Affidavit courtesy of State of New York, County of New York, Norman Goodman, County Clerk and Clerk of the Supreme Court of New York County.)

Deana M. Kearney
vs
Philip Kearney

James Winslow being duly sworn says that she resides in the city of New York, and has resided therein for sixteen years and upward. has been a house-keeper in said city for thirteen years past. is thirty years of age and upwards.

Q. Do you know Philip Kearney, formerly an officer in the U. S. Army, and if you do how long have you known him?

A. I do know him, and have since 1850. The person I refer to has lost an arm I think it was the left arm. He was called Captain & Major Kearney

Q. Was Major Philip Kearney in the habit of visiting your house, and if so, about in what years?

A. He was. He visited there in the winter of 1850, and in the summer and fall of 1850 thereafter. He came to my house to visit me.

Q. Do you know of Major Philip Kearney having carnal connexion with any woman, and if so with whom, when and where.

A. Yes. I do know he had, with myself, in the spring of 1850, in the city of New York. I also know that in the fall of 1850, he visited a lady by the name of Elizabeth Byron, and he had carnal intercourse with her about that time in the city of New York.

Jane Winslow

Subscribed and sworn to
before me this 31st day of December

Paris

Twenty-four

WITHOUT A WAR to occupy me, I built a sanctuary for Agnes and the children on the Passaic River in New Jersey. I had no desire to live in New Jersey. Though I had tried to buy land overlooking the Hudson River, none of the landowners would sell, expressing a moral repugnance at having me for a neighbor. Finding beautiful sites I wished to purchase in Red Hook and Hyde Park, I offered far more than the asking price, but the sellers were sniveling cowards who would not bargain with me.

After the tawdry episode with Diana at the Academy, Agnes and I returned to our box the following week for a concert. We faced an outpouring of wrath from twelve hundred people. The women rapped their fans against the arms of their chair, rapped them like bones, and the voices of the women rose over those of the men, shrill and harsh. They booed us so loudly that the orchestra did not strike a note until Agnes and I had left. This, after I selflessly sacrificed an arm and devoted years to patriotic service to my nation. This, after having been celebrated not ten years ago by parades and parties and long fawning editorials in the New York papers.

Poor little Agnes retired despondently to her bed for a week. My young wife lacked the strength and force of character of my old one. Agnes depended upon me for everything, was childlike in her need for my protection, and grateful for all I did for her. Everyone in New York perceived Diana as an innocent and injured little bird. I knew Diana for what she was—a bird of prey flying off and abandoning me whenever she suffered one of her jealous delusions. Agnes accepted my absences and explanations with attractive wifely forbearance and was never jealous.

After my divorce decree was granted, my uncle Archibald, a low corrupt knave, wrote these lines to me: *You have destroyed one woman by divorcing her and another by marrying her. You disgust me, disgrace your father's name, and are no longer welcome in my house.* I received similar letters from all of my elderly uncles, and none except Ravaud stood by me.

In New Jersey, we lived so peacefully, Agnes and I. No one came to call. No one wrote. Between my wife and I, there was no rancor, no verbal sparring, no vases hurling across the parlors, no grievous outpouring of emotion. No nastiness darkened our perfectly harmonious days because Agnes and I were perfectly compatible. A man who studies and practices war as an art, as a profession, and as his personal religion, enjoys peace at home. We had peace in abundance. Peace thick as the amber that traps and smothers a hornet in oozing golden splendor for all eternity.

The house and grounds, which I named Bellegrove, became my new grand passion. I wanted something in mortar and brick that would last forever and represent my ambitions; a house that spoke of my own originality, boldness, and energy through soaring roof lines, majestic towers, and asymmetrical gables. My house reflected my originality with a romantic medievalism.

Ravaud Kearny was the only relative who came to visit Agnes and me at Bellegrove. It gladdened my heart to see him. Ravaud met my daughters, Susan and Virginia, and then asked for privacy and so I took him out to the stables, where I kept twenty horses.

Ducking under the baling hook used to hoist hay up into the loft,

Uncle Ravaud sat on a bench against the bricked wall. He studied me and then said, "Diana has taken the children to Paris."

I removed a cigar from my pocket, bit the end, lit it with a match, and drew the satisfying smoke into my throat.

"Why does this concern me?"

"Diana has gone to France to live."

"She went there to escape gossip, didn't she?" I said. "In France, she might live without anyone thinking twice about her marital status. Certainly her money would go further. And Southerners are great favorites there. The French perceive Southerners as the true American aristocracy. Good riddance to her."

Ravaud said, "I correspond with Diana regularly, you know, and she has enrolled the girls at a convent school in St. Aignan, and John in a Jesuit seminary."

"Anne Lane was always putting radical ideas in Diana's head and the two of them used to speak of crossing the ocean together. Both speak French fluently." My voice trailed off because I was ruminating about how Diana's illogical decision burned me. Why would she corrupt my son by immersing him in a superstitious Papist education? My son ought to attend Columbia, as I had. I scratched my brow and leaned against a stall. "Why do you tell me this, Ravaud?"

"Because I suspect her decision was influenced by more than her friend's whim, or a desire to travel. Philip, there are some in our government who think that given Diana's deep and extensive ties to all of the great families in the South and mutual friendship with so many military men, that she is in France seeking to exert influence over Emperor Louis-Napoleon and the Empress Eugénie with regard to the South, should there be disunion."

I grimaced at him, clenched the cigar between my teeth. How preposterous! I whipped the cigar out of my mouth and blurted, "Damn it, out of respect to me, and given my service to that country, Emperor Louis-Napoleon won't receive her."

"Ah, but I hear it said that Diana and the empress might have much in common."

I ignored this bold innuendo. Ravaud hinted at the emperor's notorious and constant sexual escapades, and thus the mutual sympathy Diana and the Empress Eugénie must share as wronged wives. My uncle could be a dirty mongrel.

Ravaud rummaged in his pocket, removed a letter, and put it in my hand. I recognized Diana's handwriting instantly, the Spenserian script that she had learned in finishing school with great flourishes and curling capital letters. With Ravaud out of sight, I inspected the missive closely, touched the rising ink of her name on the thick and creamy paper, held the paper to my nose, and swore I could discern her lily of the valley scent. I tucked Diana's letter into my vest pocket and returned to my wife.

I found Agnes sitting in a window, working petit point upon a piece of linen stretched over a canvas. Our daughters sat at her feet demurely playing with their china dolls. My new world with Agnes, the empire of the mother, was a place of diapers, breast milk, and naps. Agnes smiled serenely at me when I entered the room.

"Agnes, I have decided you and the children deserve a holiday. I am taking you to Paris."

A year passed, but after closing up house, arranging to purchase fine apartments on the avenue de Matignon, Agnes and I finally arrived in Paris. Eager to be reacquainted with my old comrades, I joined General Morris as an observer with the Calvary of the Imperial Guard and offered my services to the empire.

General Morris welcomed me warmly, and by a stroke of good fortune, I soon found myself riding off to yet another war that the French had recently instigated.

Having entrained at the Gare de Lyon, we officers traveled to Mar-

seilles and thence to Genoa by sea. The French and their allies, the
Piedmontese, would take a stand against the Austrian invaders in Italy.

Pity the village of Solferino squeezed between the Austrians and the
French on June 24, 1859. Emperor Louis-Napoleon's generals quickly
learned the king could not read a map and had no idea how to deploy
and maneuver his troops into position. What did the generals expect of a
commander in chief who'd studied military history at a Swiss academy?

Upon arriving, I did as I always do. While my comrades slept and
ate, I paid local spies generously, and with them, went on reconnais-
sance, anticipating the movements of the armies in advance of the
arrival of the Austrians.

When the fateful hour arrived, His Asininity the Emperor sat high up
above the battlefield in the bell tower of the village church of Castiglione,
sweating in his gilded uniform and chain smoking, scattering the butts at
his feet and scanning our movements with his field glasses. Being wreathed
in cloud, the emperor saw nothing. As if heaven disapproved, it rained and
the rivers flooded, washing out the bridges and concealing our enemies in
a rolling fog, and the powder smoke swallowed up their hordes.

An opera-bouffe atmosphere prevailed on the battlefield. Italian
women in white gowns cheered us from their balconies, tossed handkerchiefs onto the meadow, and called out to men they recognized. The
military band played an Offenbach overture. And the flamboyant uniforms of the European armies were not to be believed. Would these
fussy European soldiers stab me or ask me to dance the mazurka?

Given the fog and blinding gunpowder smoke, we accidentally blun-
dered into enemy lines. Shortly after noon our troops seized the heights
of Solferino, and when the First Chasseurs were given the order to
charge, I defied General Morris's orders to remain on the sidelines.

Then, the battle broke in earnest and the French disemboweled their
enemy with saber and bayonet, rending men in two like hung cattle car-
casses. I had the sensation as the sun broke through the clouds, of being

surrounded by a shining bouquet of bloody hooks. I saw men clutching their own intestines in their hands like long roots dragged out of soft mulch and so I thought, to hell with the saber.

I stood in the stirrups and took the reins in my teeth to free my one hand and then relied solely upon my new repeating carbines. Blasting away at the Hungarian hussars and the dragoons of the Austrian Imperial Guard, I soon found myself well in advance of my own squadron. I shall always treasure the comic expressions on the faces of some of the Austrians when I knocked them from their saddles like nine-pins.

On that day, twenty-three thousand men died in the water-blistered vineyards and in the shorn mulberry groves. Thieves swarmed the battlefield, rifling through pockets of the dead and dying. The exhausted burial parties from Solferino buried the wounded alive in the same mass graves as the corpses. Even though the wounded men begged for mercy, their pleas were ignored and they were covered with dirt.

It is my habit to visit the hospitals immediately following a battle to cheer up comrades. Searching for my friends, I walked through the field hospital set up in a hay barn.

I followed in the wake of Emperor Louis-Napoleon. He wore his mustache waxed into ferocious upright points. The emperor stared around the barn at men packed like rats all over the floor. Spying the pile of amputated limbs leaking over the planking, Louis-Napoleon darted outside and vomited down the front of his magnificent scarlet uniform, sash, and the Legion of Honor medals he'd bestowed upon himself.

Having lost his stomach for war, the emperor secretly initiated peace talks with his enemy, Franz-Josef. Worrying that the Prussians would intervene on behalf of the Austrians, the emperor forged a peace that infuriated many who believed he had abandoned his Piedmontese allies and Italy to a terrible fate.

I returned home to poor little Agnes who breathlessly informed me that she was once again with child and we celebrated our happiness.

Come August of 1859, the French army paraded twenty abreast down the Rue de la Paix in Paris. It was a glorious hot day and the whole city had turned out to cheer on the emperor and his legions. I, wearing my somber and austere American Dragoon uniform, was flanked by gaps representing fallen comrades. As the bands played, girls darted up to the men with flowers and kisses. The Zouaves brandished stems of blue love-in-a-mist from the barrels of their muskets.

As our procession entered the Place Vendôme to the roar of the crowd, I saw Diana Bullitt Kearny standing on the curbstone surrounded by our children.

Sweat trickled over my brow. My body went cold and I felt as nauseated as I had after suffering a *coup de soleil* in Turin.

My beautiful dark-haired wife had hardly changed. She leaned forward slightly over the curb in her fashionable scarlet and blue dress, waving a tricolor, smiling her white smile, and bouncing on her toes in time to the music. Stray locks of her dark hair wisped around her rosy face. I stared in unabashed fascination at her and my children. My three girls were elegant young women in red bolero jackets tossing rose petals in the air. My son was a fair-haired, six-foot-tall boy in a pale blue summer suit and a straw hat. I heard Diana's Southern voice distinctly as I rode by her. She and the children cheered along with the crowd for my popular commanding general, calling his name. *"Vive General Morris! Vive Chasseurs!"*

I don't think Diana saw me. Or if she did, she hid her recognition, because I stared into her lovely face and big dark eyes as I passed her, but her look was one of general excitement over the event.

Look at me, damn you, I willed, but she defied me even then. I rode along chewing on the end of my mustache and considered why she tormented me.

I had a young wife, a French mistress, and countless lovers. In Paris, a city of dissipated sensualists, I was renowned as a rakish sporting man. Yet, when I thought of Diana, I knew that whatever pleasures of the flesh I might enjoy with other women were for naught.

And why? Because I, Philip Kearny, had been cursed with a monogamous soul, the like unknown before in history. Diana's very name lent itself to my ruin.

Bullitt is a corruption of the French word *boulit*, meaning "to seethe or to boil" and until I found Diana again, that is precisely what I did.

Twenty-five

AFTER OUR DIVORCE was finalized, my children could no longer attend school in America without being mercilessly harangued and taunted by their peers. So, I took them to France despite my sister Mary's objections, and though I pleaded with her to join Anne and myself and the children, she was too settled in St. Louis to begin anew. I suppose I thought that we could have a fresh start and see a little of the world besides. This was my first wild idea.

The second was that the life and the people would be somehow gentler and sweeter in a rural place. I had forgotten the first principal of any farming country; that all outsiders are instantly suspect. But the schools in Orléans had great prestige and were known for their academic rigor and given the disadvantages that life had handed them, I wanted only the best for my girls and for my son. The Sisters of St. Aignan, a profoundly intellectual order recently created by the bishop of Orléans, would educate my girls. John would attend a seminary school favored by the aristocracy.

In the Loire Valley, Anne Lane and I let an old house in Orléans that had been built in the sixteenth century for a seigneur. The marble stairs inside crumbled with age, slate tiles from the mansard roof fell like ax blades onto the footways below and behind the house, a little river gleamed like polished steel. Silverfish wiggled all over the bed curtains until I directed the servants to rub tomato vines onto the posts to repel them.

I woke one morning to find Anne sitting in a chair at my bedside with the newspapers stacked on her lap, and her walking cane leaning against her chair. Her gold hair had not grayed over the years, but had deepened in color. Anne drank from a steaming cup of chocolate and exclaimed, "The emperor has negotiated a peace in that little war with the Austrians over Italian real estate."

I groaned and kicked off the sheets, still tangled in my nightgown. "What do I care?" Hating all talk of war, I swung my legs over the side of the bed and examined my reflection in the pier glass. My feet were bare but my teeth felt as if they wore socks. I could not quite open my eyes and the hair on the back of my head gnarled like a wad of floss. I sprinkled limewater and Peruvian bark onto a toothbrush. "You haven't answered me, Annie. Why should I care about the war in Italy?"

Anne peered at me over her spectacles, slowly lowering the paper onto her lap. "Because Major Philip Kearny, who was supposedly attached as an American observer to the Cavalry of the Guard, demonstrated such courage in battle that he is said to have inspired the French to rally and win the day."

I scrubbed my teeth, squinting into the mirror and then spat.

Anne continued, "Now the papers say that Philip has accepted the Cross of the Legion of Honor. And just to think, I knew him when."

Wiping my mouth, I muttered, "So, Philip is in France."

"There is a sketch of Major Kearny in the third column. He looks as if he ought to be tying a maiden to the railroad tracks. Shifty-eyed and depraved, it's an accurate likeness, I'd say."

I rapped the toothbrush on the glass. "Does it mention his fleshy little trollop?"

"Philip and *the madam* are in France," Anne mumbled, licking her thumb and turning the page to read the story. "They probably left

America to escape the gossips. I hear they have been very roughly treated in New York. Everyone has cut them."

"But why France? France is *my* new country. Philip ought to go get his own." I snagged a hairbrush over the back of my head. My ladies' maid entered with curling tongs and a small silver pitcher of neroli oil.

"Philip would argue France belongs to him. He *was* here first, wasn't he? When was that, by the by, 1838?" Anne sighed and dropped the newspapers in the chair. "There are some stale issues of the New York *Herald* in that parcel should you care to read them." She caught my eye in the mirror and stroking her hands down both sides of my head observed, "You still love him, don't you?"

I tossed the brush onto the dressing table, opened a jar of cream, and frowned slightly at her. "Don't be silly."

"Hold still. Don't move." Anne dipped my hair comb in neroli oil, combing the sides of my hair flat as a glossy black scarf while my lady's maid heated the curling tongs over the fire.

Two hours later, having taken my breakfast, I fingered aside the curtain in one of the drawing rooms and saw a visitor arriving in the courtyard. Instantly, I recognized the ornate crest on the gilded carriage doors. Why, if I hadn't known better, I might have guessed myself honored to receive the ruling prince of a minor country. But this was Felix Dupanloup, the all-powerful bishop of Orléans, a man renowned throughout Europe as the warrior of the Church, arriving with liveried footmen and a checkered team of four, the iron wheels of his carriage smashing the gravel as his driver brought the horses around. The fifty-nine-year-old bishop alighted from the carriage slowly, with great dignity as befitted a man of his exalted rank. He patted the droop under his chin with the back of his hand.

"He has come to see the notorious American divorcée. The villagers have probably told him that you are poisoning wells," Anne whispered.

"What does he think I shall do? Roll up the whites of my eyes like some backwoods peasant and beg him for eternal salvation?"

"Be nice to him. He could be a most valuable ally to have on our side and I am told he has the ear of the empress."

"I hear he is the bastard son of a laundress from the Savoy," I said turning and watching Anne skitter out into the hall where she grabbed her umbrella from the stand.

"Where are you going?" I called after her.

She straightened her bonnet upon her head and announced, "You are much better than I at diplomacy and so I shall leave the work of charming and befriending the bishop to you. As for me, I do not take tea with Papists. I will not count beads or any other abomination of the times. I am going out for a walk."

The bishop waited for me in one of the smaller drawing rooms. When I greeted him, he turned red from the roots of his silvery blonde hair to his white linen amice—the helmet of salvation he sometimes pulled over his head like a hood to protect himself from drafts and attacks of Satan. "Welcome to Orléans, Madam Kearny," he said, and then motioned to a three-volume treatise on education on the table. "As a welcoming gift, I've brought you the books I have written. I am afraid once I began writing, it took several thousand pages to explain my theories."

"Why thank you." I touched the covers and then patted the dust from my hands. "I shall begin reading them immediately."

"I have not seen you at Mass?" Regally, he lowered himself onto the sofa, placed his hands atop his purple robe.

"So many lovely churches in Orléans. Which is yours?" I asked, tugging on the servants' cord.

"*All* of them," he said in an incredulous tone.

Ah well, by birth, I was a hereditary Presbyterian, but this cleric obviously thought I should understand things that I could not possibly have known. He asked, "Madam, isn't Bullitt a French name?"

"Yes, but my family has always been Protestant. The Bullitts fled

Nîmes after the Wars of Religion when the Catholics massacred my ancestors. You know that old story, don't you? How the Church threw the Protestants into wells and had them drawn and quartered, and so on? Ah, here is Laurence with the tea cart. Will you take refreshments with me?" I asked as Laurence shoved the cart into the room, arranging twifflers and cake forks and napkins.

Bishop Dupanloup scrutinized me with his shrewd and ambitious gaze. His hands were more suited to seining the Loire or yoking oxen than holding a missal. Not one for nuance, the old fellow got straight to the point. "Madam Kearny, I understand you are divorced."

Why was it that this true observation of my marital status still made me blush and feel slightly ashamed of myself? But I avoided his eyes, fussed with the tiered serving tray of pastries, and answered him in a steady voice. "Yes, I have been divorced two years now."

Bishop Dupanloup drew his shoulders up high and then relaxed them. He seemed to contemplate my doom while fingering a scapular bit of a holy card on a satiny ribbon around his neck. "One of my primary tasks, Madam Kearny, is the direction of souls. And the Church teaches us that divorce is a great evil."

I expected Bishop Dupanloup to hiss like a cat and wave his holy card at me. I had no doubt about the purpose of his visit. He meant to convert me. I dropped another sugary gâteau on his plate. "Yes, well, *my* people believe the most important thing about marriage is knowing when to leave it behind."

"Marriage is a sacrament." The bishop rose, stood at the window with his hands clasped at his back, his fine pale hair shining in the dull light. "A woman's silence and humility are the highest ways in which she honors God."

Conversing with the bishop was like talking to a man looking in the mirror at himself. He was a never-listening sort of fellow, just like my former husband.

Lightly tracing circles around the rim of the teacup with my fingertip, I blurted out with a sort of fierce resentment, "You see, this is the troubling part for me; why is it that all religion invariably sacrifices the innocent to save the guilty?"

His Excellency sighed. "Are you unhappy, Madam Kearny?"

"I am as happy as this world will permit."

"Yet you are content to pass eternity in mortal sin?"

"What exactly does that mean in your . . ." I made a little circle with my spoon. "I mean to say, in your Church? This mortal sin?"

"Your soul will never be one with God."

Horrified at this revelation, I held my spoon suspended in mid-air and considered being left out in the cold as everyone else was absorbed into a divine light. If there had been one constant in my life, it was the certain knowledge that God was the only sure and satisfying refuge in times of trouble and that penance naturally follows sorrow.

"Bishop Dupanloup, I hope you won't take offense if I speak plainly."

"No."

"This talk of mortal sin is making me feel positively melancholy."

He smiled benevolently. "Where is your husband?"

"My *former* husband is in Paris, in the service of Emperor Louis-Napoleon. Major Philip Kearny is a very fine killer: Arabs in North Africa, Rogue River Indians in Oregon, Mexicans in Mexico, Plains Indians on the Santa Fe Trail, and anyone else who didn't duck when he began swinging his saber." I lifted the lid of the sugar bowl and tonged lumps into the bishop's cup. Refilling it and putting the pot on the silver tray, I patted a place beside me on the sofa and smiled. "Come sit beside me and tell me all about your Church. If I have lived in sin, it is only because I have never been taught how to live without it."

At the bishop's invitation, I attended for the first time, a Catholic Latin Mass. When I arrived home, I told Anne that it had been a lot like opera because I didn't understand a word anyone was saying, the characters did incomprehensible things, but the staging, costumes, and the lighting were glorious. For the first time in years, here were strangers who were willing to listen to my story without shunning me, a warmly embracing community ready and able to offer solace. Having been disappointed in love, I actively sought to transform my life because the world I lived in was no longer enough.

On Friday afternoon, the children came running home from school, shouting for me as they burst through the front door. "The nuns say you're like Eve." Nannie flew into the room, swinging a rosary above her head like a lasso. She stopped short and bent over to catch her breath.

"How am I like Eve?"

"You gave up your paradise when you left our father."

"Oh, marriage was no paradise. And besides, I am looking forward to a greater paradise."

"What is that?"

"Spending time with you. So, come here, Nannie, and tell me about your day."

Out of sheer nervousness, Nannie had licked a red half moon of chapped skin under her bottom lip. She sat close beside me and pressed her cheek against my arm and mumbled, "I wish divorce wasn't a word."

I found there were aspects of Catholicism that I liked and those I didn't. To begin with, all of my new French friends were Catholic, and I wanted my children and me to truly belong to our new country and to share the religious interests of our friends and community. Moreover, I liked the idea of the confessional because it meant that once a week on Friday, someone would be there to listen as I poured out my heart. But I disliked kneeling on the straw-strewn cold paving stones and that nearly settled it for me, because a little kneeling goes a long way.

As if I hadn't sufficiently scandalized my family by divorcing Philip, I became more and more intrigued by the catechism. In the year that followed, I listened to the bishop's counsel and skewered myself with self-blame. Certain that I should never have agreed to divorce Philip, I was ruthlessly single-minded in my pursuit of absolution. When the bishop said that religious instruction could undo the great evil I'd done my own soul and that of my children, I believed him.

Despite Anne Lane's strenuous objections, and the outspoken, horrified disbelief of my brothers and my sister in America, who harbored deep-seated resentment and prejudice against the faith as being the last refuge of ignorant European peasants, the children and I converted to Catholicism. The bishop had not been able to contain his excitement. "What a story for Rome! The descendant of Huguenots returns to the One True Faith."

A few months later, I removed Anne and the children to Paris, to a lovely old house in the Opéra Quarter at 24 rue de Lisbonne.

Twenty-six

I HAVE NEVER SEEN a person more troubled by growing old than you are," Anne said, peering over my shoulder as the lady's maid pinned a cluster of lilies into the mass of plaits projecting like a basket from the back of my head.

"I am not troubled by growing old," I retorted. "I am fair and fat and forty and bent on enjoying the last remnants of a social life before I have to retire by my hearth with a house cap and my knitting basket."

"But you run around as if you were twenty-five, taking the children with you hither and yon to one grandee's house after another, roaming Europe as if you were the most restless creature God ever invented. Your wild traveling leaves you exhausted, as if you're trying to exorcise your demons while you roam and roam. Are you searching for something? Why are you so unsettled?"

"It is the restlessness of age, I guess." I turned my head aside, held an earring to my lobe. "What do you think of this one?" I rose from the chair and putting my fingers under Anne's chin said, "This would look better on you. The color suits you. The topaz brings out the gold in your eyes."

Anne primped in the mirror and smiled. "These do look better on me." And suddenly turning serious, she asked, "Will your beau be there? Has Baron von Raasch spoken to you about this?"

I shrugged. Anne glanced cautiously at my lady's maid and whispered, "The children say he shall surely propose marriage."

She meant the ruddy, blonde, and handsome Danish general I'd met a few months ago at a hunting party in the Orléannais. Since then, Baron von Raasch had come to call three times a week, laying siege to my parlor, waiting patiently until my other visitors had left before urging me to confide in him and tell him my story. Ever cautious, I declined to share my secrets, but this only seemed to intrigue the general and my reticence spurred his interest.

"No, Anne, that simply isn't true." I paused, noticing my maid listening intently. "Baron von Raasch is my dear friend, but I am not about to become his wife or his mistress. The last thing my children need to hear is that Paris has yet another courtesan."

"He is very persistent, the baron."

"And I am resolute," I said, tossing a wrap over my shoulders and departing.

In August of 1859, I had received an invitation to the Tuileries Palace, which was not to say the invitation in itself was unique. As many as four thousand people attended the royal parties in any given season and it was said that everyone in Paris except the street sweepers had dined at the Tuileries. Usually, the social season at court opened in January and ended on Easter, but after the summer war against the Austrians, the royal family threw over their usual routine and hosted a series of parties in the off-season.

On Monday, August 29, 1859, a humid and sultry night—I arrived alone at the Palais de Tuileries. I waited a long while as the conveyances ahead of me disgorged guests into the courtyard. When at last my door was opened, the cabin flooded with light from the entrance hall of the Pavilion de l'Horloge. I detected the distinctive moldy odor of the palace, of water on stone and the musky choking perfume worn by both the men and the women.

Under the marquee, I entered behind three young courtesans wearing stuffed hummingbirds and dead butterflies in their hair. As I passed the Swiss Guards with their useless halberds, I met my escort for the evening, a fellow Southern expatriate named Edwin De Leon. He wore white knee breeches, a fluffy lace jabot, and shining silver buckles on his shoes.

"Mrs. Kearny! I feared that you might not come after all," De Leon exclaimed, offering me his arm. The heat from many bodies and the dim gaslight in the crowded hallway was oppressive.

I snapped open my fan and fluttered it around my face. "I am tempted to put a little ice in my ears to rouse myself."

De Leon lowered his shining face close to mine and smiled. Brown decay lined his front teeth. He said, "I have it on good authority that you will be asked to join the empress for a private audience this evening."

"Well, I simply can't. I have to get home to my children."

"You must not refuse her! And she may be able to help our cause. Ah, we are going in."

I let my hand rest lightly on his forearm. "*Our* cause?" I asked. "What *cause*?"

By his expression, it was apparent he thought I was being coy. De Leon was an agent of the Southern states sent to France by rich and politically connected planters to advance the political interests of the South if Lincoln was elected. Should there be disunion, the South would need France to recognize the sovereign independence of the new Confederacy. Trade between the two nations would be essential to the survival of the cotton and sugar industries. Unlike many of my Southern kinsmen, I did not harbor delusions of a great victory. Having lived in New York, I feared that if my relatives took up arms against a people twice as numerous as our own, and with every resource on land and sea to aid them, our time of sore judgment would come sooner rather than later. Whenever De Leon raised the issue of disunion, I deflected his comments by drawing his attention to the other guests and observing peculiarities about them.

The Tuileries Palace did not inspire awe. Rather, we walked down a long hallway, squinting up at the sagging water-stained ceilings and staying clear of walls where the rats slinked into the ventilation holes. The ladies and gentlemen strutted into a huge salon to wait for the chamberlain to introduce us to our partners, who would "carry us" into the dining hall. The seating arrangement inspired gossip and was designed to amuse the emperor and empress with unlikely pairings.

The chamberlain bowed and said, "Monsieur De Leon, will you follow me?"

Left alone, I smiled hello to people I knew and amused myself observing the other women. Empress Eugénie had set the standard, for she loved blondes. All of the ladies except me had bleached their hair until it was orange as a copper pot and coarse as hay straw. The ladies wore bright blue paint on their eyelids and sweat-streaked white pearl powder that made their teeth look wolfishly yellow by comparison. Belladonna in the eyes gave them a slightly drugged, but compliant, expression. As for the gentlemen, they emulated Emperor Louis-Napoleon and wore pointy mustaches with waxed ends. Scarlet sashes slung over their shoulders and bulging middles so that every man looked like an ambassador to his own planet.

I wore no cosmetics and must have looked quaintly aboriginal by comparison. A few moments passed wherein I turned to chat with another lady. My back was to the entrance of the dining hall when the chamberlain discreetly cleared his throat behind me.

"Oh!" I was slightly embarrassed at having been caught off-guard.

The chamberlain bowed and extended a hand to his left. "Madam Kearny, may I introduce Major Philip Kearny? He will lead you in this evening."

Philip inclined his head slightly to say hello, and yet, it struck me that his demeanor was haughtier than the emperor's. Around us, fans snapped open to conceal gleeful smiles and whispers. I wanted time to stop so that I might look at him and observe the changes in him. Philip wore an American-style white cravat and tailcoat; a lean and spare man in a room filled with plump, perfumed, and delicate little courtiers with soft hands. Having just returned from Italy, his skin was sun-scorched, his hair graying, and his hairline receded on the right side.

I had thought that should I ever see Philip again, my insides would feel numb and cold. What false element in my soul made me so weak?

Standing close to him, I could smell his familiar mustache pomade— the brand he used to buy from the barber at the New York Hotel. Long ago, when he kissed me, I smelled it on my skin for hours after.

My fan hung from a chain on my wrist, I flicked it open and fanned myself, breaking gaze with him. Gradually, I became aware of the sound of beating wings, of the flapping whoosh when a flock of geese rise into the air. Startled and flushed, I glanced around and saw a hundred fans thrumming back and forth and the low excited chatter of the ladies who wielded them.

"We're providing the evening's entertainment, it seems." And then he lowered his face close to mine, so close that I could see the corners of his mouth quivering under his mustache and his eyes lit up with unexpected excitement; instantly, I understood that Philip perceived me, or rather the two of us together, as promising an exhilaratingly risky proposition for the evening. "Take my arm, Mrs. Kearny," he said, crooking his right elbow and holding steady until I placed my fingertips upon his forearm.

As we walked to our places, I suffered through a leaping flood of emotion. He glanced down at my hand as if worrying that I might take it away before he was quite ready to release me. But then we took our seats at the long table with our backs to a fireplace large enough for roasting a whole village of peasants. Philip sat on my right and Edwin De Leon on my left.

I removed my gloves for dinner, and the other ladies did the same. Tucking them on my lap under my napkin, I glanced at Philip. He was staring ferociously at his glove as the other men were sliding theirs off. I knew he did not wish to be the only one at the table eating while wearing a glove, so I leaned aside and whispered, "If you will allow me, I shall help you."

He put his hand under the table and quickly, I unbuttoned the glove. But when my thumbs touched his palm, he closed his fingers and squeezed. I met his eyes. His expression was soft and tender and yearning. Damn him.

"Open your hand, Philip," I said.

He relaxed his hand and I pushed the kidskin up his palm, released his thumb, the soft hide bunching over his calloused knuckles. He opened his mouth as if he were going to say something, but did not.

I dropped the glove on his lap.

We were pressed together from the bones of our shoulders to the muscular line of his thigh to his knee. Simply being near enough to smell him, to feel the heat of his body, gave me considerable uneasiness and a creeping hot blush covered me from forehead to breastbone. I trembled so badly that I could not lift the soup spoon to my lips without spilling it. I jerked my hand and one of the forks went flying over my shoulder. The lackey behind me jumped out of the way.

Philip made a pinching motion, "Almost got him. You were this close."

I clenched my hands together under the table, all the while shivering and swept up in my own awkwardness as I tried to recite my rosary prayer of bad memories with Philip; a long black string and each bead a betrayal, a wound he had inflicted upon my heart. But to no avail, the familiar comfort of my own resentment eluded me, my own memory betrayed me as did my own senses. Now and again, the waiters would serve me a plate and then remove it, untouched. The string quartet played behind a lattice screen and a white-wigged boy lurked behind each seated guest, while a battalion of servants rushed in and out of the dining hall.

Philip made a low grumbling sound, crooked his finger, and summoned me near. Seemingly caught in a web of his own words, he hesitated and then murmured without meeting my eyes, "After you deserted me, Diana, I kept one of your chemises, one you'd worn, and it held your scent. I crumpled it under my cheek and slept with it for years, even after I remarried. One night, Agnes came in and found it on my pillow."

I pretended to study the epergnes of sugared grapes and pears, wondering if I could endure the slow limping of the hours until I was once again free of him. I asked, "How is Agnes Maxwell?"

"Agnes?"

"Your wife. And where is she, by the by?"

"At home. She doesn't do well at these things."

"By her account or yours?"

Philip and I were conspicuously not eating, and our own promptings and hesitations were beginning to wear upon us both. We both sat rigidly upright, our faces flushed, sneaking glances at one another and yet, trying not to behave foolishly. I felt his hand clasping mine under the table linens.

"Take your hand away."

"You're my wife. I should be able to touch your hand."

"*Was.* I *was* your wife."

"Seeing you destroys the present, Diana. Why won't you understand that all I can think of is our shared past?"

"Well, don't. Eat your asparagus."

"I dislike asparagus or have you forgotten?"

"Oh, please forgive me. I've been preoccupied with other matters. For example, raising your four children all by myself."

"I have handsome children. I saw them and you at the parade."

There are some wounds in life that are very painful and the memory of my children and how each of them had learned to live without their father rushed upon me all at once. I cut the potato croquette into cubes and thought of them waiting for me at home.

"How is John?" he asked.

"John wants to be a soldier."

"He does?" Philip sat up and blinked rapidly, his face bright with pleasure.

I pushed the food around on my plate and met his eyes. "And he wishes to know why you hate him. He writes you letters every week, Philip. Why have you never answered them? He looks like you and sounds like you and has your restless nature."

Taken aback by this, Philip frowned, but asked defensively, "John thinks I dislike him? Why would he think such a thing?"

But before I could reply, Edwin De Leon tapped upon my forearm, and asked, "Does the pheasant displease you, Mrs. Kearny?"

"I wouldn't know, Mr. De Leon, as I haven't tasted it."

Edwin De Leon licked his lips and grinned mischievously. "Did you hear the uproar at the end of the table? The Comte de Kermezen ordered a second helping of soup. The emperor will think him a social monster for holding up the courses and delaying dinner."

"Diana, I must speak with you alone," Philip broke in. "It must be providence that we were brought here together," he said with a passionately solicitous frown.

I leaned aside and whispered, "I won't be tempted by you, Philip. My new faith is like armor." As if to prove my point, I made a fist of my left hand and thumped my chest, and then felt stupid for having done it. If faith were armor, mine was made of a very thin paper. Why, I could feel it shredding with every word Philip spoke, falling away in ashes as if it had never been there in the first place. Whatever my soul might want, my body had no interest in eternal salvation.

"I hadn't been aware that I was tempting you." He smiled slyly.

I reached for one of the wine goblets, wishing I hadn't said a word because neither of us could deny our slowly evolving mutual desire, a desire as palpable as the taste of the sugared lemons on our plates, a desire that lingered on the tongue, penetrated the heart, and numbed all reason.

"Pity to hide such beauty under armor." Philip raised his brows, but I drew a breath, gathered my wits, and turned away from him, devoting my attention to my other dinner partner, Edwin De Leon. The agent, irked that my attention had been divided between himself and Philip, said, "You will be given a private audience tonight and you must impress upon Eugénie a just idea of the ample resources and vast military strength of the South. You must raise the character of the South in the general estimation of the court."

Philip curled his lip at De Leon, glaring over the rim of his wine-glass as he took a sip.

"That is rather a lot for one woman to do, Monsieur De Leon," I mused. The food, served on electroplated silver, was cold, having been brought up a long a distance from the basement of the palace.

"Your brother Aleck Bullitt is owner and editor of the New Orleans *Picayune*?" De Leon asked.

Philip made his stern face. "Diana, we are almost out of time—listen to me." And then he pinched the soft skin on the top of my arm through my silk sleeve. "When we are given the signal to adjourn for smoking and music, do not go into the salon. Instead, follow me out the door into the garden so that we may speak."

"I am conversing with Monsieur De Leon."

Philip picked up his knife and drummed an impatient tattoo on the table linen. I glanced around at the other guests, who seemed to be watching us discreetly and whispering about our antics.

But agent De Leon was intent to his purpose, saying, "The *Havas-Bullier* Telegraphic and Correspondence Agency is the only telegraphic news service in France. Ask your brother Aleck Bullitt to furnish articles from the South and the *Havas-Bullier* will reprint them. News from the United States is difficult to obtain. This way, the Southern point of view will be published here." De Leon dabbed at his lips with his napkin.

Philip leaned across me so that I felt the muscles of his back against my breasts. It took all of my resolve not to clutch him to me. The back of his neck above his collar where his valet had shaved under his hairline bore the slightest stubble. When we were married, I used to brush my lips there. As he spoke to De Leon, I couldn't resist reaching up and touching him in the sunburned crease of his neck with the tip of my gloved finger.

"De Leon, you contemptible driveller! Don't involve my wife in your ugly tricks. Diana won't be part of your malignant designs."

"Well!" De Leon laughed. "I don't think you have a say, Major Kearny! You are a Southerner first, are you not, Madam Kearny?"

"I am an American first, Monsieur De Leon." This displeased the agent enormously but as he sputtered a reply, I regarded my former husband.

"Diana, meet me after dinner outside in the courtyard by the fountain of the pissing cherubs and stop talking to De Leon. Everyone in France knows he is a spy and a poor one at that, he is so indiscreet."

"Unlike *you*, Philip."

"Discretion is the soul of my nature."

Dinner concluded and the emperor and empress rose from opposite ends of the long table. We promenaded out into a reception hall where the men adjourned to smoke while the ladies assembled in the *Salon d'Appolon* for insipid warbling in the music room.

With my head down, I cut a diagonal toward the doors leading out to the garden.

Philip followed close behind me. But before the footmen could open the doors, the chamberlain raced after us and, catching me with a hand to my elbow, said breathlessly, "Please, Madam Kearny, the empress has asked for you. And Major Kearny, you have been asked for, as well."

"Just think, my ancestors left this country to avoid these people," I whispered to Philip. "Truly, I dislike being detained on such short notice."

"It will be over quickly. They aren't too bright and they've had a lot to drink. So speak in short sentences, use little words, and apologize for everything."

"I will not!"

"Diana, lower your voice." Philip gazed at me with an intensely baffled expression.

"Don't tell me what to do. You've lost that privilege."

"Kiss me before we go in." He had the audacity to try to touch my face, but I was too quick for him. "Kiss me and I will calm instantly." He bent slightly, placed his right hand on my forearm, and pursed his lips.

I jerked free of him. "I am *not your wife*. You made sure of that. I am not your wife!"

"You're my wife, whether you like it or not."

"Oh, shut up, Philip, and give me your hand."

"Why?"

"You must put your glove on before we go in."

"Oh yes, of course." Philip murmured as a smile played around his lips and his eyes moistened, grew soft, and focused intensely on me.

"Don't look love at me, I am only trying to be considerate."

"If you truly disliked me, you'd let me go in naked-handed."

"Let go of my arm. You're clinging to me like a limpet."

The next quarter of an hour was a strange foible. Emperor Louis-Napoleon impressed me as greasy little ptarmigan smelling of lilac cologne, a dementedly sensual man with stupidity finely grained into his character. The abbreviated emperor nodded grandly to Philip. "The empress and I are most interested in the temper of the American South."

Naturally, Philip hadn't taken his own advice, but he blathered on about the evil of disunion and the sheer rottenness of the South. Philip talked and he talked and he talked. While he spoke, I yawned and sighed and pressed my gloved hand to my temples as if suffering a monumental headache. I puffed air over my lips and blew stray locks of hair off my brows, and rolling my eyes, looked pointedly at him, but to no avail, his anti-South speech droned on and on.

At one moment in Philip's long dull lecture, I turned sharply and stared into the shadows across the room as if I were watching an invisible mouse scurry along the floor.

The emperor and empress both turned on their thrones to follow my gaze.

"Yes, yes, thank you, Major Kearny," the emperor finally said.

"What a fascinating man you are, Major Kearny," the empress said, having a closer look at him through her glasses. "Don't you agree . . . *Mrs.* Kearny?"

"If talking a great deal makes a man fascinating, then Major Kearny is so."

My former husband hissed like a leaking balloon. "That was unkind and uncalled for," he whispered from the side of his mouth.

Forgetting the two short fat people sitting in the big chairs, I whirled on him and said, "Did you know I would be here this evening? Is that why you came?"

"Well, of course. I had an idea . . ." He glanced nervously sidelong at the emperor.

"All of this nonsense you've been babbling about the South, well truth be told, forcing my countrymen to remain in a union against their will is like forcing a bride to the altar when she knows without a doubt that she's marrying a disgusting hedonist with no thought or care for the marriage other than satisfying his own lustful impulses."

Philip clapped his gloved hand to his forehead and rolled his eyes. "Diana, that is the oldest, dustiest, most irrelevant argument you could possibly put forth."

"No, do you know what is irrelevant to me? You. You, Philip, are irrelevant."

The empress drew a breath and released it in a slow high-pitched gasp.

"How can the father of your children possibly be irrelevant?"

"Because he's made himself so."

The emperor pressed his finger alongside his nose, glanced up at the ceiling, and asked, "Are you saying then, Mrs. Kearny, that the federal government of the United States would be the bullying groom—"

"Shh," said the empress to her husband. "I want to hear what the wife has to say."

In the grip of a blinding fury, I grabbed Philip's arm and made him look at me. "Just tell me the truth, for once in your life, tell me what I did to make you so unhappy that you had to amuse yourself with all of those other women? Be merciful just this once and tell me how I failed you, Philip, because I have blamed myself for years, I've tortured myself and thought of little else. Put my mind at ease and tell me the truth. Wasn't I pretty enough? Not stylish, not witty? Not inventive when we were alone? Why wasn't I enough?"

The empress murmured, "Ah, the major has the weakness common to all men. And I thought he might be different."

Philip shifted his weight nervously and squinted as if trying to see me through his own illusions. "Why would you think you had failed me? You never failed me."

I released his arm, threw my hands in the air, and turned my back on him. He grabbed the waistband of my dress and said through clenched teeth, "Diana, you mustn't show their majesties your back."

"Goddamn you, Philip!"

"Then don't believe me, but I have never in all of these years recovered from you abandoning me. When I'm alone, I revisit those years in Washington and New York and I try to understand, but for the life of me I cannot. I think of all of the letters I wrote to you, how I came for you and begged you to return, and yet you were so cold."

I faced him, my hands on my hips, my voice shaking with emotion. "You must really hate me to torment me in this way."

He turned aside and scrutinized me, shaking his head slowly, trembling and confused. Then he said, "I have never loved anyone but you. That is why I say these things . . . who else would I say them to but you?"

When I did not reply, but spun on my heel and started for the door, he followed, calling to me. "Very well then, if it makes a difference, I accept responsibility for having destroyed our happiness. I was wrong. I betrayed you. And I have regretted it because it has cost me you, my family, the respect of my friends and relatives, and the admiration of my countrymen."

We had nearly reached the door when the Spanish-born empress leaned forward slightly, tapping her fan into the palm of her gloved hand as she said to her husband, "Watching these two is better than going to the theater, don't you agree?" And raising her voice, she called loudly across the vast throne room, "Major Kearny? Madam Kearny? Come to Compiègne for a *série*. Mind, Major, we are inviting *only* you. And mind, Madam Kearny, we are inviting *only* you."

"Thank you, I'm afraid that simply isn't going to be possible," I said, but Philip glared aghast at me, and with crushing force, stepped on my foot. "Hush, Diana."

"Don't you hush me."

A few minutes later, we backed out of the throne room, bowing and scraping as if grateful for the dreary episode. Once the doors closed, he puffed out his chest. "Well, I think they admired me. Don't you?"

"You have always preferred being flattered by an insignificant mind to being treated as an equal by an honest one."

Undeterred, Philip grasped my hands and pleaded, "Stay and dance with me."

"No, thank you, I'd prefer to avoid the fret of wrestling with you on the dance floor. And besides, you don't dance, Philip, or have you forgotten?"

"Then come with me for a drive. Take a glass of wine with me."

I flicked my hand at a footman and sent him searching for my cloak. "It is hastening onto midnight and I am tired."

The footman summoned my carriage and tossed my shawl over my shoulders. As the evening was in full swing, we were alone under the marquee. Gathering my shawl around me, I couldn't help smiling up at Philip. The blustering old fool was delighted with himself. He stroked his mustache with his thumb and forefinger and grinned. "Like old times, wasn't it? Didn't you and I have fun?"

"That was a long season ago."

"Kiss me good night, Diana."

I began to make my excuses, but he drew me against him and I felt his body pressing urgently against mine as he lowered his face. His mouth quivered at the corners, but as our lips were about to touch, I quickly raised my fan as a barrier and Philip ardently kissed the bunch of peacock feathers. Grimacing, he wiped his mouth with the back of his hand. "Don't you think it slightly ridiculous to play coy at this point in our lives?"

"I'm not playing coy. I am in the company of a married man who is behaving badly."

Shutting the carriage door, he stood up on the pedal and leaned in the window.

"Diana, I shall see you at Compiègne."

"But I am not going to Compiègne."

"You must! You can't decline a royal invitation. They'll cut off your head."

"I can do whatever I please. We rebels can do as we please. Drive on."

"But when will I see you?" he asked, refusing to jump off the pedal.

"In another eight years, perhaps? Good night, Philip," and rapping the ceiling with my fan, I let the curtain fall over the window.

Twenty-seven

I CAME HOME that night in a fever. Seeing Diana brought back the world I had loved my whole life. As a young man, my impulsivity had blown my prospects to the wind but I would change all of that. Believing procrastination to be the thief of time, I set to work, did not sleep, but went directly to my writing desk, opened the humidor, clipped the end of the cigar, lit it, and squinting through the smoke, wrote to Diana explaining my intentions.

And what were my ignoble intentions? I wished to begin an affair of intrigue with my own damn wife and felt a fool for it. Yet, I wrote into the small hours. It took acrobatic effort to stand on my dignity while groveling for her favor. A thousand infallible arguments about why I ought to gain her heart poured forth from my pen. Pausing only to sip Madeira and light yet another cigar, I couldn't help thinking of her mouth, for it was dark and ripe as a blood plum. I will say this of Diana; she has ever been uphill work.

At seven in the morning, still sitting in my chair with a hand to my forehead, I looked up to see Agnes in the door. Wordlessly, she walked behind me, her taffeta skirts rustling as she reached for the curtains, opened them, and tucked them into their braces. Light fell over my head and neck, and yawning, I signed the twenty-page letter.

"Where were you last night?"

"At the palace." I placed a wax wafer over the flap of the envelope, lifted the globe from the lamp and held my brass stamp in the flame until the metal glowed. Then, I pressed the stamp with my initials into the wax.

"But after . . . were you up all night writing?"

"Yes."

"To whom?" Her voice wavered.

"A military friend at home."

"Which one?"

"Agnes, see to breakfast."

"Oh, look at your face, Philip. How lovelorn you are! You are thinking of Diana, aren't you?"

I pushed the chair back and stood and felt her taking me in with her eyes. How had she intuited that? Despite all of the years that had passed, I could never hear Diana's name without a beating of my heart. "Nonsense, Agnes, why would you think such a thing?"

"Because you will always love her the most, and you love her because she was the only woman who ever defied you," she whispered.

Clutching the letter in my hand, I brushed by her and went into the hall. There, I told one of the footmen to deliver it to the rue de Lisbonne and dropped a few francs into his hand.

Agnes followed me, staring after the footman as he descended the steps and went down the street. "Where is he taking that letter?"

"The lamp in my study is smoking. Tell the chambermaid to soak the wick in vinegar and see that it is well trimmed."

Later that day on a beautiful summer's morning with the windows open, Agnes sat behind the piano; I had fallen asleep sitting in the chair. I woke with a start to hear Agnes warbling a love song. Groggy with fatigue, I walked by her, grabbed the music from the piano, and crumpled it into a ball.

At three o'clock in the afternoon my valet woke me from a nap and pressed an envelope into my hand. Without lifting my head from the pillow, I opened it.

Diana had replied to me.

> *Your letter came this morning. I shall meet you*
> *tomorrow afternoon at one o'clock at the villa in the*
> *Bagatelle Gardens in the Bois de Boulogne.*

At the appointed hour, I rode to the *bois*, expectant and happy as a boy. I'd brought Diana a gift of a fan, a beautiful ivory, pearl, and gold fan that had cost me a small fortune, the silk and parchment center had been hand-painted with scenes of Diana the huntress. With my gift in my pocket, I waited in a cloud of insects, listening to a mossy trickle of water out of a fountain by the rose garden. I opened my watch and checked the time every three minutes. At a quarter past one o'clock, a woman in an open carriage, holding a parasol over her head halted on the graveled road, and sheltering her eyes with her hand, called, "Philip? Philip, is that you?"

"Agnes!"

"But what are you doing here?"

"Did you follow me?"

I could see by her simpering smile that she most surely had followed me.

"Philip, I don't understand. Why are you here in the rose garden? Why this place is famous for assignations."

"Go home, Agnes. Go home where you belong."

"I would rather wait with you."

Without replying to Agnes, I said to the driver, "Take Mrs. Kearny home now."

"Yes, sir," said the driver. He knew who paid his wages.

Though I waited more than an hour for Diana, she never came.

Thinking we must have misunderstood one another, I rode to her house on the rue de Lisbonne and presented myself at her door.

Diana's stone house was typical of those in the Opéra Quarter, four stories high and narrow, with a mansard roof. All of my good intentions were folly and wasted upon a frivolous woman who could not be troubled to keep her appointments even though I had generously supplied her every means of comfort and luxury. I paused on the walk and looked up at the noble facade of the grand old place. Leaning from the upper-story windows were two girls and a boy, whom I supposed to be my children. The young man resembled me so much it was like going back in time through a mirror.

I am quite certain now that Diana raised my own children to hate me. Many times over the years I thought to write to them, considered trying to visit them, but to what purpose? My children regarded me from the window with benign curiosity, and then went back to their bantering, which I could hear from the street. One of my daughters playing a piano, one daughter sang a tune, and the boy talked to them over the music.

I grabbed the old-fashioned knocker and pounded on the brass plate. A maid opened the door and greeted me. Sitting behind her on the stairs was an eleven-year-old girl in pantalets and a tartan party frock. Upon seeing me, a look of utter disappointment crossed her pretty face and she sank down on the step with her chin in her hand.

"Is Mrs. Kearny in?" I asked in French.

"Who is calling?" the maid replied.

"That is a private matter."

"If you will not announce yourself, I cannot admit you, sir." The maid began to close the door but I forced it open with my walking stick. Had I not been impeccably dressed, the maid might have been more alarmed, but as I pushed by her and stood in the hall looking around, she was merely chagrined.

The child came around to have a better look at me. She was a beautiful fine-boned girl with enormous dark eyes like Diana, and yet, too, I saw myself in the nobler refinement of her features.

"May I tell Mama who is calling?"

"What is your name?"

"I am Elizabeth Kearny."

"Ah." Here was my youngest child, conceived the night Diana and I came home from the opera, the child my father held in his arms before dying, and dismissed as having a religious nature.

"What is your name?" she asked, poking her finger into the receiving dish filled with *cartes des visites*, swirling the cards around and then plucking out one of mine. Of late, it had become the fashion to leave a photograph instead of a name card. My picture must have displeased the girl, because she wrinkled her nose and dropped it back into the receiver.

The maid said something to discourage this conversation but the girl would not be deterred.

I tried a trick on her to test her response. "Is your father at home?"

"No, sir, my father is dead."

"Dead! How did your father die?"

"In childbed. He died when I was born."

Clearly, my daughter's French convent education had failed her.

"Who told you that nonsense?"

"Me. It is something I tell myself."

"Do you ever wonder about him?"

"About whom?"

"Your father, girl."

"No."

"But why not?" I asked impatiently. Why wouldn't she think of me? It was damnably unnatural.

"I have never known him. It is impossible to miss someone you have never known. And Mama says he was awful and wicked to her. So, I am glad he is dead."

While I digested this poison nugget, the child clasped her hands at her back, glimpsed herself in the hall-stand mirror, and toed a circle upon the old limestone floor. "But I should like to think that my father would look exactly like the Baron von Raasch, as the baron is the most handsome man I think I have ever seen."

This took me aback. "Baron von Raasch, the Danish general? How do you know him?"

"He is our friend and protector." The child bowed forward a little, put her hand beside her mouth, and whispered, "Baron von Raasch has been begging Mama to marry him. He is with her in the study. Would you like me to lead you in?"

I did not need her help. I strode down the hall to the second parlor where I could hear Diana's soft laughter and von Raasch murmuring something. I halted at the door.

Peering through the crack like some disgusting voyeur, I saw my wife sitting on a chair and von Raasch across from her, his knees touching hers. Diana, with teacup and saucer in her hands, inclined forward, lifted her face to him and von Raasch touched her cheek with his fingertips. Diana's lips parted as they met his and von Raasch kissed my wife slowly and languorously in such a way that I knew instantly they had been lovers for a long while.

Outraged by her infidelity, I kicked open the door and stood there, as I saw no reason for words. Diana whipped around and looked at me, her eyes dark and fierce and vibrant. Von Raasch jumped to his feet and reached into his coat for his sidearm, but Diana put her hand across his chest.

She crossed the room, stood on the threshold opposite me, and I will swear until the day I die that her eyes were brimming with tears. Had I, in that instant, reached for her, had I demanded that she come away with me and sit at my table and sleep in my bed, I know that my future would have changed. But for once in my life, I hesitated.

"You were not at the *bois*. Who is that man?" I demanded.

"Have you ever wondered how I felt all of those nights when I knew you were sleeping in the arms of other women? Well, Philip, it felt just like this." And calmly, deliberately, Diana shut the door in my face and turned the key in the lock.

To hell with her! Let her rot in old age and loneliness and regret her crimes against me.

Once again, Diana had wronged me to the utmost.

Twenty-eight

A T FIRST, when I received Philip's love letter, an ardent and poetic elegy to all the reasons and the times he had loved me, I was ready to run to him. More than a love letter, he had written a prayer for things I could not grant. Despite all, I told myself, I would not judge of any of his past actions until I knew the particulars. *I wish to love you, too,* was what I thought. But had I done so, it would have given lie to what I had salvaged of myself from the wreckage of my marriage. There is a time to let go of the rope, and so, I let go. This is not to say that I did not know the sickening swoop as I bent over the ledge to watch the last remnants of my love drop the long drop into the blackened gorge. I closed my eyes and for all the world felt myself extending my arms and plummeting after, down into the smooth choking darkness. Final farewells are deathly, after all.

After Lincoln was elected president in the autumn of 1860, war became certain and agent Edwin De Leon pressured me to accept the empress's invitation to Compiègne. But I had no wish to be thrown into company with Philip and so declined to go. It seemed a year of declinations, for after much contemplation, and with great regret, I even refused the Baron von Raasch. After a time, he stopped calling upon me and I heard that he had married another. As a Catholic, I could never remarry, for the Church and most people of my acquaintance considered remarriage a greater sin than divorce. All well and good, for I had had enough of marriage to last any woman a lifetime.

Anne Lane grew worried about her family in St. Louis. Fearing they might need her in the coming crisis, we bid one another a tearful farewell, and promised to reunite as soon as time and circumstances allowed.

In the evenings, I took my ease in the second parlor; a velvet and garnet room where I'd hung the portrait of my sisters in our white dresses over the fireplace. Some days, as I drank my tea, I'd stare at it and find it hard to believe twenty-six years had passed since we sat together on the summer lawn under the ash trees. I put on my spectacles, and standing before the painting, scrutinized it for wear and telltale cracks and it gratified me that no matter how much time had dwindled away, in this painting at least, we were all beautiful, strong, young, and hopeful about our futures. I often wondered how our lives might have differed had we never married, but lived happily ever after as spinsters under one rooftree.

Nearing Christmas of 1861, Nannie and Di came running into the parlor carrying a large brown paper parcel tied in string, addressed from my sister Mary. I sat in a chair close to the fire with my feet up on a stool, my workbasket at my side and a blanket over my lap, hemming handkerchiefs for my girls. Di, a young lady of seventeen with hair black as treacle and fair skin, wore the new short skirts favored by the empress, a wide dome three inches off the ground. Nannie, in braids and pantalets, flew in behind her. Elizabeth followed, carrying her pet turtle in her hands. John, now sixteen, was out riding with friends from seminary school.

Out of long habit and education, the girls spoke only French at home.

"Open the package, Mama! We want to read the news."

"The letter opener is on my writing desk, Di. Why don't you open the parcel for us?" I said, slipping a porcelain thimble over my thumb. The three girls sat side by side on the sofa, bowing their heads over the treasures inside. Di sorted through the envelopes and papers as Nannie blurted out the contents.

"Newspaper articles written by Uncle Aleck in the New Orleans *Picayune*. Uncle Aleck has written, *Direct these articles to Mr. Edwin De Leon to be given to* Havas-Bullier Telegraphic News. Oh, and look, here is a letter from Aunt Mary marked urgent, read immediately!"

I put my sewing aside and reached for the letter from Mary. "How odd," I said. "It is postmarked Fairfax County, Virginia. Why is Mary in Virginia?"

"Visiting family, perhaps?"

"A letter from a lady named Emily V. Mason!" Nannie shouted.

"Lower your voice, Nannie. You sound like a foghorn."

I slipped my spectacles over my nose as I unfolded the letter from my sister. Her ordinarily bold handwriting was little more than a faint scrawl. Di came up behind my chair, and peering over my shoulder, read along silently. I handed the pages to her as I finished them, and Di gave them to Nannie, who gave them to Elizabeth.

> *My Dear Sister Diana,*
>
> *I am in the deepest possible distress. I have been making a visit to our cousin, Miss Emily Mason, whom you will remember having met at White Sulphur Springs in happier times. During our stay here in Fairfax County, Virginia, I took a fever, and have been so ill, that the doctor says soul cannot help but separate from body. I only hope the Lord in His infinite mercy will interpose on my behalf. More than my own troubles, I worry over Miss Mason, who has been burdened with looking after*

me. Could you come back, if only for a short while, to
comfort me in the time I have left?
    Your affectionate sister,
    Mary

Removing my spectacles, I folded them, and slid them into the velvet pouch, thinking a moment. The girls were silent and watchful, whispering speculation to one another. I patted the arms of the chair, and smiled brightly at them. "How would you feel about living awhile in Virginia?"

Elizabeth lifted her turtle and stroked the top of his shell. "Why, the mere idea makes me so unhappy! There are wild Indians in Virginia, aren't there, Mama?"

"But I don't wish to go back to America. Everyone says there is going to be a terrible war!" Di exclaimed, her face scarlet with worry.

"If there is a war, no harm will come to Virginia," I said, rising and poking at the coal fire.

"Why not?" Elizabeth asked.

"Because Virginia is the mother state of all of the Union. President Lincoln wouldn't dare hurt anyone in Virginia."

"I hear Americans live in tents and eat raw buffalo." Nannie studied the ends of her braids and brushed her cheek with them. "Is there any food in America? Are we going back there only to starve to death?"

Elizabeth whispered, "America is the land of guns and honey."

Di said to Nannie, "We'll have to carry pistols and dirks wherever we go."

"Why, daughters, do you forget you are Americans?"

They all three stiffened slightly as if I had insulted them.

I went to my writing desk and penned a letter to Mary and to Emily Mason. I told my sister to have hope for I would soon be with her. I begged indulgence of Miss Mason, thanking her for her exertions on behalf of my family. I asked Miss Mason not to move my sister for fear she might suffer from the exercise of travel and change of atmosphere. That accomplished, I set the children and the servants to work dismantling the house and packing trunks. I could not afford to ship my furniture to America, as the custom would have broken my finances, but I did take clothing, and uncertain what the future might hold, I took the *Bullitt Sisters as the Fates*.

I thought it might cheer Mary to see it one last time.

≈ Native Soil ≈

Twenty-nine

ONE WINTER MORNING in Paris as I chewed my croissant and sipped my coffee, perusing the *Journals des Debats*, I read a crowing article written by my former brother-in-law Aleck Bullitt about South Carolina seceding from the Union.

I made plans to return to America, impatient to leave Paris, fearing I would miss the war and fighting. In the next few months, I arranged our return to Bellegrove in New Jersey. We sailed in March and two weeks later, I rode up in advance of Agnes's carriage. The grounds-keeper scrambled to open the gate for me, but I beat him to it, and jumped my horse over. In high spirits, I galloped down the quarter-mile drive bordered by pine trees and flowering viburnam shrubs. The care-taker, housekeeper, and my whole household staff gathered on the steps, waving their handkerchiefs and bobbing curtseys as we pulled around.

From the baggage wagon, I grabbed the valise I always kept packed with spare clothing and incidentals for emergencies. Agnes was unfas-tening her cloak and handing it to the maid.

"Philip? Where are you going?"

"To Washington and then to Albany to obtain a commission. New York may very well make me a division commander on the spot. Who knows, President Lincoln may soon put the entire army under my command. I have more battlefield experience than any other army officer in the country."

"But we have only arrived at home. Won't you wait until tomorrow?"

"No." And I ordered the groom to bring a fresh horse around.

"But, Philip!" She came down the stairs and startled me by taking the bridle in her hands.

"Release the horse, Agnes."

"If you really love me, don't go. Don't do this. Stay with me and we shall enjoy our peace. I promise I shall make you happy."

What a crowning piece of folly. I hadn't guessed poor little Agnes for a clinging and eccentric woman. Surely, I loved Agnes as well as I could love anyone, but her ultimatums recoiled on her and we parted with harsh words.

In Washington, I obtained a glowing recommendation from my old commander, General Winfield Scott, and then I presented myself in Albany.

I did not let the abuse Agnes and I had suffered in New York taint my patriotism. As a high-toned gentleman, vastly superior to these political tricksters and contemptible dogs, I put my patriotic duty to my country and the Union before my wounded pride. A fine and noble revenge, I thought, to approach my native soil and offer my services despite New York having treated Agnes and me so shabbily. I would ignore the slights and the injustices. I would defy my secret enemies and do my duty for my country as an officer and an aristocrat.

The states were required to raise volunteer quotas and to commission officers to lead those men. Being a native New Yorker, and my family having two hundred years history here, I assumed my services would be welcome.

I went to Governor Morton's office. But all that afternoon, I waited on the sofa like a beggar. Merchants and haberdashers filed past me into the governor's office and came out as brigadier generals. Men who'd never fired a weapon, men who'd never seen combat or commanded troops were put in charge of whole divisions. After waiting three hours in a moldy anteroom to see Governor Morton, his secretary came creeping out and informed me that the governor would not see me.

In a boiling fury, I threw down my documents and demanded to know why.

The little worm said, "Major Kearny, you are divorced. And a divorced man is morally incapable of leading impressionable young men into battle. The public outcry! Why, the scandal would be too great."

I bolted from the building, cursing Americans. How I hated them, hated them all, ruled as they were by unfit men and their own prejudices.

But I did not surrender. Instead, I went to Newark. There, I sought out my old friend and sometime lawyer, Cortlandt Parker, one of the first men of New Jersey and legal adviser to President Lincoln. Fuming and outraged, I explained my predicament. Cortlandt sat behind his massive desk with his feet up, his head back in the chair, his fingers tented. The sunlight gleamed on his bald head and at long last he said, "How would you feel about leading a brigade of Jersey men?"

Though I had hoped for a division at least, I settled for the brigade. My commission came through, and upon receiving orders, I embarked immediately for Alexandria, Virginia.

Thirty

THERE WERE SOME DAYS when I felt I had passed my whole life being driven from pillar to post. We made the long trip to Fairfax County on a freezing, shivering sort of morning. Upon arriving in late January of 1861, we were delayed by a spell of northeast weather. Taking the train, we were in a car with wooden seats, a pair of benches on each side of the car, and no cushions. We ate from a basket of ham biscuits and drank from a stone jar of London Brown Ale.

John was so restless, making mischief, chattering constantly, irritating his sisters and the other passengers, that I opened my valise and removed a skein and a pair of knitting needles and taught him to knit. Thereafter, he was as content as you could imagine, knitting long red ropes. My daughters peered through the windows as we came into Fairfax County: a land of tangled swamps, dripping trees, and muddy roads paved with long cedar planks that curled up like tobacco leaves from the floods. I could judge the place from what I saw; coffins piled high in the wagons and people dead of the climate fevers.

At the station, a colored man in a slouch hat pushed a wheelbarrow up and offered to take my trunks. But upon seeing our heap of baggage, he politely declined the job. Instead, I hired one of the hacks lined up along the rails and a wagon besides. As the porters loaded our things, I took special care to instruct them about firmly tying the portrait of my sisters in a safe spot. Before we set off, I double-checked the flannel blankets swaddling the frame.

"The Episcopal Seminary in Fairfax County," I said to the driver. "The home of Miss Emily Mason."

"Mama is there a shortage of whitewash in America? Why do none of these people paint their houses?" Di asked, looking positively distressed, her spoon bonnet nearly falling off her head.

"Houses!" Nannie cried. "I thought those were hog sheds!"

Elizabeth strained to see past her sisters as a boy in a long red coat drove a yoke of oxen into the field. John worried with his hair, stroking his fringe of bangs until I thought he'd wear a bald spot over his forehead.

We arrived at three o'clock in the afternoon to find Emily Mason's house ominously quiet. I gathered that the servants had run off. I hurried up to the house, but opening the front door and standing in the main hall with my hands on my hips, I smelled the strong odor of chloride of lime. The house had been washed down with disinfectants.

My three daughters huddled together in the doorway like a covey of pastel-colored partridges, clutching at one another, and staring around the echoing and vacant hall. John made a face, wrinkling his nose, and said, "Smells like they're worried about fever sickness spreading, doesn't it?"

I raised my face to the stairs and then turning said sternly, "Girls, wait for me in the carriage. I shall come out for you but I do not wish to expose you to the sickness in this house until I am sure it is not catching."

"But, Mama!" Di protested.

"Do as I say. John, I have a special request of you. I want you to go out and fetch the painting and bring it up. I don't want it to get damp."

"Hear that Di? She doesn't care if you get damp, now does she?"

"Hear that, John, Mama doesn't care if you catch a fever, now does she?" Di snapped back.

"You be quiet, Di."

"No, you, John."

I found Emily Mason, a small woman, grave and dignified, in a second-floor room sitting on a ladder-back chair reading scripture to my sister, the red marker ribbons over her hands as she held the book open. It was a bright, sparely furnished room with white curtains and a pitcher on a washstand. Upon seeing me, Miss Mason smiled sadly, and marking the page with the ribbon, closed the book and met me out in the hall. "We have had damp northeast weather, which has made her cough return."

"How is she, otherwise?"

"Our family physician says she has a cancer of the blood. She is fearfully thin, but tenacious. The doctor says she might live a month or two. She might live to see summer, but she is much too weak to be moved."

Seized with apprehensive dread for my beloved sister, I drew my shawl tightly around my shoulders and remembered my cousin's many courtesies. "We have imposed such burdens on you, Miss Mason."

"Oh, you mustn't think that. We are kin. And besides, I like looking after her as it takes me away from my own selfish cares. Sometimes, I grow weary of thinking of myself all the while."

"The house is deserted. But where have all of your people gone?"

"To Alexandria. The federal army is there and one morning I woke to find all of my servants had run away to the Yankees. Such ingratitude I never did see, as I devoted myself to them for years and this is how they repay me. Have you ever heard of such disloyalty? Ah well, your sister will be delighted to see you."

Quietly, I entered the room alone. My sister wore a nightdress and her throat had been painted with iodine. I sat on the side of the bed and touched her brow, but hardly recognized her. She looked eighty years old, her skin hung in pleats, her eyes were sunken, and even her low gentle voice, which had sung me to sleep all those nights of my childhood, had been destroyed by her long illness.

"Sister?" I asked, wetting a bit of gauze in the pitcher of water and pressing the damp cloth to her lips. "Sister?"

Her eyes fluttered open but they were not the bright and wide blue eyes I had known. Her glance was opaque and shaded.

"You've come home," she sighed.

"Yes," I said, wringing out the cloth.

"How long I have waited."

"I am sorry to have made you wait."

The flapping curtains broke the stillness in the room.

"Seeing you gives me a sharp attack of sore throat," Mary said. I reached aside for the pitcher and poured a glass of water for her but she refused it. "Miss Mason tells me the federals are fast approaching."

"If it is true, I have seen no sight of them."

"Yet it worries me not; wasn't my own husband a general? No harm will come to us," Mary said.

"I agree entirely, no army would dare to cause us grief. Now calm yourself. Ah, thank you, John! Mary, here is your nephew with a surprise for you."

My son brought forth the ladder-back chair and carried in the painting. His hair stuck up on one side as if he'd just awakened and his trousers sagged and threatened to drop to his heels. The boy was a stick, and he had no hips. At sixteen years of age, John weighed one hundred thirty pounds in his broadcloth shirt and cotton trousers and his voice sounded like a cracked clarinet.

"Hullo, Aunt Mary."

"It is good to see you again, John. My, you've grown so tall I can hardly believe my eyes. You've grown at railroad speed."

John carefully positioned the *Bullitt Sisters as the Fates* upon the chair. Weary from travel and bone-sore, I sighed and untied my bonnet strings, removed my gloves, and bent over to unlace my boots.

With thumb and forefinger, Mary flicked the crown of my head.

"Why did you do that?" I asked, rubbing my scalp.

"Your head may be empty but that doesn't mean it is transparent. I can't see around you and I can't see the painting of us." Mary squinted. "Well, now. I can remember sitting for that portrait clearly as if it happened yesterday."

My son leaned against the door frame. "You all look old-fashioned. I can hardly believe ladies ever dressed in such clothes. What year was it painted?"

"In the year of grace 1834," Mary said. "Now, John, please leave us. I wish to have some private talk with your mother."

My boy hurried from the room and shut the door. I stretched my legs and folded my arms over my waist.

Outside, I could hear my girls chattering and complaining in the carriage.

"When is she going to let us come out?"

"My legs are cramped from sitting so long."

"Nannie, stop pinching me!"

"Well, Di, you stop bossing me."

"Mama!" Elizabeth howled from below. "Mama set us free else we shall all die in a heap down here!"

"The girls send their love," I said.

Mary laughed softly. I walked over to the window and shut it, for the rains were blowing in and the white curtains flew like flags of surrender. When I slammed the old sash down with a bang Mary startled, but then she smiled and said, "Come lie beside me, Sister. As we did when we were children in Louisville."

I took the sliver of space on the edge of the bed, my skirts falling all down the side, my wet stockings brushing against the blanket. Lying back in her pillow, Mary looked content and stroked her feathery hand over my hair.

"I am sorry he was unkind to you. I am sorry he has made you so sad," Mary said, closing her eyes, the lids wrinkled and jaundiced. "Love is like the chance effect of an idle wind, isn't it? Love can pull down the whole fabric of the world around you."

My head ached. I rested my cheek beside hers on the pillow.

I said, "Promise me you won't go. If you go, I'll be left alone. I'll be the last one."

"Don't fret, Sister. I am too anxious to die just yet."

In her last days, to ease her pain, my sister was given morphine, and thus, wasn't in her right mind, but talked to people she'd loved and who had passed on years before her. Leveling a look on me, she'd relate stories about the Indian Wars, and the frightening massacres of white settlers and of whole villages of red people. Sometimes, she'd speak to an Indian woman she called Bright Sun and then again, she'd ask me if I were one and the same. Of course, I said, and this seemed to ease her mind, but the wrong answers I supplied made her grimace and scold me. Then, too, she imagined herself in the company of her deceased husband, the old general, to whom she'd been so devoted, and then, her whole countenance changed and brightened, and her voice sounded young again. She became a vivacious bride of twenty-two, reliving her happiest moments as a wife and mother, playing with her children, or conversing with her husband about a dancing party they'd attended in St. Louis.

When Mary was lucid, she'd watch me as I sat beside her, my hands working fabric and needle, mending Miss Mason's linens.

"You must rest," I'd say, rising to bring her water, or beef tea.

"I'd like to rest," Mary sighed, "but they keep sending me back."

"Whom do you mean?"

"Our people who've gone before me. They keep sending me back."

Mary died in April, shortly after the rebel guns fired upon Fort Sumter, and I arranged to have her body sent to our family plot in Cave Hill Cemetery in Louisville, where she would rest beside her husband

and her five children who had died before her. I stood at the train station beside the caisson bearing her coffin and as the porters lifted her remains into the last car, I bid my sister farewell and I wished her a good journey home.

It had been a spring when full-pond showers beat down the roads and the crops drowned in the fields. Then came news that the federals would surely invade, and the road in front of Emily Mason's house took on the appearance of a wagon yard. People packed everything and left.

I planned to return to Paris with the children, but first wished to set Miss Mason's house to rights. Without servants, she could not manage the house or the gardens and as I returned each morning from gathering eggs from the chicken coop, while John fed the horses, we'd find her humming tunelessly, pressing ferns into the pages of a book, refusing to believe the worst was about to befall her. And though I urged Emily to go to her relatives in Morristown, New Jersey, she said, "I am too old to run. I will stay and throw myself into the hands of the Lord. I was born in this house, my grandparents were born in this house, and I will not turn it over to the Yankees without a fight."

In the first week of May of 1861, on a rainy morning when the landscape was obscured by a river-thick fog, Emily left shortly after dawn, carrying a large basket. She walked two miles through the cedar swamp into a clearing in the woods where the strawberries grew all over the hillside. I promised to finish ironing the laundry, and then help her preserve the strawberries she'd picked.

With the fires roaring in the brick summer kitchen, I opened the lid of the ten-pound iron, scooped coals from the hearth, and poured them into the hollow before latching the lid. Setting to work on Miss Mason's heavy chambray work skirts, the coal iron softly thumping on the ironing board, I thought of Philip, and wondered where he might be. Surely, the shadow of God's displeasure had fallen over my suffering country.

After they'd had their breakfast, I sent Di, Nannie, and Elizabeth a half mile off to the dairywoman's to fetch four pails of milk and a crock of butter for Miss Mason's larder.

At ten o'clock, realizing with growing alarm that Miss Mason had been away for four hours, I descended the stairs, wiping my hands upon my apron. In the opaque gleam of the overcast morning, my girls came up the dirt drive under light yokes with pails swinging from them, followed by Elizabeth, who hugged a stoneware jar against her chest. John turned the horses out into the paddock and grumbled as he went back and forth from the stalls, mucking them out with a pitchfork and tossing the straw and manure into a pile.

"Di? Have you seen Miss Mason?" I asked.

Di and Nannie groaned and bending their knees, freed themselves of the yokes, carefully lowering the sloshing pails onto the ground. "No, we haven't seen her. But Mama! Mama, we saw soldiers!"

Nannie jumped in, "We saw a half-dozen soldiers milling about but we hid from them when they passed us; we ducked low and we hid behind a cattle trough."

"And they didn't see us!" Elizabeth cried, letting the butter crock thump into the mud at her feet.

I brushed the hair from my face, trying to quiet my fear. "Which soldiers?"

The girls looked at each other and frowned. "We don't know."

"Miss Mason is out there alone and in danger. You must tell me what color those soldiers were wearing?"

Nannie grumbled defensively, "With this fog and rain, the light is changeful and when we weren't squinting in the glare of the sun trying to break through the mists, we were trying to see through the gloom and the shadows."

Di and Elizabeth appeared to think upon my question and they spoke over one another. "Muddy, drab-colored uniforms. Dull uniforms of a dreary color!"

"Oh, you girls are hopeless," I said, but Elizabeth blurted, "They were carrying guns, Mama! And after they went off, we ran awhile and Di and Nannie spilled some of the milk, but I didn't spill any of the butter."

"Why do you worry, Mama? We only saw six soldiers."

"That was a scouting party." I tapped my fingers against my lips, worrying about Miss Mason. I called, "John! Tack up the horse and bring him out!"

"You can't go for a ride now, Mama. It's about to rain. Mops of rain are falling from the sky."

"Don't leave us!" Elizabeth squealed.

But I could think of no woman less capable of defending herself than Miss Mason, and I could not repay her kindness to my sister with cowardice, hiding in her house, while she might very well have been taken prisoner by a Yankee detail, or worse.

"Bring the milk and butter inside," I called, and gathering my skirts in my fists, I ran to the house, clapped a stiff straw hat upon my head, fastened an India rubber cape at my throat, tugged my riding boots over my calves and searching my trunk for my pistol, tucked it into my waistband. Returning out front as my son brought the horse around with a sidesaddle, I sat up high, and taking the reins, I looked down at my children's faces, upturned and shining with rain. Tense, pale, and silent, they stared at me.

"John, keep watch from the parlor window. Chances are, we won't see those soldiers again, but all of you must keep your wits. If soldiers come this way, hide in the coal cellar. I will be back shortly, but until then, lock the doors and stay together."

Like any good hunter, I took notice of the light and of the wind as the horse cantered down the road. Upon reaching a crossroads, then veering left, I entered the cedar swamp where ribbons of mist curled over the water and the horse's hooves sank to the fetlocks in a rotten spongy turf. A cottony fog concealed the riding path and the hazards of rock and root.

An hour deep into the woods, I nervously scanned for sight of the strawberry meadow, but did not see it. Stopping a moment to tie a kerchief around my neck and shoulders to guard against the clouds of mosquitoes whirring around my head, I listened to the branches dripping green and chill in the sodden air, felt the cold rain beading off the brim of my hat, trickling down my neck under my cape.

Lifting my chin, I drew a breath, inhaling the dank odors of waterweed, fungus, and moss. I would not have been surprised to find tombstones leaning up between the nettles, for surely this earth was the nesting ground of specters and the pale people of my dreams.

Had I somehow lost the path? I turned and looked back from whence I had come and then directly ahead, but six rods distance, the dirt trace was overgrown with wild Virginia roses, big as tea saucers, spilling in pink and crimson profusion into the ravine, and humming with bees.

Fighting panic and gathering my wits, I dismounted, tied the horse to a dogwood tree blooming with starlike flowers. Removing my gloves, I reached into my skirt pocket for a compass, wiped the rain from the glass, and studied the needle.

A sharp noise came from my right where the juniper loomed like black cinder mounds between the cedars. And sounded again, a distinctive noise, the snap of a stout stalk or twig. Silent as I could be, all breath and heartbeat and unresolved terror, keenly primed for ambush, knowing in that juniper thicket, some predator had taken a bead on me, and even now had me in his sights, I stepped back and around the horse. The rose thorns tore at my skirts and scratched my legs as I crept backward up the hill, away from the path.

Sinking down into the roses so that nothing but the crown of my straw hat could be seen, I waited and listened. A deer came lunging down the ravine, over a mossy trickle of water and through a cloud of insects, emboldened by his own shadowlessness, breathing in harsh pants as if he had run a great distance. His ears cupped and twitched at the sound of my breathing. He paused to rest so close to me that I could see the dun fretting in his pelt, but then he bounded as if revived and disappeared into the undergrowth.

A man appeared on the trace, riding through the roses to where my horse stood on the path. The reins were loose on his lap and his black India cape fell askew revealing the empty left sleeve of a general's uniform. As he approached, he fixed his gaze in my direction. He held a field glass in his right hand and the emotions moving over his face stirred my heart, an expression of astonishment and disbelief that he did not bother to hide.

Standing slowly so as not to startle him, rising from my hiding place on the hillside, we did not speak, but merely looked at one another. It seemed hours that we remained in that suspended state, as if I had no power over my limbs, and yet, my mind had never been so clear. There was Philip, dismounting slowly and squinting at me through the rain, his dark eyes and his finely chiseled features shadowed by the leather brim of his military kepi.

He stared up at me and I looked down at him, both of us awe-stricken and saddened with the ache of life. Despite all, the current of sympathy between us was still strong and devastating.

He broke the silence first, his voice hoarsening upon my name. "Diana? Come down from there. I should like to speak with you, if only for a short while."

As I sidled down the hill toward him, he pocketed his field glass and extended a hand. But when his hand gripped mine, we both stood motionless, paralyzed with cautious desire, remorse, and yearning.

He cleared his throat and murmured, "Of course I recognized you, even at a distance, and through the rain."

I nodded and looked down at my hand in his. "I came here looking for a lady friend whom I fear is lost. But I'll go now."

Yet he would not release my hand, and I did not move away for I could feel his heartbeat to the end of his fingers, and my own pulse, too.

"This lady is of middling years and slender," I said.

"Carrying a basket? Yes, I saw her on the road, she is unharmed."

"But the children saw soldiers?"

"My pickets will not disturb you or yours."

Noticing the telltale double pair of gold buttons on his coat, I observed, "They've made a brigadier general of you."

Nodding, he reached up and touched the smallpox scar on his neck just below his jaw and fixed his gaze upon the rain-soaked hill. "My troops are in Alexandria and I often scout these woods."

"The federals are moving this way, then?"

He looked at me with such intensity that I stepped back as he urged, "You must leave as soon as you can. Why are you here, Diana?"

As I explained the reason for our visit, the deadweight of loss and the years having passed between us slowed my talk, and then I stopped speaking altogether. He appeared thin and gray of complexion. How would he survive the rigors of camp life and the malarial heat of summer when he seemed to be so sick and weak? Yet, I felt the full weight of his desire mingled with a defensive scorn.

"Were you ever happy with me?" he asked in his keen and rapid manner, digging the heel of his left boot into the mud. He glanced side-long at me, awaiting my answer.

"Sometimes more than happy, if you will believe that."

"More than happy?"

"Yes." Then, knowing it was my turn, I did not meet his eyes. "And you?"

"I have never loved anyone but you." And then he fell silent as if what he'd said had pained him. What this confession cost him, I could not tell, for his past behavior gave lie to his sweet words. "I wish you could forgive me, Diana. And I, you. Can't we find some peace between us, even now?"

"You have injured me too deeply to ever forgive me."

He thought upon my words and then laughed sharply, his laughter ending in a raspy cough. "You have injured *me* too deeply to ever forgive *me*, woman."

"At last we are agreed about something, and that in itself must be good, don't you think?"

Looking down, his eyes fixing on mine, he took my hand and whispered, "A truce between us, then? A real truce?"

I couldn't help smiling at him, but took my hand away. Both of us were suddenly and acutely aware of one another, of our too sensitive flesh and the delicate and bewildering crossroads we had reached in our lives. The strain of life had been so sharp that I could not reconcile my sadness over our failures or the even sadder disillusionment of our mutual successes.

Removing the itchy straw hat, I tossed it onto the rosebush and scratched my temples.

He drew me close, my cheek brushed against his, and hesitating, our eyes met but I tucked my head against his shoulder, under his chin. Philip touched my arm and his hand came to rest on my waist as he pressed his mouth against the crown of my head. A great wave of desolation and loneliness pressed on me, an inexpressible longing for him.

We made for ourselves a bed of his blanket over a mound of pine straw and draped his canvas tarp over the branches of the dogwood trees and so built a shelter from the rain. With cold and trembling fingers, we unbuttoned our clothes, kneeling and kissing all the while, shivering as we clung to one another, our hands and mouths revisiting familiar pleasures and places. I had nearly forgotten the taste of him, how it felt to press my nose to his chest or to feel the weight of his body upon mine.

We breathed in the sweet rich scent of Virginia roses, the very blooms he'd given me on our wedding day. My husband whispered his secret joys and regrets, as if speaking made eternal in his heart the memory of us together.

As he embraced me, I knew that all of the harm we had done our souls had been our undoing. What we had striven for together might end in nothing. Yet, all we had been and done would be part of both of us as long as we lived, and we would remember, always.

Thirty-one

THE LONG RAINS have come. It rains every day on the peninsula and the roads are wonderfully bad. The wagons bog up to the axles. The heavy cannon and the batteries fire around the clock and never hit a thing except that fellow who had his leg blown off below the knee because of a stupid blunder on his part. The idiot tried to stop a cannon ball rolling through camp, and deceived by its slow progress over the furrows, tipped his boot and the centrifugal force tore his limb in two.

To think, out of my sense of patriotism, I lavished person and treasure on my country only to find all of my brilliant victories saving this army have been smothered up out of jealousy by this treasonous buffoon McClellan. He pays the newspapers to squash news of me and to write instead, myths, damnable nursery stories about his own false efforts.

Why? He is in league with the Confederacy! McClellan intends to surrender to the South at the first opportunity, appease Richmond, reunite the country, and run for the presidency! The Peninsula Campaign has been a masterwork of errors thanks to that goddamned Virginia Creeper, George McClellan. For two years, during 1861 and 1862, our army has ignobly and lazily reposed within sight of the steeples of Richmond.

As inertia ruled our days, I sometimes left my camp in Fairfax

County for weekend visits to friends in Washington. In the evenings, I'd ride by my old house on K Street, where I spent those early years with Diana.

Though she had long ago returned to Paris, on some nights, I sat outside our old house, smoking in the saddle and peering up from the curbside at the windows as if I expected to see my wife moving through the rooms in her nightdress with a candlestick, her black hair falling long down her back and our Susan nestled against her shoulder.

My troops encamped about three miles outside Alexandria near the area of the Episcopal Seminary, an ideal compound for a hospital, quartermaster's storehouse, and fine quarters for my staff. The troops inhabited a wilderness of tents and wagons. I established my camp with my fourgon carriage—like a tinker's house on wheels, but staffed by a French chef and stocked with every delicacy a man might enjoy on Sevres china.

I slept in the field with my men when the weather was poor, or if the skirmishing with confederate pickets was heavy, or if I believed a battle might ensue. The men knew that if they were sleeping in a tent on a rainy night, so would their commanding officer be. I could not remember having been so weary and unwell since I had the typhoid fever. I had been sick with fever and dysentery and had lost twenty-five pounds and sleep had deserted me.

Since our meeting in the Virginia woods, I had not returned home to Agnes or Bellegrove. I wrote to Diana every night no matter how weary I might be, wrote to her while the mosquitoes hung so thick in my tent they threatened to put out the lamp and the fleas swarmed over me from ankle to knee. Her letters came from Paris, three months delayed, and the few I'd received from her, I kept in a breast pocket of my uniform, tied in ribbon.

In this place, neither death nor life matters a great deal. Sometimes, on the battlefield, the dead fell in a perfect line one quarter of a mile long, lined up as if for final judgment, like wheat flattened by a cyclone. I could have walked over the hill on their bodies and my feet would not have touched the mud.

On September 1, 1862, we had come to a farm called Chantilly on Ox Hill in late afternoon, but the heavy weather and gunpowder obscured all light, and you would have guessed it for a winter's night.

I turned in the saddle, wiped the rain from my face, and looked down at the men. Unshorn and bewildered, they slogged miserably along the muddy turnpike, retreating as Jackson harassed our rear units all along the road. I rubbed my eyes and my skin felt briny with filth. My right hand felt numb and my knuckles were puffy and stiff under my glove.

When the troops refused to move through the cornfield to support General Birney's right flank, I determined that I would lead them. But Colonel Clark balked like a horse that won't jump a ditch. He dug in and refused to move.

"Those are Georgia troops, sir. There are rebels on the other side of the field. Please listen to me, General, that isn't our army. I don't know how many troops the rebels got. Hell, sir, we caught two of their men and have them prisoner now," Colonel Clark insisted.

If Colonel Clark would not take his men to join Birney's right flank, I would reconnoiter for him. So, I went looking for our troops, certain that it was General Birney's men on the other side of the cornfield.

Damning the colonel's want of nerve, I urged my horse into the deep and sticky mud between the grain stalks. Felt the wet leaves cutting against my trousers and smelled the thick moldy wind. The odor of the cornfield hung heavy over the smells of gunpowder and the dead, as if God had taken pity and had let this one field grow.

I rode through the showery darkness and saw spurs of light from distant musket fire on the hill. Blinded by rain and the murky twilight, I brought the horse up side-slope out of the grain and into a grassy meadow.

Beyond the clearing I heard men moving in a line in the woods and muffled steps in the darkness of a heavy tree line.

There were pickets before the trenches where a huddled form swung a greasy lamp.

"What troops are these?" I called, for I could not see them.

"Forty-ninth Georgia," someone answered.

And then someone in the line shouted, "That's a Yankee! Fire at will, boys!"

You should have seen the sunlight break through the woods. The minie balls pelted the cornfield, each shining lead ball a raindrop seeded with light and soaring as if the very sun itself melted in a watery gossamer and flew right at me.

I imagined myself back in our house in New York, running up the stairs to Diana's bedroom, where the painting of her and her sisters hung above the marble mantel in a red velvet bedroom furnished with old walnut furniture. The afternoon light seemed to animate the women under the ash trees and Diana's dark eyes were so lifelike, brilliantly focused on me as she smiled and welcomed me to her. She wore such a proud expression, but then pride comes easily to the young.

I found Diana's chemises, nightdresses, and stockings folded in the chest of drawers. The fabric so fragile, tied with silk ribbons, still smelling of her skin when I held them to my nose. It had been so long since I had inhaled her scent that I sank on the side of the bed kneading the gauzy muslin in my hands, and for the first time in years, felt anguished. Virginia rose petals dried in a gathering basket on a small table under the window, and the wind blew the petals all over the floor.

I opened the wardrobe where her gowns hung on the hooks. Closing my eyes, I immersed my hands in the sumptuous silk folds of her skirts, cool and sliding over my hands. Seized with a mad frenzy, I yanked her gowns off the hooks, threw them on the bed, and lay face down upon them. My skin felt like a humid shroud encasing my heart, my heart constricting at the memory of her.

A wind came up so strongly it blew the air from my lungs and I felt cold as the seeps of winter.

As I fell from my horse and lay face down in the muddy clearing just short of the cornfield, I heard the troops of the 49th Georgia approaching and congratulating one another on having shot me. I buried my hand in the soft cool folds of her dresses and wished to see her face once more. I felt the cold mud against my cheek and smelled the dense green odor of the field and tasted my own blood in my mouth.

Did I still love Diana Bullitt? I dreamed about her nightly, dreamed of the taste of her on my lips, the scent of her so close I believed the intervening years between our wedding and this moment had been a frivolous interval and then I had my answer.

When the enemy came near me, one of them kicked my leg.

I tried to rise but Diana held me to her breast on the shores of that pond in the territory, smiling over me as my back scraped the cotton-wood tree, her black hair falling around me like the darkest curtain, warming me, comforting me, inviting me to lose myself in her.

My heart opened to her at the closing of my life. I heard voices in the rain-laden silence, accusing whispers flittering against my ear like a moth wing, but just as quickly, the sounds vanished.

Thirty-two

S OME PEOPLE say that the grace of God flies faster than a bullet, but I don't think God was anywhere to be found on that battlefield, on the first of September 1862, on the day Philip died. When he left me, I felt no hint of his passing, no instinct made me seize with grief, no portent in the heavens let me know that he'd gone. Yet, like everyone else in Paris, I read of his death in the newspaper, and looked into the eyes of my son as the paper fell from my hands. As I frantically searched one paper after another, I learned the details of the battle only by degrees; some journals said Philip had died a hero, while others reported that his death had been a wasteful folly.

When I could not bear to read anymore, I reached for my parasol. Stepping out onto the walk in front of my house, I felt the sunlight striking the steel stays of my bodice, warming my heart, and suspected in some measure it was an act of kindness from him. With my face set like stone but my heart torn in pieces, I ventured toward his building on the avenue de Matignon, for it seemed the worst thing in the world to sit quietly in my parlor when the news might have been wrong, when Philip might have returned to Paris to convalesce in his apartments. But though I stood opposite his dwelling place for hours until the light dwindled away, I saw no sight of him, and finally understood that there had been no mistaking the news.

After the war was over we reluctantly returned to America, and only because Philip had, in a last generous gesture, left all of his fortune and the mansion at Bellegrove to our son, John. In the autumn of 1866, I escorted my grown children back to New Jersey, but found I could not enter Philip's house, halting on the drive as if he himself were denying me entry. Our children climbed the steps quietly and reverently, but I could not understand my own hesitancy. I heard Di and John, Nannie and Elizabeth commenting upon the irony of their situation, and yet, expressing intense curiosity about the dark and brooding old house.

My limbs were heavy and try as I might, I could not summon the courage to step foot in the sanctuary he'd built for himself and for Agnes. Rather, I sat upon a stone bench under a spreading oak tree, and looked down at my hand, at the wedding ring he'd given me, the one I still wore on my third finger. And in that instant, I understood why I could not, indeed why I *should not* enter his house. What use would my life be in all of the years to come if I did not break faith with Philip? If there was to be any purpose in the years before me, I *must* break faith with him. After a time, I made my excuses and I left my children to their explorations—they were adults after all, and finally enjoying the shelter of their father's house.

Instead, I traveled alone to Cape May, New Jersey, where a cousin of mine had recently opened a hotel, having written me long boastful letters about the certain bright future of the little seaside village. A few months later, I built a Queen Anne–style cottage on the ocean and opened my house to my family and friends.

And every autumn, when the heavy winds blew, when there were dark rollers and the weedy waters broke over beaches strewn with upended green skiffs, I thought of Philip, but more often, I thought of my children and of my numerous grandchildren. We did not observe formalities, nor did we keep rules, but came to the table straight from the ocean, with wet hair, in our bathrobes, and sand gritty between our toes. On Cape May, my guests complained, everything tasted like sand. When the wind came up and the grass made a rasping noise over the dunes, I sometimes imagined the land was giving a voice to Philip, and to all of the boys who reposed in their native soil, in this weary country.

Our daughter Di put a match to the wick of the kerosene lamp and the light flared in the dark morning room. Tossing a gray woolen blanket over her shoulders, in bare feet with her long dark hair in ringlets, Di shivered as she peered out the windows at a squall on the tide line. Glass rattled in the window frame as she gazed at the sea.

She was the only one of our children who still carried some memory of Philip. Turning, she asked me in a tone that while not accusing was tinged with bitterness, "Mama, why couldn't the two of you have been happy together?"

And I honestly told her, I didn't know why. Sitting beside her, a cup of coffee warming my hands, I felt her disappointed scrutiny.

Di brushed the hair from her eyes, tugged the blanket around her arms and said, "Sometimes it all just seems a great waste, I mean to say, the way father died. Nobody even remembers him anymore. In five years' time, he has been utterly forgotten. And for what? I remember his obituary, all of those famous men saying he was the bravest of the brave, but look where it got him. Look where his bravery got him!"

For some reason, it seemed important to refute what she'd said, for while I had always hated his wars, it didn't seem right that she think of her father's life as having been somehow sadly thrown away in one moment of recklessness. If nothing else, Philip had loved the path he'd chosen, and his country had benefited from his devotion to his profession. So, I told her how Abraham Lincoln had expressed his hope in August of 1862 that Philip would be the general to stop Robert E. Lee in Virginia. How, in my heart, I always knew that if he had been made commander of the Union Army, the Civil War would have been a two-month campaign, and a mere footnote in the history books that we the people would have looked back on as a slight and embarrassing detour in our shared national destiny. I described the way President Abraham Lincoln had called Philip "my general" and told my daughter that Emperor Napoleon III had admiringly said her father was "a bird of prey."

Di pulled a chair away from the table, and sat, cupping her chin in her hands, her expression doubtful. Hearing the laughter from her sisters and their children in the parlor, she asked, "And what, I wonder, will they say about you, Mama?"

I glanced at her, and couldn't help but smile as, leaning, I lowered the glass globe over the flickering bit of lamp wick. Brushing a bit of dust from my hands, I rested them on my hips and lifting my chin, I spoke the truth.

"Those who knew Philip and who knew me will say that between the two of us, I was the better hunter."

Since You Asked . . .

While the lives and the private and published papers of General Philip Kearny and Diana Moore Bullitt Kearny have inspired this novel and the major events in this story have a basis in historical fact, the characterizations of Philip and Diana are wholly my creation. Dr. Roger Nichols, Professor of History at the University of Arizona at Tucson, kindly allowed me to read Diana Bullitt Kearny's correspondence, written from 1834 to 1862. Archivist Dennis Northcott, at the Missouri Historical Society Library, graciously made other collections available. I obtained additional Bullitt Family letters from the Filson Club. (See also, Coles, Therese Langhorne Bullitt. *My Life.* Privately Published, 1910. And see, Bullitt, Thomas W. *My Life at Oxmoor, Life on a Farm in Kentucky Before the War.* Louisville, KY: Filson Club, 1995.)

I am profoundly grateful to Mary Patton for obtaining General Kearny's letters from the New Jersey Historical Society. However, interested readers can find the general's correspondence in *Letters from the Peninsula: The Civil War Letters of General Philip Kearny*, ed. William B. Styple, Kearney, NJ: Belle Grove Publishing, 1998.

After the death of Thomas Bullitt in 1824, Mrs. Bullitt's creditors pressured her to dissolve her household. Though her daughter Diana Bullitt possessed significant real estate holdings, including residential, commercial, and undeveloped lands purchased on speculation in Ohio and Indiana, the young woman owed thousands of dollars to various creditors in 1840. To pay her debts, Mrs. Bullitt sold the Louisville house and she and Diana went to live with Diana's sister, Mary Bullitt Atkinson, wife of Brigadier General Henry Atkinson, commander of the Sixth Infantry and administrator of Jefferson Barracks in Missouri. General Atkinson helped Diana to manage her finances and become solvent. *(Brigadier General Henry Atkinson to Thomas Ludlow Alexander, June 1840. Brigadier General Henry Atkinson to Diana Bullitt Kearny, February 21, 1842.)*

Philip surprised Diana with a visit to Jefferson Barracks on Friday, June 18, 1841, and proposed marriage with such urgency that the young woman's family was reluctant to consent. Overcoming their objections, Philip and Diana were married at the Jefferson Barracks chapel on Thursday, June 24, 1841, attended by witnesses Anne Lane and Owen Bullitt. *(Mary Bullitt Atkinson to Thomas Ludlow Alexander, July 1, 1841.)*

According to Diana's affidavit, she and Philip had five children: Susan Kearny *(b. April 1842)*, Diana Kearny *(b. January 4, 1844)*, John Watts Kearny *(b. July 25, 1845)*, Anne De Lancey Kearny *(b. June 9, 1847)*, and Elizabeth Watts Kearny *(b. October 7, 1848)*.

Contemporaries of the young couple observed that Philip and Diana were deeply in love though they were unable to live peacefully together. When the Kearnys separated in August of 1849, their friends exchanged a flurry of letters assigning blame. William Carr Lane of St.

Louis characterized the split in this way. "Poor Diana Kearny! I pity her from the bottom of my heart. There may have been faults on her side, little ones, as well as faults—stupendous ones—on his side, but she has not deserved so sad a fate." On the other hand, Anne Lane was accosted by a Washington, D.C. matron who claimed to have known the couple and who blamed Diana's bad temper for the disintegration of their marriage. (Lane Manuscript Collection, Missouri Historical Society.)

Shortly after writing to Diana and asking her to return to him, Kearny wrote in his journal on June 1, 1851, "Praise God my birthday! I have changed in a few months, constitutionally, mentally and in temperament from being over-young to being over-aged for my years. My life has certainly been strangely admixed. Impulsiveness has been like a runaway steed. My fortune and love of pleasure made me appear to others deficient in character, I am *NOW changed*." (Emphasis Kearny's. *Rogue River Journal*. Courtesy Division of Special Collections & University Archives, University of Oregon Library System.)

Kearny pursued his wife for years and tried to reconcile with her on numerous occasions. Her friends observed that Diana came very close to returning to Philip, even though they urged her not to. (Lane Manuscript Collection, Missouri Historical Society.)

Victorian Americans perceived divorce, like suicide, as being so scandalous that they frequently purged all mention of it from family records. Thus, I am extremely grateful to Norman Goodman, and the kind people at the office of the County Clerk and Clerk of the Supreme Court of New York County, for clambering over dusty boxes in the vaults and discovering the curled and yellowing Kearny divorce records rolled up with brown ribbon. The divorce documents contain a routine boilerplate clause required by New York law in the 1850s preventing Philip Kearny as the "guilty" party from remarrying in the state, while granting Diana, as the innocent plaintiff, the right to remarry at will.

(Kearny divorce papers courtesy of the Clerk of the County of New York. See also, Basch, Norma. *Framing American Divorce from the Revolutionary Generation to the Victorian.* Berkeley, Calif.: University of California Press, 1999.)

Beverly Robinson, Philip Kearny's divorce lawyer, paid Jane Winslow to testify in the Kearny divorce case. Winslow asserted that she was a "housekeeper" in New York and that she had sexual intercourse with Kearny in 1850. Jane Winslow was indeed a housekeeper—by the late 1840s she had earned a fortune as one of New York's most notorious and successful whorehouse madams, operating a brothel at 73 Mercer Street. Dr. Timothy J. Gilfoyle, Professor of History at Loyola University of Chicago, kindly corresponded with me about Jane Winslow, and writes about her in his excellent history of New York prostitution. (Gilfoyle, Timothy J. *City of Eros, New York City, Prostitution and the Commercialization of Sex, 1790–1920.* New York: Norton, 1992.)

While numerous military historians have meticulously examined Kearny's important role in the Peninsula Campaign and in the Seven Days' Battles, as of April 2005, a good biography about the general based on primary sources had not been written. However, David Welker has written a superb analysis of the Battle of Chantilly. (Welker, David A. *Tempest at Ox Hill, The Battle of Chantilly.* Cambridge, MA: Da Capo Press, 2002.) The archivists at the U.S. Army Military History Institute at the U.S. Army War College and Carlisle Barracks were most helpful.

In 1869, John Watts De Peyster, Philip Kearny's cousin, wrote a biography of the general, but omitted Kearny's personal life, believing it too scandalous. The biography is mostly De Peyster's exegesis into arcane military history with regrettably brief glimpses into Kearny's life and career. (De Peyster, John Watts. *Personal and Military History of Philip Kearny, Major-General United States Volunteers.* New York:

Rice & Gage, 1869 and Newark: Bliss, 1869.) Thomas Kearny, the general's grandson, wrote a biography of Philip in 1937, but relied heavily on a servant's recollection of the Kearny marriage; the servant's version differs sharply from the letters written by Kearny's contemporaries. It is inconsistent with New York divorce law in the 1850s and with the court documents. (Kearny, Thomas. *General Philip Kearny, Battle Soldier of Five Wars.* New York: G. P. Putnam's Sons, 1937.) A third biography of Kearny written for the juvenile market was based on the two previously mentioned works with fictional flights of fancy about Kearny's life and military career that primary sources have revealed couldn't possibly have been true. (Werstein, Irving. *Kearny the Magnificent: The Story of General Philip Kearny.* New York: John Day, 1962.)

Philip Kearny recounted his experiences in Algeria in a crisp and colorful memoir. (Kearny, Philip. *Service with the French Troops in Africa by an Officer of the United States Army.* New York: 1844.) His good friend and adviser Cortlandt Parker unflinchingly but compassionately recounted Kearny's strengths and sins and, in the balance, made his subject even more admirable because he made him human. (Parker, Cortlandt. *Philip Kearny: Soldier and Patriot: An Address Delivered Before the New Jersey Historical Society.* Newark: Northern Monthly, 1868).

Women who knew him or had met him had wildly different perceptions of General Philip Kearny. Sarah Emma Edmonds disguised herself as a Union soldier named Franklin Thompson, and was one of several acting orderlies for General Kearny, serving as his courier. She recorded several fascinating anecdotes about Kearny and deeply admired him, going so far as to steal a horse from the enemy camp and then presenting it as a gift to the general on the battlefield. (Edmonds, Sarah Emma. *Nurse and Spy or Unsexed, the Female Soldier.* Hartford, Conn., 1864;

later reprinted in Philadelphia.) In her diary, prominent New Yorker Maria Lydig Daly lamented his death but described Kearny as "immoral" while Emily Mason of Virginia despised him for taking her home by force and making it his headquarters. (See, Hammond, Harold Earl, ed. Maria Lydig Daly. *Diary of a Union Lady 1861–1865*. Lincoln, Neb.: University of Nebraska Press, 2000. See also, Mason, Emily V. *Memories of a Hospital Matron*. Reprinted. *The Women's War in the South*. Nashville, Tenn.: Cumberland House, 1999.)

Ms. Carol Howardson at the New Jersey Bar Association provided fascinating records about Kearny's lawyer friends and relatives. Kearny's Columbia school notes are archived at the Beinecke Rare Book & Manuscript Library, Yale University. Philip Kearny's correspondence with portraitist Miner Kellogg is at the Archives of American Art, and his father's estate records were gathered from the New York Historical Society. Thanks also to the Colorado Library System, the National Archives in Washington, D.C., the Seymour Library Archives at Knox College, the National Archives in College Park, Maryland, and the Library of Virginia Archives.

I am grateful to Elizabeth Bullitt Godfrey and Henry "Hank" Bullitt of Louisville, Kentucky, for giving me a tour of Oxmoor, the old Bullitt family homestead in the heart of the city, and for sharing family stories about their illustrious ancestors.

Stimson Bullitt's painstakingly detailed and entertaining Bullitt genealogy proved most valuable, as did his wise counsel on numerous historical matters. (See, Bullitt, Stimson. *Ancestral Histories of Scott Bullitt and Dorothy Stimson*. Seattle, Wash.: Willows Press, 1994.)

Mrs. Mary Kennard Perry of New Jersey kindly provided the portraits of her beautiful great-grandmother—thanks also to Mr. Walter Perry of New York City for permission to reprint the portraits of Diana Bullitt Kearny, and for his kind conversation about family genealogy.

I am also indebted to the descendants of Cortlandt Parker for providing archival information about the amazing Parkers of New York and New Jersey, particularly, Ms. Nancy Parker Wilson of Boston and Greenvale Vineyards, Rhode Island, and those very kind citizens of the Garden State, Mr. and Mrs. Henry Hoyt and Mr. John "Boly" Shurtleff.

number LC-USZ62-117045), by B. B. Russell ca. 1868, Boston, MA, and *Philip Kearny at the Battle of Williamsburg*, ink wash by Waud (reproduction number LC 262-7005-6172): 167, 285, 333. Special thanks to Khadijah Camp. Still Picture Branch (NWDNS) National Archives at College Park, College Park, MD for *Philip Kearny* (reproduction number NWDNS–111-B-307), *Philip Kearny in Hussar Cloak* (reproduction number NWDNS–111-B-6113), and *Philip Kearny in Profile* (reproduction number NWDNS–111-B-4429): 90, 318, 352. Mary Kennard Perry and Walter Perry for *Diana Bullitt Kearny* ca. 1840, *Diana Bullitt Kearny* age 30, and *Diana Bullitt Kearny* age 40 from the Perrys' private collection: 6, 294, 358. The Speed Art Museum for *Oakland House and Race Course, Louisville*, oil on canvas, 28 1/4 x 35 3/4 in. (71.8 x 90.8 cm), by Robert Brammer, American, active 1839–1853, and Augustus A. von Smith, American, active 1835–1841, purchase, Musuem Art Fund, 1956.19: 1. Special thanks to Lisa Parrott Rolfe. Bill Styple Collection at the U.S. Army Military History Institute for *Philip Kearny in Civilian Clothing*, taken in Paris in 1859: 286. Special thanks to Randy Hackenburg, photo historian. The Woodcock Foundation for the Appreciation of the Arts: http://Woodcockmuseum.umsl.edu for *Buffalo Bull, Grazing*, lithograph with hand coloring, 1844 by George Catlin (1796–1872): 89. Special thanks to Dr. Julie A. Dunn-Morton, Woodcock Curator of American Art.

About the Author

MICAELA GILCHRIST is the author of *The Good Journey,* winner of the Women Writing the West Award and the Colorado Book Award. She lives with her family in Colorado.